THE EXPRESS TRACK TO SUSPENSE!

"Derailed me for a couple of nights . . . what a neat, twisty, well-written thriller!"
—James Patterson

"Fast-paced . . . full of twists and surprises . . . a page-turner."
—*Newsday*

"Tautly written and cleverly plotted, with plenty of roller-coaster turns."
—*USA Today*

"Clever, gripping . . . will hold readers spellbound, turning the pages faster and faster."
—*Tampa Tribune*

"Seizes you, intrigues you, titillates you, and finally cuts you loose."
—*Washington Post*

"Gripping . . . relentless . . . powerfully real . . . mesmerizing from the first chapter . . . full of whiplash turns, compelling characters, and visceral and wrenching dramatic moments. Like only a few of our best thriller writers can do, Siegel left me limp and gasping."
—James W. Hall

"Siegel skillfully weaves this gripping plot . . . compelling."
—*Sunday Oklahoman*

"Intense and startling . . . a top-notch novel of suspense with unexpected twists that are shocking and satisfying . . . will keep readers hooked to the last page. With complex characters, tight plotting, and powerful writing, DERAILED is high-quality entertainment."
—Nelson DeMille

"Genuine surprises . . . impressive." —*Cleveland Plain Dealer*

Please turn this page for more reviews and turn to the back of his book for a preview of James Siegel's new novel, *Detour*.

Also by James Siegel

Epitaph
Detour

DERAILED

JAMES SIEGEL

WARNER BOOKS

NEW YORK   BOSTON

This book is a work of fiction. Names, characters, places, and incidents are the product of the author's imagination or are used fictitiously. Any resemblance to actual events, locales, or persons, living or dead, is coincidental.

Copyright © 2003 by James Siegel
Excerpt from *Detour* copyright © 2005 by James Siegel
All rights reserved.

Cover artwork copyright © 2005 by Miramax Film Corp.

Warner Books

Time Warner Book Group
1271 Ave. of the Americas, New York, NY 10020
Visit our Web site at www.twbookmark.com.

Printed in the United States of America

Originally published in hardcover by Warner Books
First Trade Edition: September 2005

10   9   8   7   6   5   4   3   2   1

The Library of Congress has cataloged the hardcover edition as follows:
Siegel, James.
    Derailed / James Siegel.
        p. cm.
    ISBN: 0-446-53158-8
        1. Attica Prison—Fiction. 2. English teachers—Fiction. 3. Murder for hire—Fiction.
    4. Prisoners—Fiction. 5. Extortion—Fiction. 6. Adultery—Fiction. 7. Prisons—Fiction.
    8. Revenge—Fiction. I. Title.
    PS3569.I3747 D47 2003
    813'.6—dc21   2002073572

ISBN: 0-446-69669-2 (pbk.)

To Mindy, who tends to her family as she tends to her garden—
with great love, ceaseless devotion, and unflagging enthusiasm.

ACKNOWLEDGMENTS

I would like to thank both Sara Ann and just plain Sarah for their immense help in structuring this story, Larry for believing in it, and, of course, Richard, for unapologetically championing it.

DERAILED

ATTICA

I spend five days a week teaching English at East Bennington High and two nights a week teaching English at Attica State Prison. Which is to say, I spend my time conjugating verbs for delinquents and dangling participles for convicts. One class feeling like they're in prison and the other class actually being in one.

On the Attica evenings, I eat an early dinner with my wife and two children. I kiss my wife and teenage daughter good-bye and give my four-year-old son a piggyback ride to the front door. I gently put him down, kiss his soft brow, and promise to look in on him when I get home.

I enter my eight-year-old Dodge Neon still surrounded in a halo of emotional well-being.

By the time I pass through the metal detector at Attica Prison, it's gone.

Maybe it's the brass plaque prominently displayed on the wall of the visitors room. "Dedicated to the Correction Officers who died in the Attica riots," it says. There is no plaque for the prisoners who died.

I have only recently begun teaching there, and I can't quite decide who's scarier—the Attica prisoners or the corrections officers who guard them. Possibly the corrections officers.

It's clear they don't like me much. They consider me a luxury item, like cable TV, something the prisoners did nothing to deserve. The brainchild of some liberal in Albany, who's never had a shiv stuck in his ribs or feces thrown in his face, who's never had to peel a tattooed carcass off a blood-soaked floor swimming with AIDS.

They greet me with barely disguised contempt. It's the PHD, they mumble. "Pathetic Homo Douchebag," one of them scrawled on the wall of the visitors bathroom.

I forgive them.

They are the outnumbered occupiers of an enslaved population seething with hatred. To survive this hate, they must hate back. They are not allowed to carry guns, so they arm themselves with attitude.

As for the prisoners who attend my class, they are strangely docile. Many of them the unfortunate victims of the draconian Rockefeller drug laws that treat small purchases of cocaine like violent felonies. They mostly look bewildered.

Now and then, I give them writing assignments. Write something, I say. Anything. Anything that interests you.

I used to have them read their work in class. Until one convict, a sloe-eyed black named Benjamin Washington, read what sounded like gibberish. It *was* gibberish, and the other convicts laughed at him. Benjamin took offense at this and later knifed one of them in the back over a breakfast of watery scrambled eggs and burnt toast.

I decided on anonymity there and then.

They write what interests them and send it up to the desk unsigned. I read it out loud and nobody knows who wrote what. The writer knows; that's good enough.

One day, though, I asked them to write something that

would interest me. The story of them. How they got here, for instance, to Mr. Widdoes's English class in the rec room at Attica State Prison. If they wanted to be writers, I told them, start with the writer.

It might be enlightening, I thought, maybe even cathartic. It might be more interesting than the story "Tiny the Butterfly," a recent effort from . . . well, I don't know, do I? Tiny brought color and beauty to a weed-strewn lot in the projects until he was, unfortunately, *crushed like a bug* by the local crank dealer. Tiny, it was explained at the bottom of the page, was *cymbollic*.

I gave out the assignment on Thursday; by next Tuesday the papers were scattered across my desk. I read them aloud in no particular order. The first story about an innocent man being framed for armed robbery. The second story about an innocent man being framed for possession of illegal narcotics. The third story about an innocent man being framed . . .

So maybe it wasn't that enlightening.

But then.

Another story. Hardly a story at all (although it had a title); a kind of introduction to a story. An invitation to one, really.

About another innocent man.

Who walked on the train one day to go to work.

When something happened.

DERAILED

The morning Charles met Lucinda, it took him several moments after he first opened his eyes to remember why he liked keeping them closed.

Then his daughter, Anna, called him from the hallway and he thought: *Oh yeah.*

She needed lunch money, a note for the gym teacher, and help with a book report that was due yesterday.

Not in that order.

In a dazzling feat of juggling, he managed all three between showering, shaving, and getting dressed. He had to. His wife, Deanna, had already left for her job at P.S. 183, leaving him solely in charge.

When he made it downstairs he noticed Anna's blood meter and a used syringe on the kitchen counter.

Anna had made him late.

When he got to the station, his train had already left—he could hear a faint rumble as it retreated into the distance.

By the time the next train pulled in, the platform had been

repopulated by an entirely new cast of commuters. He knew most of the 8:43 crowd by sight, but this was the 9:05, so he was in alien territory.

He found a seat all by himself and immediately dived into the sports pages.

It was November. Baseball had slipped away with another championship for the home team. Basketball was just revving up, football already promising a year of abject misery.

This is the way he remained for the next twenty minutes or so: head down, eyes forward, brain dead—awash in meaningless stats he could reel off like his Social Security number, numbers he could recite in his sleep, and sometimes did, if only to keep himself from reciting other numbers.

Which numbers were those?

Well, the numbers on Anna's blood meter, for example.

Numbers that were increasingly and alarmingly sky high.

Anna had suffered with juvenile diabetes for over eight years.

Anna wasn't doing well.

So all things being equal, he preferred a number like 3.25. Roger-the-Rocket-Clemens's league-leading ERA this past season.

Or twenty-two—there was a good round number. Latrell Sprewell's current points per game, accumulated, dreadlocks flying, for the New York Knicks.

Numbers he could look at without once feeling sick.

The train lurched, stopped.

They were somewhere between stations—dun-colored ranch houses on either side of the track. It suddenly occurred to him that even though he'd ridden this train more times than he cared to remember, he couldn't describe a single neighborhood it passed through. Somewhere along the way to middle age, he'd stopped looking out windows.

He burrowed back into the newspaper.

It was at that exact moment, somewhere between Steve Serby's column on the state of the instant replay rule and Michael Strahan's lamentation on his diminishing sack total, that it happened.

Later he would wonder what exactly had made him look up again at that precise moment in time.

He would ask himself over and over what would have happened if he hadn't. He would torture himself with all the permutations, the what ifs and what thens and what nows.

But he did look up.

The 9:05 from Babylon to Penn Station kept going. Merrick to Freeport to Baldwin to Rockville Centre. Lynbrook to Jamaica to Forest Hills to Penn.

But Charles clearly and spectacularly derailed.

ATTICA

Two nights later after dinner, my four-year-old climbed onto my lap and demanded I do treasure hunt on his back.

"We're going on a treasure hunt," I whispered as I traced little steps up and down his spine. "*X* marks the spot . . ." as he squirmed and giggled. He smelled of shampoo and candy and Play-Doh, the scent that was clearly and uniquely *him*.

"To get to the treasure, you take big steps and little steps," I murmured, and when I finished he asked me where this treasure was exactly, and I answered him on cue. This, after all, was our routine.

"Right here," I said. And hugged him.

My wife smiled at us from the other side of the table.

When I kissed them all good-bye, I lingered before stepping out into the driveway. As if I were attempting to soak up enough good vibes to last me through the night, straight through the redbrick archway of Attica and into the fetid rec room. Like a magic aura that might protect me from harm.

"Be careful," my wife said from the front door.

*   *   *

When I went through the metal detector, it went off like an air raid siren.

I'd forgotten to take my house keys out of my pocket.

"Hey, Yobwoc," the CO said while patting me down. "Keys are like . . . metal." Yobwoc was Cowboy backward and stood for Young Obnoxious Bastard We Often Con.

PHD was just one of my monikers here.

"Sorry," I said, "forgot."

As soon as I entered the classroom, I could see there was another piece of the story waiting for me at my desk. Eleven pages, neatly printed.

Yes, I thought. *The story is just getting started.*

Other sections soon followed like clockwork.

From that first day on, there would be another piece of the story waiting for me every time I entered the classroom.

Sometimes just a page or two—sometimes what would constitute several chapters. Placed flat on my desk and all, like the first one, unsigned. The story unfolding piecemeal, like a daytime serial you just can't pull your eyes away from. After all, it would end up containing all the staples of soap opera—sex, lies, and tragedy.

I didn't read these installments to my class. I understood they were solely for me now. Me and, of course, the writer.

Speaking of which.

There were twenty-nine students in my class.

Eighteen blacks, six Hispanics, five pale-as-ghosts Caucasians.

I was reasonably sure that none of them had ever ridden the 9:05 to Pennsylvania Station.

So where was he?

DERAILED TWO

An expanse of thigh—that's all at first.

But not just any thigh. A thigh taut, smooth, and toned, a thigh that had obviously spent some time on the treadmill, sheathed by a fashionably short skirt made even shorter by the position of the legs. Casually crossed at the knees. All in all, a skirt length that he'd have to say fell somewhere between sexiness and sluttiness, not exactly one or the other, therefore both.

This is what Charles saw when he looked up.

He could just make out a black high-heeled pump jutting out into the aisle, barely swinging with the motion of the train. He was directly facing her, his seat backward to the city-bound direction of the train car. But she was blocked by the front page of *The New York Times,* and even if she wasn't blocked by the day's alarming if familiar headline—MID-EAST BURNING—he hadn't yet looked up toward her face, only peripherally. Instead he was focusing on that thigh and hoping against hope she wouldn't turn out to be beautiful.

She was.

He'd been debating his next move: whether to turn back to

his sports stats, for instance, whether to stare out the grime-streaked window, or scan the bank and airline ads lining each side of the car, when he simply threw caution to the wind and peeked. Just as *The New York Times* strategically lowered, finally revealing the face he'd been so hesitant to look at.

Yes, she *was* beautiful.

Her eyes.

They were kind of spectacular. Wide and doe shaped and the very definition of tenderness. Full, pouting lips she was ever so slightly biting down on. Her hair? Soft enough to cocoon himself in and never, ever, come out.

He'd been hoping she'd be homely or interesting or simply cute. Not a chance. She was undeniably magnificent.

And that was a problem, because he was kind of vulnerable these days. Dreaming of a kind of alternate universe.

In this alternate universe, he wasn't married and his kid wasn't sick, because he didn't have any kids. Things were always looking up there; the world was his oyster.

So he didn't want the woman reading *The New York Times* to be beautiful. Because that was like peeking into the doorway of this alternate universe of his, at the *hostess* beckoning him to come inside and put his feet up on the couch, and everyone knew alternate universes were for kids and sci-fi nuts.

They didn't exist.

"Ticket." The conductor was standing over him and demanding something. What did he want? Couldn't he see he was busy defining the limitations of his life?

"Ticket," he repeated.

It was Monday, and Charles had forgotten to actually walk into the station and purchase his weekly ticket. The time change had thrown him off, and here he was, ticketless in front of strangers.

"Forgot to buy one," he said.

"Okay," the conductor said.

"See, I didn't realize it was Monday."

"Fine."

Another thing had just occurred to Charles. On Mondays he stopped at the station ATM to take out money he then used to purchase the weekly ticket. Money he also used to get through the week. Money he didn't, at the moment, have.

"That's nine dollars," the conductor said.

Like most couples these days, Charles and Deanna lived on the ATM plan, which doled out cash like a trust fund lawyer— a bit at a time. Charles's wallet had been in its usual Monday morning location, opened on the kitchen counter, where Deanna had no doubt scoured it for loose cash before going off to work. There was nothing in it.

"Nine dollars," the conductor said, this time impatiently. No doubt about it; the man was getting antsy.

Charles looked through his wallet anyway. There was always the chance he was wrong, that somewhere in there was a for-gotten twenty tucked away between business cards and six-year-old photos. Besides, looking through your wallet was what you were supposed to do when someone was asking you for money.

Which someone was. Repeatedly.

"Look, you're holding up the whole train," he said. "*Nine* dollars."

"I don't seem . . ." continuing the facade, sifting through slips of wrinkled receipts and trying not to show his embarrassment at being caught penniless in a train of well-to-do commuters.

"You got it or don't you?" the conductor said.

"If you just give me a minute . . ."

"Here," someone said. "I'll pay for him."

It was her.

Holding up a ten-dollar bill and showing him a smile that completely threatened his equilibrium.

DERAILED THREE

Of all the things they talked about—and they talked about all sorts of things—there was one thing they didn't talk about.

Commuting to work? Yes.

I was thinking the other day, she said, *that if the U.S. government was run like the Long Island Rail Road, we'd all be in trouble. And then I realized that maybe it is, and we are.*

The weather? Of course.

Fall's my favorite season, she said. *But where did it go?*

Baltimore, Charles answered.

Jobs? Absolutely.

I write commercials, Charles said. *I'm a creative director.*

I cheat clients, she said. *I'm a broker.* After which she added: *Just kidding.*

Restaurants dined in . . . colleges attended . . . favorite movies. All spoken of, discussed, *mentioned.*

Just not marriages.

Marriages, the plural, because she wore a wedding band on her left ring finger.

Maybe marriage wasn't considered an appropriate topic

when flirting. If flirting was what they were doing, of course. Charles wasn't sure; he was kind of rusty at it and had never been particularly at ease with women to begin with.

But as soon as she'd pressed the ten-dollar bill into the conductor's hand, Charles protesting all the while—*Don't be silly, you don't have to do that*—as soon as the conductor gave her one dollar in return, Charles still protesting—*No, really, this is totally unnecessary*—he'd gotten up and sat in the empty seat next to her. Why not—wasn't it the polite thing to do when someone helped you out? Even someone who looked like her?

Her thighs shifted to accommodate him. Even with his eyes glued to her heartbreaking face, he'd managed to notice the movement of her legs, a memory that stayed with him as he spoke to her about the banal, trivial, and superfluous—a good name, he thought, for a law firm specializing in personal injury suits.

He asked her, for example, which brokerage house she worked for. *Morgan Stanley,* she answered. And how long she'd been there. *Eight years.* And where she'd worked before that.

McDonald's she said.

My high school job.

She was just a little younger than he was, she was reminding him. Just in case he hadn't noticed.

He had. In fact, he was trying to think of just the right word for her eyes and thought it was probably *luminous.* Yeah, luminous was just about perfect.

"I'll give you your money back as soon as we get to Penn Station," he said, suddenly remembering he was in her debt.

"Tomorrow's fine," she said. "Ten percent interest, of course."

"I've never met a woman loan shark before. Do you break legs, too?"

"Just balls," she said.

Yes, he guessed they *were* flirting after all. And he didn't seem half-bad at it, either. Maybe it was like riding a bicycle or having sex, in that you never actually forgot how. Although it was possible Deanna and he *had*.

"Is this your usual train?" he asked her.

"Why?"

"So I know how to give you your money back."

"Forget about it. It's nine dollars. I think I'll survive."

"No. I've got to give it back to you—I'd feel ethically impugned if I didn't."

"*Impugned?* Well, I wouldn't want you to feel impugned. By the way, is that an actual word?"

Charles blushed. "I think so. I saw it in a crossword puzzle once, so it must be."

Which got them onto a discussion about what else? Crossword puzzles. She liked them—he didn't.

She could make it through Monday's with *both eyes closed*. He needed both eyes and a piece of brain he didn't possess. The one that provided focus and fortitude. His brain liked to roam around a little too much to sit down and figure out a five-letter word for . . . say . . . *sadness*. All right, all right, so that was an easy one. *Grief*. That place where his brain insisted on spending so much of its time these days. Where it had set up house and resolutely refused to budge. Except, of course, when it was imagining that alternate world of his, where he could flirt with green-eyed women he'd just met not five minutes before.

They kept talking about other mostly inconsequential things. The conversation a little like the train itself, moving along at a nice, easy clip, if briefly stopping here and there to pick up some new topic of discussion before gathering steam once again. And then suddenly they were under the East River and almost there.

"Well, I'm lucky you were here today," he said, entombed in darkness as the fluorescent train lights flickered off and all he could see was the vague shape of her body. It seemed like he'd just got on, like he'd just been asked for nine dollars he didn't have, and she'd just untangled her thighs and paid for him.

"Tell you what," he said. "Take the same train tomorrow and I'll pay you back then."

"You've got a date," she said.

For the rest of the day, even after he'd shaken her hand good-bye and watched as she disappeared into the Penn Station crowd, after he'd waited ten minutes for a cab uptown and was greeted with his boss, Eliot, telling him to brace himself just two feet into the office, he'd think about her choice of words.

She could've said fine, sure, meet you tomorrow. She could've said good idea. Or *bad* idea. Or just mail it to me.

But she'd said: *You've got a date.*

Her name was Lucinda.

DERAILED FOUR

Something was up.

Eliot informed him their credit card client was coming in to speak with them. Or, more likely, to scream at them.

Blown deadlines, poor tracking studies, unresponsive account executives—they could take their pick.

Even though the actual reason was the same reason it always was these days.

The economy.

Business simply wasn't good; there was too much competition, too many clients with too many options. Groveling was in, integrity out.

This was going to be a visit to the principal's office, a sit-down with Dad, an audience with the IRS. Where he'd have to stand and assume the position and say thank you, sir, too.

One look at Ellen Weischler's sour expression when he walked into the conference room pretty much confirmed this.

She looked as if she'd just tasted curdled milk or sniffed something odious. He knew *what*, too. The last commercial they'd done for her company was a triumph of mediocrity.

Badly cast, badly written, and badly received. It didn't matter that they'd recommended another one to them. That they'd begged and pleaded and, yes, even groveled in an attempt to get them to choose a different board. It didn't even matter that the first cut of the commercial had been almost good—clever, even hip—until the client, Ellen in particular, had meddled with it, changing copy, changing shots, each succeeding cut more bland than the previous one, until they'd ended up with the current dog wagging its tail five times a day on network buys across the country. It didn't matter because it was *their* spot, and the buck—or to be perfectly accurate, the 17 percent commission on the $130 million account—stopped there.

There being, of course, Charles.

He greeted Ellen with a chaste kiss on one cheek he thought better of halfway into his lean—thinking you should probably shake hands with she who was about to deck you.

"So . . . ," Ellen said when they'd all taken their seats. All being Charles, Eliot, two account people—Mo and Lo—and Ellen and hers. *So,* the way Charles's mother used to say it when she'd found a *Playboy* under his bed. *So.* A *so* that demanded explanation and certainly contrition.

"I guess you're not here to raise our commission," Charles said. He'd meant it as a joke, of course, only no one laughed. Ellen's expression stayed sour; if anything, she looked worse than before.

"We have some serious issues," Ellen said.

We have some serious issues, too. We don't like you telling us what to do all the time. We don't like being repudiated, belittled, ignored, screamed at. We actually don't like sour expressions. This is what Charles wanted to say.

What he actually said was: "I understand." And he said it with a hangdog expression he was perfecting to the point of artistry.

"It seems like we talk and talk but no one listens," Ellen said.

"Well, we—"

"This is just what I mean. *Listen* to me. Then speak."

It occurred to Charles that Ellen had transcended angry and gone straight to rude. That if she were an acquaintance, he would have already walked out of the room. That if she were a client worth significantly less than $130 million, he would've told her to take a hike.

"Of course," Charles said.

"We all agree on a strategy. We all sign off on it. And then you consistently go off in other directions."

Those directions being wit, humor, entertainment value, and anything else that actually might make a consumer sit up and watch.

"This last commercial is a case in point."

Yes, it is.

"We agreed on a board. We said it was going to be done in a certain way. Then you send us a cut that's nothing like what we agreed to. With all this *New York humor* in it."

If she'd uttered a profanity, c—t, say, she couldn't have looked more distasteful.

"Well, as you know, we're always trying to make it—"

"I said *listen.*"

She'd definitely entered *rude* and might actually be edging into *humiliating*. Charles wondered if this was something one was capable of recovering from.

"We have to send cut after cut back to you just in order to get it to the board we originally bought in the first place." She paused and looked down at the table.

Charles didn't like that pause.

It wasn't a pause that was finally inviting a response. It wasn't even a pause meant to let her catch her breath. It was a pause that portended something worse than what preceded it. The kind of pause he'd seen from girlfriends before they dropped the ax and dashed all hope. From unscrupulous salesmen about to get to the fine print. From emergency room interns about to tell you exactly what's wrong with your daughter.

"I think maybe we need a change of direction," she looked up and said.

Now what did that mean? Other than something bad. Was it possible she was firing the agency?

Charles looked over at Eliot, who, strangely enough, was looking down at the table now, too.

Then he understood.

Ellen wasn't firing the agency.

Ellen was firing him.

Off the account. Ten years, forty-five commercials, not an insignificant number of industry awards—it didn't matter.

The answer was no. You couldn't recover from this. Eliot could, but he couldn't. And it seemed to him that Eliot must've known, too. You don't take a step like this without informing someone in advance.

Et tu, Brute?

No one was speaking. The pause wasn't merely pregnant, it was pregnant with triplets—angry, bawling ones; something Charles was scared he himself was about to start doing—just lay his head on the table and begin crying. He didn't need a mirror to know he was turning bloodred. He didn't need a psychiatrist to know his self-esteem had taken a mortal hit.

Ellen cleared her throat. That's it. After repeatedly admonishing him for speaking out of turn, she was waiting for him to say something after all. She was waiting for his resignation speech.

"You don't want me on the business anymore."

He'd meant it to sound emotionless and maybe even slightly defiant. But he'd failed. It sounded whiny and defensive, maybe even pathetic.

"We certainly appreciate all the great things you've done," she began. Then he kind of tuned out. He was thinking that a ballsy company, a ballsy *president,* might've stood up to them—said we pick who works on your business here, and Charles is the guy. Maybe. If the account were less significant, if business were better, if they all weren't spending so much time on their knees.

But Eliot was still staring down at the table, doodling now as a way to give him something to do while Charles was being publicly eviscerated. Or perhaps he was just doing the math—$130 million versus Charles Schine—and coming up with the same answer every time.

Charles didn't let her finish.

"It's been fun," he said, finally striking the right note, he thought. World-weary cynicism with a touch of noblesse oblige.

He exited the conference room engulfed in a kind of hot haze; it felt like walking out of a steamroom.

And into an entirely different climate. Word had spread. He could see it on their faces, and they could see it on his. He barely acknowledged his secretary, walked into his office, shut the door.

Later, after everything fell apart for him, it would be hard to remember that it all began this morning.

In this way.

As for now, he sat behind closed doors and wondered whether Lucinda would be on the train tomorrow.

DERAILED FIVE

She wasn't.

He took the same train, stood on the very same spot on the platform.

He walked the train from car to car—first back, then forward—scanning each face the way people do in airports when they're expecting relatives from overseas. Faces they know but don't know, but long to know now.

"Remember the woman who bailed me out yesterday?" he asked the conductor. "Have you seen her?"

"What are you talking about?" The conductor didn't remember him, didn't remember her, didn't remember the incident. Maybe he was used to berating commuters on a regular basis; yesterday's drama wasn't worthy of recall.

"Never mind," Charles said.

She wasn't there.

He was a little amazed that it mattered to him. That it mattered to the point where he'd walked the cars like a rousted homeless man seeking warmth. Who was she, anyway, but a married woman he'd harmlessly flirted with on the way to work? And that's what *made* it harmless—that they hadn't done it again. So why exactly was he looking for her?

Well, because he wanted to talk, maybe. About this and that and the other thing. About what happened to him at the office yesterday, for instance.

He hadn't been able to tell Deanna.

He was all ready to. Honest.

"How was work today?" she'd asked him at dinner.

A perfectly legitimate question, the question, in fact, he'd been waiting for. Only Deanna had looked tired and worried—she'd been peering into Anna's blood sugar journal when he walked into the kitchen.

So Charles had said: "Work's fine."

And that was it for talk about the office.

When Anna first got sick, they'd talked of nothing else. Until it became apparent what the future held for her, and then they'd stopped talking about it. Because to talk about it was to acknowledge it.

Then they created a whole *canon* of things they were not to talk to each other about. Anna's future career plans, for example. Any article in *Diabetes Today* involving loss of limbs. Any bad news in general. Because complaining about something other than Anna diminished Anna.

"I was monitored by Mrs. Jeffries today," Deanna said. Mrs. Jeffries was her school principal.

"How did it go?"

"Fine. Pretty much. You know she always throws a fit if I deviate from accepted lesson plans."

"So did you?"

"Yes. But the composition I gave out was 'Why we like our principal.' So she couldn't really complain, could she?"

Charles laughed. And thought how that was something they used to do a lot of. The laughing Schines. And he looked at his wife and thought, *Yes, she's still beautiful.*

Dirty blond hair—with a little help from Clairol, maybe—

tousled and curly and barely constrained by a white elastic headband; dark brown eyes that never looked at him without at least a modicum of love. Only there were tired lines radiating out from the corners of those eyes, as if tears had cut actual tracks into the surface of her skin. Like those lines crisscrossing NASA photographs of Mars—*dry riverbeds,* the astronomers explain, where torrents of water once surged across the now dead landscape. Which is sometimes the way he thought about Deanna—all cried out.

After dinner they both went upstairs. Charles attempted to help Anna with her eighth-grade social homework—the separation of church and state, something she was trying to do with MTV tuned to the volume of *excruciating.*

"What steps did the United States take to separate church and state?" Charles said, only he mouthed the words so that maybe Anna would get the point—that there should be a separation of homework and TV.

She refused to take the hint. When he finally stood in front of the television so she'd stop sneaking peeks at Britney or Mandy or Christina and concentrate on the business at hand, she told him to move.

"Sure," he said. And jerked his arms and legs in a reasonable facsimile of the funky chicken. *See, I'm moving.*

At least that elicited a smile, no small accomplishment from a thirteen-year-old daughter whose general demeanor ranged from sullen to dour. Then again, she had good cause.

When he finished helping her, he gave her a kiss on the top of her head and she grunted something that sounded like *Good night* or *Get lost.*

Then he entered his bedroom, where Deanna was lying under the covers and pretending to sleep.

The next morning he ran into Eliot by the elevators.

"Can I ask you something?" Charles said.

"Sure."

"Did you know they were coming in to ask me off the business?"

"I thought they came in to *complain* about the advertising. Asking you off the business was how they registered the seriousness of their complaint."

"I just wondered if you knew it was coming."

"Why?"

"*Why?*"

"Why do you want to know if I knew it was coming? What's the difference, Charles? It was coming."

When the elevator doors opened, Mo was standing there with two legal pads and the new head creative on the business.

"Going down?" she said.

DERAILED SIX

Lucinda," he said. Or yelped.

That's what it sounded like to him—the noise a dog makes when its tail is stepped on.

She was back on the train.

He hadn't seen her when he sat down; he'd opened his paper and immediately burrowed into the land of the Giants: "Coach Fassel lamented the lack of pressure by his front four this past Sunday. . . ."

Then that black pump, the stiletto heel like a dagger aimed at his heart, as he looked up and bared his chest for the kill.

"Lucinda . . ."

A second later, that perfect face edging out into the aisle to peer at him, eyes sheathed in black-rimmed spectacles—*she hadn't worn glasses before, had she*—followed by a full-wattage smile. No, more like one of those soft-glow bulbs, the kind of light that takes the edge off and makes everything look better than it actually is.

And she said: "Hi." Such a sweet "hi," too, as genuine sounding as they come, a woman who seemed glad to see him. Even though she was four rows and three days away from their scheduled assignation.

"Why don't you come over here," she whispered.

Yes, why not.

When he reached her, Lucinda pulled her impossibly long legs off to the side to let him pass.

"Just in time," she said. "I was ready to call the police and report the nine dollars stolen."

He smiled. "I looked all over for you the other day."

"I'll bet," she said.

"No, really, I did."

"I was *kidding*, Charles."

"So was I," he lied.

"So," she said, hand out, impeccably manicured fingernails polished bloodred, "pay up."

"Sure." He reached for his wallet, opening it up to a picture of Anna and hiding it immediately, as if it were an admonishment he didn't wish to hear. He placed a crisp ten-dollar bill in her hand, the tips of his fingers grazing her flesh, which felt slightly moist and hot.

"Your daughter?" she said.

He blushed, was sure he blushed, even as he answered, "Yep."

"How old?"

"Too old." The wise-guy-ish you-wouldn't-believe-the-travails-of-fatherhood tone. The good-natured *I love her and all, but I wouldn't mind wringing her neck on occasion.*

"*Tell* me about it."

So she had children, too. Of course she did.

"Daughters?" he asked.

"One."

"All right, I showed you mine, now you show me yours."

She laughed. *Score one for Charles, the cutup.* Then she reached into her bag, one of those cavernous things you could've gone camping with if it wasn't made of such obviously expensive leather. She fished out her wallet and flipped it open for him.

A very photogenic little girl of about five, blond hair flying in all directions, caught in midair on a playground swing somewhere in the country, maybe. Freckle faced, knobby kneed, and sweet smiled.

"She's adorable," he said, and meant it.

"Thanks. I forget sometimes." Mimicking his tone of parental weariness. "Yours looked lovely, too—what I could see of her."

"An angel," he said, then immediately regretted his choice of words.

The conductor asked them for their tickets. Charles was tempted to ask him if he remembered the woman *now*. After all, he was doing everything possible to sneak peeks at her legs.

"Here," she said to Charles after the conductor managed to pull himself away and move on. She'd put a dollar bill in his hand.

"I thought I owed you interest," he said.

"I'll let you slide. This time."

He wondered about *this time*.

"I didn't remember you with glasses," he said.

"Getting new contacts," she said.

"Oh. You look great in them, by the way."

"You think?"

"Yeah."

"Not too serious for you."

"I like serious."

"Why's that?"

"Why do I like serious?"

"Yes, Charles. Why do you like serious?"

"Seriously . . . I don't know."

She smiled. "You're kind of funny, aren't you?"

"I try."

They were passing Rockville Centre, the movie theater where he often took Deanna plainly visible from the train car. And for one surreal moment, he imagined he was looking out on his past life. That he was firmly ensconced in this new universe of his—snug as a bug in *Charlesville.* Just Lucinda and him, newly married and on their way to work. Still chitchatting about their recent honeymoon—*where* had they gone, exactly? Kaui—yes, two weeks at the posh Kaui Hilton. Already starting to think about having kids, too—after all, they weren't getting any younger, were they? One of each, they'd decided, though it didn't really matter. As long as they were, of course, healthy. . . .

"Busy day today?" she asked him.

"Busy? Sure." Busy fending off disgruntled clients looking for his head and bosses looking to betray him. And for a second, he felt like telling her exactly what had been going on there and finding a nice soft spot on her shoulder to cry on.

"Me too."

"*What?*"

"It's going to be a busy day for me, too."

"I imagine you're getting a lot of angry calls these days."

"Well, if you consider death threats angry."

Charles smiled. "You're kind of funny, too."

"You think?"

"Yes. Clients must have loved you when times were good."

"Are you kidding? Then you weren't making them enough money. They all had a cousin or brother-in-law or grandmother whose stock split sixty-four times. Why couldn't I sell them one of *those?*"

"Well, admit it. It was kind of like throwing darts."

"Sure. Now they're throwing them at me."

He thought he detected the slightest accent. What, though?

"Were you born in New York?" he asked her.

"No, Texas. I was an army brat," she said. "I grew up every-
where and nowhere."

"That must have been tough." The usual platitude one was
supposed to offer at that kind of statement, he guessed.

"Well, your best friend changed identity just about every six
months. On the other hand, it was kind of neat because *you*
changed identity, too, if you wanted to. If you screwed up in
Amarillo, they didn't have to know about it in Sarasota. You
were able to start clean."

"I can see the benefit of that," Charles said. The man across
from them was pretending to read the paper, but what he was
actually doing was the very same thing the conductor had
done. That is, taking every opportunity to stare at Lucinda's
thighs. Charles felt a certain pride of ownership—even if ownership consisted solely of the forty-five-minute ride into Penn
Station.

"Did that happen a lot?" Charles asked.

"What?"

"You screwing up?"

"Once or twice," she said. "I was rebelling against authority."

"Is that what you called it?"

"No. That's what *they* called it. I called it getting lit."

"Who's they? Your parents?"

"Yeah. And the army psychiatrist they made me go to."

"How was that?"

"Have you ever *met* an army psychiatrist?"

"General incompetence? Major malpractice? No."

She laughed. "See, I told you you were funny," she said.

Yes, an absolute laugh riot. "Maybe you wouldn't mind calling my clients up and telling them that."

"Sure. How *are* things at the office?"

"Fine."

"You said you were in what . . . advertising?"

"Yes. Advertising."

"So? How is the ad biz these days?"

"It has its good days and bad days."

"And . . . ?"

"And . . . ?"

"These are the bad days?"

"Well, no one's threatening to kill me." No, just to demote him into insignificance.

"Come on, I complain about my job—you complain about yours. Fair's fair. . . ."

And so, what the hell. He did tell her.

Initially not intending to reveal much more than that he'd had a little trouble with a client, but once he started he found himself more or less unable to stop. Listening to himself spill out the details of office Sturm und Drang with genuine amazement at his utter lack of control. Seething Ellen Weischler. Backstabbing Eliot. The unfairness of it all.

He supposed she could have stopped him at any point. She could have said enough, or do you really want to be telling me this, or even begun to laugh at him.

She did none of those things, though. She listened. And when he finished, she said:

"And they think brokers suck."

"I don't know what made me tell you that," he said. "Sorry." Although he wasn't, actually. Embarrassed? Sure. But at the same time *purged.* As if he'd finally thrown up last night's rancid meal and could finally get back to the table.

And then she did more than just listen to him. She reached out and massaged his right shoulder. More like a soft, soothing pat, a friendly rub, a supportive and sisterly squeeze.

"Poor baby," she said.

And Charles couldn't help thinking that certain clichés are belittled out of nothing but jealousy. *Her touch felt electric,* for instance. A cliché knocked as pure hokum by people unlucky enough not to be feeling it. Which, at any given moment, was *most* people. Because, well, her touch *did* feel electric; his body was suddenly humming like one of those power lines they string across the dry Kansas plains.

They blew into the East River Tunnel—*the tunnel of love,* he thought—and for just a moment he was afraid he was going to lean over and do something stupid. That he'd end up being taken away in handcuffs for this stupid thing on the platform at Penn Station.

Then something happened.

The train car went pitch black, the lights zapping off as they always did when the train burrowed under the East River. It felt as if he were sitting in a darkened movie theater waiting for that phosphorescent glow to come rescue him. Or for something else to rescue him; he could smell her there in the darkness. Lilac and musk.

And then her breath was by his ear, soft and humid. Her mouth was close enough to kiss as it whispered something into his ear.

Then the lights blinked on, blinked off, and settled back into full ghostly fluorescence.

Nothing had really changed.

The unrepentant voyeur sitting directly across from them was still peeking at Lucinda's thighs. The woman with varicose-veined legs was dozing across the aisle from them. There was the pinch-faced banker, the college kid slumped over his textbook, the court stenographer warily guarding her Teletype.

Lucinda also looked just like she had before, turned face forward like everyone else.

Wasn't she turning back to her newspaper, checking the Amex and the Nasdaq and the overseas indexes and municipal bonds?

He waited a while to see if she'd look over and resume speaking with him, then looked out the window, where they passed a massive billboard that said, "Lose Yourself in the Virgin Islands."

When the train settled into Penn Station, he asked her if they might have lunch sometime.

You're the sexiest man I've ever met.
That's what Lucinda whispered to him on the train.

DERAILED SEVEN

Okay," Winston said, "okay. Seven players who hit forty or more home runs with eleven letters in their last name."

"Yastrzemski," Charles answered, immediately going for the local boy made good, the BoSox star who'd been raised on a Long Island potato farm.

"Okay," Winston said. "That's one."

Winston Boyko. Mailroom employee. Baseball fan. General raconteur.

He'd been stepping into Charles's office ever since he'd spied Charles in his faded Yankees T-shirt.

Charles had asked him if he wanted anything, and he'd said, *Yes, the starting lineup of the 1978 Yankees, including DH.*

Charles had gotten every one with the exception of Jim Spencer—first baseman—and that, more or less, had started a friendship. Of sorts.

Charles couldn't tell you where Winston lived or what his middle name was, or even if he had a girlfriend or wife. It was a let's-talk-baseball-trivia kind of friendship, a relationship conducted in the ten minutes a day Winston delivered the mail—once in the morning, once in the afternoon.

Right now, it was morning and Winston was grinning because Charles was having trouble coming up with any additions to the great Yaz.

Killebrew—sorry, nine letters.

Petrocelli—good guess, only ten.

"How about you give me till this afternoon?" Charles asked.

"You mean so you can look it up on-line and then pretend you didn't?"

"Yes."

"Okay," Winston said, "sure."

Winston wasn't your average mailroom employee. For one thing, he was white. For another thing, he was easily smart enough to be writing copy.

Charles had wondered on more than one occasion why he'd ended up delivering office mail—but he'd never asked him. They weren't that kind of buddies.

On the other hand, you never knew. Wasn't Winston looking at him with a hint of genuine concern?

"You okay, chief?" he asked him.

"Sure. I'm fine."

Only he wasn't fine. He'd been handed a pain reliever account from Eliot, his boss and betrayer. By note, too—"Till something better comes along," he'd written at the bottom of the page. Only when was *that* going to be?

And he was thinking about what he was going to be doing for lunch today. Who he'd be having lunch *with*. The woman with the luminous eyes.

And Charles thought: *I have never cheated on Deanna.*

Not once.

Not that he hadn't been tempted here and there. Sorely tempted, sometimes experiencing actual physical symptoms not unlike the warning signs of a heart attack—a faint sweat, a dull ache in the chest, a slight nausea. It's just that whenever he contemplated going further, he experienced the very same symptoms.

Only worse.

The problem was that he looked at infidelity pretty much the way he imagined Deanna did—not as a fling, but as a *betrayal*. And betrayal was the kind of word he associated with Benedict Arnold and the 1919 Black Sox. The kind of act that gets you either banned or executed. Besides, he was sure that he loved his wife. That he loved at least the constant unalterable presence of her.

Then again, this was before life betrayed *him*. Before he started dreaming about life in a more Charles-friendly universe.

"You look kind of sick," Winston said. "I'm worried it might be contagious."

"It's not." You couldn't *catch* what he had, could you?

"That's what Dick Lembergh said."

"Dick Lembergh? Who's that?"

"Nobody *now*. He's dead."

"Thank you. That's comforting," Charles said.

"I'll give you a hint," Winston said.

"A *hint?*"

"About the other six players. Three of them were American Leaguers."

"Why didn't you say three of them were National Leaguers?"

"Hey, you're *good*."

Winston might not have a blue-collar mind, but he had a workingman's body. That is, he looked like he could beat you up if he ever felt like it. He had a tattoo on his upper arm—*AB*, it said.

A mistake I made, he'd once told Charles.

Getting the tattoo?

Nah. Dating that girl—Amanda Barnes. I like the tat.

"By the way," he said now, straightening up to leave, "I'm not a hundred percent sure if it's seven players with eleven letters in their last names or eleven players with seven letters in their last names. A guy told it to me in a bar around two in the morning, so it's anybody's guess."

They met at an Italian restaurant on 56th and Eighth where it was reputed that Frank Sinatra used to eat on occasion.

Lucinda was dressed for success—if success was making Charles's eyes water with adoration and arousal. A silk V-neck blouse that didn't hang, drape, or cover—it *clung*.

Of course, it could have simply been nerves he was feeling. It was like having lunch with a supplier, neither one exactly sure what to expect.

So Charles asked her what any friendly business acquaintance might ask another. What her husband did.

"Play golf," said Lucinda of the lovely eyes.

"For a living?"

"I hope not."

"How long have you been . . . ?"

"Married? Long enough to have to think about it. And you?"

"Eighteen years," Charles said. He didn't have to think about it—didn't particularly want to think about it, either. On the other hand, wasn't talking about their spouses a sign that nothing untoward was going on here, that everything was pretty much innocent?

"Eighteen years ago I was in grade school," Lucinda said.

He'd wondered how old she was—around thirty, he guessed.

"So," Lucinda asked him, "any new backstabbings to report?"

"Well, I have a new account."

"Yes?"

"An aspirin. Recommended by doctors two to one over other aspirins."

"That's great."

"Except doctors don't recommend aspirin anymore. But if they did . . ."

"So what are you going to . . . ?"

"I don't know. It's a headache."

Lucinda laughed. Lucinda had thin wrists and tapered fingers that she used to brush her thick dark hair out of her eyes—*one* eye, actually. He thought of Veronica Lake in *This Gun for Hire*.

"How did you get into . . . ?"

"Advertising? Nobody knows how they get into advertising. It's a mystery. Suddenly, you just are."

"Kind of like marriage, huh?"

"Marriage? I don't follow."

"Well, believe it or not, I can't remember actually *wanting* to get married. I don't even remember saying *yes*. I must've, though."

She twisted her diamond ring as if to make sure it was actually there—that she was, in fact, married. Maybe it was Charles's charm that was making her forget?

"Your husband. Did you meet him in Texas?" Charles asked.

"No. I smoked pot in Texas. And hung out in backseats."

"Oh, right—I forgot—you were a juvenile delinquent."

"They call it *hell-raiser* in Amarillo. How about the teenage Charles? What was he like?"

"Oh. I was a heck-raiser, I guess." The teenage Charles read a lot of books and handed in every homework assignment and term paper on time.

"Oh, right—you were the guy we made fun of."

"Yeah. That's me."

Charles was basking in the afterglow of lunch.

Unfortunately, he was also staring at a file that said "Account Review" on the cover.

The thing about being given a pain reliever account was that you didn't necessarily want to accept it. Pain relievers, dishwasher detergents, deodorants. They were signposts to a kind of advertising Siberia. "Downward Spirals This Way." They existed in a place where no one much noticed what you did, save the clients themselves. And they made you test, retest, and test some more, even though odds were good you'd still end up with a housewife holding the product up to camera and telling you how it changed her life.

In addition to inheriting the account, he inherited a commercial that seemed to be well into the preproduction process. That is, it had already been tested, retested, and tested again and then sent off to three production houses for bids. One of them—Headquarters Productions, Charles noticed—had been recommended by the agency. He knew their rep—Tom Mooney, old style and annoying, a Fuller Brush man with reels.

The account executive on his new account, Mary Widger, had sent him the TV board for his perusal. As it turned out, it wasn't a housewife holding the pain reliever up to camera and telling the world how it changed her life. It was a housewife holding the pain reliever up to camera and telling her husband instead.

He called David Frankel, an agency producer he'd never worked with before, since David worked on the kinds of commercials he'd be doing from now on but hadn't up till now.

"Yeah," Frankel answered the phone. "Who's this?"

"Charles Schine."

"Oh. Charles Schine."

"I think we're going to be working together."

"It's about time," David said. Charles wondered if he was expressing friendliness or simply satisfaction at Charles's demotion into the land of analgesics.

He'd pick friendliness.

It was the agency producer's job to bid out the board, work

the numbers to everyone's satisfaction, then go off and shoot it with you.

"This job seems a little high," Charles said. He was referring to the bid price penciled in at the bottom of the page—already forwarded to the client for approval after factoring in editing, music, and all the other postproduction costs. Plus agency commission.

Nine hundred and twenty-five thousand dollars for a two-day shoot.

"They always pay that," David said.

"Okay. It just seems a little high for two actors and an aspirin bottle."

"Well, that's the price," he said flatly.

"Fine." It wasn't as though money were something Charles was supposed to concern himself with—only if the clients themselves were concerned about it. And according to David, they weren't.

But it did seem high.

"Why don't we get together next week and go over every-thing," Charles said.

"I count the minutes," David said.

Charles guessed friendliness wasn't what David had been ex-pressing after all.

Their second lunch date was still more *lunch* than date. Still just two people who found each other interesting, if unavail-able.

When dessert arrived—two biscottis with cappuccinos—she said: "You never mention your daughter. What's she like?"

"Normal," Charles said.

"Normal?"

"Yeah. Normal."

"That's it? I've heard gushing parents before . . ."

"Rude. Moody. Generally embarrassed I'm her father. *Normal.*"

Of course he hadn't told her *why* his daughter was rude and moody a lot of the time.

But she was looking at him with an expression that looked kind of reproachful, so he did.

"She's sick."

"Oh."

"Juvenile diabetes. And no, you don't just take insulin and everything's okay. Not this time."

"Sorry," she said.

"So am I."

Lucinda was a first-class listener.

He realized this about ten minutes into his mostly uninterrupted monologue about just *how* sorry he was. How eight years ago he and Deanna had brought this normal little girl into the ER and left with someone else. A kid he had to give shots to twice a day and monitor closely so she wouldn't dive into hypoglycemic shock. A kid for whom he had to go buy special insulin made from pig cells because it was the only one she'd really respond to, but whose general condition was in free fall anyway. A kid like that.

His kid.

She listened with empathy and concern. She shook her head, she sighed, she politely asked him questions when she didn't understand something. *Pig insulin—why was that?*

He answered her as best he could, and when he finally finished spilling his guts, she resisted feeding him even one moronic platitude. He appreciated that.

"I don't know how you manage," she said, "I really don't. How's Anna dealing with it?"

"Fine. She's renting herself out as a pin cushion."

One of the ways *he* was dealing with it, of course, was this way. The lame joke, the stale bon mot, laughing in the face of disaster.

"How's that working out for you?" Lucinda asked him after he mentioned *needling* Anna about taking her pig's insulin on time.

"How's what working out?" Charles said. Playing dumb.

"Nothing," Lucinda said. "Never mind."

What do you talk about when you can't talk about the future?

You talk about the past.

Sentences begin with "Remember when . . ." or "I passed Anna's old nursery school today . . ." or "I was thinking about that vacation we took in Vermont. . . ."

After he and Deanna spent dinner reminiscing about the heatless ski shack in Stowe where Anna's milk bottle had frozen solid, after they finished eating and stacked the dishes and Charles went upstairs and checked Anna's feet, which she only grudgingly displayed for him, they both ended up in bed with the TV on.

Then somehow, her hand ended up touching his. His leg sidled up to her leg. It was as if their limbs were doing it on their own, their bodies finally saying, *Enough of this, I'm cold. I'm lonely.*

Charles got up and locked the door. Not a word about what they were doing. He slid back into bed and embraced her, heart colliding with his ribs, kissing her and thinking how he'd really and truly missed this.

Only somewhere in the middle of becoming lovers again they became strangers. It was odd how that happened. As he was moving on top of her and beginning to enter her, his mouth searching for hers—a sudden awkwardness to their motions. They were like two jigsaw pieces refusing to match— turn them this way and that way, and they still wouldn't fit. She pushed against his chest, he fell out of her, he went to kiss her, she turned her head the wrong way. She smiled in encouragement, he moved back into her, she froze, he shrank and slunk away.

They untangled slowly and drifted to opposite sides of the bed. Neither of them said good night.

DERAILED EIGHT

How did they get from lunch hour to the cocktail hour?

From tuna Niçoise and biscottis to cosmopolitans and salted nuts?

Lunch, after all, was something you did with a friend. Drinks was something you did with a good friend. Lunch involved a call to Lucinda, but drinks required a call to Deanna. An explanation for his lateness. It required *lying*.

And he was as bad a liar as he was a joke teller.

Then again, practice makes perfect.

"I'm working late tonight," he told Deanna over the phone on the afternoon of their first nighttime date.

"I'm working late *again*," he told her the next time.

And the time after that.

Slowly becoming aware that life was changing for him. That he was spending most of his time more or less waiting for the *next* time he'd see Lucinda.

Temple Bar.

Keats.

Houlihan's. Where both of them finally had to acknowledge where this was heading.

Maybe it was the drinks. He'd decided to forgo his usual Cabernet and had opted for a margarita instead. Or two. At a bar where they didn't skimp on the tequila.

By his second drink, he was seeing things. Or not seeing things. For instance, the rest of the bar patrons had faded away, leaving only Lucinda.

"I think you're trying to get me drunk," she said.

"No. I'm trying to get you drunker."

"Oh right. I forgot. I'm already wasted."

"You look beautiful wasted," he said.

"That's because *you're* wasted."

"Oh yeah."

She did look beautiful—glassy eyes had nothing to do with it. Dressed tonight in something ridiculously short and impossibly snug, stretched *this* tight over her glossy nylon thighs.

"What did you tell your wife?" she asked him.

"I told her I was having drinks with a beautiful woman I met on the Long Island Rail Road."

"Ha," she said.

"What did you tell your husband?"

"Same thing. That I was having drinks with a beautiful woman I met on the Long Island Rail Road." She laughed, holding her pink cosmopolitan away from her body so it wouldn't spill on her.

Her husband. Stolid, dependable, nearly twenty years older than her, and poisonously boring, she'd complained to him. Passionate only about golf these days.

"You know . . . ," he said. "You know . . ."

"What?"

"I forget." He was going to say something that he had the vague notion he was going to regret later, but he'd lost it when she turned to look at him with those soft green eyes. If jealousy

was the *green-eyed monster,* what was love? The green-eyed
angel?

"What are we doing, Charles?" she said, looking kind of
solemn now. Maybe she was about to say something she was
going to regret, too.

"We're having a drink."

"I meant what are we doing after we have a drink?"

"Having another drink?"

"After that."

He was thinking of a possible answer for that one, but suddenly there *was* someone else in the bar; they *weren't* the only
two people left in the world. A man of uncertain age had
pushed himself between them to get the bartender's attention.

Only his attention went elsewhere—as soon as he got a look
at Lucinda's legs, that is.

"May I buy you a drink?" he said to her.

"No," she said, showing the cosmo still in her hand.

"Okay. May I buy you the bar?"

"Sure, go ahead."

"Excuse me," Charles said; the man was nearly standing on
his shoes.

"I don't want to buy *you* a drink," the man said.

"That's funny. It is. Only I was talking to the woman here."

"So was I."

Charles couldn't tell whether the man was being funny or
just being himself, which could be anything from rude to
homicidal. It was hard to tell these days.

"You know, actually, he *was* talking to me," Lucinda said to
the man. "So . . ."

"A needle pulling thread."

"All right, *we'll* leave," she said.

"Oh, *stay,*" he said.

"Excuse me," Lucinda said, getting up from her bar stool and trying to push past him.

"Something I said?"

"*Excuse* me."

"Great. The cunt's leaving," he said.

Charles hit him.

As far as he knew, he'd never hit anyone before; he was surprised that hitting someone was just as painful as being hit. He was also surprised that the man actually went down, with genuine blood on his lip.

"He said something very rude to me," Lucinda explained to several waiters who'd suddenly materialized and stepped between them.

A flushed-looking man came rushing up from the nether regions of the restaurant—the manager, Charles guessed.

"Maybe you should all leave," he said after ascertaining what had transpired. It wasn't difficult—the man Charles had punched to the floor was still in the process of getting up, and Charles was still rubbing the hand that punched him.

"Sure," Charles said. "Why not."

He retrieved Lucinda's coat from the cloakroom, aware that all eyes were on him, though the only eyes he cared about were green and widened with gratitude.

Well, weren't they? Hadn't he just kicked sand on the bully, rescued the maiden, defended her honor?

It was blustery outside, cold enough to turn his breath to vapor.

"Get a cab to Penn?" she asked, her eyes tearing up from the chill—or was it from the emotion of the moment? From the exhibition of his *prowess?*

"Forget the train," he said. "I'll call a car. I'll get a car and drop you home."

"You sure?"

"Yes."

"Maybe that's not a good idea."

"Why's that?"

"I don't know. Someone may see us." The first open acknowledgment of illicit doings.

"Someone might see us on the train, too."

"That's the train. Strangers sit on trains. Its different."

"Okay. Whatever you want." His arm was on her arm—he hadn't realized he'd put it there, but he had, and he could feel her body heat beneath the coat. Like the fever beneath a chill.

"I just don't think the car's a good idea."

"Okay."

"I might do something I shouldn't do."

"Like pass out?" He was trying to be funny again—emphasis on *trying*—but maybe it wasn't the time to be funny, because he could almost swear she was leaning in toward him, that she'd somehow gotten closer than she'd been before.

"Like maybe *eat* you," she said.

"That settles it," he said. "I'm getting the car."

She kissed him.

But kissing doesn't quite do it justice. It wasn't kissing as much as mouth-to-mouth resuscitation, because he felt himself coming back from the dead.

When they pulled apart, and they didn't do that for what seemed like a day and a half, they both caught their breath as if just beached from the sea.

"Uh-oh," she said.

His sentiments exactly. Or maybe just *oh*. An exclamation of wonderment and unbridled joy—okay, not *totally* unbridled, since there were just a few complications lurking around somewhere.

Yet those complications—which had names and faces and legitimate claims to his love and loyalty—suddenly seemed to recede like the bar patrons from moments ago and fade away into a peripheral world.

*   *   *

In the car ride home they snuggled in the backseat, *snuggling* the kind of word you generally stop using past a certain age. It felt both warmly familiar and achingly new.

They kissed again, too. And he kissed not just lips, but several parts of her, the nape of her neck, the faint scar on the inside of her arm—*playground accident*—her dark, downy eyebrows. One eye on the driver, who now and then would glance in his rearview mirror, the other eye on each other, and he'd have to say that each other looked pretty good. Flushed faces—hers for sure, and he could also feel the heat on his own, though *it wasn't the heat, it was the humidity.* As if they were enveloped in a swollen raincloud ready to drench them to the bone and him all ready to dance through the puddles afterward like Gene Kelly.

When they lip-locked over Van Cortland Avenue, when they squeezed hands past the shadow of Shea, when they nuzzled on the exit ramp to the Grand Central Parkway—he was willing to wager that no one had felt exactly like this before, even though he knew it was a lie. The number one sin of the hopeless addict: denial. And he *was* addicted, wasn't he? It seemed as if he couldn't go two exits without kissing her. That he couldn't make it through three songs on the radio—101.6 FM, Music to Make Out By—without running his hands up and down her body.

"Slow down," she said once they made it off Exit 8E of the Meadowbrook Parkway—no meadow, no brook, just parkway. She was saying it to the driver, but she might as well have been talking to him, because if he didn't slow down, it was possible that he would overheat—one of those unfortunate victims you see littering the highway on their way to somewhere important.

"I don't want you to drop me in front of the house," she said. "My husband's home."

"Where *is* your house?"

"A few blocks up. Over here is fine."

They stopped at the corner of Euclid Avenue—the name of a tree that no longer exists on Long Island.

And Lucinda said: "Meet me on the train tomorrow."

DERAILED NINE

It was called the Fairfax Hotel. The kind of hotel that had fallen into disrepair and anonymity. The kind of hotel most people would choose to bypass for something better.

But not Charles, and not now.

He was on his way there to spend the morning with Lucinda.

He'd finally screwed up the courage to ask.

They'd had two more dinners and two more car rides where they'd made out like overly hormonal high school kids. They'd kissed and petted and snuggled, and now it was time to *take the relationship further*. He'd actually used those words. Surprised they'd actually made it out of his mouth and eternally grateful she hadn't laughed at him. Even more grateful for her response, which after several moments of silence had been: *Sure, why not.*

He'd asked her this over two cups of coffee in Penn Station, and then they'd walked out onto Seventh Avenue arm in arm and shared a taxi, even though he'd be going approximately seventy blocks out of his way to drop her off—but then that was seventy more blocks of her company—embracing and clinging to this new idea of them. And she'd said, *Where?* Good question, too. Where exactly were they going to consummate things? And they'd passed one hotel in the taxi—*No,* she said, *too close to Penn;* and then another—*too stuffy looking;* and then one more when they'd made it all the way downtown.

The Fairfax Hotel.

Flanked by a Korean deli on one side and a woman's health center on the other. Kind of dingy, yes, but wasn't that the kind of hotel made for these things?

And she'd said, *Fine, yes, that one looks fine.*

And they'd made a date.

The train ride into Penn Station.

Both of them were surprisingly quiet, he thought, like boxers before the biggest bout of their lives.

He spent most of the time counting the minutes between stations: Merrick to Freeport to Baldwin to Rockville Centre. Under the darkness of the East River, she grabbed for his hand and locked fingers. They felt ice cold, as if all the blood had rushed out of them, frozen with . . . what? Guilt? Shame? Fear?

There was something nonspontaneous about all of this. Before, they'd been sort of fumbling around in the dark, but now it was all coolly premeditated. On the walk to the taxi stand, she leaned against him not so much from desire as from inertia, he thought. As if he were dragging her there—lugging dead weight up the escalator and through the entranceway.

He understood. It was one thing to make out in a car and another thing to check into a hotel with the intention of having sex.

The inside of the Fairfax Hotel looked pretty much the way the outside looked—shabby and faded and just this side of destitute. The lobby smelled of camphor.

When they walked up to the desk, he could feel Lucinda's

white-knuckled grip somewhere up by his throat. He told the deskman that he'd be paying in cash and was given a key to room 1207.

They rode the elevator up in silence.

When the doors opened on twelve, he said, "Ladies first."

And Lucinda said, "Age before beauty."

So they walked out together. The floor was in need of a few more light bulbs, he thought, since the only light seemed to be coming from a half-draped window to the left of the elevator. The carpet smelled of mildew and tobacco.

Room 1207 was way down at the end of the hall where it was darkest, and Charles needed to squint just to make out the numbers on the door.

This is what they got for ninety-five dollars in New York City: a room smelling of disinfectant, with one queen-size bed, one lopsided table lamp, and one table, all pretty much within two feet of one another.

A room that was virtually equatorial—with no discernible thermostat to help.

There was a white paper sash encircling the toilet lid. Charles did the honors; he had to go the moment he entered the room. Nerves.

When he came out of the bathroom, Lucinda was sitting on the bed, playing with the TV clicker. Nothing was actually appearing on the TV screen.

"I think you have to pay extra," she said.

"Do you want to . . . ?"

"No."

There was an awkward politeness to their mannerisms, he thought, as if they were a couple on a blind date. Jitters masked as solicitude.

"Why don't you sit down, Charles?" she said.

"Fine." He sat in the chair.

"I meant *here*."

"Oh. Right." He slipped off his coat and hung it up in the closet next to hers. Then he walked over to the bed—a very short walk given the dimensions of the room—and sat down.

I shouldn't be here. I should get up and leave. I should . . .

But she laid her head on his shoulder and said: "So. We're here."

"Yes." He was sweating right through his shirt.

"Okay." She sighed. "Do you want to stay, or do you want to go?"

"Yes."

"*Yes?* Which is it?"

"Stay. Or go. What do *you* want to do?"

"Fuck you," she said. "I think I want to fuck you."

It happened when they were ready to leave.

They'd dressed quietly, and Charles had searched the room to make sure they hadn't left anything.

Then they'd walked to the door.

He opened it to usher her out. She moved past him, and he could smell the perfume she'd just dabbed on in the bathroom. Then he smelled something else.

There were two of them standing there—Lucinda and him, and then suddenly there were three.

He was knocked backward onto the floor.

He was kicked in the ribs, then kicked in the stomach as the air was forced out of him. Lucinda was thrown on top of him, then not on top of him, then she was lying there beside him.

The door slammed. The lock turned.

There were two of them, and then there were three.

"Make one fucking sound and I'll blow your heads off," the one who wasn't either Lucinda or himself said.

A man with a gun—Charles could see him, could see the gun, too, something stunted looking and oily black. He was panting, as if he'd just run a long distance to get there.

"I'll give you all my money," Charles said. "You can have it."

"*What?*" The man was black but Hispanic, Charles thought, a kind of accent, anyway. "*What the fuck d'you say?*"

"My money—it's yours."

"I told you to shut the fuck up." He kicked him again, not in the ribs this time, but lower down. Charles groaned.

"Please," Lucinda said in a trembling little girl's voice, a voice that didn't seem capable of coming out of a grown woman. "Please . . . don't hurt us. . . ."

"*Don't hurt us,*" the man said, mimicking her, taking pleasure in making fun. Of her fear. That little-girl voice . . . like she was going to cry or something. "Oh, I ain't gonna *hurt* you, baby . . . uh-uh. . . . Now throw me your fucking wallets."

Charles reached for his pocket, through the folds of his down jacket saturated with sweat—reached in and grabbed his wallet with a shaking hand.

This only happens in movies. This only happens on the front pages. This only happens to someone else.

He threw his wallet to the man with the gun. Lucinda was fumbling inside her pocketbook, looking for hers, the one with the picture of a five-year-old girl on a swing somewhere in the country. Somewhere other than here—the threadbare floor of room 1207 in the Fairfax Hotel.

By the time she threw him her wallet, he was already looking through Charles's, pulling the cash out of it—quite a bit of cash, too, the cash Charles was going to use to pay for the room. But after the man took the cash, he kept looking at the wallet—grinning at something.

"Well, look at this," he said.

He was looking at Charles's pictures—Anna and Deanna and him. The Schine family.

"Funny," he said. "That don't look like you . . ." talking to Lucinda. "That sure as *shit* don't look like you."

Back to Charles. "That don't look anything like her, *Charles.*" Smirking at them.

Then, looking through her wallet and finding a picture of *hers.* "Ain't that something," he said. "*This* guy don't look like you, Charles. Uh-uh. This guy *ain't* you, Charles."

He snorted, laughed, giggled; he'd figured something out.

"Let's see here. Know what I think? Hey"—he kicked Charles again, not as hard this time, but hard enough—"I *said,* Know what I think?"

Charles said, "What?"

"*What?* What? I think you guys are fucking around with each other. Stepping out on the old lady, huh, *Charles?* Getting some *strange,* my man. That what you doing, *Charles?*"

Charles said, "Please, just take my money."

"*Just take your money?* Just take your money? Thanks, but I already took your fucking money. See"—holding the cash out to him—"this is your money. I *got* your fucking money."

"Yes," Charles said. "I see. I promise we won't go to the police."

"You promise, huh? That's fucking nice of you, that's real fucking *kind* of you, Charles. I can take your word on that, huh? You won't go to the police. Well then . . ."

He waved the gun around in little looping circles, first toward him, then her, then back again. Inky black, snub-nosed barrel. . . .

"Well then . . . if you ain't gonna go to the police and all . . ."

Lucinda was trembling beside him, shaking like a wet stray.

"Hey, baby," the man said. "Hey, *baby* . . ."

"Please . . . ," Lucinda said.

"How is she, *Charles?* Better than the old lady, I bet. Nice pussy, Charles? Nice *tight* pussy?"

Charles started to get up. He was back in the bar and the man was insulting her, and Charles would have to set him straight, to show him what's what. Except the man pistol-whipped him across the face and Charles went flying back again. Hearing a crack before feeling the pain—first one and then the other, first the sound of his nose being broken, then the nauseating *pain* of his nose being broken. And the blood starting to seep out on the floor.

"What was that, my man? I didn't hear you, *Charles*. What'd you say? You said you can fuck her if you want? Why, thank you, Charles. That's fucking kind of you. Letting me have your bitch and all."

"No," Lucinda moaned. "No . . ."

"*No*? Didn't you hear him say that I could fuck you, *Lucinda*." It was the first time he'd said her name—in a way, it seemed every bit as horrible as kicking them to the floor and stealing their wallets. "That's what the man said. You giving it to him—you can give it to me. Whore's a whore, *baby*. Am I right, Charles? Am I?"

Charles was choking on his own blood. It was pouring down his throat and clogging his windpipe—he was drowning in it, sputtering for air.

"Sit up here, Charles." The man pulled him up, led him over to the lone chair, which had fluff seeping out of a ripped cushion decorated with a faded floral design. He sat him down on it. "Feeling better there, Charles? Take a deep breath. That's right—in, out. You'll want a good seat for this, Charles. *Championship* fucking, my man. Twelve rounder. You don't want to miss this."

Lucinda ran.

She'd caught him by surprise—the man with the gun, lying there trembling like that, and then suddenly springing up and making a run for it. She made it all the way to the door.

She even turned the knob and got it half-open before he reached her and pulled her back in. By her hair. That dark, silky hair that tasted of shampoo and sweat, so soft you could comb it by hand—twisted in his fist as she screamed.

"You want to shut the fuck up, *Lucinda*." He'd put the barrel into her mouth, straight in, knocking it up against her teeth. Lucinda stopped screaming.

Charles was still wheezing through his own blood, dizzy enough to pass out, a white light searing the bridge of his nose. Watching as the man laid Lucinda onto the floor as if they were engaged in some eerie kind of dance, some modern pas de deux, laying her down and standing over her. As he pulled her skirt up above her waist. As he snorted and wolf whistled and slowly, slowly pulled her black lace panties down to her knees.

As he unzipped his pants.

DERAILED TEN

He passed out, more than once he passed out, but each time the man brought him back, slapping water onto his face, whispering into his ear.

Don't fade on me, my man. Round two . . . baby. Round three . . . four . . .

It was like bad porno . . . the kind you don't really want to see, but your friend just happens to have it, so you watch. Even as you pull your eyes away, you watch. The woman with the dog, the scat tape where she swallows it all—sickening, really, can't believe she's really doing that, but she is, and you're watching it. Your stomach churning, your guts heaving, makes you want to throw up, but you have to look at it. Don't know why, but you do.

Him and Lucinda. Beautiful naked Lucinda and him.

And she was beautiful. As he placed her on hands and knees and put it into her ass. Telling Charles what he was doing, too—keeping up a kind of running commentary. . . .

See, Charles—they love it in the ass. They tell you they don't, but all whores do.

Telling her to moan for him. Putting the gun up by her head as he rode her and *making* her moan. Moans of pain, probably, but they sounded like moans of pleasure. Moans were moans. Hard to tell which were which, except for the fact that her eyes were squeezed shut, her mascara streaked and running, and she was biting into her lip until it bled.

And Charles watching, sitting there in the chair as if he were tied down, even though he wasn't tied down.

See this, Charles—a born cocksucker. . . . That's right, baby . . . suck that big daddy dick. . . .

The tableaux changed, no longer fucking her in the ass, but standing in front of her, hands cradling her face, that beautiful Lucinda face. And Lucinda choking, gurgling, the sounds spurring him on . . . *Oh yes . . . oh yes . . . you watching this, Charles, Charley . . . don't want to miss the cum shot . . . gotta see the money shot . . . oh yes . . .*

And later, Lucinda lying there—how much later? Charles didn't know, later that morning, later that afternoon. Lucinda lying there covered with sweat and cum, hardly moving. Was she dead? No, she was still breathing, if only barely. Charles looked down at the dried blood on his hands and wondered whose it was, forgetting that it was his, that his nose must be broken.

And now the man was rubbing himself, naked except for his sweat socks and sneakers, staring at Lucinda on the floor and jerking himself. For another round. Round . . . *what?* Five, six?

"Still with us, *Charles?*" the man said. "Hang in there, bud. More to come. . . ."

And there was.

The man taking her again, propping her up against the bed as if she were a marionette, all loose arms and legs, twisting her into his vision of lewd. Legs up by her ears, hands spreading herself—giggling at this. Taking his time, placing her just right, an inch here, an inch there. Lucinda slack jawed, just a prop, a blowup doll.

And Charles decided to give it one more shot—not *him* deciding, his *machismo* deciding, his reptilian cortex, maybe—pushing him up off the chair in the general direction of the man who was about to rape Lucinda for the fifth or sixth time.

The first thing was—he was dizzy. It was blindman's buff and he'd been spun around the room like a top and couldn't tell which way was which. He staggered, he teetered, he wobbled—the man not even aware of him yet because he was still positioning Lucinda and had maybe forgotten that Charles was even in the room. So Charles eventually righted himself and actually made it all the way over to him. He grabbed the man from behind, around the neck, and squeezed.

He squeezed for all he was worth, he squeezed like there was no tomorrow, a virtual *death grip* of steel. But the man calmly, almost lazily, stood up and sloughed Charles off him as if he were dumping garbage onto the sidewalk. Charles ended up splay-legged on the floor, wondering what happened, as the man grinned and shook his head.

"Charles . . . Charles . . . what the fuck's the matter with you? Giving you the show of a lifetime. *Championship* fucking—you've never seen fucking like this. And this is the thanks I get. *Shit.* I ought to kick your ass, Charles. I ought to kick the *shit* out of you."

Charles mumbled something back at him. *What* did he say? He didn't know. . . .

"Okay, *Charles.* Let's calm down. Let me count to ten. You just wanted some for yourself, that it? Watching the *fuck machine* got you hot, that it? I understand. Only not today, my man. It ain't your turn, understand?"

Lucinda was still stuck in that pornographic position, like a bored model waiting for the shutter. Only she didn't look bored as much as dead, not even turning to look at her would-be savior, who in the end had simply traded one seat for another. One in the balcony for one in the front row.

As the man—fully erect, the clumsy violence had apparently invigorated him—knelt between her white thighs, the thighs Charles had lain between not two hours before, and began again. So close to him, Charles could almost touch him, even if he couldn't hit him, even if he couldn't *stop* him.

"Oh, Charles," he whispered, "like velvet. Like *smooth,* fucking velvet. . . ."

It took a while after the man left to *know* the man had left.

Charles heard the door slam, even saw him walk through the door before he heard the door slam, even heard the man say good-bye to them—*Hate to go, but* . . . And Charles continued to sit there on the floor as if the gun were still trained at his head. As if the man were still moaning into Lucinda's hair, that grotesque ass pumping up and down mere inches from his face.

And Lucinda, too. Still with her legs apart like something wanton, like those Amsterdam hookers who lounge in shop windows with their legs spread in an open invitation. Only their expressions not quite as horrified looking, their hair not matted to their chins with sweat and blood and dried cum.

Eventually Charles moved.

One leg at a time, tentatively, like a man testing the water. As if to prove he *could* move even if he wasn't quite willing to believe it. And then after he'd moved his legs, his arms, and then his whole body, getting up off the floor and standing, a little wobbly, but up on his own two feet again. And when he moved, so did she.

Not saying anything, nothing at all, but slowly bringing one thigh over to the other, hiding that open part of her that resembled a raw wound. And then slowly picking herself up off the floor and trudging over to the bathroom, where she went in and closed the door.

He heard the water running, heard the sound of towel rubbing skin, then what sounded like retching. A toilet flushing once, then twice.

He still hadn't cleaned himself up yet. Bloody hands, blood all over his face, too, no doubt—his nose feeling twice its normal size, as though he had a clown nose on his face. And maybe he did—maybe that was entirely appropriate. Charles the clown, getting whacked in the head and booted in the bottom while the circus master had his way with the star attraction. Who was opening the bathroom door now. Still not saying anything to him—what, after all, do you say to a clown? Still looking dazed and battered, if a little more cleaned up. Still naked, too, as if that didn't matter, as if she could never be more naked than she was fifteen minutes ago—spread open and violated, and after that, what could clothes do for you? And maybe something else—that clowns don't count, they're superfluous in the scheme of things, and it doesn't matter what they *see* if they can't act.

Are you all right? he started to say to her. He almost had the words out of his mouth until he realized how hopelessly inadequate they were. How could she be all right, how could she ever again be all right?

"I should take you to a hospital," he said.

"No." Her first word to him in what must have been hours.

"You should be looked at."

"No. I've been looked at enough for one day." Her voice sounded dead, the way bad actors sound, wooden, no real emotion there. It was scarier than screaming, more frightening than tears. If she'd cried, he'd have put his arms around her and comforted her. But there was nothing he could do for her.

She began to get dressed, slowly, one item at a time, not covering up, no coyly turning away from him like before. So Charles went into the bathroom, where he flinched at his own reflection, thinking at first that it was someone else staring back at him. It couldn't possibly be him. But this was *Charles the clown*, remember? He of the bulbous nose and red paint and fright wig.

He pressed a wet towel up against his nose, where it stung, as if he'd applied iodine. He smoothed down his hair and tried to wipe the blood away from his cheeks.

When he came back into the room, she was more or less dressed. One stocking ripped, skirt slit where it wasn't before, yet she was put back together in a reasonable facsimile of a dressed woman. The way a mannequin is a reasonable facsimile of a dressed woman—minus the thing that actually makes a woman alive.

"What do we do?" Charles asked her, not just her, but himself as well, because he didn't know.

And she said, "Nothing."

Nothing. It sounded so ridiculously preposterous. So blatantly ludicrous. The criminal was still at large, his victims beaten and bleeding, and what does she propose doing? Nothing.

Only the opposite of nothing is something, and he couldn't *think* of a something.

Go to the police?

Of course you go to the police. You've been robbed and raped and beaten, so you go to the police. Only . . .

What were you doing at the Fairfax Hotel?

Well, we were . . .

What were you doing at the Fairfax Hotel in the middle of the morning?

Well, the thing is . . .

What were the two of you doing at the Fairfax Hotel?

If I could take a minute to explain . . .

Maybe they could ask for some discretion here, maybe you were *allowed* to ask for a little discretion, and the police detective would wink at them and say, *I understand.* That he'd be sure to keep this just between them, no need to worry. Only . . .

There was a criminal here, and sometimes criminals get caught—you report them to the police, and sometimes the police actually apprehend them and bring them to court. And then there are trials, public forums that make the front pages, where witnesses have to get up and say, *He did it, Your Honor.* Those witnesses being him. Him and Lucinda.

And what were you doing at the Fairfax Hotel?

Well, we were . . .

What were you doing at the Fairfax Hotel in the middle of the morning?

Well, the thing is . . .

Just answer the question.

What do we do? *That* was the question.

Nothing. Maybe not as ludicrous as it first appeared. Maybe *not* so ridiculous.

Yet was it possible that they could just ignore what had happened to them? That she could just forget about it, like a rude comment or a vulgar gesture? Go to sleep and wake up and *poof*—gone.

Lucinda said, "I'm going."

"Where?"

"Home."

Home. To the blond five-year-old who never met a playground swing she didn't like. To the husband with the nine handicap who might or might not notice the sudden pallor in her cheeks, the bit lip and shell-shocked disposition.

"I'm sorry, Lucinda," he said.

"Yes," she said.

He was sorry for everything. That he'd asked her up here in the first place. That he hadn't seen the man lurking in the stairwell opposite their room. That he'd sat and watched as the man raped her again and again. That he hadn't protected her.

Lucinda trudged to the door—that amazingly elegant gait turned plodding and ungainly. She didn't look back, either.

Charles thought about offering to call a car for her, but he knew she'd turn him down. He hadn't been able to provide the one thing she'd really needed him to. She'd want nothing more from him.

She opened the door, stepped through the open space, and shut it behind her.

ATTICA

Sorry, I have to interrupt here.

I think I should come clean.

Three things happened.

On Wednesday, a man rang our doorbell to see the house. He'd gotten the listing from a real estate agent, he said.

My wife answered the door and told him the house wasn't for sale. It must be some kind of mistake.

Your husband's a teacher, isn't he? he said.

Yes, she said. But it was still some sort of mistake. The house wasn't for sale.

The man apologized and left.

He didn't look like a man who was in the market for a house, she told me later.

Well, what did he look like? I asked her.

Like one of your students, she said.

A high school kid? I said.

No. Like one of your *other* students.

Then the second thing happened.

A CO called Fat Tommy informed me in the lounge that I was going to be ass out soon.

What did that mean? I asked him.

It means you're going to be ass out soon, he said.

Fat Tommy was over three hundred pounds and had been known to sit on unruly prisoners who'd been shackled face-down on the floors of their cells.

Why? I asked him.

Cutbacks. I guess somebody finally realized they've got better things to do with our taxes than teach coons to read.

I asked him if he knew when.

Nah, he said. But I wouldn't start teaching them *War and Peace.*

When Fat Tommy laughed, his three chins jiggled.

Then the third thing happened.

The writer penned a note on the bottom of chapter 10. At first I thought it was just part of the story, something Charles said to Lucinda or even to himself. But it wasn't. It was to me—a kind of editorial aside.

"Like the story so far?"

That's what he wrote.

The answer, by the way, was no.

I didn't.

For one thing, the story lacked suspense.

It was missing the one crucial ingredient needed to make it suspenseful.

Surprise.

Because suspense depends on not knowing what's going to happen.

But I did know what was going to happen.

I knew, for example, what would be on the other side of the door of room 1207. I knew what was going to come in when they opened that door. I knew what that man was going to do to Lucinda over and over for the next four hours.

I remembered it all from a previous life.

In this previous life, I woke up every morning wondering why I preferred to remain sleeping.

I showered and dressed and tried not to look at a blood meter sitting on the kitchen counter. I took the 8:43 to Penn Station, with the exception of one morning in November when I didn't. The morning my daughter made me late and I took the 9:05. The morning that I looked up from my paper and was asked for a ticket I didn't have.

This was my story.
I'll take over from here.

DERAILED ELEVEN

After Lucinda left, I went to the doctor.

It was 130 blocks uptown from the Fairfax Hotel. I walked because the man had taken my wallet and all my cash in it.

I had a broken nose and a bloodstained jacket, but no one seemed to notice. There were other things to look at, I suppose—a homeless man with no clothes on, for instance. A woman on Rollerblades dressed entirely in purple. A black man shouting about something called the Sons of Jonah. My swollen nose and bloody jacket slipped right under the average city dweller's radar.

A funny thing happened as I walked. And walked and walked.

I started counting blocks but ended up counting blessings.

Because there *were* blessings. I was alive, for instance. That was blessing number one. I'd been half-sure the man was going to shoot me. So being alive was a blessing. And then there was my wife and daughter. Blessings, both of them. My *unknowing* wife, blessedly ignorant of the fact that I'd just spent the morning in room 1207 of the Fairfax Hotel with a woman other than her. Watching that woman get brutally and repeatedly raped, of course—but still.

And Anna . . . how could I have done a thing like this to *her?* I felt as if I'd been deathly sick for a long time and that my fever had finally broken. I could think clearly again.

Dr. Jaffe asked me what happened.

"I fell getting out of a cab."

"Uh-huh," Dr. Jaffe said. "You'd be surprised how many times I hear that."

"I'm sure."

Dr. Jaffe set my nose and gave me a sample bottle of codeine. "If the pain gets bad," he said.

I felt like telling him that the pain was already bad, but then I was kind of welcoming the discomfort. Like the 130 blocks of arctic air I'd just stepped out of, it grounded me.

I walked all the way to the office. I suppose I could've gone home, but I was going to make this a day like any other. A late-starting day, a day with a morning I'd rather not think about, but wasn't there a whole afternoon ahead? And another morning and afternoon after that, and so on? I was jumping back in with both feet.

When I got to the office, I trotted out the same story for anyone who asked. And everyone who saw me did. Winston, Mary Widger, and three-quarters of my creative group. The cab, the street hole, the unfortunate fall. They were all sorry for me; they all tried not to look at my nose and the two raccoonlike rings appearing under both eyes.

When I finally sat down in my office, I felt the kind of relief that comes with being back in your own environment, an environment that had been feeling a little sad and hopeless lately, but suddenly felt warm and welcoming. Life *itself* feeling warm and welcoming—richer than I'd been willing to give it credit for. There were all my *things*, for example. My very own phone and computer and couch and coffee table. And all those industry awards I'd managed to garner—gold and silver and bronze—and who could say, despite recent setbacks, that there wouldn't be more to come? And on my desk, a photograph of *us:* Deanna and Anna and me, taken somewhere on a beach in the Caribbean. My *family,* secure in the knowledge of my love. And I did love them.

But looking at that picture made me think about that *other* picture, the one in my wallet. The one the man had ogled, then polluted by holding in his hand. The one he still had with him.

"Darlene," I called.

"Yes?" My secretary appeared at my door, wearing a look of motherly concern.

"I just realized I lost my wallet. It must've fallen out when I broke my nose."

"Uh-oh."

"Can you call the credit card companies for me and cancel the cards?"

"No."

"What?"

"*No.* You've got to call them yourself. They'll only listen to the cardholder."

"Oh. Right." I probably should've known that. I probably should've known a lot of things. For instance, that shabby-looking hotels look shabby for a reason—because they *are* shabby. The kinds of places that attract lowlifes and persons with criminal intent. Persons who loiter in stairwells, waiting for persons with adulterous intent to cross their paths. I was in my forties and still learning.

I called the card companies. American Express and Visa and MasterCard. Canceling your cards is an easy thing to do these days; you just tell them your mother's maiden name—*Reston*—and poof. Your card number ceases to be. And I pictured the man standing in some store being told that his card was no good. That one, too. And this one as well. All of them no good.

Only I suddenly pictured Deanna in a store, being told the same thing. I had to call her. It was after three—she'd be home.

She picked up on the fourth ring, and when I heard her voice saying, "Hello," I was overcome with a kind of gratitude. Grateful to God, I suppose—assuming that there was one, assuming that he'd care enough to see that I'd made it out of the Fairfax Hotel in one piece. Minus a whole nose, maybe, minus a *lover*, sure, but other than that, reasonably intact.

"You won't believe the day I had," I told her. And she *wouldn't* have believed it.

"What happened?"

"I broke my nose."

"You broke your *what?*"

"My nose. I fell down getting out of a cab and broke my nose."

"Oh, Charles . . ."

"Don't worry. It's okay, it's fine. The doctor set it and gave me enough codeine to sedate a horse. I'm feeling no pain." That wasn't true—I *was* feeling pain, but this pain was a kind of penance and tempered by that other thing I was feeling, which was unmitigated relief.

"Oh, *Charles*. Why don't you come home?"

"I told you. I'm fine. I have a few things to do here." Like say three hundred Hail Marys and lick my wounds.

"You sure?"

"Yes." I was moved by the obvious empathy in her voice, the kind of empathy made possible only through years of sticking together through thick and thin. Even if we couldn't communicate it lately—even if we couldn't physically express it—it was there. It had always been there. And I nearly felt like confessing and throwing myself on the mercy of the court. But then I'd never have to, would I? Life was back where it started, before I'd looked up from my paper and noticed a white thigh and swinging black pump.

"One other thing," I said.

"What?"

"I lost my wallet. When I fell out of the cab. I told you, you *wouldn't* believe the day I had."

"A wallet's just a wallet. I'm more concerned about you."

"I already called the credit card companies and canceled them. Just wanted you to know—you better cut them up and throw them away. They're going to send us new ones by tomorrow—at least they say they are."

"Fine. Consider it done."

I said good-bye, whispered, "I love you," and started to hang up.

"Oh, I almost forgot," she said.

"Yes?"

"Mr. Vasquez called."

"Mr. *Who?*"

"Mr. Vasquez. He said he had a business lunch with you at the Fairfax Hotel. He forgot to tell you something.

"Charles . . . ?"

"Yes?"

"Why didn't he call you at the office?"

DERAILED TWELVE

I called Lucinda at the work number she'd given me.

Hello, this is Lucinda Harris at Morgan Stanley. I'm not here at the moment, but if you leave your name and a brief message, I'll get back to you.

So I did leave a brief message of sorts. *Help.* Not saying the actual word, of course, but then it's the thought that counts.

"I've got to talk to you," I said. "That . . . *person* from the hotel called me." I tried to keep the panic out of my voice, the same way I'd tried to keep it out of my voice when Deanna had told me that *Mr. Vasquez* had called. I failed both times.

Are you okay? Deanna had asked me.

It's the codeine, I'd said. *It's making me woozy.* I had wanted to say, *It's Mr. Vasquez, he's making me terrified.*

Eliot came into my office to offer condolences about my nose. Maybe to try to patch things up, too—after all, we were friends, weren't we? More than co-workers, than simple boss and employee. Eliot had been my rabbi all these years—hadn't he promoted me and talked me up and provided me with more than generous raises? I'd been mistaken to blame Eliot for my dismissal from the credit card account—that had been their doing, not his. Ellen Weischler and her gang of four. Eliot was burying the hatchet and saying let's be friends again.

And I needed a friend right now.

How much do you love me? I used to ask Anna when she was very small.

From the earth to the moon, she'd answer me. And sometimes, *To infinity.*

Which might be how much I needed a friend right now. A need as infinite as it was immediate.

I felt like unburdening myself to him. *I'd like to tell you something that happened to me,* I'd say to him. *I know it's hard to believe—I know it's kind of ridiculous. I met this girl.* And Eliot would wink and nod and smile, because Eliot had met girls before, too—three marriages to prove it and number three on life support these days.

I met this girl, I'd say, *married,* and Eliot's smile would grow only wider, if that were possible, because he'd met married girls, too. *We went to a hotel together*—and here Eliot would lean in even closer, all ears, because was there anything quite as delicious as listening to a buddy give up the details, other than recounting the details yourself?

We went to a hotel together, I'd continue, *only when we got to the room, someone else came in there with us.*

And Eliot would lose that smile. Because this story took a vicious left turn and ended with this someone who came into our room raping the woman and calling my house. Talking to my *wife.*

Eliot asked me if something was the matter.

"No," I said.

"Maybe you ought to go home," Eliot said. "You look a little pale."

"The nose," I said.

"Yeah—the nose doesn't look so good."

"No."

"Well, go home, then."

"Maybe I will."

Eliot patted me on the back—friends again, after all.

So I went home.

Why did he call you at home, Charles?

To prove that he could, Deanna.

I took money out of petty cash to pay for the train ride—the scene of the crime. The crime of coveting—another man's wife, another man's life. One night when I was eight years old and my parents' constant sniping had reached a full-out conflagration, I'd packed my football helmet with a change of underwear and announced I was running away from home. Down the block I went—one block, two blocks, long enough to realize that no one was going to be coming after me. Eventually I stopped amid the swirling autumn leaves and started back. Thirty-five years later, I'd run away from home again. But this time I was running back.

My cellular phone rang. For a second, I wondered if it was *him*—my business associate from the Fairfax Hotel. But it couldn't be him, he didn't have the number. But someone else did.

"Hello," Lucinda said.

She sounded different from this morning. Emotion was back in her voice after all, only a different kind from what I was used to. *Dread,* I'd say. First dead, then dread, all in the space of one afternoon.

"He called my *house,* Lucinda," I said.

"Welcome to the fucking club," she said.

"What?"

"He called *mine,* too," speaking in a whisper, as if she were trying to keep someone else from hearing. Was her husband somewhere in the house?

I'd been very much hoping that Mr. Vasquez hadn't called my house. Or that a Mr. Vasquez had, but that it was simply someone who'd found my discarded wallet in a vestibule of the Fairfax Hotel and called as a Good Samaritan. Or for a reward. Ridiculous, maybe. But there was always hope, wasn't there?

Not anymore.

"You spoke to him?"

"Yes."

"What did he want?" I asked. That, after all, was the million-dollar question here—you have to know what a man wants before you know what to do.

"I don't know what he wanted."

"Well, what did he *say?* Did he—"

"He asked me how he was."

"How he *was?* I don't—"

"Did I enjoy it? He wanted to know if I *enjoyed* it. He wanted affirmation—isn't that what men ask you after they . . ." But she couldn't bring herself to finish the sentence. I guess even false bravado has its limits.

"I'm sorry, Lucinda."

Another apology. I had the feeling I could apologize to her every day for the rest of my life, then keep on apologizing to her into the afterlife, and it still wouldn't be enough. And then I'd have all those other people to apologize to as well.

"I think he wanted to know . . . ," she said.

It suddenly occurred to me that I was speaking louder than I should've been. Either louder or softer—because I was drawing glances from the sparsely filled train—from the woman surrounded by Bloomingdale's shopping bags sitting across from me and the two girls with nose earrings holding hands on the other side of the aisle.

"What did he want to know?" I asked.

"Whether we'd done anything. Gone to the police. . . ."

We won't go to the police, I'd promised him. The kind of

promise most victims of violent crime probably make in the heat of terror. Only in this case, a promise *Vasquez* could more or less believe if he chose to. *This woman don't look like you,* he'd said to Lucinda. *And this man—he don't look like* you.

Vasquez might've jumped anybody this morning. But he'd gotten lucky. He'd found the perfect victims. Because we had to hide the fact we *were* victims.

"What do we do now?" Lucinda asked me now, the same question I'd asked her back in the hotel room. Because suddenly *nothing* wasn't enough. Not anymore.

"I don't know."

"Charles . . ."

"Yes?"

"What if he . . ."

"Yes?"

"Never mind."

"What if he *what,* Lucinda?" But I think I knew what she was going to ask me. I just didn't wish to hear it said out loud—not now, not yet.

"Okay, so what do we *do,* Charles?"

"Maybe what we should've done before. Maybe we have to go to the police."

"I'm *not* telling my husband."

She'd gotten real emotion back in her voice after all. A sudden and undeniable firmness that brooked no further discussion. "If *I* can manage it, then you can." *I was the one raped,* she was saying to me. *I was the one raped six times while you sat there and did nothing. If I can choose to be quiet about it, then you can. Then you* have *to.*

"Okay," I said. "Okay. If he calls again, I'll talk to him. I'll find out what he wants."

Deanna mothered me when I got home. So did Anna— maybe she was finally happy to see someone else in need of medical attention. She brought me a warm compress to lay against my swollen nose and gently rubbed my arm as I lay half-dead on the bed.

I was back in the bosom of my family—content, grateful, the very picture of domestic bliss.

Except each time the telephone rang, I flinched as if punched in the stomach.

A friend of Deanna's. A mortgage broker's cold call. My secretary wanting to know if I was all right.

But there was always the next call, wasn't there?

And they insisted on hearing about the accident. Anna wanted to know how I could have been so *spastic*. Stepping out of a cab, for God's sake. Into a *hole?*

I said I didn't want to talk about it. And I wondered if repeating the same lie was the same as telling different lies. If one was worse than the other. Neither one felt particularly good, not when my daughter was offering me a warm towel and my wife her unconditional love.

I tried to watch some basketball in the den, to root for the struggling Knicks. But I found it hard to focus; my mind kept wandering. There was a player on the Indiana Pacers, for instance, who looked a little like . . . Black, but Hispanic. Lopez, his name was—a backup guard. Taller of course, but . . .

"What's the score?" Anna asked me. She'd stopped watching basketball with me at age nine, but I supposed she was trying to be kind to her bruised and battered father.

"We're losing." It was a safe answer these days, even if you didn't actually know what the score was.

Just then it turned up in the left corner of the screen. The Knicks had rallied within four.

"Eighty-six to eighty-two," Anna recited.

"A close one," I said. "We've got a shot."

"Daddy?"

"Yes?"

"Daddy—did you ever play basketball?"

"Sure."

"On a *team?*"

"No. Not on a team."

"Then how'd you play?"

"With friends. At the park—you know." Murray Miller, Brian Timinsky, Billy Seiden. They were my best friends growing up—but slowly, one by one, they'd faded away. Years ago, I'd seen Billy Seiden in a Pathmark supermarket, but I'd left without saying hello.

I hugged Anna. I wanted to tell her something, about love and life and how it can be fleeting if you don't hold on—that you have to jealously guard what's important to you—but I couldn't think of the right words.

Because the phone rang.

Anna picked it up after the second ring.

"For *you,*" she said.

"Who is it?"

"Some Spanish guy," Anna said.

DERAILED THIRTEEN

The conversation:

"Hello there, *Charles*."

"Hello." His voice seemed out of context. It belonged in a hotel room smelling of blood, not here in the safety of my own den. Unless my den wasn't safe anymore.

"How's things, *Charles?*"

"What do you want?"

"You doin' okay, Charles?"

"Fine. What do you want?"

"You *sure* you doin' okay, Charles?"

"Yes, I'm doing okay."

"Not getting stupid on me, Charles, right? Not running to the cops?"

Lucinda was right; he wanted to know if we'd gone to the police. "No," I said.

"I know you promised and all, but I don't know you that well, know what I'm sayin'?"

"I haven't gone to the police," I said. I was speaking softly; I'd ushered Anna out of the room, but that didn't mean she wouldn't come in again. And then there was Deanna, who just might pick up the phone and wonder who I was talking to.

"That's good, Charles."

"What do you want?" I asked him again.

"What do I want?"

"Look, I—"

"You're not going to get stupid on me, Charles, right? You tell the cops, you got to tell the *little woman,* right, Charles? You got to tell her how you're fucking *Lucinda,* right, Charles? Why you want to do that, huh?"

He'd laid it out for me. The crux of the situation, just in case I'd missed it.

"I'm not going to the police," I repeated.

"That's good, Charles. Here's the thing—I need a loan."

Okay. It was the question Lucinda had begun to ask me on the phone. *What if he . . .* Not exactly finishing, but if she had, she would have said: *What if he asks for money?*

"I *hate* to ask, know what I mean?" he said. "But I'm a little short, see."

"Look, I don't know what you think—"

"Not much, Charles. A little loan, you know. Say ten grand. . . ."

"I don't have ten grand."

"You don't have ten grand?"

"No." I'd thought it was over, but it wasn't over.

"Shit. That's a problem."

"Look, I don't have cash just lying around like that. Everything's—"

"That's a real problem, *Charles.* I really need that loan, see."

"I just don't have—"

"I think you better get it for me." Leaving unsaid *why* I better get it for him.

"Everything's tied up. I just can't—"

"You're not listening to me, Charles. I'm talking here and

you're not listening. I need ten grand, Charles. Okay? That's the deal. You're a *big fucking executive*, Charles. Says so right on your business card. Senior"—saying it like señor—"creative director. Ex-ec-u-tive vice pres-i-dent. That's pretty fucking impressive, Charles. And you don't *got* ten grand? Who the fuck you kidding?"

No one, I thought.

"Charles."

"Yes."

"I don't give a fuck about your *cash flow,* okay? I want ten grand from you. You understand me?"

Yes.

"If you understand, then say you will give me ten grand."

Deanna was calling me from the kitchen. "Do you want some chicken soup?"

"I'll get it for you," I said.

"You'll get what for me?"

"I'll get you the ten thousand."

"Great. Thank you. Hated to ask you and all, but you know how it is."

"Where?"

"I'll call you again, okay, Charles?"

"Can you please call at the office? Can you—"

"Nah. I like calling here. I'll call you back *here,* okay, Charles?"

Click.

What if he asks us for money? Lucinda had wondered.

Even though he'd taken our money, even though he'd said, *See, I got your money, right here,* he didn't have *all* our money, did he?

And as long as we weren't going to the police, he could go ahead and ask for it.

The Knicks lost at the buzzer.

Deanna asked me what was wrong, and that's what I told her—the team lost and I'd been pulling for them.

"Poor baby," she said.

Which is exactly what Lucinda had said to me that day on the train. *Poor baby*, as she'd patted me on the arm and whispered something into my ear. Something about me being sexy.

Which maybe I was, back before I'd turned into a clown.

Vasquez wanted ten thousand dollars.

I didn't have ten thousand dollars just lying around. It wasn't sitting under the mattress or accruing interest in a bank account, either. What I did have was approximately $150,000 worth of stock certificates sitting in a file cabinet in my office attic. Company stock, handed out to me each and every year thanks to Eliot's beneficence.

Deanna and I had a name for those stock certificates—a designation that left no doubt as to their purpose. Not our vacation fund, or our retirement fund, or even our rainy day fund. *Anna's Fund.* That's what we called it. Anna's Fund, there for whenever and whatever might come in the future. Call it a hedge against a coming depression.

An operation, for instance.

Or ten operations. Or other things I didn't necessarily want to contemplate.

Anna's Fund. Every paper penny of it.

But what else could I do but *pay* him?

I lay in bed with Deanna, Deanna already starting to doze even though it couldn't be much past nine. Those twenty-six third graders take a lot out of her—and now this, what would *this* take out of her? If she knew, that is—if she found it. If I broke down and told her, not breaking my promise to Lucinda, not exactly, not telling the *police*. Just her.

Then I wouldn't have to give Vasquez his money, would I? Unless . . .

Unless Vasquez threatened to tell someone else. Unless he said, *Fine, your wife knows—great, but Lucinda's husband—he* doesn't. Lucinda's husband, whom she'd sworn would never know, no matter what, never know she'd gone to a hotel room with another man to have sex and ended up having more sex than she'd bargained for.

If I can manage it, then you can, Lucinda had said to me.

I owed her that, didn't I? After letting another man rape her—after sitting there and *watching* another man rape her? We were in this together.

Besides, I could fantasize all I wanted about telling Deanna, but the truth was, I could no more imagine telling Deanna what I'd been up to than I could imagine telling *Anna.* I could rehearse the very words; I could imagine the burden being lifted. *See? No burden.* But it was make-believe—it wasn't real.

After Deanna was safely asleep, I went upstairs to the attic to rummage through our file cabinet. Under *A* for Anna's Fund.

Only to find it, I had to wade through a few other things first, the file cabinet having surrendered over the years to general disorganization and chaos. High school diplomas, college degrees, birth certificates—a record, more or less, of *us.* The Schines. Milestones, achievements, life-changing events. A tiny pair of footprints courtesy of Anna Elizabeth Schine. A degree from Anna's kindergarten. And farther back—a marriage certificate. "Charles Schine and Deanna Williams." Promising to love and honor—a promise I'd callously discarded in a downtown hotel.

There was a surreal quality to taking my stock certificates out of the file cabinet in order to pay off a rapist. There was no manual for this sort of situation, no self-help books promising to make it all better.

On the way out of the den, I passed Anna's room—a sleeping Anna bathed in moonlight, or was it simply her night-light?

She'd begun plugging it into the wall again soon after she'd gotten sick. Because she was suddenly scared to death to be alone in the dark. Because she worried she'd wake up hypoglycemic and wouldn't be able to find her sugar tablets—or maybe that she wouldn't wake up at all.

Sleep seemed to relieve her of all her anger and sadness, I thought.

I tiptoed in and leaned over her bed. Her breath brushed against my face like butterfly wings (remembering now how I'd once pinched a monarch's wings between my thumb and forefinger to show it to a four-year-old Anna before carefully placing it into a cleaned-out jelly jar). I planted a kiss on one cool cheek. She stirred, groaned slightly, turned over.

I went downstairs and slipped the stock certificates into my briefcase.

DERAILED FOURTEEN

I met Lucinda at the fountain on 51st and Sixth.

When I called and told her what Vasquez wanted, she'd lapsed into silence and then asked to meet me there.

I'd been sitting there ten minutes when I saw her cross 51st Street.

I stood up and began to raise my hand in greeting. But I stopped—she was with another man. She continued toward me, and for a moment I was caught between sitting down and standing up, between saying hi and saying nothing. I sat back down; something made me lie low.

I stayed seated right there on the rim of the fountain as Lucinda and the man walked right by me without a glance.

The man was dressed in a respectable blue suit and recently shined shoes. Fiftyish, hair just beginning to thin, lips pursed in thought. Lucinda looked almost normal again, I thought, which was to say gorgeous, if you didn't look too closely. If you didn't peer intently at the faint rings under her eyes—not like the rings under mine, which resembled football black, but undeniably there. A woman who looked as though she hadn't slept much lately, who's tossed and turned despite the two Valiums and glass of wine.

She seemed to be speaking to the man, but whatever she was saying was swallowed up by a cacophony of New York clatter—car horns, bicycle bells, piped music, bus engines. They passed within five feet of me and I couldn't hear a word.

I waited as they headed for a side street. I was surrounded by the usual mix of tourists with craned necks, afternoon smokers puffing away with undisguised desperation, and the odd street person mumbling to himself.

I stared at the Christmas decorations on Radio City Music Hall across the street. "Spectacular Christmas Show," it said, the entire marquee wreathed in holly. A sidewalk Santa was ringing a bell by the front doors and shouting, "Merry Christmas, everyone!" Here by the fountain it was cold and raw.

I waited five, then ten minutes.

Then I saw Lucinda coming back, hurrying around the corner and staring straight at me. So. She'd seen me after all.

"Thank you," she said.

"You're welcome. For what?"

"For not saying hello. For not saying anything. That was my husband."

That was my husband. The golfer. The one who would never know.

"Oh," I said.

"He surprised me at the office. With flowers. He insisted on taking the cab uptown with me. Sorry."

"That's okay. How have you been?"

"Just terrific. Couldn't be better." The tone of her voice suggested that I was kind of stupid for asking her that, like one of those TV reporters at a scene of unimaginable tragedy asking the victim's remaining family how they're feeling these days.

"Has he called you again?" she asked me.

"Not since he asked for ten thousand dollars. No."

"And?" she said. "Are you going to give it to him?"

"Yes."

She looked down at her hands. "Thank you."

"Don't mention it." And I *didn't* want her to mention it, either. Because every time I mentioned it, it became realer, something that was going to actually take place.

"Look," she said, "I have one thousand dollars here. A little account my husband doesn't know about." She reached into her pocketbook.

"It's okay," I said. "Forget it."

"Take it," she said as if she were trying to pay for the Milk Duds and soda and I was insisting on being old-fashioned about it and covering the entire date.

"No. I'll take care of it."

"Here," she said, and forced ten hundred-dollar bills into my hand. After a brief tug-of-war, I gave up. I put the money into my pocket.

Then she said: "Do you think it's going to stop here?"

Which was the real question, of course. Would it stop here, or would it not?

"I don't know, Lucinda."

She nodded and sighed. "What if it *doesn't*? What if he asks for more money? *Then* what?"

"Then I still don't know." *Then we're doomed, Lucinda.*

"How did it happen, Charles?" she said, so softly that at first I wasn't sure I'd heard her.

"What?"

"How did it happen? *How?* Sometimes I think I dreamed it. It seems impossible, doesn't it? That it actually happened to us? *Us?* Sometimes . . ."

She dabbed at her eyes—they'd turned liquid, and I thought how her eyes were the second thing I'd noticed that morning on the train. First her thighs, maybe, then her eyes. I'd seen a tenderness in them, and I'd said: *Yes, I could use that. I need that now.*

"Maybe that's the way you should think of it," I said. "A bad dream."

"But it wasn't. So that's stupid."

"Yes. That's stupid."

"If he found out, it would kill him," she said.

Her husband—she was talking about her husband again.

"If he found out, he'd kill *me*."

"He won't find out." We were in this together, I was assuring her. We may have cheated on our spouses, but we wouldn't on each other.

"What did you say to your wife?" she asked me. "About your nose?"

"I fell."

"Yes," she said, as if that were what she'd have thought of, too.

"Look, I wanted to tell you . . ." Tell her what, exactly? That I'd failed her, I suppose, that I'd failed her, but I wouldn't fail her again.

"Yes?"

"I should've . . . you know, stopped him."

"Yes."

"I tried. Not hard enough."

"He had a gun," she said.

Yes, he had a gun. He had a gun he sometimes pointed at me and sometimes didn't. While he was raping her—he didn't. The gun was there on the floor, three feet from me, maybe, that's all.

"Forget about it," she said. But I could tell she didn't mean it—that she *did* think I should've tried harder, that I should've saved her. And I remembered how I'd defended her in the bar that night and how she'd kissed me afterward for it. Bar bullies are one thing, of course, and armed rapists are another.

"I don't think we should talk to each other again, Charles," she said. "Good-bye."

"Happy so far?" David Frankel was asking me.

"What?"

"Happy so far? With the commercial?"

We were finally shooting the aspirin commercial. Stage ten at Silvercup Studios in Astoria.

"Yes. It's fine."

"Yeah. Corinth's an old pro."

Well, he was old, I felt like saying. Robert Corinth was the director of the aspirin commercial. He was short and balding, with a silly-looking ponytail beneath a half-moon of sunburnished skin. The ponytail said: *I may be succumbing to the indignities of aging, but I am still cool, I am still with it.* We were on take twenty-two.

"Who's doing the music for the spot?" I asked him.

"Music?"

"Yes, the track. Who's doing it?"

"T and D Music House."

"I never heard of them."

"Oh, yeah. They're good."

"Okay."

"They do all the tracks for my stuff."

"Okay. Fine."

"You'll like them. They always give us a good price."

I was going to ask him why he was smiling at me like that. But I was interrupted by Mary Widger whispering in my ear.

"Charles," she whispered, "can I have a word with you?"

"Sure."

"Mr. Duben thinks the aspirin bottle should be higher."

"Higher?" Mr. Duben was my new client. He'd greeted me by saying, *So you're the new blood.*

Yes. Type O, I'd answered him, and he'd laughed and said, *Great, that's just what we need.*

"Higher. In the frame."

"Sure. Can you tell Robert to put the bottle higher in the frame, David?"

"No problem," David said. "I live for stuff like that."

Later in the afternoon, somewhere between takes forty-eight and forty-nine, Tom Mooney cornered me by the craft service table.

"Hey, buddy," he said.

Tom wasn't my buddy. He was the rep for Headquarters Productions, and his modus operandi was to make himself annoying enough to cause clients to give him work in an effort to make him go away. He'd been fairly successful at it, too.

"How are you, Tom?"

"Me, I'm fine. The question is how are you?" He was looking at my face.

"I fell," I said. For the hundredth time.

"I meant workwise."

Tom knew exactly how I was, workwise. He knew, for instance, that up till just a few weeks ago, I'd been in charge of a showcase credit card account but now was solely in charge of this aspirin account. He knew this because advertising was a small community, and as in most small communities, news traveled fast, and bad news faster.

"Great," I answered him.

He asked me if I'd gotten his Christmas card.

"No."

"I sent you a card."

"I didn't get it."

"No?"

"No."

"Well, Merry Christmas. Christmas gift to follow," he said.

"No gifts necessary, Tom."

"Don't be silly. Uncle Tommy never forgets a client."

"If it's a Headquarters hat—I've got one," I said.

"Who's talking hats?" Tom said. "Did I say anything about hats?"

"I've got a Headquarters T-shirt, too."

"Hey, you're a Headquarters *client* now."

"Yes, that's me."

"So think of me as Santa Claus."

"That's funny. You don't look like Santa Claus." With his slicked-back hair and hyperkinetic mannerisms, Tom resembled Pat Riley on amphetamines.

"How do you know? Did you ever *see* Santa Claus?"

When Anna was small, five and a half, maybe, she'd asked me how Santa shopped at Toys R Us if he lived in the North Pole. I'd inadvertently left the store sticker on a My Little Pony.

"Nice to meet you, Santa."

"And what does little Charley want for Christmas?"

If Tom had all day, I could've told him.

"Nothing, Tom. I'm fine."

"Hey, you're shooting with me, right?"

"Right."

"You're working with Frankel, right?"

"Frankel? Yes, sure."

"Okay. Ask him what he gets for Christmas."

What did that mean?

"All I want for Christmas is a good spot, Tom."

"Then why'd you use *us?*" he said.

But when I didn't laugh, he said: "Just kidding."

That night, Vasquez called my house and told me to meet him in Alphabet City at the corner of 8th Street and Avenue C.

DERAILED FIFTEEN

They called it Alphabet City because it stretched from Avenue A to D in lower Manhattan. It used to be the stomping ground for Hispanic gangs, till it was invaded by an artsy crowd and became both dangerous and hip. Bodegas and galleries coexisted side by side, serving empanadas and op art.

I hadn't been down here since I was in my early twenties. I vaguely remembered a cab ride to no particular destination that had ended here—seven of us stuffed in one cab looking for a good time. I couldn't remember how the night ended.

Today I wasn't looking for a good time.

I was looking for Vasquez.

Deanna had picked up the phone when he called. *How are you, Mrs. Schine?* he'd said to her. She'd looked just a little puzzled when she'd handed it over to me.

Business call, I'd told her later.

Vasquez had asked me if I had the money: yes. He'd asked me if I was still being a good boy (translation—no police): yes. He'd told me to meet him here in Alphabet City.

When Deanna left the room, I told him it was ten thousand and no more, did he understand? This was it.

Vasquez said sure thing, bro.

The corner of Avenue C and 8th at eleven in the morning was an accurate reflection of the neighborhood. Five Latino kids were killing time on the hood of a high-rider while a street artist was putting up a sign offering henna tattoos. No Vasquez yet.

A black man bumped into me.

"Why the fuck you don't look where you going?" he said.

I hadn't been going anywhere, of course; I'd been pretty much just standing there. "Sorry," I said anyway.

"Sorry, huh?" The man was bigger than me, approximately the size of a typical SUV.

"Yes," I said.

"What if sorry ain't good enough?"

"Look, I didn't see you. . . ."

The man laughed.

"That's okay," he said. "That's fine. *Charles,* huh?"

He knew my name—the man who'd accused me of not looking where I was going knew my name.

"Charles," he said again. "Right?"

"Who are you?"

"Didn't I just ask you a question? You Charles or not Charles?"

"Yes, I'm Charles."

"They call you *Chuck?* If you were my crimey, that's what we'd call you."

"No." *Chuck, Chuck, bo buck, banana fana fo fuck* . . . A song other kids in the neighborhood used to have a lot of fun with when I was eight. "Where's Vasquez?" I asked him.

"I'm gonna bring you to him. What the fuck you think I'm here for?"

I didn't want to be brought to him.

"Why don't I give you the money and—"

"You ain't givin' me nothin', understand? We're gonna take a little walk."

"How far?"

"How far?" imitating me. "Just up the street."

He started walking, looking back to make sure I was following him, and I remembered how I used to do the same thing when Anna was small, walking with her but not with her, making sure she wouldn't wander off in a dangerous direction. Only I was already going in a dangerous direction.

When we passed an alley between two renovated tenements, the man stopped and waited for me, then began steering me into the narrow passageway. I tried to stand my ground, until the man's grip threatened to crush my arm and I gave up.

He threw me up against the wall. *This is what happens in alleys, isn't it,* I thought: *beatings and stabbings and robberies. Sometimes in hotel rooms, but mostly in alleys.* I waited for the inevitable, which was going to be swift and brutal and complete.

Only the beating never came.

"Let's see here," the man said. And he groped me instead, running his hands up and down my legs, chest, and back. He was patting me down.

"No fuckin' wire on you, Charles, that's good. . . ."

"I told him I didn't go to the police."

"Yeah. And he believes you."

"Look, I really need to get back," I said, hearing the panic in my own voice and trying to inch away from the wall.

"Come on," he said, "just over here. . . ."

I'd gone *just over here* when I first sat down next to Lucinda, and then just over a little more when I took her to the Fairfax Hotel, and now I was being asked to go just over here again, when all I really wanted to do was go back to that place called yesterday.

I followed the man out the other side of the alley and down a block that smelled of sauerkraut and pomade. We passed a hair salon specializing in dreadlocks and hair tattoos. The man took a left into the vestibule of a partially renovated tenement.

He buzzed a name and was buzzed back.

"Come on," he said, holding the scratched glass door open for me. *Come on* again. I was taking orders these days, a new recruit in the army of the morally dispossessed. Aware that I was treading deeper into enemy territory with each and every step, but not at liberty to refuse. In this army, deserters were subject to possible execution.

Vasquez was in an apartment on the first floor. He was there, just behind the door when it opened and let us in.

I flinched when Vasquez put out his hand. I'd seen that hand do other things—to Lucinda and me. But Vasquez wasn't looking for a handshake.

"Money," he said.

He was dressed in do-rag chic—low-slung pants with a hint of Calvin Klein peeking out of the waistband—a ratty green sweater hanging off his shoulders. I was getting my first good look at him. And I was surprised how different he appeared from what I'd remembered, at least in the overall impression. He seemed less physically imposing, thinner and distinctly bonier. And I wondered how many criminals had gone to the chair on erroneous eyewitness testimony—plenty, probably, it being hard to get a fix on someone when he's beating your brains in or raping your girlfriend.

I handed over the ten thousand dollars in crisp hundred-dollar bills. Feeling as if I were making another domestic purchase—a washing machine, a big-screen TV for the den, patio furniture—only this domestic purchase, of course, purchasing domesticity itself. Five thousand for Anna and five thousand for Deanna. No money-back guarantee, either. A strictly good-faith purchase when there wasn't any.

"Nine thousand nine hundred . . ." Vasquez diligently counted to the last bill, then looked up at me with that awful smile, the one I remembered from the hotel room.

"Almost forgot," he said, and punched me in the stomach.

I went down.

I couldn't breathe; I began to claw the air for breath.

"That's for canceling your cards, Charles. It was kind of inconvenient for me, seeing as how I was in the middle of buying something."

The other man thought the whole thing was funny—he started laughing.

Then Vasquez said: "We'll be leaving now, Charles."

It took me five minutes to breathe normally again, then another five minutes to actually get up, using the wall as support. The five minutes I spent on the floor trying to breathe was spent crying, too, partially from the punch to my solar plexus and partially from the realization of where I was.

Down on the floor next to a roach-infested container of two-day-old Chinese takeout.

DERAILED SIXTEEN

I stayed late at the office the next day.

I was feeling kind of jumpy and ashamed at home these days—not in any particular order. Every time I looked at Anna, I'd think about the ten thousand dollars I'd robbed from her fund; and every time the phone rang, I suffered through that interminable pause before someone actually answered it— imagining actual dialogue that always ended with Deanna tromping into the bedroom or den or basement to accuse me of ruining her life and killing our daughter.

I preferred that moment happen over the phone—seeing that I couldn't imagine actually having to look her in the eyes as she recited my litany of crimes. In the office I could shut the door and turn off the lights and stare at my reflection in the computer screen, which was stuck in perpetual sleep state—which was the state I wished I could somehow place myself. I could think about ridding myself of this awful thing that threatened to derail my life. At home I could only suffer its consequences.

At the moment, I was trying to look up the T&D Music House.

I wanted to call them tomorrow about the track for the aspirin spot. Something emotional without being maudlin. Something that might disguise the banal dialogue and wooden delivery of the actors.

I couldn't find a listing for them, though. T&D—wasn't that what Frankel had said? Or was it some other letters? No—I was pretty sure it was T&D.

Maybe the postproduction guide I was using was out-of-date. Maybe—

I heard a loud bump.

It was past eight, and the custodial staff had already finished their rounds. I was fairly certain nobody was burning the midnight oil but me.

I heard it again.

A kind of scraping now, a few clinks, a thud. Someone next door—Tim Ward's office, and I'd seen Tim with my very own eyes sprinting off for the 6:38 to Westchester.

Then something else.

Someone was whistling "My Girl." Temptations, 1965.

Maybe it was a member of the custodial staff after all—some piece of unfinished cleaning up that needed to be taken care of while the office slept—custodians, like a shoemaker's elves, appearing mostly at night to magically leave behind the fruits of their labor. A new carpet, freshly painted walls, a renovated air-conditioning system. Sure, it was just one of the elves.

Clink. Thud. Boom.

I stood up from my chair and walked across my paper-strewn carpet to see. When I opened the door, the noise stopped. So did the whistling. I thought I heard a sharp intake of breath.

There was a light on in Tim Ward's office—the desk light, I guessed; a cool yellow was radiating through the glazed glass like sunlight caught behind morning fog. For a moment, I was unsure what to do. You don't *have* to do anything when you hear someone whistling late at night from the office next door. You can, but you don't have to.

I opened the door to Tim's office anyway.

Someone was doing something to Tim's computer—an Apple G4, same as mine.

"Hello," said Winston Boyko. "I'm fixing it."

Only Winston didn't seem to be fixing it.

He seemed to be stealing it.

"Tim said it was flickering on and off," he said, but he looked flushed and his voice was unsteady. The computer was connected to the wall with a thin steel cable Winston must've been in the process of cutting. I figured this out because Winston had what looked like a wire cutter in his hand.

"Tim asked *you* to fix it?" I said.

"Yeah. I'm pretty good with computers, didn't you know that?"

No, I didn't.

"We've got a computer department, Winston. To fix computers."

"Well, what do you know? Guess I don't have to, then."

"Winston?"

"Yes?"

"Tim didn't ask you to fix his computer," I said.

"Not in so many words. No."

"You don't know anything about computers, do you?"

"Sure I do."

"Winston . . ."

"I know how much they sell for." And then he shrugged. *Okay, the charade is up,* he was saying. *Can't blame a guy for trying.*

"Why are you *stealing* computers, Winston?" Maybe that was an odd question to be asking the person stealing it. After all, why does anyone steal anything? To make money, of course. But why Winston—the human baseball encyclopedia and all-around agreeable guy. Why *him?*

"I don't know. Seemed like the right thing to do at the time."

"Jesus . . . Winston . . ."

"You know what a G4 sells for? I'll tell you. Three thousand used. How about them *Apples?*"

"It happens to be illegal."

"Yeah—you got me there."

"And I *saw* you stealing it. What am I supposed to do?"

"Tell me not to do it again?"

"Winston . . . I'm not sure you—"

"Look. I didn't steal it, right? See—the computer's still here. No harm done."

"This is the first time?"

"Sure."

But now I remembered hearing something about missing computers. That's why they'd fastened them to the wall with steel wires in the first place, wasn't it?

"Look," Winston said. "It would really be inconvenient for me if you said anything."

And for the first time, I felt a little uncomfortable. A little nervous. This was Winston here—my baseball trivia partner and mailroom buddy. But this was also a *thief,* standing here late at night with no one else around, with a wire cutter in his hand. I wondered what kind of weapon it'd make and decided probably a good one.

"So can we just forget about it? Okay, Charles? Promise I won't do it again."

"Can I think for a second?"

"Sure." Then, after that second went by, and then another one: "Tell you what," Winston said. "I'll tell you why it would kind of fuck me over. Aside from getting fired from this job, of course, which wouldn't be the biggest deal in the world, relatively speaking. I'll be honest with you, okay?"

"Okay."

"Here's the deal." He sat on Tim's chair. "Sit down, you look like you're going to jump through a window."

I sat down.

"The thing is . . . ," Winston said.

Winston had served time.

"Nothing major," he assured me. "I was a recreational drug user."

"That's it?"

"Well, I was also a recreational drug *pusher*."

"Oh."

"Don't look at me like that. It wasn't like I was dealing H. Mostly E."

When did drugs become designated by letters of the alphabet? I wondered. Was there one for each letter now?

"It was my college job," Winston said. He scratched his upper arm over by his tattoo. "I suppose I could have worked in the school cafeteria. This seemed easier."

"How much time did you . . . ?"

"Sentenced to ten. But my bid was five. Five and a half up at Sing Sing. Which is like a hundred years old."

"I'm sorry." But I wasn't sure if I was sorry about Winston going to prison or sorry about catching him in the act of stealing a company computer, which might necessitate his having to go to prison again. Maybe both.

"*You're* sorry. Talk about a bad career move. I came out and I'm six years behind everybody else. I've got no college degree. I've got no work experience except for stacking books in the prison library, and I don't think that counts. Even if I did have a college degree, no one would exactly be welcoming me into the executive ranks. I carried a three-point-seven GPA my first year and now I'm pushing mail."

"Do they know you served time?" I asked him.

"You mean *here?*"

"Yes."

"Sure. You should come down to the mailroom sometime. We're a liberal's wet dream. We got two ex-cons, two retards, an ex-junkie, and a quadriplegic. He's our quality control man."

"When you came out—why didn't you go back to college?"

"Were you going to pay my tuition?"

Winston had a point there.

"Look, I'm on parole," Winston continued. "They have these rules when you're on parole. You can't go out of state without permission. You've got to check in with your parole officer twice a month. You can't associate with any known criminals. And—oh yeah—you can't steal computers. I may have fucked up on that one. On the other hand, there's this *other* rule they have when you're on parole. You can't earn a living—not really. Know what they pay me to deliver your mail?"

We could talk sports all we liked, but we were on two different sides of the socioeconomic spectrum, Winston was saying. I was an executive, and he was just a mail boy.

"How many computers, Winston?"

"Like I told you, this is the first time—"

"You got *caught*. I know. How many times didn't you get caught?"

Winston leaned back and smiled. He flexed his arm—the one with the wire cutter in it. He shrugged.

"A couple," he said.

"Okay. A couple." I suddenly felt tired; I rubbed my forehead and looked down at my shoes. "I don't know what to do," I said out loud. I might have been saying that about everything now.

"Sure you do. I just bared my soul to you, man. I was stupid, I admit it. Won't happen again. Promise."

"All right. Fine. I won't say anything." Even as I was saying this, I wondered exactly why I'd come to that decision. Maybe because I felt like no less of a thief than Winston. Yes. Hadn't I stolen money from Anna's Fund? Late at night, too, when no one could see me—just like Winston? Wasn't that criminal etiquette—never turning in a fellow criminal? Do the same for me, wouldn't he?

"Thanks," Winston said.

"If I hear about another computer being stolen . . ."

"Hey—I'm larcenous. Not stupid."

That's right, I thought. *The stupid one is me.*

DERAILED SEVENTEEN

Daddy . . ."

The word you almost never tire of hearing during the day, becoming the word you dread waking to in the middle of the night. It came like a fire alarm in a pitch-black movie theater, and right in the middle of the film, the current feature a kind of domestic drama involving me and Deanna and a woman with green eyes.

"Daddy!"

I heard it again, and this time I woke up for good and nearly fell off the bed.

Memories of other nights like this clamored for my undivided attention even as I tried to deflect them, to concentrate on the physical act of standing up and running barefoot across a dark and frigid hall.

To Anna's room.

I flipped on the lights even as I entered it—one hand pressed against the switch, the other already reaching out for her. Even with my eyes squinting from the sudden brightness, I could see that Anna looked exceptionally and spookily weird. She was, I was fairly certain, smack in the middle of hypoglycemic shock.

Her eyes were rolled back, to that part of her brain that was reeling from lack of sugar, her body caught in one unending stutter. When I put my arms around her, it was like holding on to a frightened puppy, all shake and quiver. Only if Anna was frightened, she was incapable of telling me.

When I shouted at her, she refused to shout back. When I shook her head and whispered into her ear, when I slapped her gently—no response.

I'd been told what to do when this happened. I'd been prepped and trained and reminded and warned. I just couldn't remember a word of it.

I knew there was a syringe sitting in a fire-engine-red plastic case. I thought the case was downstairs in a kitchen cabinet. I believed that the case needed to be opened and the syringe filled with a brown powder that was also in the case. And water—some amount of water was to be added.

These things were flying through my mind like a dyslexic sentence I couldn't quite grasp. I caught the general drift, though, which was horrifying and merciless.

My daughter was dying.

Suddenly Deanna was right behind me.

"The shot," I said to her, or possibly yelled.

But she already had it in her hand. I felt a momentary surge of pure love for her, this woman I'd married and created Anna with, even in the midst of terror feeling like falling to my knees and hugging her. She opened the case for me, calmly plucked out the syringe, and studied the bold-lettered directions on the way into Anna's bathroom. I cradled Anna in my lap, whispering that it would be okay, Anna, yes, it would, *you'll be fine, Anna, yes, my darling,* as I heard the water running in there. Then Deanna was back out, shaking the syringe in her hand.

"Deep," Deanna said, handing the shot to me. "Past the fat into the muscle."

I'd dreaded this moment—had imagined over and over what it'd be like. When they'd first trained me on the fine art of insulin giving, pricking thin quarter-inch needles just into the fatty tissue on hip, arm, and buttock—they'd also mentioned *this*. That eventually there would come a moment when I'd probably have to use it. Not *every* parent had to, but given that Anna had an especially virulent case and given that Anna had gotten it so young . . . This needle *not* a quarter inch long, more like four inches, and thick enough to make you turn your eyes away. Because it had to get its pure sugar mix into the brain cells fast enough to keep them from starving.

This syringe was in my hand now, only my hand was quivering as much as Anna was, because it was like stabbing her, even if it was with the gift of life. I placed it by her upper arm, but since we both were shaking, I was afraid to push it in, afraid I'd miss and blunt the needle, waste the liquid.

"Here—" Deanna took the needle from me.

She put it against Anna's hip, hand steady, and stuck it all the way in. Then she slowly pushed the plunger down till all the brown liquid was gone.

It was almost instantaneous.

One minute my daughter was lost. Then suddenly her eyes rolled back into focus, and her body gently quieted and settled back onto the bed.

And she cried.

Anna cried, worse even than the morning she was diagnosed and we told her more or less what was in store for her. Worse than that.

"Daddy . . . oh Daddy . . . oh Daddy . . ."

So I cried, too.

*   *   *

I took her to the hospital—the children's wing of Long Island Jewish, just to be on the safe side. I hadn't been back since those first excruciating weeks, and the very smell of the place was enough to take me back to the time when I'd paced the halls at four in the morning, knowing that the best part of my life was over. Anna felt it, too; she'd managed to calm down on the twenty-minute ride to the hospital, but the moment we entered the waiting room, she'd shrunk back into my body and hid there, so that I nearly had to carry her inside.

It was 2:00 A.M.; we were given an Indian intern who seemed overworked and distracted. Deanna had been calling Anna's doctor when we'd left the house.

"What happened, please?"

"She was hypoglycemic," I said. "She had an episode." Anna was sitting on the examining table, virtually slumped against me.

"You administered the shot?"

"Yes."

"Uh-huh . . ." He was examining her even as we spoke, doing all the things doctors do—heart, pulse, eyes, ears—so maybe he was competent after all. "We'd better take her blood sugar, no?"

I wondered if he was asking me for my medical opinion or simply being rhetorical.

"We took it before we came. One forty-three. I don't know what it was before she . . ." I was going to say *passed out, fainted, became unconscious* but felt reticent to say it in front of Anna. I noticed a bruise had already formed where Deanna had given her the shot and thought that other parents who bruise their children are brought up on charges and locked away.

"One forty-three, yes?"

"Yes."

"Well, we'll see. . . ."

He asked for Anna's hand, but Anna had no intention of giving it. "No," she said, and meant it.

"Come on, Anna, the doctor has to take your blood sugar to make sure everything's okay. You do this four times a day—it's no big deal."

But of course it was a big deal. *Because* she did it four times a day and now they were asking her to do it a fifth—actually sixth, since I'd taken it before we came here. It was a big deal because she was back in the hospital where she'd first been told she wasn't like everyone else, that her body had this terrible deficiency that could kill her. It might not be a big deal to the doctor, or even to me, but it was to her.

Still. She was sitting in LIJ at two in the morning because she'd almost died, and now the doctor needed a blood sample. "Come on, Anna, be a big girl, okay?" remembering back to those first days at home when I'd have to beg her to give me her arm, sometimes having to take it from her, brute force preceding brute pain, each time convinced I was committing the worst kind of assault.

"I'll do it *myself*," Anna said.

The doctor was losing patience now; so many patients and so little time. "Look, miss, we have to—"

"She said she'll do it herself," I said, remembering something else about back then. How after her diagnosis, Anna had spent two weeks here learning how to deal with this thing called diabetes, with hospital protocol demanding that all patients administer one insulin shot to themselves before they could be discharged. And Anna, who feared needles the way other people fear snakes, or spiders, or dark cellars, had made me promise that she wouldn't have to do that. And I'd said, *I promise*. And on the day she was due to be discharged, the nurse had come in and asked Anna to do it—to fill up the shot with two kinds of insulin and inject it herself into her already bruised arm. And at first both parents, Deanna and me, had

said nothing, letting the nurse gently and then not so gently ca-
jole the patient into doing what she was so clearly terrified of.
And finally, with the silence from her only allies nearly deafen-
ing, Anna had looked over at me with pure naked pleading.
And even though I knew that it probably was a good thing for
Anna to give herself a shot, I still told the nurse, *No. She doesn't
have to do that.* I'd made a promise to her and I kept it. Her
body might have betrayed her, but her father hadn't. It was the
kind of moment you feel like bronzing—the one you take out
of the cabinet and hold up to the light later on, when you've
betrayed everything else.

"She'll do it herself," I repeated.

"Okay," the Indian said. "Well then, please let her do it already."

I gave her the lancet pen and watched as Anna shakily
brought it up to her middle finger and snapped the top, a
bright bubble of blood already forming as she took the pen
away. I offered to hold the blood meter for her, but she took it
from me and managed it herself—little Anna not so little anymore, a fighter if there ever was one.

Her blood sugar was fine—122.

I told the intern that my daughter's endocrinologist, Dr.
Baron, would be coming by any minute.

But Dr. Baron wasn't coming by. The intern's beeper sent him
scurrying out of the ER, and when he came back, he said: "Dr.
Baron says she can go home."

"He's not coming?"

"No need. I told him her numbers. He said she can go
home."

"I thought he would come to see her."

The intern shrugged. *Doctors,* he was saying, *what are you
going to do?*

I said, "That's great."

"Could I please have a word with you?" he said.

"Sure." I followed the intern to the other side of the ward, where a Chinese man was sitting in a chair, looking down at his bloody hand.

"How is her sit, please?"

"Her *what?*"

"Her sit."

Her *sight.* "Okay," I said. "She uses glasses for reading. She's supposed to, anyway," thinking that it had been a while since I'd actually seen them on her. "Why?"

He shrugged. "There is some damage there. It's no worse?"

"I don't know. I don't think so." Feeling that familiar ache in the pit of my stomach again, as if something were lodged in there that even Long Island Jewish Hospital couldn't surgically remove.

"Okay," the intern said, and gave me a pat on the shoulder. Overworked, a little impatient, maybe, but friendly after all.

"Is there something I should be telling Dr.—"

"No, no." The intern shook his head. "Just checking."

After I signed a few papers and handed over my new credit card, we were told we could leave.

Outside in the quiet winter air, our breath merged on the way to the car, one vaporous cloud that followed us all across the parking lot. *It should be a* black *cloud,* I thought—wasn't that the metaphor for ill luck?

"Hey, kiddo," I said, "you seeing okay these days?"

"No, Dad, I'm blind."

Well, her blood sugars might be running wild, but her sarcasm was intact and healthy.

"I was just wondering if you noticed anything, that's all. With your eyes."

"I'm fine."

But on the ride home, Anna snuggled against me, the way she used to when she was small and needed to nap.

"Remember that story, Dad?" she asked me after several blocks.

"What story?"

"The one you used to tell me when I was little. You made it up. About the bee."

"Yes." A story I'd put together on the spot, after Anna had been stung and I'd told her the bad bee was dead to make her feel better. Only it hadn't made her feel better; she was horrified that bees *die* when they sting, even the bee who'd stung her.

"Tell it," Anna said.

"I don't remember it," I lied. "What about the one about the horses? You know, the old man who goes looking for adventure?"

"No," she said. "I want the bee story."

"Gee, Anna, I don't even remember how it starts."

But she did. "There was a little bee," she began. "Who wondered why he had a stinger."

"Oh yeah. That's right."

"Tell it."

Why that story, Anna?

"He wondered why he had a stinger," I said.

"Because . . . ," Anna said impatiently.

"Because he saw that every time the other bees used their stingers, they died."

"His best friend"—she nudged me—"and—"

"His best *bee* friend," I corrected her, "his aunt Bee, his uncle Bumble, all of them used their stingers and then died."

"He was very sad about this," Anna said softly.

"Yes, he was sad about this. Because he wondered what was the point, then. Of having a stinger, of being a bee."

"So then . . ."

"So then. He asked everyone this question. All the other animals in the forest."

"In the *garden*," Anna corrected me.

"In the garden. But no one could help him."

"Except the owl."

"The *wise* owl. The owl said, 'When you use it, you'll know.'"

"And . . ."

"One day, the bee was in the forest—the garden—and he saw a peacock. Of course he didn't know it was a peacock. He didn't know what a peacock was, exactly. Just an ordinary-looking bird, apparently."

"You didn't say *apparently* when I was little," Anna said.

"Well, you're not little anymore. Apparently."

"No."

"Just an ordinary-looking bird. So he thought. Until he landed on it and asked it the same question he'd asked all the other animals. Why do I have a stinger?"

"Why?" Anna said, as if she really wanted to know the answer to the question, as if she'd forgotten and needed to hear it again.

"And the peacock said to the bee, 'Buzz off.' Whereupon the bee got angry."

"And stung the peacock," Anna said, finishing for me. "And the peacock went ouch, and all its feathers stood out. All of them. All the colors of the rainbow. And the little bee thought it was the most beautiful thing he'd ever seen. And died."

When we turned into Yale Road, Vasquez was there. Standing like a sentinel under a street lamp.

I drove right past him and almost up onto the facing sidewalk.

"Daddy!" Anna was suddenly not snuggling anymore, but up and alert and maybe even alarmed.

Somehow I managed to steer the car back into the street, then up the driveway to 1823 Yale.

"What's wrong?" Anna said.

"Nothing." As insincere a "nothing" as ever left a person's mouth. Certainly mine. But Anna was too polite to question me any further, even when I grabbed her by the arm and nearly yanked her into the house.

When Deanna was up and waiting. Coffee brewed, lights on, kitchen TV set to the Food Channel as she waited for the loves of her life to return home safely.

Anyway, we'd returned.

It's possible she mistook my expression of dread for the night's events—waking up to find our daughter unconscious and in shock. What else would she think caused me to turn white and pace up and down the kitchen floor?

"Is she all right?" Deanna asked. She'd already directed this question to Anna herself, who with her teenage sullenness back in full working order had simply tramped by her and up the stairs to her room.

"Yeah," I said. "Fine. Her blood sugar was down to one twenty-two."

"How is she? Scared?"

"No," I said. *I'm scared.*

Anna was a trooper, and Anna was going to be a-okay. But *Charley* here—that was a different matter. I was trying to deflect my wife's attention from the door, where any minute now the man who was blackmailing me might ring the bell.

Vasquez was no more than forty yards away from my wife and child.

I walked to the window and stared out into the dark.

"What are you looking at?" Deanna asked me.

"Nothing. I thought I heard something . . ."

She was behind me now. She laid her head against my neck and stood there half leaning on me, one of us thinking the danger had passed, the other one knowing it hadn't.

"Is she really okay?" Deanna asked me.

"What?" I felt momentarily calmed by the warmth of her body.

"Maybe I should sleep with her tonight."

"She wouldn't let you."

"I can slip in after she falls asleep."

"I think it's okay, Deanna. She'll be fine tonight." The operative word being *tonight,* of course. Couldn't vouch for tomorrow night or the night after that. Of course, it was possible *we* wouldn't be fine tonight.

Why had Vasquez come here? What did he want?

"Why do you look so worried, Charles? I thought that was my department."

"Well, you know . . . the hospital and all."

"I'm going to sleep," she said. "I'm going to try."

"I'll be up later," I said.

But after Deanna walked up the stairs, I counted to ten, then went over to the fireplace and picked up a poker. I swung it back and forth a few times.

I opened the front door and went outside.

It was approximately twenty-five steps from my front door to the beginning of the driveway. I knew this because I counted every one. As something to do—anything to do—instead of panic. Of course, it was possible I was *already* panicking. After all, I was walking down the driveway with a fireplace poker in my hands.

When I made it all the way down to the sidewalk, I took three deep breaths and saw that Vasquez wasn't there.

The streetlight illuminated a starkly empty corner.

Was it possible I'd imagined it? Was I starting to see Vasquez even when Vasquez wasn't there—my very own personal spook?

I was honestly willing to believe it—in fact, desperately *wanted* to believe it. But it wasn't until I dutifully walked all the way to the corner and even called out his name—not loudly,

no, but loud enough for the neighborhood setter to start barking—then reversed field and walked back past my driveway to
the opposite corner and *still* saw no Vasquez, that I was willing
to embrace it as gospel.

Maybe I *was* seeing things. I'd had a near death experience
tonight—my daughter's, maybe, but still. You have one bad
fright, you're due for another. Chalk one up for my old pal fear.
Or my *new* pal—we were spending so much time together
these days.

But when I passed the oak tree that established the borders
of my property, I noticed a wet stain running down its gnarled
trunk. And I smelled something.

Acrid, tart—the smell of Giants Stadium at halftime. So
many beers consumed and so many beers given back, the stadium like one enormous urinal. That's what it smelled like
here.

Courtesy of a passing canine? Fine, except for a simple law
of physics. A dog just couldn't reach that high on the trunk—
not Curry, not the neighborhood setter, not even a Great Dane.
Dogs pissing on trees is a very solemn ritual, or so I'd read—a
way of marking their territory.

That's why Vasquez had done it.

I hadn't been imagining things. No.

Vasquez had come calling and had left a calling card. *See,* he
said, *this is my territory—your home, your life, your family.*

It's mine now.

DERAILED EIGHTEEN

Hello, Charles."

It was 10:15 Wednesday night. I was sitting in the den, where I'd been standing guard over the telephone. It was unnerving—every time it rang I'd pick it up and wait to see who'd say hello. The fastest answering machine in the West—one ring and it was sitting in my hand. I knew he'd be calling; I didn't want Deanna picking it up first.

"Why were you outside my *house?*" I said.

"Was that me?"

"I'm asking you what you were doing here."

"Must have been taking a walk."

"What do you want? What?"

"What do *you* want?"

Okay, I was a little taken aback—this answering a question with a question.

"What do I want?"

"That's right. You tell me."

Well. For one thing, I wanted Vasquez to stop coming by my

house. For another thing, I wanted him to stop calling my house. That would be nice.

"I want you to leave me alone," I said.

"Okay."

"I'm not clear what you mean. . . ."

"Something about *okay* you don't understand? You said you want me to leave you alone, I said okay."

"Great," I said, stupidly letting some vague tenor of hope enter my voice, even though I knew, I *knew*—

"Just give me some more money."

More money.

"I gave you money," I said. "I told you—"

"That was then. This is now."

"No." The till was empty, the cupboard bare. I'd taken once from Anna's Fund. No more.

"You fucking stupid?"

Yes. Probably.

"I don't have any more money for you," I said.

"Look, *Charles*. Pay attention. We both know you got the money. We both know you're gonna give it to me, 'cause we both know what's gonna happen if you don't."

No, I didn't know. But I could guess.

So I asked him how much he was talking about. Even though I didn't really care how much he was talking about, because it was already too much.

And Vasquez said: "Hundred thou."

I shouldn't have been surprised, but I was.

That was inflation for you—ten thousand to a hundred thousand in the blink of an eye. But then—how much is a life worth, exactly? Are *three* lives worth? What *is* the going rate for a wife and daughter these days? For being able to look them in the eye without seeing disgust staring back? Maybe a hundred thousand was cheap. Maybe I was getting a bargain here.

"I'm waiting," Vasquez said.

He would have to keep on waiting. It was a bargain I simply couldn't afford.

Besides, it was never going to stop *here* anyway. Wasn't that the point of blackmail? Wasn't it governed by its own immutable laws, like the universe itself, and, just like the universe, never ending? Vasquez might say it would stop, but Vasquez was lying. It would stop only when I stopped Vasquez. A simple truth even an idiot could understand—even someone *fucking stupid* could grasp that. Only I couldn't stop Vasquez— I didn't know how. Other than to say no and take my chances.

"I don't have it," I said.

And hung up the phone.

When Winston delivered my mail the next morning, he found me slumped over the desk.

"Are you dead," Winston asked me, "or just pretending?"

"I don't know. It feels like I'm dead. Could be."

"Can I have your computer, then?"

I looked up, and Winston put up his hands and said: "Just kidding." Since the night in the office, Winston had been exactly like the Winston *before* the night in the office. No tiptoeing around, no bowing and scraping, no false humility. If I'd scared Winston straight, you wouldn't have exactly known it. On the other hand, I hadn't heard about any missing computers lately, so maybe Winston had reformed.

"Seriously," Winston said, "something wrong?"

Where to begin? Then again, much as I might want to, I couldn't tell Winston a thing.

"What was it like?" I asked him instead.

"What was what like?"

"Prison?"

Winston's face darkened—yes, a definite change from sunny to cloudy, with possible thunderstorms lurking in the area. "Why are you asking?"

"I don't know. Just curious."

"It's hard to describe unless you've been there," he said flatly, maybe hoping I'd just say okay and leave it at that.

But I didn't say okay. And though Winston was under no obligation to answer me, maybe he *saw* himself as having an obligation to me now. Because he did answer me.

"You really want to know what prison was like?"

"Yes."

"What was it like? It was like . . . walking a tightrope," he said, letting that simple statement lie there for a while. "Walking a tightrope, but you can't get off. All that concentrating on not falling and getting yourself killed. Constantly—twenty-four hours a day, understand? You tried to not get involved in things—that was your mantra, because if you did get involved in things, it was almost always trouble. So you tried to ignore everyone, to walk around with your head up your ass. But that takes enormous concentration. To act like you're blind. Because all kinds of shit is going on around you—the worst kind of shit. Rapes, beatings, stabbings—all this gang warfare. You try to be invisible. You know how *hard* it is to be invisible?"

"I can imagine," I said.

"No, man, you *can't* imagine. It is the hardest possible thing to do. It's not doable. Sooner or later, you're going to get involved, because someone is going to make you get involved."

"And someone made you?"

"Oh yeah. I was prime meat in there. I was unaffiliated, and so I was prime meat."

"You were . . . ?"

"Bitched up? No. But only because I fought someone who tried, and did two months in lockup. You can't go out of your cell. Except for showers. No rec. Nothing. Which was kind of okay, since I knew when I *did* get out of my cell, I was in trouble, since the guy I fought was affiliated."

"So what did you do?"

"I got affiliated."

"With who?"

"A gang. Who do you think runs things in there?"

"Just like that?"

"No. I had to earn it—you don't get anything for nothing there, Charles. There's always a price."

"What was the price?"

"The price? The price was I had to stick a shank in someone. Like a blood initiation, only the blood was someone else's. That's how you get into a gang. You make someone else bleed."

"Who were they?"

"Who was who?"

"The gang?"

"Oh, just a bunch of guys. Nice guys, really, you'd like them. They had some very pronounced beliefs, though. Like for instance, they believe all blacks are subhuman. And all Hispanics—them, too. They don't like Jews much, either. Other than that—they're terrific."

And now I noticed something again. Winston's tattoo. AB. Maybe not Amanda Barnes after all.

"You got that tattoo in prison, didn't you?"

Winston smiled. "Can't put anything over on you. Proud member of the Aryan Brotherhood. We have a handshake and everything."

You had to admire Winston, I thought. He found himself in a terrible situation, and he did what he had to. Maybe there was a lesson in that.

"See you this afternoon," Winston said. "But no more questions about prison, okay? It kind of ruins my day."

DERAILED NINETEEN

When I disembarked at Merrick station I called Deanna to pick me up. I thought about walking, but a steady wind was whipping in from the ocean and I was nearly blown back into the train when I stepped off onto the platform.

But when Deanna answered the phone, she asked me if I could wait ten minutes. The chimney guy I'd hired was there, and she didn't want to leave him alone in the house with Anna.

So I told her I'd walk after all.

Christmastime had turned what was generally a quiet and reserved residential street into something akin to the Vegas strip. All those flashing lights. All those plastic reindeer pulling plastic Santas on their plastic sleighs. A plastic manger or two. Several stars of Bethlehem precariously perched on once stately arborvitaes.

I pulled in gulps of air that felt strangely heavy and saturated with moisture as I walked past and took in the show.

And then, suddenly, rescue.

A car horn beeped, then beeped again.

I turned and saw my neighbor's Lexus purring by the side of the curb.

I walked up to the passenger door as my neighbor Joe cracked open the window.

"Hop in," he said.

You didn't have to ask me twice. I opened the door and slid into a kind of primal warmth—what the first cavemen must have felt when they created those first licks of flame and finally, miraculously, stopped shivering.

"Thanks," I said.

"Cold out there, huh?" said Joe, who was nothing if not observant.

"Yes."

Joe was a chiropractor, which either was or wasn't a legitimate profession. No one had ever been able to explain it to my satisfaction.

"How's the kid?" Joe asked.

"Okay," I answered, thinking I sounded like Anna now. One-word answers to any question. "And yours?" Joe had three children spaced a year apart, including a girl around Anna's age who was academically oriented, athletically gifted, and disgustingly healthy.

Joe said they were fine.

"How's things at the office?" he asked me.

"Fine." People politely asked you things that they didn't actually want answers to, I thought—but what if I did answer him? What if I said, *Glad you asked, Joe,* then gave him an earful about Eliot and Ellen Weischler. *I was fired off the account I worked on for ten years, and now they have me working on a shit account that no one cares about.* And while I was at it, I could fill him in on Vasquez and Lucinda, too. What would he say then?

But instead I said: "How are things with you?"

"People always have bad backs," Joe said.

Even after they've gone to you for treatment, I felt like saying. But didn't.

"Doing anything for the holidays?" Joe asked me. We were stopped at a traffic light that was generally acknowledged to be the slowest traffic light in Merrick. Whole days would pass and this traffic light would stay red. Kingdoms rose and fell, presidential administrations came and went, and the light obstinately refused to change.

"No. Going over to Deanna's mom like we do every year."

"Uh-huh."

Then after I asked Joe the same thing, and Joe told me he was going down to Florida for a few days, the car went quiet as we both realized that was pretty much it—we'd run out of small talk.

"Boy, it's cold," Joe finally said, repeating his comment from earlier in the ride.

"Go through the light, Joe," I said.

"What?"

"Go through the light." Something had just come to me.

"Why should I—"

Deanna had asked me to wait at the station. Because the chimney cleaner I'd hired was there and she didn't want to leave him alone in the house.

"Go through the *fucking light.*"

I hadn't hired a chimney cleaner.

"Look, Charles, I don't want to get a ticket and I don't see what the big rush is—"

"Go!"

So Joe did. The evident panic in my voice finally spurred Joe into action; he gunned the engine and went right through the traffic light, swinging into Kirkwood Road just two blocks from our homes.

"If I got a ticket, you'd pay it," Joe said, trying to regain a little of his dignity now that he'd blindly obeyed his neighbor for no good reason. *What did I mean, coming off like that, ordering him around?*

"Stop here," I said.

Joe had obviously intended to steer the car into his own driveway and let me walk next door. But I couldn't wait. For the second time in two minutes, Joe did as he was told. He stopped the car in front of 1823 Yale and I jumped out.

When I flung open my front door, I saw Deanna leaning against the banister, in the middle of telling someone that Curry didn't like everyone this way, that he was selective with his affections.

And then the person she was telling this to.

"Mr. Ramirez said he's giving us a special price," Deanna was saying.

We were sitting in the living room, the three of us.

"But only because he likes Curry and vice versa," Deanna continued. She was talking about the price of cleaning the chimney. Deanna always managed to settle into an easy rapport with handymen of one kind of another, befriending them, regaling me later with stories about their wives and children.

"Yeah," Vasquez said. "I'm just a dog lover." He was smiling, the same smile he'd had when he was propping Lucinda up against the bed to rape her for the last time.

"Mr. Ramirez—" Deanna said, but she was interrupted.

"Raul," Vasquez said.

"Raul said our chimney has a broken . . . what was that again?"

"Flue."

"Yes, we have a broken flue."

"Yeah. It's an old chimney," Vasquez said. "When was this house built?"

"Nineteen twelve," Deanna said. "I think."

"Yeah. It's probably never been touched."

"Then I guess it's about time," Deanna said.

"That's right. Sure."

I hadn't said anything yet. But now they were waiting for me to say something, some acknowledgment of the problem at hand and what I was going to do about it. I hadn't said anything yet because I couldn't imagine what to say.

"So," Deanna continued, "Raul is prepared to fix it and clean the chimney. But it's up to you."

"You don't want to live with a broken flue," Vasquez said. "The thing could be dangerous. All that carbon dioxide can back up, man—it'll *kill* you while you're sleeping, understand?"

Yes, I understood all right.

"There was this family I knew that didn't fix their flue," Vasquez said. "One night they went to sleep, and in the morning they didn't wake up. All of them, dead. A whole family."

"So, what do you say?" Deanna asked me, looking alarmed now. "What do you want to do?"

Anna wandered into the living room, dressed in pajamas.

"What's the capital of North Dakota?" she asked me.

Two questions before me now, but I only felt like answering one.

I'll take state capitals for one hundred, Alex.

"Bismarck," I said.

"Anna, this is Raul," Deanna said, always the hostess.

"Hi," Anna said, flashing him her most polite smile, the one she trotted out for distant relatives, old friends of her parents, and, apparently, handymen.

"Hello," Vasquez said, and reached out and tousled her hair. That hand on my child's head.

"How old are you?" Vasquez asked her.

"Thirteen," Anna said.

"That right?"

He hadn't taken his hand off her head. Instead of coming off

the way it was supposed to, it was lingering there uncomfortably, five, then ten, then fifteen seconds; Anna was starting to
squirm.

"Look just like your mom," Vasquez said to her.

"Thanks."

"You like school?"

Anna nodded. My daughter, who generally tried to refrain
from offending anyone, obviously wanting that hand off her
head now, but evidently unsure just how to accomplish that.
She looked at me for help.

"Look . . . ," I said.

"Yeah?" Vasquez stared right back at me. "You say something?"

I said: "Why don't you run upstairs and finish your homework, Anna."

"Okay." She wanted to do that, yes, but the problem was that
Vasquez hadn't taken his hand off her head yet. So she stood
there, her eyes still beseeching me for assistance.

"Go *on*, honey."

"Okay."

But Vasquez was *still* not removing his hand, still standing
there and smiling at me as the room finally went quiet. One of
those awkward moments—like watching a friend of the family
kiss your wife just a little too intimately at a drunken party and
not knowing whether to stand by and watch or challenge him
to a fistfight.

"I have to do my homework," Anna said.

"Homework? Aww . . . pretty girls like you don't have to do
homework. You gotta get the boys to do it for you."

This was where I was supposed to act. Where I was supposed
to say please get your fucking hand off my daughter's head because it's fucking making her uncomfortable and she wants to
go upstairs, understand fucking English?

The silence was loud enough to split eardrums.

Then: "She likes to do her homework herself," Deanna said. Ending it. And finally, mercifully, insinuating herself between Vasquez's arm and Anna's head, physically and decisively ushering our daughter out of harm's way.

When Anna padded out of the living room, she glanced back at me with an expression that seemed to admonish me. Apparently, her face said, she'd been looking to the wrong parent for help.

I heard her footsteps going up the stairs at double speed.

Quiet again. Then:

"So . . . ?" Deanna said, clearing her throat. "Maybe you want to think about this, honey?" Apparently this was one hired help she wasn't going to befriend after all.

"I wouldn't take too long," Vasquez said, still smiling. "You don't want to take chances with your family's safety, right?"

I felt something acidic deep in my guts, something ice cold and broiling hot at the same time. I thought I might need to throw up.

"No," I said. "I'll get back to you soon."

"Okay, you get back to me, then."

"Yes."

"Why don't you see Raul out," Deanna said, evidently eager to get him out of the house.

So I walked him to the front door, where Vasquez turned and put his hand out, just as you'd expect from your friendly neighborhood chimney cleaner.

"Know what they taught us in the army, Charles?" he whispered. "Before I got kicked out?"

"What?"

Vasquez showed me.

Leaving one hand exactly where it was, proffered in friendship, but using the other one to grasp my testicles. Crushing them in his fingers.

My knees buckled.

"Grab 'em by the balls. Their hearts and minds will follow."

I tried to say something but couldn't. I wanted to cry out but couldn't. Deanna was not twenty feet behind me and completely oblivious to the excruciating pain radiating down my legs and threatening to make me scream.

"I want the money, Charles."

I felt my eyes begin to water. "I'll . . ."

"What? Can't hear you. . . ."

"I'll . . ."

"I'll never hang up on you again? That's cool, apology accepted. I want the fucking money."

"I can't breathe. . . ."

"A hundred thousand dollars, okay?"

"I . . ."

"What?"

"Plea . . ."

"A hundred thousand and I give you your balls back."

"I . . . pl . . ."

And then he did.

He did give them back. At least temporarily. He opened his fingers, and I slumped against the doorjamb.

"Honey," Deanna said, "can you bring the recycling bin out to the curb?"

DERAILED TWENTY

I was looking over the bid for the aspirin job.

Think of this as a kind of avoidance therapy. If I was looking over the bid for the aspirin job, I couldn't be asking myself *What was I going to do? How was I going to survive this?*

So that's what I was doing.

Meticulously going over that aspirin bid; something was wrong with it, but I didn't know what. What *was* wrong with it?

This avoidance strategy was only partially successful.

In the middle of scanning down a line of neatly typed-in figures, I saw Vasquez with his hand on my daughter's head.

If he didn't get one hundred thousand dollars, he would be coming back.

I thought about telling Deanna.

But as much as I tried to say, *She will forgive me, she will.* As much as I told myself that Deanna loved me, and wouldn't that love survive an indiscretion? As many times as I postulated the theory that every marriage has its ups and downs and that okay, *this* down might be subterranean, but wouldn't it naturally be followed, after much anguish and restitution, by another upswing? As much as I rationalized, ruminated, debated, and what have you—I couldn't quite convince myself that I could for one minute withstand that look in Deanna's eyes. The one that would inexorably come immediately after she found out what I'd been up to.

I'd seen that look before. I'd seen it the morning they'd diagnosed Anna in the emergency room. The look of being utterly and hopelessly betrayed. I'd had to stare it full in the face as the news slowly sank in and she'd fastened on to me like a swimmer being pulled off by an undertow.

I didn't think I could bear to see it again.

Back to the sheet in front of me. It listed every expense associated with the commercial.

Director's fee, for instance. Fifteen thousand dollars day rate. Which was about average for a B director, A directors being somewhere up at twenty or twenty-five. Then there was set construction. Forty-five thousand—pretty much the going rate for one suburban kitchen on a New York stage set.

All these thousand dollars reminding me of the thousands I myself didn't have. Why was I looking at this estimate, anyway? There was something wrong with it. What, exactly? I didn't know.

There was editing. Film-to-tape transfer. Color correction. Voice-over costs. And there was music. Yes, T&D Music House; that was the name all right. Forty-five thousand dollars. Full orchestra, studio record, mix. Seemed okay.

I called David Frankel.

"Yep," David answered.

"It's Charles."

"I know. It says your extension on my phone."

"Right. I've been trying to call the music house, but I can't seem to find the number."

"*What* music house?"

"T and D Music."

"Oh. What are you calling them for?"

"What am I calling them for? I wanted to talk to them about the spot."

"Why don't you talk to me about the spot. I'm the producer of the spot."

"I've never heard of T and D Music," I said.

"You've never heard of T and D Music."

"No."

"Why are we having this conversation, exactly?" David sighed. "Did you talk to Tom?"

"You mean ever?"

"Look, what do you want the music to be? Just tell me."

"I'd rather talk to the scorer."

"Why's that?"

"Because I want to convey my feelings directly."

"Okay, fine."

"Okay, fine, *what?*"

"Convey your feelings directly. Go ahead."

"I need their *number.*"

Another sigh now, the kind of sigh that said he was dealing with an idiot here, a complete and utter moron.

"I'll get back to you on that," David said.

I was going to ask why David needed to get back to me since all I was asking for was a number. I was going to ask him why he was acting as if I were brain-damaged. I was going to remind him that a producer's job was to produce, and sometimes that meant producing something as simple as a phone number.

But David hung up.

It was only then, as I heard that familiar question whispering in my ear again—*What are you going to do, huh, Charles?*—that I realized I was a little brain-damaged after all. That I'd been a little slow on the uptake here.

T&D Music House.

Tom and David.

Tom and David Music House.

Of course.

I followed Winston for five or six blocks in subzero temperature.

Winston smoked a cigarette. Winston window-shopped—a Giuliani-ized video store—once plastered with triple-X-rated posters promising the raptures of the flesh, now plastered with kung fu posters promising the pulverizing of it. Winston leered at two teenage girls in miniskirts and woolen leggings.

I hadn't intended to follow Winston. What I'd intended to do was walk right up to him at closing time and ask him if he wanted to have a beer with me. But I'd felt strangely reticent about doing it.

It was one thing to joke around twice a day with a man who delivered your mail, to ask him what left-handed baseball player had the highest batting average in history, to trade wisecracks and earned run averages. It was another thing to go drinking with him. I wasn't sure Winston would *want* to go drinking with me.

On the other hand, hadn't we traded confidences? Or hadn't *one* of us done that? And now the other ready to do the same? But that brought me to the other reason I hadn't been able to just walk up to Winston and suggest a drink.

Winston blew on his hands. He waltzed through a traffic light, narrowly avoiding a taxicab seemingly intent on mayhem. Winston stopped at a pretzel man and asked how much.

I was close enough to make out the words. I wished Winston would turn around and acknowledge me. A few more blocks and I was in danger of freezing to death.

Across the street was a Catholic mission with a biblical statement I remembered from Sunday school emblazoned over its door: "Oh Lord, the sea is so large and my boat is so small." *True enough*, I thought.

When I looked back toward Winston, he wasn't there. I ran over to the pretzel man and asked him where his last customer had gone to.

"Eh?" the pretzel man said.

"The tall guy you just sold a pretzel to. Did you see where he went?"

"Eh?"

The man was Lebanese, maybe. Or Iranian. Or Iraqi. Whatever he was, he couldn't speak English.

"One dolla," he said.

I said never mind. I walked away and thought: *I will talk to Winston tomorrow. Or maybe tomorrow I will change my mind and not talk to him at all.*

Someone grabbed me by the arm.

I don't want a pretzel, I started to say. But it wasn't the pretzel man.

"Okay, Charles," Winston said, "why the fuck are you following me?"

DERAILED TWENTY-ONE

On Christmas Eve I got drunk.

The problem was my mother-in-law's special eggnog, the special part being that it was two-thirds rum.

"Come to Daddy," I said to Anna after I'd finished one and a half of them, but she didn't seem to like that idea.

"You look dopey," she said to me.

"Are you drunk, Charles?" Deanna asked me.

"Of course not."

Mrs. Williams had an upright piano that must've been seventy years old. Deanna had taken lessons on it until she'd mutinied at ten years old and said enough. No more "Heart and Soul" and "Für Elise." Mrs. Williams had never quite forgiven her for that; her punishment was having to bang out Christmas songs on the piano we were all forced to sing to. "Hark the Herald Angels Sing," for instance. Neither Deanna nor I was particularly religious, but there are no atheists in foxholes. I belted out, "God and sinners reconcile . . ." as though my life depended on it, my syncopation slightly askew, as I was already into my third eggnog.

"You *are* drunk, Daddy," Anna said dourly. She liked singing songs with Grandma about as much as she liked giving herself shots.

"Don't talk to your father like that," Deanna said, stopping in midchord. Deanna, my defender and protectress.

"I'm not drunk—both of you," I said. "Want to see me walk a straight line?"

Apparently not.

Instead Anna snorted and said: "Do we have to sing these stupid songs?"

". . . . in Bethlehem," I sang, focusing on the Christmas star on top of the tree. It was faded from years of use, no longer sparkling the way it'd been when Anna needed to be held up in my arms during the Christmas sing-alongs to see it. A tarnished star now; you could see that it wasn't a star at all—just papier-mâché pockmarked with glue.

"Well, that was fun," Mrs. Williams said when we finished. Then when no one answered her, "*Wasn't it?*"

"Yep," I said. "Let's sing another."

"Get bent," Anna said.

"What does that mean?" I asked.

"It means *no*," Deanna said.

"That's what I thought it meant," I said. "Just checking."

"No more eggnog for you," Mrs. Williams said.

"But I *love* your eggnog."

"I think you love it too much. Who's going to drive home?"

"I will," Deanna said.

"When are we going?" Anna asked.

After dinner, we opened Mrs. Williams's presents. Anna would get hers tomorrow morning: two new CDs, including one by Eminem. Two tops from Banana Republic. And a cell phone. These days if you didn't have a phone of your own, you were some kind of dweeb. After all, you never knew whom you'd need to call: a girlfriend, a boyfriend, an ambulance.

Mrs. Williams received a lovely new sweater from Saks. She dutifully thanked us all—even me, who of course had no idea what was going to come out of the box.

"I'd like to propose a toast," I said.

"I took away your eggnog," Deanna said.

"I know. That's why I want to propose a toast."

"Geez, Charles, what's gotten into you?"

"I know what's gotten into him," Mrs. Williams said. "My eggnog."

"Damn fine eggnog, too," I complimented her.

"*Charles.*" Deanna looked mad.

Anna giggled and said: "Oh my, Daddy said 'damn.' Call the police."

"No," I said. "No police. Not a good idea."

"Huh?"

"Just kidding."

Mrs. Williams had put up some coffee. "Coffee, anyone?" she asked.

"I'm sure Charles would love some," Deanna said. As it happened, I wouldn't have loved some. It was clearly a plot; they were trying to sober me up.

Meanwhile Anna was whispering to Deanna. Something about getting off her back. "I'm behaving fine," I heard her say.

I'd sunk into the living room couch and was wondering if I'd be able to get up when the time came to leave.

"How's your nose, Charles?" Mrs. Williams asked me.

"Still there," I said, and touched it for her. "See?"

"Oh, Charles . . ."

Mrs. Williams had put on the TV station with the yuletide log. I stared into the flames and started to drift. It felt warm and pleasant. Until I began drifting into dangerous waters and it became unpleasant. That frozen street corner in the city.

The Charles that was all liquored up with the holiday spirit was screaming at me not to think about it.

But I couldn't help it.

I don't want a pretzel, I'd started to say. Remember?

I'd wanted something else.

Okay, Charles, why the fuck are you following me?

Winston with his arm casually around my shoulder, although I could feel the strength in it, and what's more, I thought Winston *wanted* me to feel that strength.

"I wasn't following you," I said. Lying seemed to be my first instinct here—and besides, I wasn't following Winston as much as procrastinating about following him.

"Yes, you were. Sing Sing gave me eyes in the back of my head, remember?"

"I was just going to ask you to have a beer. Really."

"Why? You finally figured out the seven players with eleven letters in their last names?"

"I'm still working on that one," I said, not exactly sure how to proceed.

"So why didn't you just ask me? If you wanted to have a beer so badly?"

"I saw you walking a block ahead. I was just trying to catch up."

"Okay," Winston said. "So let's have a beer."

And he smiled.

We went to a place called O'Malley's, which looked very much like what you would expect a place called O'Malley's to look like. It had a pool table in the back, a dartboard in the corner, and a TV tuned to an Australian football match. It had two resident drunks, at least I assumed they were more or less regulars, since one of them had his head laid flat on the bar and the bartender wasn't bothering to wake him. The other one Winston knew, because he said, "Hey, man," and briefly clapped him on the back when we walked by.

"What'll you have?" Winston asked after we took our seats at the bar.

"I'm buying," I said.

"Hey, you did me a favor, remember?" Winston retorted.

Yes, I remembered. Enough to think Winston might do me a favor in return.

"A light beer," I said.

Winston asked the bartender for two. Then he turned back to me.

"So, everything okay?" he asked. "You looked a little depressed the other day. Is it your kid? Isn't she sick or something?"

I'd never told Winston about Anna, but word gets around, I suppose.

"No, it's not that," I said.

He nodded and watched as the bartender put two beers in front of us.

"I have this problem," I said, finding a certain comfort in that word. Problems, after all, were manageable things. You had problems and then you figured out a way to solve them.

"Look, if it's a pang of conscience about that night, forget it. Have you heard about any more computers being stolen? I told you I wouldn't, and I haven't."

"Yes, I know," I said.

"So what is it?"

Winston took a long sip of beer. I hadn't touched mine yet—there was an ever-widening pool of water under the glass, making the bar beneath it look dark as blood.

"I did a stupid thing," I said. "I went a little crazy. With a woman."

Winston looked just a little confused. I understood—he was probably wondering why someone who wasn't a friend in the strictest definition of the term was talking to him about other women, about things you talked only to *best* friends about.

"You had an affair or something?"

"Or something."

"Okay. So, it's over, or what?"

"It's over, yes."

"So what is it? You're guilty about it. You wanted to unburden yourself? Fine. Don't worry about it. Everybody in the office is having an affair. Even with each other. What do you think we talk about down in the mailroom? Who's screwing who."

I sighed. "It's not that."

"Okay," Winston repeated. "So what is it?"

"Something happened."

"What? She's pregnant?"

"No. We were caught by someone," I said.

"Huh?"

"In the hotel room."

"Oh," Winston said. The wife, he was thinking.

"A man came in and attacked us," I said.

"*What?*"

"He jumped us as we were leaving the room. He robbed us and . . . raped her."

I had Winston's full attention now. Maybe he was still asking himself exactly why I was telling him all this, but at least he was interested in what I was saying.

"He raped her. In a hotel?"

"Yes."

"What hotel?"

"Just a hotel. Downtown."

"*Fuck,* Charles. What happened? Did he get away? They didn't catch him?"

No, they didn't catch him. In order to have to have caught him, they would have had to be told that he'd done something that necessitated his having to be caught.

"We didn't report it," I said.

"You didn't report it." Winston had fallen into the unfortunate habit of repeating every other thing I said. Probably because every other thing I was saying was a little hard to believe.

"We *couldn't* report it," I said, "understand?"

"Oh," Winston said, finally comprehending the situation. "Yeah. Okay, sure. So he took your money and disappeared?"

"No. He *didn't* disappear." I finally took a sip of beer—it tasted flat and warm. "That's the problem."

Winston looked confused again.

"He's blackmailing us," I said. "I guess that's what you call it. Asking us for money so he won't tell Deanna. My wife. And her husband."

Winston sighed and shook his head. *That's some situation you've got yourself into,* this sigh said. *I feel for you.*

I wanted Winston to do more than feel for me. I wanted him to *act* for me. And that would take more than sympathy. It would take a kind of quid pro quo; it would take *another* kind of blackmail.

"So—did you pay him what he wanted?" Winston asked.

"Yes and no."

"Well, did you or didn't you?"

"I did. He wants more now."

"Uh-huh," Winston said, taking another sip of beer. "I guess that's kind of par for the course, isn't it. Don't they always want more?"

"I don't know. It's the first time I've ever been blackmailed."

Winston almost laughed. Then he caught himself and said: "Sorry, Charles. Really, it's not funny, I know. It's just that it's kind of hard to imagine—I mean, *you.* In this kind of shit?"

He lifted his glass again and sucked down foam. "So . . . what are you going to do?"

Winston had finally reached the million-dollar question.

"I don't know," I said. "There isn't much I *can* do. I can't pay him. I don't have the money."

"Uh-huh. So you're going to let him tell your wife," he said, adding up all the variables but coming up with the wrong answer. "Sure—fuck him. She loves you, doesn't she? So you fucked around—who hasn't? She'll forgive you."

"I don't think so, Winston. I don't think she will forgive me. I don't think she could. Not with our daughter and all. . . ."

I explained the rest. How Lucinda refused to let her husband know, either. How I felt I owed her that.

"Shit," Winston said. Then, after a long moment of silence: "Been a great couple of months for you, Charles, hasn't it?"

He was referring to losing the credit card account, I guessed—even the mail department must've weighed in on that one.

"So," Winston said softly, "what do you do now?" as if asking himself that question, putting himself in that situation, maybe, and wondering what *he'd* do. And it's possible that it was then, that very moment, that he finally understood why I'd asked him here, why I'd followed him four blocks in the freezing cold to get him to have a beer with me. Maybe because he said to himself, *If it was me, I'd kick that blackmailer's ass. I'd kill him. I would.* Dismissing that as a reasonable alternative for me, of course, since I wasn't exactly the violent type. No, you had to have a little muscle to do something like that, you had to have a little experience in these matters, gotten your hands dirty now and then, or at least your fists bloody. Didn't you?

Winston put his glass down—midswallow he put it down and looked at me.

"What the fuck are you asking me?" he said. He'd finally put two and two together; he'd finally figured it out.

"I was hoping—"

"You were hoping *what?*" Winston cut me off. "What?"

"You'd help me."

"You were hoping I'd help you." There he went, echoing me again, but this time not because he couldn't believe what I was saying, but because he *could*.

". . . and the Sydney Black take the ball upfield . . ." The TV was still tuned to the Australian football match, which had evidently reached the do-or-die point of the game, because the crowd was roaring now, on their feet screaming for victory.

"Look," Winston said, "I like you, Charles. You're okay. I'm sorry about your daughter, man. I'm sorry about this blackmail thing, I am. But you're not my brother, okay? You aren't even my best friend. I have a best friend, and I'd do just about anything for him, but even if he asked me what I think you're about to—I'd say, *Go fuck yourself.* Do we understand each other?"

"I just thought maybe you'd . . . see him."

"*See* him. What the fuck does that mean? And when I see him, what would I be supposed to say to him? Huh? 'Could you be a nice guy and stop bothering my friend?' Is that before or after I kick his ass for you?"

Winston was no dope—a 3.7 GPA, and even with a history of drug abuse, his brain cells were still more or less intact.

"I'd pay you," I said.

"You'd pay me. How nice of you. Great."

"Ten thousand dollars," I said, plucking the figure out of the air. I'd paid ten thousand to Vasquez already, hadn't I—ten thousand seemed about right. Out of Anna's Fund again, but maybe there'd be a way to replenish it—that I *had* been giving a little thought to.

"Ten thousand," Winston said. "Or *what?*"

"What do you mean?" I said, even though I knew exactly what Winston meant. I'd been trying to leave that part of it unsaid.

"Or what?" Winston repeated. "If I don't take the ten thousand. And ten thousand is a lot of money for me—I'll admit it. But if I turn you down anyway. *Then* what?"

"Look, Winston . . . all I'm asking you—"

"You're asking me to commit a felony. I'm just wondering why you thought I'd say yes."

Then, after I didn't answer him: "How did *he* put it to you, Charles? The rapist. The blackmailer."

"What?"

"When he asked you for money—he said you pay such and such to me. Or else. Isn't that how he said it? More or less? So that's what I'm asking you. I'm asking what the *or else* is."

"Look, I think you misunderstood—"

"No, I understand perfectly. You're not asking me for money—you're *offering* it—I understand, very generous of you. But if I turn it down, if I say no thanks—then what? What's my alternative here?"

He wanted me to say it out loud. That's all.

I caught you stealing. I caught you stealing, and I can tell. Delivering mail is no great shakes, but prison is a lot worse. Right?

I might have offered to buy him a beer like a long-lost friend, but it wasn't friendship I was banking on.

But I couldn't bring myself to say the words.

I'd hoped Winston might do it as a favor—I'd let him off the hook once, and now Winston would get me off *mine*. That ten thousand dollars might do the trick here. But now that Winston was forcing me to issue the actual threat, I found I couldn't.

And I thought: *I'm not Vasquez.*

"Ten thousand dollars, huh," Winston said. He turned back to the football match: ". . . ball kicked upfield, Dover has it in the left corner . . ." He looked over at the sleeping drunk, who'd momentarily roused himself before sticking his head back down on the bar. He tapped his fingers on the edge of his beer glass—*tink, tink, tink,* like a wind chime caught in a sudden breeze.

And then he turned back to me and said: "Okay."

Just like that.

"Okay," he said. "Fine. I'll do it."

DERAILED TWENTY-TWO

I called Tom Mooney and told him I wanted to talk to him about something.

About music production.

It was the three-day work week between Christmas and New Year's. The time of year when people attempt to put their affairs in order and make a New Year's resolution or two. To lose those few extra pounds, for instance. I was formulating a weight-loss plan of my own. I had approximately one hundred and eighty extra pounds sitting on my neck. I needed to get rid of it.

Tom showed up five minutes early and made an elaborate show of taking off his coat and closing the door.

"Okay," Tom said when he sat down, "so what do you want to talk about?"

"Kickbacks," I said.

But maybe I'd been too blunt, because Mooney suddenly edged back in his chair. Was it possible there was a kind of code you were supposed to use for these things, a language of men in the know?

"Kickbacks—what's that?" Tom said. "Are we in the Teamsters or something? The last time I looked, we shoot commercials."

"T and D Music," I said. "So you also write songs."

"Hey, we're a full-service production company. Whatever it takes."

"And that's what it takes?"

"Have you seen Robert's reel lately?" He was trying to be funny, I guess, because he seemed to be waiting for me to laugh.

I didn't feel like laughing today.

"How long has this been going on?" I asked. "You and David?"

"Look, Chaz. Did you call me over here for an interrogation? Because maybe I missed something when you called me. I thought you called me over here for another reason. Correct me if I'm wrong."

I blushed. Maybe there *was* another language, or maybe I knew the language but was incapable of speaking it. First with Winston in the bar and now here. I had called Mooney over here for another reason, not to condemn him, not even to sweat all the dirty little details out of him. Just to put out my hand and say, *Count me in.*

So maybe it was time I dropped the air of moral superiority—that's what Tom was saying. And what's more, he was right.

"Twenty thousand," I said.

Kind of amazed that the words had actually made it all the way out of my mouth. *Twenty thousand* as a bald statement of fact—no equivocation, no rising consonant lilting into a plea. Twenty thousand—for the ten I owed Winston and the ten I'd already given out. And I wondered if this was the way it was done—or if I'd been expected to slide a scrap of paper across the table with the figure scrawled in pencil.

But Tom smiled again—the kind of smile that says, *You are one of us, aren't you.*

I felt a bit queasy—but less than I expected. Was this how it happened? Losing yourself a little at a time until suddenly there was no *you* there anymore? Someone who used your name, slept with your wife, hugged your kid, but wasn't actually you anymore?

"Hey," Tom said. "I told you I was Santa Claus, didn't I?"

The next day, I met Winston one block north of the number seven subway tracks in the mostly empty parking lot of a Dunkin' Donuts in Astoria, Queens.

Winston's idea. *Aren't you supposed to meet in out-of-the-way places?* he'd said after asking me if I knew the only pitcher with five Cy Young Awards.

Roger Clemens, I'd said.

Winston was waiting for me in a white Mazda with non-matching hubcaps and a busted taillight. The windshield was covered with spiderweb cracks.

I drove up in my silver Mercedes sedan and felt embarrassed about it. I parked at the far end of the lot, hoping Winston wouldn't see me. But he did.

"Over here," he yelled.

When I made it to the car, Winston leaned over and opened the passenger door.

"Hop in, bud."

Bud hopped in.

"Know my favorite song?" Winston asked.

"No."

" 'Money.' By Pink Floyd. Know my favorite artist?"

I shook my head.

"Eddie Money."

I said: "Yes, he's good."

"My favorite movie? *The Color of Money.* Favorite baseball

player of all time—Norm Cash. Second favorite—Brad Penny."

"Yes, Winston," I said, "I have your money."

"Hey, who was asking for *money?*" Winston said. "I was just making conversation."

A number seven train rumbled over the el, showering sparks down onto the street.

"But now that you mention it," Winston continued, "where is it?"

I reached into my pocket. *It's burning a hole in my pocket—* isn't that the expression? A messenger from Headquarters Productions had dropped off the manila envelope yesterday.

"Five thousand," I said. "The other half after."

"You see that in a movie?" Winston asked, still smiling.

"What?"

"The 'other half after' stuff? You see that in a movie or something?"

"Look, I just thought—"

"What's the deal, bud? I believe, when I said I'd do this, from the goodness of my heart, by the way—because you're a pal and you're in trouble—you said *ten* thousand."

"I know what we—"

"A deal's a deal, right?"

"I understand."

"What were the terms?"

"I think one-half—"

"Tell me what the terms were, Charles."

"Ten thousand," I said.

"Ten thousand. Right. Ten thousand for what?"

"What do you mean?"

"What are you giving me ten thousand for? Because you like me? 'Cause you want to send me back to college?"

"Look, Winston . . ." I suddenly wanted to be somewhere else.

"*Look,* Charles. I think maybe there's some kind of confusion. I want to review the terms with you. You ask someone to do something like this for you, you have to know what the terms are."

"I know the terms."

"You do? Then state them for me so there's no confusion. What are you giving me ten thousand for?"

"I'm giving you ten thousand to . . . make Vasquez go away."

Winston said: "Yeah, right—that's what I thought the terms were. Ten thousand to make Vasquez go away." He pulled something out of his pocket. "Here's my *argument* to make him go away," he said. "What do you think? Think he'll listen to it?"

"A gun." I felt myself recoil; I edged back against the window.

"Hey—you're good," Winston said. "You sure you haven't done this before?"

"Look, Winston, I don't want . . ."

"What? You don't want to look at it? Neither will he. What did you think I was going to do, Charles—ask him nicely?"

"I just want . . . you know . . . if at all possible . . ."

"Yeah, well, just in case it's not at all possible."

"Okay," I said. "Okay." I had been thinking in euphemisms all this time—*making Vasquez go away.* Doing something about him. Taking care of him. But this was the way a Vasquez was taken care of, Winston was saying. Sometimes it was this way.

"Okay what?" Winston said.

"Huh?"

"'Okay, here's your *ten thousand,* Winston'?"

"Yes," I said, giving up.

"Great," he said. "For a second there I thought you were only giving me half."

I took the envelope out of my pocket and handed it over.

"You're too easy, Charles," Winston said. "I would've settled for three-quarters."

Then, after he'd counted it all, he said: "Where?"

DERAILED TWENTY-THREE

Under the West Side Highway.

One week into the new year.

I was sitting next to Winston in a rented metallic blue Sable with leather seats. Winston had his eyes closed.

I could see a lone tugboat chugging its way up a Hudson River so black, it was as if it weren't there. Just an empty black space where the river ought to be. It was cold and sleeting; thin slivers of glass were exploding onto my face through the open window.

I was shivering.

I was trying not to think about something. I was trying to stay calm.

There was a hooker standing on the corner across the street. She'd been standing there ever since I entered the car.

I was looking at her and wondering where her customers were.

A fair question, since it was only a little past ten, and she was wearing a sheer red negligee and shiny black boots. She'd been dropped off by a Jeep with New Jersey license plates and was waiting for some other car with New Jersey license plates to come along. But it had been ten minutes and she was still stuck out there in the sleet. Doing nothing much but looking across the street at the blue Sable, which didn't seem to be moving, either.

She looked as if she were freezing. She had a small fake fur wrap around her shoulders, but other than that nothing, lots of pasty white flesh out there where her customers could see it and put a price tag on it.

But where *were* her customers?

The insurance salesman from Teaneck, the broker from Piscataway, the truck driver on his way to the Lincoln Tunnel?

I was under the West Side Highway because that's where Vasquez had told me to meet him.

Do you have the money? he'd asked me.

Yes, I did.

You'll meet me ten o'clock at Thirty-seventh and the river.

Yes, I would.

You'll tell nobody—understand?

Yes, I did. (Well, maybe just one other person.)

You'll show up alone.

Yes, I would. (Well, maybe not exactly alone.)

How long *had* the hooker been standing there without a customer? I thought again. How long, exactly?

Then she began to walk over to me.

In the middle of the street now, closer *to* me than away from me, so I knew that she wouldn't be turning back. Her boot heels echoing as she made a beeline for the blue Sable that had been sitting there all this time without moving an inch.

"Want a date?" she asked me when she reached my window. I could see actual goose bumps on her breasts and legs, because her breasts were only half-hidden by the red negligee and her legs were naked save for those calf-length boots.

No, I didn't want a date. I wanted her to leave.

"No."

"Uh-huh," she said. Her face was young but old, so it was practically impossible to tell her age. Anywhere from twenty to thirty-five. "You got a cigarette?"

"No."

But there was a pack of cigarettes sitting on the seat between Winston and me—Winston's cigarettes. She could clearly see them there, one or two cigarettes even peeking out of the torn wrapper.

"So what are *those?*" she asked me.

"Wait a minute," I said. I reached for the pack, but when I picked it up I got a piece of Winston's brain matter on my hand—the pack was smeared with it. I pulled one cigarette out anyway and handed it to her through the window.

"Thanks," she said, but she didn't sound as though she meant it.

Then she asked me for a light.

"I don't have one."

"What about him?" She meant Winston, who still had his eyes closed.

"No," I said.

"Maybe *he* wants a date?"

"I don't think so."

"What's wrong with him? He drunk?"

"Yes, he's drunk. Look, I gave you a cigarette, so . . ."

"What good's a cigarette without a light? What am I sup-posed to do—*eat* it?"

"We don't have a light, okay?"

I saw the reflection first—a flickering puddle of red in the middle of the street and then the sound of tires crunching glass.

A police cruiser.

"Get out of here," I told her.

"*What?*"

"Look, I just want to be left—"

"Go fuck yourself," she said. "You don't go telling me to get outta *nowhere*. Understand?"

"Yes, okay . . . I just don't want a date, okay?" trying to be nice now, trying to be polite about this so that maybe she'd go away. Because Winston still had his eyes closed, and the police cruiser was almost up to our car. And the hooker—she wasn't leaving, now that I'd made her good and mad at me.

"I'll stay where I damn please," she said.

And the cruiser rolled right up to the car; and the side window rolled down.

I expected the policeman to yell at me. Tell me to get out of the car, maybe—me and Winston. I expected the policeman to get out of the cruiser and shine a flashlight into the front seat, where he'd notice that Winston had his eyes closed and, if he looked closer, something else. That half of Winston's head was gone.

"Hey," the policeman said.

"Hey yourself," the hooker answered. Like old friends.

"How you doin', Candy?"

"How d'ya think," she said.

"Great night to work, huh?"

"You got that right." Just making conversation, one pal to another.

I was sitting there listening to them. But I wasn't actually hearing them.

I was remembering.

When I'd arrived at the pier, I saw Winston sitting in the rented blue Sable, just as he was supposed to be. I watched him sitting there for ten minutes, then fifteen, before I noticed that a window was open. That Winston wasn't moving a muscle— hadn't moved his head in all that time. Hadn't lit a cigarette, hadn't coughed, or yawned, or scratched his nose. Stock still, still as a still-life: *Man in Blue Car.* Something was wrong. That open window, for instance—the sleet blowing straight in. Why was that?

I crossed the street finally to take a quick look, *quick* because I was expecting Vasquez any minute, and I was supposed to have come alone. Winston's eyes were closed as if he were sleeping. Except he didn't appear to be actually *breathing*. And the window *wasn't* open; it was broken.

I got into the car and tapped Winston on the shoulder, and Winston ignored me. And then I leaned across the front seat to get a better look at Winston's hat, which was when I realized that it wasn't a hat. It was pulp. Half of Winston's head was gone. I threw up—my vomit mixing in with the various pieces of Winston's head. And I was about to run out of the car screaming when I saw the hooker being dropped off by that Jeep. So I stayed put.

Did you see anyone get in or out of the car? they'd ask her.

And she'd say no.

Unless she decided to walk across the street and ask for a cigarette.

The Sable was starting to smell. Even with the broken window letting in steady gusts of frigid air.

"You're keeping safe, right, Candy?" the policeman was saying.

"You know me," she said.

No one had bothered to say anything to me yet.

I was tempted to turn the ignition and take off. There were two problems with that, of course. One was that Winston was sitting behind the wheel. And the other was that the policemen, who so far were still ignoring me, would more or less have to *notice* me if I suddenly gunned the engine and took off.

But now, finally, one of them did look inside the car.

"You," he said.

"Yes?"

"You conducting a transaction with Candy here?"

"No. I just gave her a cigarette."

"Something wrong with her?"

"What? No . . . she's fine."

"That's right, Candy's a honey."

"I just was . . . having a smoke."

"Are you married?"

"Yes."

"Your old lady know you go around looking for hookers?"

"I told you. I was just—"

"What about your buddy here? He married, too?"

"No. No . . . he's single." He's *dead*.

"Both of you out looking for hookers and you aren't doing any business with Candy? Why's that?"

"Officer, I'm sorry if you misunder—"

"What are you apologizing to me for? Tell *her* you're sorry. Freezing her ass out here and you two guys don't give her the time of day. What's with your friend over there?"

"He's . . ." *Dead, Officer.*

"Maybe you should show Candy some appreciation."

"Sure."

"Well?"

"Oh . . ." I fumbled for my wallet. My hand was shaking so hard, it was difficult to actually get it into my back pocket. I finally managed to grab an indeterminate bunch of bills and held them out to her.

"Thanks," Candy said listlessly, taking them and stuffing them into the top of her negligee.

"What about him?" the policeman asked. "What's your name?" he asked Winston.

Winston didn't answer him.

"I *said*, What's your name?"

Winston still didn't answer him.

I was picturing myself in the back of the police car, being driven *downtown*—wasn't that the expression? I was picturing myself being booked and fingerprinted and given one call. I didn't even know a lawyer, I thought. I was picturing facing Deanna and Anna through a scratched plastic partition and wondering where on earth to begin.

"Okay. Last time," the policeman said. "What's your *name?*"

And then.

A sudden crackle, and a staticky voice broke through the excruciating silence like a clap of thunder on an oppressively humid afternoon.

". . . we have a . . . uh . . . ten-four . . . corner of Forty-eighth and Fifth . . ."

And suddenly the policeman was no longer asking Winston what his name was. He was saying something to Candy instead—"Catch you later," it sounded like. And the police car left—just like that, *vroooom,* gone. Mere seconds from discovering a man with half a head and another man sitting calmly next to him in a front seat covered with vomit and brain matter, and it was suddenly, inexplicably, over.

And finally, at last, I could let it out.

I could cry for Winston.

DERAILED TWENTY-FOUR

It occurred to me almost by accident. I was driving to nowhere in particular. I was following the West Side Highway and trying to keep from shaking.

Winston was dead.

Winston was dead, and I'd killed him.

Hadn't I cornered him in the bar that night and more or less *forced* him into doing this?

I tried to work it out—what happened, exactly? Vasquez had said come alone, but maybe Vasquez hadn't trusted me to come alone, so he'd come early to sniff around. Is that what happened? There was Winston in a blue Sable just sitting there, and maybe Vasquez got suspicious and confronted him, and maybe Winston got belligerent—remembering this was a man who'd been in prison, who was used to doing things to people before they did it to him. Only not this time. And Winston had ended up with half a head.

That made sense, didn't it? It was hard to tell if it *really* made sense, because I was scared senseless.

I was almost suffocating from the stench inside the car now.

And it was then that I remembered *another* awful smell sniffed from the front seat of a moving automobile. The mind worked like that sometimes, playing a kind of charades with you— *stench* and *car* and what do you get?

Memories of Sunday afternoons spent motoring down to Aunt Kate's house in southern New Jersey. To get there, we had to take the Belt Parkway down to the Verrazano Bridge, then go straight through the heart of Staten Island. Passing not much of anything along the way, just a supersize mall here and there with a megaplex cinema showing seventeen different movies all playing at once. Then, smack in the middle of nowhere, it would hit with terrifying swiftness. A vomitous odor would suddenly assault us through the cracked-open windows, through the air-conditioning vents and sunroof. The odor of garbage, the stench of landfill. Huge mounds of dun-colored earth on either side of the highway circled by clouds of screaming gulls. Fishkill.

I'd close the windows, Deanna holding her nose right next to me and Anna screeching in the backseat. I'd turn off the air-conditioning and make sure the sunroof was locked tight, but the odor would still come in. It was like sticking your head in a garbage pail, and no matter how fast I drove—and I'd hit the accelerator for all it was worth—I couldn't drive fast enough. I couldn't outrun the smell, not until I'd traveled a good fifteen minutes or so and the landscape turned sweetly suburban.

An hour later, drink in hand on Aunt Kate's backyard deck, I could still sniff it on my clothes.

That's where I headed.

I took Canal down to the Manhattan Bridge, then up the Belt to the Verrazano. Traffic was light this time of night—a good thing, considering Winston was decomposing right next to me. *Have you got half a brain?* I used to complain to Anna when I lost my temper. And Winston did have half a brain, the other half spread in pieces around the car.

I was thinking ahead to the tollbooth. If it would be a problem paying—if the toll collector would be able to see inside the car. If he or she would be able to *smell* the car. Trying to take this thing one obstacle at a time—like Edwin Moses, whom I'd once heard on ESPN explaining his method in the hurdles as just that: one hurdle at a time and never look at the finish line.

The finish line for me was Winston safely disposed of and me back in bed. And Vasquez paid off in full—oh yes, a hundred thousand was seeming kind of cheap right at the moment—all of Anna's Fund, maybe, but still kind of cheap, things being what they were.

The toll collector was humming vintage James Brown—"I Feel Good." Not if she sniffed the car, she wouldn't be. Not if she took a peek at my traveling companion and noticed the brain schematic sitting on his shoulders. I'd pulled out the money in advance and had it out there waiting for her. She'd had a kind of cool rhythm going with the cars in front of me— arm out, arm in, money in, change out, like one of those funky dances from the sixties, the *swim* or the *monkey*. But when I rolled up to her window with cash in hand, she told me to wait a minute. She started to count bills inside the booth and left my money sitting right where it was—in my sweaty palm.

It was maddening. I began to worry about the other toll collector now, the one to my right and therefore closer to the dead body. I wondered if they carried guns—toll collectors? It didn't really matter, since I knew they carried radios. A simple message to the police station up ahead and I was dead meat.

Finally, after another half a song—Little Stevie Wonder circa 1965—she reached out and took the money from me.

And I breathed again—shallow breaths, of course, head turned toward the window because the stench was enveloping me like steam. Winston was the second dead person I'd ever seen. I'd attended an open-coffin funeral when I was fourteen—a friend of the family who'd succumbed to cancer—and

I'd more or less kept my eyes on my shoes, peeking just once at a face that seemed oddly happy. Not so with Winston, his mouth half-open as if caught in midscream, his eyes squeezed shut. He'd gone complaining about it.

I killed Winston, I thought again.

Just as if I'd pulled the trigger myself. Adultery, fraud, and now murder? It didn't seem so long ago that I'd been one of the nameless good guys. It was a little hard to reconcile that Charles with this one—this one driving a dead man through Staten Island on the way to the dump. It was a little difficult to digest. Yet if I could only make it to the dumping grounds without being apprehended by the police; if I could dispose of Winston's body and the bloody car; if I could make Vasquez go away with one hundred thousand dollars . . .

One hurdle at a time.

First I had to find a way into the landfill. It had to be close; the stench in the car had been joined by another one that was even worse.

I reached the exit for the dump. At least I thought it was, because the next exit said Goethals Bridge. I exited onto a deserted two-lane road with no street lamps. Winston slumped against the window as I turned right.

I followed the road for five minutes or so, not a single other car in either direction. I imagined the only traffic that found its way here was either coming or going to the landfill, and at this time of night no one was doing either of those things. Except for me.

I squinted into the blackness, looking for a gate that might let me in, slowing to a crawl so I wouldn't ride past and miss it.

There.

Just up ahead, a gate all right—a barbed-wire fence ending in two swinging doors and a sentry box. A gate in—which might have made me weep for joy, or shout in exultation, or at least sigh in relief, if it wasn't for the fact that it was locked solid.

Well, what had I expected? This was city property, wasn't it, not a public dumping ground for anyone with a dead body to get rid of.

I got out of the stinking car only to find that it smelled worse outside the car than in it. It was as if the air itself were garbage, as if all the putrid smells of New York City were dumped here, too, along with all that solid stuff. Landfill and airfill both, and the seagulls feeding on all of it and crying out for more. *Rats with wings*—wasn't that what they called them? And now I understood why.

An entire flock of them had descended by my feet—lifting their wings and cawing at me as if I were after their food. As if I *were* their food. Sharp yellow beaks all pointed at me, and I wondered if they could smell Winston's blood on me, if, like vultures, they could sniff out the dead and dying.

I felt hemmed in, surrounded by encroaching seagulls and stench, and I yelled and flapped my arms, hoping to scare them away. But the only one scared seemed to be me; the gulls hardly moved, one or two of them beating their wings and lifting an inch or two off the ground. I retreated to the car, where I sat in the front seat and stared at the locked gate.

I reversed the car and began to meander up Western Avenue again, tracking the fence and looking for anything that might constitute a way in.

"Come on, surprise me," I said out loud. Life had thrown me a few nasty ones lately—thinking that maybe I was due some good ones. Even *one* good one, right now, here in the asshole of Staten Island, where all the waste exited and lay rotting.

And then my headlights caught a piece of torn fence as the road curved right. Just big enough for one man to get through—even one man dragging *another.*

He must have a mother somewhere, I suddenly thought. I pictured her as a typical suburban mom. I didn't know where he'd grown up, so maybe she wasn't a suburban mom at all. But that's the way I imagined her. Divorced, maybe, disillusioned by now, but still proud of her grade-school son with the 3.7 GPA. That pride tested through the years, of course, as Winston got into drugs, then into dealing drugs, and then, God help her, into *prison* for dealing drugs. But wasn't he putting his life back together again? Wasn't he the owner of a legitimate job these days—okay, just delivering mail for *now*, but you couldn't keep a good man down for long, could you? Not with his brains. Before you knew it, he'd be running that company, sure he would. And such a good-hearted boy, too, and likable— everyone but everyone liked Winston—and he never forgot her birthday card, not once. She still had that lopsided clay ashtray he'd made her in second grade, didn't she—sitting up some-where on the mantelplace. Winston's mom, who wouldn't be getting a birthday card from him this year or any other year from now on.

I wished I'd asked Winston more about his life. Anything about his life. If he *did* have a mom waiting for his Christmas cards every year, or a girlfriend sitting up tonight and wonder-ing just where Winston was exactly, or a brother or sister or fa-vorite uncle. But all I'd asked him about was baseball and prison, that's it, and then I'd asked him to do something that had gotten him killed.

I stopped the car right by the section of torn fence, then sat there for a while to make sure I was really alone. Yes, as far as I could tell, I was very much alone, alone at the dump, alone in the universe. "Deanna," I whispered, my partner in life, but only the one she knew about—Charles the nine-to-five adman, as opposed to Charles the adulterer and accessory to murder.

I got out of the car, I walked around to the other side, I opened the door and watched helplessly as Winston fell over onto the ground. I would try to think of it as the *body*—the thing that's left behind when the soul, what made Winston Winston, had already departed. It was easier that way.

I lifted the body by its arms and began dragging, and I immediately realized that the term *dead weight* was not a misnomer. Dead weight was the immovable object, panic the irresistible force, but who said the irresistible force wins out? I could barely move the *body*; an inch or three at a time. It felt as though it were pulling back—tugging at my shoulder sockets, at my elbow joints and aching wrists. At this rate, I'd have the body through the fence by daybreak, just in time for a fleet of sanitation workers to point me out at the police lineup. *That's him,* they'd say—the man pulling the deceased into the garbage dump.

But slowly, torturously, I made progress, working out a kind of routine: one huge pull, then a dead stop to catch my breath, shake my hands, and rev up for another. In this fashion, I got the body all the way to the torn section of fence without suffering a single heart attack. And still hours from sun break, too—twelve-thirty, according to my luminescent-dial Movado, a forty-second-year birthday gift from Deanna, who was probably starting to wonder where I was. She *worried,* and she did it better and with greater dedication than anyone I knew.

I fished my cellular phone out of my coat pocket, flipped it open with a now throbbing wrist, and pressed 2—my home number. Number 1 in automatic dialing was Dr. Baron's office.

"Hello?" Deanna, sounding, yes . . . upset.

"Hi, honey. I didn't want you to worry—it's taking longer than I thought."

"Still at the office?"

"Yeah."

"Why are you calling on your cellular?"

Yes, why was I?

"I don't know. I walked down the hall for coffee and suddenly realized how late it was."

"Oh, okay. How much longer do you have?"

Good question. "An hour or so, maybe . . . we have to show these stupid aspirin boards in the morning." I was kind of surprised how adept I'd become at telling lies, surprised too that I was having this perfectly normal domestic chat—*I'm working late, dear*—while standing over a man with half a head.

"Well, don't work too hard," Deanna said.

"Yes, I won't." Then: "I love you, Deanna," saying her name this time, which on the scale of I love yous ranked somewhere near the top, uttered as something meant as opposed to just another way to end a conversation. Love you—love you, simply a more intimate version of good-bye, but *not* when you put a name there. Not then. . . .

"I love you, too," Deanna said, and I knew she meant it, no name necessary.

I put the phone back in my pocket, put one foot through the open hole, reached down, and began to drag Winston through.

The stench was worse over here—hard to imagine, but it was. Outside the fence I was smelling it, but inside the fence I was *eating* it, ingesting it smell by smell and beginning to turn sick to my stomach.

I pulled the body farther into the dump, closer to the edge of the enormous mound of ground-up garbage. Now that I was this close to it, it looked like one of those temples to the sun I'd seen in Mexico City on a long-ago trip with Deanna. Pre-Anna, and we'd spent the mornings sight-seeing and the afternoons soaking our livers in tequila. Lots of lovemaking, followed by long drunken naps.

Now what?

You could think in the general all you wanted, but sooner or later the specific starts snapping at you for answers. I'd gotten the body to the dump, I'd dragged it through a barbed-wire fence, I'd brought it to the very foot of the temple of the garbage god.

I looked down at my hands, the very hands that hugged Deanna, that gave insulin shots to Anna, that once upon a time had explored every inch of Lucinda, now being asked to moonlight on a very different kind of job. To shovel a grave.

I dug in, scooping out handfuls of ground-up waste, sharp pieces of tin and bone, glutinous pieces of gristle and fat, manmade fibers of cardboard and Sheetrock.

If I'd been trying to remain dispassionate before, I took it up like religion now. As if my soul depended on it, my very life, this objectification of tonight's events. Merely smells, merely hands, merely a body. Focusing solely on the act of digging—so much material removed at such and such a rate, leaving an ever widening hole.

By now, I had garbage all over me, up to my elbows in garbage—dangerously close to *becoming* garbage.

I heard something from far off, the sound of a thunderstorm that might or might not be coming this way—but maybe it wasn't a thunderstorm after all. The sound was a little too thin for thunder—and as far as I could tell, it was a more or less cloudless night. I heard it again—ears wide open this time—and finally recognized it for what it was. And in recognizing it, I pictured it, too: black pointy ears, snub tail, and sharp white teeth practically dripping with saliva.

And it was getting closer. The junkyard dog of my nightmares.

I dug quicker, scooping out the worst kind of shit with broken-nailed fingers like a dog digging for bones. And every passing minute I could hear the *real* dog getting louder—distinct barks and growls drifting around the mounds of garbage and over to me, just as my scent must have been drifting back the other way.

The hole was big enough. I stood up and breathed once, twice—getting myself ready for my last physical expenditure of the night.

A cloud of seagulls suddenly passed in front of my eyes—a screaming thundercloud of them, swollen with panic. I could see two glowing eyes staring at me from across the dump.

All those clichés of fear—of where real fear first makes itself known to you: *in the pit of your stomach . . . up and down your spine*. They were all true. And I could feel it in places you might not expect, either. The back of my neck, where it felt as if each little hair were standing on end. The hollow of my chest, which was vibrating like a bass woofer.

The two eyes advanced and with them a sound that grated on what little nerve I had left. Not a bark, no, one low, sustained growl. The kind that said, *I am not happy to see you.*

I began to back up, slowly, one baby step at a time, even as the dog—I couldn't make out what breed, exactly; let's say human retriever—padded closer and closer.

Then I turned—and ran. Maybe I shouldn't have; maybe it would have been wiser to stare it down. *Never show a dog fear*—wasn't that the old wives' adage you're taught from youth? It makes them mad, gets their blood up, stirs up their carnivorous impulses.

But something else stirs up their meat-eating instincts even more. Meat. And I had magnanimously left the dog a lot of it. In the person of Winston.

It took several minutes—several minutes I spent scurrying out through the fence hole and into the car—to realize that the dog wasn't following me.

And then I heard it. A sound of gnashing teeth—of tearing flesh—of lascivious guttural consumption.

The junkyard dog was eating Winston.

DERAILED TWENTY-FIVE

I had to get rid of the blue Sable.

It had been rented from Dollar Rent A Car by one Jonathan Thomas. One of the four driver's licenses Winston had stuffed in his otherwise depleted wallet.

The easiest thing to buy—identities, Winston had confided in me. And Winston had four of them. Back when I was young and idealistic, searching for your identity was an expected rite of passage. Winston, on the other hand, simply bought his—or stole it—making sure he had a few extras just in case.

Just in case someone asked him to get rid of someone else.

Now I had to get rid of the car.

That sort of took care of itself. On the way back down Western Avenue, I passed the highway; it was dark, and I was replaying the sounds of canine feeding in my head—hitting the rewind button against my better judgment and listening to it over and over again. When you're hearing the sounds of someone being eaten, it's easy to miss things like highway signs. I ended up in a part of Staten Island I hadn't known existed—farmland, actual rows of fallow field with an honest to God silo sitting in the distance. Two ticks from every sin of urban congestion, and I was suddenly in Kansas.

But not *every* sin of urban living was missing. I passed a massive car dump. It looked like a watering hole for wrecks, being as they were all grouped around a mud pond, some of them half-submerged in it. One more wreck would hardly be noticed, would it?

I gently swerved off the road and into the bumpy lot, driving the car to the very edge of the water. I took one last look around the car—trying not to touch the pieces of flesh stuck to carpet and leather, opening the glove compartment, and finding a surprise in there. A gun. Winston's, I remembered, the one that must've never made it into his hand because another gun took his head off before it could. I delicately placed it into my pocket. Then I put the car in neutral, stumbled out of the front seat, and with a gentle push forward let the car slip quietly into the pond, where it finally came to rest with just its antenna poking out of the muck.

I wasn't much for religion—I didn't know any prayers to really speak of. But I stood there for a minute and whispered something anyway. In his memory.

I turned away and began to walk.

How I was going to get home?

I could have called a car service, I suppose, but I knew they kept records. I needed to find my way back to midtown, where Charles Schine taking a car ride home would be like any other late night at the office.

I passed a gas station. I could see a lone Indian-looking man reading a magazine in a barely lit cubicle. I walked around the side, looking for a bathroom. I found one.

Gas station bathrooms were much like bathrooms in Chinatown, which were much like black holes in Calcutta, or so I now thought. There was no toilet paper. The mirror was cracked, the sink filled with sludge. But I needed to wash up. I would have to find a bus or train that would take me back into the city, and I smelled like garbage.

The sink had running water. Even a little soap left in the holder, a thick scummy yellow. I washed my hands—I threw water on my face—I took my shirt off even though the bathroom was frigid and I was exhaling clouds of vapor every time I breathed. I rubbed my chest and under my arms. *A whore's bath*—isn't that what they called it? And I was a whore in good standing these days. I'd prostituted every single thing I'd believed in.

I put my shirt back on. I zipped up my jacket. I went back outside and began walking.

I just picked a direction. I wasn't going to ask the gas station manager, who just might remember a shell-shocked-looking white man who'd showed up without his car.

A half hour later I discovered a bus stop. And when an empty bus came to a stop there a half hour after that, I took it. I was lucky. It was headed to Brooklyn, where it eventually let me off by a subway station.

I made it back to Manhattan.

Home.

Something I appreciated after a night of grave digging. Four solid walls of clear yellow shingle and black-pitched roof with one impressive chimney poking through. The real estate agent who'd sold it to us described it as a center hall colonial. A substantive ring to it—nothing much could happen to you in a center hall colonial, now could it? Of course, outside the center hall colonial, all sorts of things.

When the car dropped me off, I walked to the back door and tried to open and close it as silently as I could, but I could hear Deanna stirring from our upstairs bedroom.

I made one more foray to the bathroom—this bathroom a lot cheerier than the previous one. Cleaner, too. Nice fluffy yellow towels hanging from the wall and a Degas print over the toilet—*Woman Bathing*?

This time I undressed down to my boxers and used a towel generously soaked in soap to rinse myself down. That was more like it—I smelled almost bearable. I took the gun out of my pants and put it into my briefcase.

Then I went upstairs to the bedroom, where I maneuvered my way through the pitch black—one stumble over a high-heeled shoe—and into bed.

Deanna said: "You washed up." Not as a question, either.

Of course; she smelled the soap, she'd heard the faucet, too. Now, why would a working-late husband wash himself before climbing into bed? That's what she was asking herself—and I was having trouble coming up with an answer.

Don't be silly, Deanna, I could say. *I haven't been with another woman.* (See: Lucinda.) *I've been busy burying a body. This hit man and friend I hired to get rid of someone who was blackmailing me because I was with another woman* before. *Got it?*

"I worked out today," I said, "and I never took a shower."

Not a great excuse when you thought about it—not at this hour of the night. I mean, why couldn't I have just waited till morning? But maybe it would do.

Because Deanna said: "Uh-huh." Maybe she was suspicious about it, maybe she was suspicious about a lot of my recent behavior, but maybe she was too tired to hash it out. Not at two in the morning. Not when she'd stayed up all night waiting for me to come home.

"Good night, sweetheart," I said, and leaned over to kiss her. Milky and warm: home.

I had a dream that night, though—when I woke in the morning I could remember several details.

I'd been visiting someone in the hospital. I had flowers with me, a box of candy, and I was in the reception room waiting to be called up to the sick person's room. What sick person, though? Well, the patient's identity changed several times in the dream, which is what happens in dreams—first they're one person and then they're someone else. At first I was visiting Deanna's mom, but when I finally got up to the room it was Anna lying there. She was plugged into a spider's web of IVs, and she barely acknowledged me, and I demanded to see the doctor. But when I turned to look at her again, it was Deanna who was lying there in just this side of a coma. Deanna. I remembered the next part of the dream clearly: shouting in the hall for the doctor to come see me, even though there *was* a doctor there—Dr. Baron, in fact, who kept explaining that they couldn't get hold of the doctor, not possible, but I was having none of it.

Finally my shouting seemed to do the trick; the doctor *did* come to see me. But he changed identities, too—first Eliot, my boss, then someone who might've been my next-door neighbor Joe, and finally and last, Vasquez. Yes, I woke up remembering Vasquez's face there in the hall with me. By turns impassive and malevolent and snide, but consistently deaf to my pleas. Deanna was dying in there and he was doing nothing to help her. Nothing.

In the morning, after Deanna left for work and Anna for school, I made another trip into the file cabinet, another furtive visit into Anna's Fund.

DERAILED TWENTY-SIX

On the train in the morning, I did *not* read the sports page first. Did not read about the Giants' last lamentable defeat, about the Yankees signing yet another platinum-priced free agent, about the Knicks' eternal search for a point guard.

For one day, at least, my Hebraic reading of the daily newspaper (that is, back to front) was put aside, and I read the paper like a concerned citizen. Concerned about the festering situation in the Middle East, the ongoing congressional gridlock, the roller-coaster tendencies of the Nasdaq. And, of course, the recent upswing in urban crime. Murder, for instance.

I had listened to the 1010 on your dial morning news flash in the shower and been pleased to hear nothing of the sort. Someone was murdered all right—someone was always getting murdered in New York City. But this someone was female, twenty-one, and French. Or Italian. A tourist, anyway.

The *Times* "Metro" section yielded no male victims. Likewise the local Long Island paper. Of course, even if someone *had* been discovered, it would've been too late to make it to print.

But these were modern times. The first thing I did when I arrived at the office, after saying hello to my secretary, was to get on the Net.

I searched the on-line editions of two newspapers. There was nothing about a male murder victim in New York City.

Good.

I spent the rest of the morning trying not to think about Winston's body. Trying not to think about the hundred thousand dollars of Anna's Fund that was no longer Anna's. About how I was giving up—finally and futilely giving up.

It was easier said than done—at lunchtime I made another visit to David Lerner Brokerage on 48th Street.

It helped that I had to go to an editing house to look over the nearly finished aspirin commercial with David Frankel. He had the editor play it several times for me. It wasn't the best testimonial commercial ever done. It wasn't the worst, either. I took particular notice of the music bed, which sounded like something borrowed from a stock music house—or thrown out by one. It probably *was* stock, of course—something purchased for three thousand dollars, then billed at forty-five.

David, the *D* of T&D Music House, seemed much more personable today. As though I were a true partner in this endeavor now. Maybe because we *were* partners now. Partners in bilking the agency and client out of their dubiously earned cash.

"Trust me," David said after the editor—Chuck Willis, his name was—had played the spot another three or four times, "the client will love it."

And I thought how on the accounts I *used* to work on, it didn't matter if the client was going to love it. That was always secondary to whether or not *we* loved it. But it was hard to love a spot where a housewife basically read the product's attributes off an aspirin bottle.

Still, I had to look it over and act like I cared. Like it was worth looking over and making helpful hints about, suggestions for improvement.

I pointed out places where I thought the film could be trimmed. I asked them to look for a better voice-over. I would've mentioned doing something about that saccharine music bed, but then someone might've discovered we'd illegally made over forty thousand dollars off of it.

When I got back to the office around two, someone I'd never seen before was placing my mail onto Darlene's desk. Of course—my new mailroom guy.

I asked him where Winston was. I would've been expected to ask him that.

The man smiled and shrugged. "He didna come in," having trouble pronouncing each word correctly. I wondered if this was one of the disadvantaged people Winston had told me about.

"Oh," I said, acting surprised. "I see."

Darlene smiled at the new mail deliverer and said: "You're better looking than him, anyway." *Than Winston.*

The man blushed and said: "Tank you. . . ."

I watched him walk away with a sickening feeling. *Life goes on,* people say when someone dies, *it goes on.* And there was the proof right in front of me. Winston had been gone just one day, and his replacement was making the rounds already. It both belittled and magnified what had transpired last night—it did both. It made me sick.

Later that afternoon, I held a creative briefing.

Just the thing to get my mind somewhere else, I hoped. The meeting took place at three-thirty in a conference room dutifully reserved by Mary Widger.

My band of unhappy creatives dutifully listened to me—with pads and pencils, too, no less, managing to look halfway interested in what I was saying. They were unhappy because it was another assignment for their new account—a combination cold and headache pill—instead of an assignment for their *old* account, which might've meant a commercial worth doing and putting on their reels. And they were also unhappy because I was more or less reading verbatim from a strategy statement prepared by Mary Widger. Strategy statements much like Foucault's theorem—obtuse, complex, and understood by no one. In my bygone halcyon days, I'd simply ignored them; we'd write the commercial, fall all over ourselves laughing, and write the strategy statement from that.

Not anymore; now I read words like *target audience,* like *comfort level* and *saturation,* without once turning red. A dutiful drone doing what drones do—droning on interminably, or until the said strategy was read down to the last period.

I went back to my office and closed the door. I called Deanna.

"Hello," I said. I wasn't sure why I was calling her, but I remembered the days when I used to call her *daily* from work, and more than once, too.

When we'd stopped talking to each other, really talking, when we'd started talking about inconsequential things only— I'd stopped calling her three times a day. And there were days I didn't call her at all, entire twelve-hour periods when not a single word passed between us.

And now there were so many things I couldn't talk to her about, too—things I was ashamed of, things I could barely bear to think of.

But I called her anyway.

"Hello yourself," Deanna said. "Everything okay?"

"Yes, fine."

"You sure, Charles?"

I wouldn't realize till later that Deanna wasn't merely making small talk here. That she *knew* things weren't okay with me— not the details, but enough.

But I didn't take advantage of the opportunity—not yet. I couldn't.

"Yes, everything's fine, Deanna," I said. "I just wanted to say . . . hi. I just wanted to see how you're doing today. That's all."

"I'm doing okay, Charles. I am. I'm worrying about you, though."

"Me? I'm fine. Really."

"Charles . . . ?"

"Yes?"

"I don't want you to think . . . well . . ."

"Yes?"

"I don't want you to think you can't *talk* to me." There was something heartbreaking about that statement, I thought. Talking—surely the easiest thing two people can do with each other. Unless they can't. And then it's the *hardest* thing two people can do with each other. The most impossible thing on earth.

"I . . . really, Deanna. There's nothing. I was just going to say hi. To say . . . I love you. That's all."

Silence from the other end of the line. "I love you, too."

"Deanna, do you remember . . . ?"

"Remember what?"

"When I played the magician at Anna's party? I bought those tricks from the magic store. Remember?"

"Yes. I remember."

"I was good, too. The kids loved it."

"Yes. Me too."

"When I turned over the hat, remember? And they thought they were going to get soaked with milk. Confetti came out. Oohs and aahs." I'd been thinking about that for some reason today, maybe because I was searching for another kind of magic now.

"Yes, David Copperfield has nothing on you."

"Except a few million dollars."

"But who's counting."

"Not me."

"Thinking of changing careers?"

"I don't know. It's never too late, is it?"

"Yeah. Probably."

"That's what I thought."

"Charles?"

"Yes?"

"I meant what I said. About *talking* to me. Okay?"

"Sure."

"Be home normal time?"

"Yes. Normal time."

"See you then."

When I hung up the phone, I thought it might actually be possible to make everything turn out okay. Not everything, but the important things. I knew what the important things were, too—they were staring at me from the ten-by-twelve picture frame on my desk.

But that's when everything began to go wrong.

DERAILED TWENTY-SEVEN

The phone call came maybe two minutes later.

Two minutes after I'd hung up with Deanna, after I'd stared at the picture of my family and thought that maybe I could make it all work out in the end.

The phone rang. And rang again. Darlene was probably down the hall swapping boy stories with her fellow executive assistants—which is what secretaries liked being called now in lieu of decent salaries.

So I picked it up.

There were over one hundred people who could have logically been on the line—much later, I counted them as an excuse for something to do. Everyone I knew, basically—maybe a hundred people, all in all, who could reasonably be expected to pick up a phone and call me. Not that I wasn't expecting this call, of course. In many ways, it was the only call I *was* expecting. But I imagined it very differently. I imagined it was going to be *Vasquez* on the line.

But it wasn't Vasquez.

It was her.

Only her voice was strangely reminiscent of another time, another place. That little-girl voice again. Terribly cute when it's coming from a little girl, but nauseating when it's not.

"Please, Charles," the voice pleaded. *"You have to come here. Now."*

I was thinking several things at once. For instance, where *here* was. Her home, her office? Where? For another, I was wondering what it was that was causing her to sound like a frightened child again. Even though I knew what it was. I knew.

"You *have* to . . . *Oh God . . . please,"* she whispered.

"Where *are* you?" I asked her. A good logical question, one of the four Ws they teach in journalism. What, When, Why, Where? Even if I was asking it in a voice that sounded as panicked as hers. Even then.

"Please . . . he followed me . . . he's going to . . ."

"What's going on, Lucinda? What's wrong?" Which, after all, was the real question here.

"He's going to hurt me, Charles. . . . He . . . he wants his money . . . he . . ." And then her words got muffled and I could picture what was happening. I saw the phone being yanked out of Lucinda's hand, the receiver covered by a large black fist. I pictured the room, which looked like the room in Alphabet City even if it wasn't. And I imagined her face—even as I tried to avert my eyes, I did. Don't look . . . don't . . .

And then someone was speaking again. But not her. Not this time.

"Listen to me, *motherfucker."* Vasquez. But not the one I was used to. That phony ingratiating tone was gone, the carefully controlled fury. Fury had been let out for a stroll, and it was kicking up its heels and break-dancing on whoever got in its way.

"You thought you could fuck with me. You thought you're gonna set *me* up? You miserable piece of shit. *Me?* You put some pansy in a car, and he's gonna what? Kick *my* ass? You fucking crazy? I got your *girl* here, understand? I got your whore right here. Tell me you understand, motherfucker."

"I understand."

"You understand *shit*. You think you're some kind of gangsta or something? You send some clown to fuck me over? *Me?*"

"Look . . . I understand. I—"

"You understand? You get your ass over here with the hundred grand or I will fucking kill this stupid whore. You understand *that,* Charles?"

"Yes." After all, who couldn't understand that? Was there anyone on earth who couldn't grasp the gravity of that statement?

Now we were down to Where again. I asked for an address.

This time it was uptown—Spanish Harlem. A place I'd never been to except in passing while on my way to somewhere else—Yankee Stadium or the Cross Bronx Expressway.

I called Vital for a car. I opened my locked drawer and stuffed the money into my briefcase—I had it sitting there, waiting for the moment to arrive. I saw something else sitting there, too: Winston's gun. For a second I thought about taking it with me, but then I decided against it. What, after all, would *I* do with it?

On the way downstairs I passed Mary Widger, who asked me if anything was wrong.

Family emergency, I explained.

In fifteen minutes I was traveling up Third Avenue. The car slithered, it squeezed, it maneuvered its way excruciatingly through an obstacle course of stationary refrigeration trucks, FedEx vehicles, moving vans, commuter buses, taxis, and gypsy cabs.

But maybe we weren't moving as slowly as I thought—maybe I was simply picturing what Vasquez was going to do to Lucinda and thinking that I couldn't let it happen again, not twice in one lifetime. It seemed that I'd look up at a street sign—64th Street, for instance—and five minutes later I'd still be looking at the same sign.

Halfway through the ride, I realized the hand that was holding my briefcase had gone numb. I was gripping the handle so tightly, my knuckles had taken on the color of burnt wood—ash white. And I remembered a game Anna used to play with me, a kind of parlor trick—asking me to hold her forefinger in my fist and squeeze for five minutes, not a second less, and then release, always giggling as I tried to open my now paralyzed fingers. That was the way I felt now—not just my hands, but all of me: paralyzed. The way I'd felt back in that chair in the Fairfax Hotel. The woman I'd fallen in love with being raped not five feet from me, and I like a victim of sleeping sickness, able to perform all the functions of life save one. To act.

Eventually, the tonier sections of the East Side fell away. Boutiques, handbag stores, and food emporiums turned into thrift shops and bodegas as more and more Spanish words began showing up on passing storefronts.

The apartment building was on 121st Street between First and Second Avenues.

It was surrounded by a check-cashing place, a hairdresser, a corner bodega, and two burned-out buildings. A man selling roasted chestnuts and what looked like unpeeled ears of corn had set up shop in the middle of the block. Another man who looked suspiciously like a drug dealer was checking his beeper and talking into a fancy-looking cellular phone in front of the building.

I asked the car to wait for me. The driver didn't seem very happy with the idea, but he had the kind of job where you couldn't exactly say no.

"I may have to circle," he said.

I didn't answer him—I was staring at the building and wondering if I could make it through the door. There were three men loitering in the entranceway, and none of the three looked like anyone you'd ask for directions. They looked like three-fifths of a police lineup, men you don't put your hand out to unless it contains your wallet.

And I was carrying more than my wallet today; I was carrying my wallet plus one hundred thousand dollars.

As soon as I eased myself out of the car, I heard the click of the door locks. *You're on your own*, they said. And I was; and on 121st Street between First and Second Avenues, I was pretty much the center of attention, too. I imagined that Lincoln Town Cars made very few stops here, as did well-dressed white men carrying expensive leather briefcases. The chestnut seller, the drug dealer, the three men guarding the entranceway of building number 435, all were looking at me like a hostile audience demanding something entertaining.

I didn't know whether to run up the steps like a man in a hurry or walk up the steps like a man on a stroll, and I ended up somewhere in between—a man who's not quite sure where he's going but is still anxious to get there. When I reached the landing where the cracked asphalt was liberally scribbled with chalk and spray paint (*"Sandi es mi Mami; Toni y Mali . . ."*), I ended up acknowledging the three doormen the way most New Yorkers acknowledge anyone: I didn't. I kept my eyes averted—on the doorstep, an island of worn tire tread separating brown cement from curled yellow linoleum.

"Hey . . ."

One of the men had said something to me. I was hoping the man had been addressing one of his friends, but I was pretty sure he'd been talking to me. A man wearing oversize yellow basketball sneakers and dress pants—all that I could actually see of him, since I had my eyes trained down by my feet.

I looked up into a middle-aged Spanish face that might have been okay behind the counter at McDonald's, but not in the middle of Spanish Harlem with one hundred thousand dollars sitting in my briefcase. Besides, the face looked upset with me, as if I'd just complained about the Happy Meal having no French fries in it, and where exactly was the pickle on my burger?

I kept moving, continued to make like a halfback in the opposing secondary as I kept those legs pumping. Just about through the door, too—since the door was permanently half-ajar and offered no resistance.

"Where *you* going?"

The same man as before, speaking in heavily accented English, with the emphasis on *you*, the intonation important here, since I might've thought the man was being helpful otherwise: *Tell me where you're going and maybe I can help direct you there.* No—the man was questioning my very validity for being there.

"Vasquez," I said. The first thing that entered my head, besides *Help*. If you gave a name, it sounded aboveboard. Maybe they knew that name, and maybe they wouldn't want to fuck with it. And maybe even if they didn't know that name— *Vasquez, who's that?*—they'd still be leery of poaching in someone else's territory. A man alone was fair game, but when he wasn't alone, who knew?

Anyway, it worked.

I kept walking through the doorway, and they didn't stop me. There was no elevator, of course; I took the steps two at a time. Lucinda was waiting for me—*He's going to hurt me, Charles.* Maybe the end was waiting for me, too.

The stairway smelled of bodily fluids: piss and semen and blood. I slipped on a banana peel that turned out to be a used condom and nearly fell down the stairs. I could hear ghostly laughter coming from somewhere I couldn't see, the kind of laughter that might be funny or might not be. It was impossible to tell.

When I knocked on the door, Vasquez opened it. I got one word out before I was dragged in and slammed up against the wall. He slapped me across the face. I tasted blood. I dropped the briefcase onto the floor and tried to cover up. He slapped me again. And again. I said, "Stop it—I have it, there . . . there." He kept slapping me, open-handed wallops that sneaked in between my upraised arms.

And then, suddenly, he stopped.

He dropped his arm, uncurled his fist, took a deep breath and then another. He shook his head; he exhaled. And when he finally spoke, he sounded almost normal. As if he'd just needed to vent his anger a little bit before coming back to himself.

"Shit," he said, as if he were saying glad that's over with. "Shit." Then:

"You got the money?"

I was breathing too fast, like an asthmatic searching for air. My face stung where Vasquez had slapped it. But I managed to point to the floor. To the briefcase. The apartment had at least two rooms, I thought—I could hear someone from the room next door. A soft sniffling.

"Where is she?" I said, but my lip was swollen and I sounded like someone else.

Vasquez ignored me. He was opening the briefcase and turning it upside down, watching as stacks of hundred-dollar bills slithered across the floor.

"Good boy," Vasquez said, the way you might to a dog.

I could hear her clearly now from the next room. The apartment—what I could see of it—had almost no furniture. The walls were streaked with dirt and scarred with cigarette burns. They were painted the color of yolk.

I said: "I want to see her."

"Go ahead," Vasquez said.

I walked through the half-open door, which led to the rest of the apartment. The room was dark, the window shades pulled down. Still, I could make out a chair against the back wall. I could see who was sitting on that chair.

"Are you okay?" I said.

She didn't answer me.

She was sitting very still, I thought. Like a child on a church pew who's been told repeatedly to be quiet. She didn't look hurt, but she was sitting there dressed only in a slip.

Why was she in a slip?

I could hear Vasquez counting the money from the next room: "Sixty-six thousand one hundred, sixty-six thousand two hundred . . ."

"I gave him the money," I said.

But maybe not soon enough. I'd said, *Sorry, I don't have it*— and Winston had ended up dead and Lucinda had ended up here in her underwear. I wanted her to move, to answer me, to stop sniffling—to understand that no matter what had happened to her, no matter how many times I'd failed her, the end was within sight. I wanted her to walk across the finish line with me and not look back.

But she wasn't moving. She wasn't responding.

And I thought: *I have to do something now*. I'd taken Anna's money, I'd gotten Winston killed, I'd let Lucinda be snatched off the street. I'd done this all to keep a secret, and even if Lucinda was one of the people who'd wanted me to keep it, I had to do something.

Vasquez walked into the room and said: "It's all here."

I was going to get out of here, and I was going to go to the police. It had gone too far. It was the right thing to do. Only, even as I told myself in no uncertain terms what was necessary here, even as I steeled myself for what would be an unpleasant—okay, even horrible—duty, I could hear that *other* Charles beginning to whisper into my ear. The one who was telling me how close we were. The one who was saying that what's past is past, and now I was *this* close to getting out of it.

"Okay, Charles," Vasquez said. "You did good. See you. . . ."

He was either waiting for me to leave or was about to leave himself.

"I'm taking her with me," I said.

"Sure. You think I want the bitch?"

Lucinda still hadn't said anything. Not one word.

"Maybe you better stay home from now on, Charles. Back in *Long Island*." He had my briefcase in his hand. "Do me a favor, don't try some crazy shit like before—you ain't gonna find me anyway, see? I'm . . . relocating."

And he left.

I stood there listening to his footfalls growing softer down the stairs, softer and softer till they disappeared completely.

I'm . . . relocating.

For some reason, I believed him, but maybe only because I wanted to. Or maybe because even Vasquez knew you could bleed someone only so much before the body was declared officially dead.

"I thought he was going to kill me this time," Lucinda whispered slowly. She was staring at a point somewhere over my head. Even in the darkness I could see she was trembling. There was blood on the inside of her thigh. "He held the gun to my head and he told me to say my prayers and he pulled the trigger. Then he turned me over."

"I'm taking you to a hospital, Lucinda, and then I'm going to the police."

Lucinda said: "Get out of here, Charles."

"He can't get away with it. He can't do this to you. It's gone too far. Do you understand me?"

"Get out of here, Charles."

"Please, Lucinda . . . we're going to report this, and—"

"Get out!" This time she screamed it.

So I did. I *ran*. Down the stairs, out the front door, back into the waiting car, feeling all the while one distinct, overpowering, and guilty little emotion.

Overwhelming relief.

DERAILED TWENTY-EIGHT

For two weeks or so, I believed.

Believed that possibly the worst was over. That, okay, I'd been tested, tested severely—a modern-day Job, even—but that it was entirely possible things were going to work out in the end.

Yes, it was *hard* to look Anna in the face these days, very hard. Knowing that the money I'd painstakingly accumulated for her was, for all intents and purposes, gone. That my carefully constructed bulwark against her insidious and encroaching enemy was virtually depleted.

It was hard, too, looking at Deanna—who trusted me, maybe the very last thing in life she *did* trust—knowing what I'd done with that trust.

Hardest of all, of course, was thinking about the people I couldn't look at. Lucinda, for instance—whom I'd failed not once, but twice. And Winston. Whom I'd failed right into the grave. Their pictures clamored for my attention, like needy children demanding to be seen. *Look at me . . . look.* I tried not to, I tried tucking Winston away in places where I couldn't find him. But I always did. When I picked up an ordinary piece of office mail, or read an article about the winter baseball meetings—he'd say hello. I'd see him lying there the way I'd left him. I'd close my eyes, but the pictures wouldn't go away. Like the flash of a camera that remains seared on your eyelids.

Still, I was hopeful.

Hoping for two things, really. That Vasquez had actually meant what he said, that he realized the well was good and dry now and he wouldn't be coming back. That he *had* relocated.

And I was hoping that I could rebuild Anna's Fund. That through diligent and constant *cheating,* through the auspices of the T&D Music House, I could build it back to where it was before. That I could do this before I might actually need it. Before anyone noticed it, either.

For two weeks, then, this is what I clung to.

Then there was a man waiting for me in reception. That's what Darlene said.

"What man?" I asked her.

"He's a detective," Darlene said.

I thought of Dick Tracy. At first I did—remembering the Sunday comics I used to press into Play-Doh, then stretch into funhouse mirror versions of their former selves.

"A detective?" I repeated.

"Yeah."

"Tell him I'm not here," I said.

Darlene asked me if I was sure.

"Yes, Darlene. I'm sure." Letting just a touch of annoyance into my voice—because annoyance covered up what I was actually feeling, which was, okay, fear.

"Fine."

And the detective left. After which Darlene informed me that it was a *police* detective who'd been waiting for me.

The next day he was back.

This time he was sitting there in full view as I exited the elevator. I wasn't actually aware he was the police detective until he got up and introduced himself as such.

"Mr. Schine?" he said.

And I immediately noticed that if he was a rep, he was devoid of reels, and if he was someone seeking employment, he was minus a portfolio.

"I'm Detective Palumbo," he said, just like in the movies and TV. That New York accent, the kind that always seems somehow phony in the darkness of a movie theater.

Purpetration . . . dufendunt . . . awficcer.

That's how Detective Palumbo sounded—only no matinee looks here. A genuine double chin and a stomach that never met the Ab Roller +. Of course, he carried a real badge.

"Yes?" I said. A dutiful citizen just trying to be helpful to an officer of the law.

"Could I have a word with you?"

Of course. No problem. Anything I can do, Officer.

We walked past Darlene, who gave me a look that seemed somewhat reproachful. *I asked you if you really wanted me to tell the detective you weren't there, didn't I?*

We walked in, I shut the door behind us, we both sat down. And all that time, I was having a disturbing conversation with myself. Asking myself myriad questions that I couldn't answer. For instance, what was the detective here for? Had Lucinda reconsidered and gone to the police herself?

"Do you know Winston Boyko?"

No. Detective Palumbo was here about someone else. He was here about Winston.

"What?" I said.

"Do you know Winston Boyko?"

Okay. What were my options here? *No, I don't* wasn't one of them. After all, there were a number of people who could swear just the opposite—Darlene, Tim Ward, and half the sixth floor.

"Yes."

Detective Palumbo was scribbling something in his little notebook that he'd produced almost magically out of his coat, scribbling away and seemingly waiting for me to embellish a little.

(A detective comes to see you and asks you if you know this obscure mailroom employee and you say . . . what is it? *Yes. That's it.* No curiosity about *why?*)

"Why do you want to know, Detective?"

"He's missing," Detective Palumbo said.

A lot better than *He's been found dead.* I could cry all I wanted about this unexpected interrogation, but a Winston missing was better than a Winston found.

"Really?" I said.

Detective Palumbo had a red mark on the bridge of his nose. Contacts? A slight nick on his chin where he'd cut himself shaving? I checked out his face as if it might hold a few answers for me. For instance, what he thought I knew.

"For over two weeks," Palumbo said.

"Hmmm . . ." I was down to monosyllabic responses now, being as my brain was off somewhere else furiously constructing alibis.

"When was the last time you saw him?" Detective Palumbo asked.

Good question. Maybe even a trick question, like who was the last left-handed batter to win the American League MVP award? Everyone says Yastrzemski, everyone, but it's a trick—it's really Vida Blue, left-handed wunderkind pitcher for the Oakland As. The kind of question Winston would have loved, too.

When did you last see him?

"Gee, I don't know," I finally said. "A few weeks ago, I think."

"Uh-huh," Palumbo said, still scribbling. "What exactly was your relationship, Mr. Schine?"

What did *that* mean? Wasn't *relationship* the kind of word you used for people who *had* one? Lucinda and me, for instance. If Palumbo was asking me what kind of relationship Lucinda and I had, I would've said *brief*. I would've said sex and violence, and you can forget the sex.

"He works here," I said. "He delivers my mail."

"Yeah," Palumbo said. "That's it?"

"Yes."

"Uh-huh." Palumbo was staring at the picture of my family.

"So I guess you're interviewing . . . everyone?" I asked, hoped.

"Everyone?"

"You know, everyone who works here?"

"No," Palumbo said, "not everyone."

I could've asked him, *Why me, then?* I could've asked him that, but I was afraid of the answer I might get back, so I didn't. Even though I was wondering if Palumbo was *expecting* me to ask him that.

"So . . . is there anything else I can—" I began, but was interrupted.

"When was that again? The last time you saw him?" Palumbo asked, pencil poised and waiting—and I was reminded of an image from one of those British costume dramas that continuously turn up on Bravo: the Crown's executioner holding the ax above his head, only awaiting the signal to strike.

"I don't remember, exactly," I said. "Two weeks ago, I guess."

I guess. Couldn't hold someone to a guess, could you? Couldn't drag them downtown and haul them before the court on a wrong *guess*.

"Two weeks ago? When he delivered your mail?"

"Yes."

"Did you ever get together with Mr. Boyko, you know, socially?"

Yes, once in a bar. But it was business.

"No."

"Did Mr. Boyko ever talk to you about himself?"

"How do you mean?"

"Did Mr. Boyko ever talk about himself? To you?"

"No, not really. About mail . . . you know."

"Mail?"

"Deliveries. Where I wanted something sent. Things like that."

"Uh-huh. That's it?"

"Pretty much. Yes."

"Well, what else?"

"Excuse me?"

"You said *pretty much*. What else did he talk to you about?"

"Sports. We talked about sports."

"Mr. Boyko is a sports fan, then?"

"I guess. Kind of. We're both Yankee fans," trying hard to keep in the present tense when I was talking about Winston—not so easy, when I could picture him lying stiffly at the foot of the mound of garbage.

"That's all, then. You talked about mail and sometimes about the Yankees?"

"Yes. As far as I can remember."

"That's it?"

"Yes."

"Would you know how Winston came into ten thousand dollars, Mr. Shine?"

"What?" *You heard him.*

"Mr. Boyko had ten thousand dollars in his apartment. I was wondering if you had any idea how he got it."

"No. Of course not. How would I . . . ?" I was wondering something: if the police were allowed to check with David Lerner Brokerage and see how much stock I'd sold. It wouldn't look good, would it? It would look, okay, suspicious. But then, why would they suspect me of giving ten thousand dollars to Winston? I was panicking for no good reason.

"There were some computers stolen from your agency. One from this floor."

"Yes, that's right."

"Did you ever see Mr. Boyko up here when he wasn't supposed to be?"

Computers. Palumbo was asking me about computers. Of course. *Winston the thief.* Winston the ex-con. He was talking to me because he suspected Winston had gotten that money from stealing some computers. He needed witnesses. Winston had stolen some computers and he'd made some money and taken off.

"Now that you mention it, I did see him up here one night when I was working late."

"Where, exactly?"

"Just around, you know. In the hall here."

"Was there any reason for him to be up on this floor after work?"

"Not that I can think of. I thought it was kind of strange at the time." I was killing him again, I thought. First when he was alive and now when he wasn't.

"Did you challenge him about that? Ask him what he was doing there?"

"No."

"Why not?"

"I don't know. I just didn't. He was down the hall—I was in my office. I really didn't know if he was supposed to be here or not."

"All right, Mr. Schine." Palumbo shut his notebook and placed it back into his hip pocket. "I think that's all I have for you today. Thank you for taking the time to talk to me."

"You're welcome," I said, even as I wondered about that word. *Today.*

"I hope you find him."

"So do I. You know, Mr. Boyko was pretty good about seeing his parole officer. He hadn't missed a meeting. Not one. You *did* know he'd been in prison, right?"

"I think I may have heard something about that. Yeah, sure. Is *that* who told you he was missing? His parole officer?"

"No," Palumbo said. Then he looked straight into my eyes, the way lovers do when they want you to acknowledge the sincerity of their feelings.

"Mr. Boyko and I had a kind of working relationship," he said. "Understand?"

No, I didn't understand.

As I walked Detective Palumbo out into the hall, wondering if the detective was going to go interview someone else—he didn't. Still not understanding that statement: *Mr. Boyko and I had a kind of working relationship.*

And what kind of relationship was that?

It was only when I replayed the interview later in the day, wondering if I'd been okay with my answers, meticulously going over each Q&A to see if I'd slipped up, given the detective any cause, no matter how minute, to distrust me, that it occurred to me what kind of relationship any ex-con can have with any police detective.

What were the terms?

Because something else was bothering me. Something that didn't make sense. It was this. People are reported missing all the time—isn't that the usual quote you hear from bored and jaded police detectives on the evening news? The distraught parent complaining about police inaction, how their teenage daughter or son was missing for God knows how long, and the parents knew something was wrong, of course, they *knew,* but still the police did nothing much but take a report. Because people disappear all the time. That's what the bored detectives say. And if they looked for every kid who didn't come home, they'd have no time left to go after the serious criminals.

And these are kids they're talking about—*kids* that they don't exactly jump into action after. And Winston was not a kid. He was a grown man—and by the usual social standards, not a very important one. In fact, on the scale of important people, of people the police need immediately to start looking for, he'd probably be next to last, just above black transvestite heroin addicts, maybe.

Yet just two weeks after this ex-con doesn't show up for work, a police detective is there looking for him.

What were the terms?

So I replayed the detective's words again. *Mr. Boyko and I had a kind of working relationship, understand?*

And yes, I *was* beginning to understand now.

What were the terms?

I'd seen all the movies, I'd watched the TV shows, I'd read the papers. Police detectives were allowed to lean on ex-cons for information. Ex-cons were inclined to give it to them so as not to be leaned on. So that maybe they'd look the other way when they were trying to supplement their income with, say, a little computer theft.

What were the terms?

I know the terms, Winston.

Why don't you state them for me so there's no confusion.

That night in Winston's car by the number seven train.

Why don't you state them for me.

And why was that? Why *did* Winston need me to state them for him, need to hear me say the words out loud? Because in the end, it's the words that'll set you free. You need to give them the words if they're ever going to believe you.

State them for me.

Policemen and ex-cons with only one kind of working relationship, really, and this is the way it works. This way. They ask and you tell. You whisper. You snitch.

State them.

If you don't have the words, if you don't have them sitting there on some tape somewhere, how will they ever believe you? A company big shot, a bridge and tunneler, an honest to God white-collar commuter, and he wants you to *what?* Say again, Winston. . . .

State them.

No, not everyone, Palumbo said.

Just you.

DERAILED TWENTY-NINE

Things happen for a reason. That's what Deanna believed. That things aren't as random as you might expect—that there was some kind of unseen and only hinted-at plan out there. That the orchestra might be out of tune and all over the place, but there was a maestro somewhere in that hidden orchestra pit who knew exactly what he was doing.

I'd always treated that kind of thinking with a healthy skepticism, but now I wasn't so sure.

Take the Saturday after my interrogation. Freakishly warm, pools of soft mud sucking at my shoes as I meticulously picked up after Curry in the backyard. I was concentrating on this task—covering every inch of the yard with eagle-eyed dedication—as a way to keep from concentrating on other things.

I was holding in fear and panic; I was trying not to let them out.

So when Deanna called out to me from the back door—something about auto insurance—I barely acknowledged her.

She needed to renew our insurance, she was saying. Yes, that's what it was. I nodded at her like one of those bobble dolls they stick on the dashboard of cars—reflexive motion caused by the slightest disturbance in the air. She needed to renew our insurance, and she wanted to know where our policy was.

So I told her. And went back to the business at hand.

It was ten or fifteen minutes later when she appeared at the back door wearing an expression I was all too familiar with. The one I'd hoped to never see again.

At first, of course, I thought, *Anna. Something happened to Anna and I must throw down my garbage bag and run into the house.* Where I would no doubt find my daughter comatose again. Only at that very moment I saw Anna pass her upstairs bedroom window, where the latest from P. Diddy was streaming through the closed sill. She looked fine.

What, then? So my mind backtracked, scurrying down the recent road to *here*—searching furiously for clues that might explain the nature of this particular disaster.

I'd been cleaning the yard; she'd come out to tell me something—yes, our insurance needed renewing. She'd asked me where our policy was; I'd told her.

In the file cabinet, of course. Under *I* for insurance. Right?

Except this was *auto* insurance. Automobile insurance that needed renewing. So in the haphazard and admittedly chaotic filing system of the Schines, it was possible that this policy wasn't under *I* after all, but under *A. A* for automobile. In the *A* file.

All this occurring to me at lightning speed and, as lightning would, leaving me dazed and scorched. Possibly even *dead.*

Which is when I wondered about things happening for a reason. Why, for instance, our auto insurance had needed to be renewed now, right this minute, *today.* Why? And why at the very moment she'd asked me for help in finding our policy, I'd been so preoccupied with staying preoccupied that I hadn't had the wherewithall to tell her I'd go get it myself.

"Where's Anna's money, Charles?" Deanna asked me. "What have you done with it?"

Maybe I'd always known the moment would come.

Certain things were just too massive to be hidden successfully—their very dimensions make them impossible to conceal. Their edges stick out in the open, and sooner or later someone is bound to notice them.

Or maybe I *wanted* to be found out—isn't that what any psychiatrist worth his salt would say? That I might've been cleaning up the garden, sure, but at the same time I was yearning to clean up my life.

Hard to believe that I would've gone through all I had only to throw it all away on purpose. But then, things weren't that simple anymore.

"What have you done with it?" she asked me.

And at first, I was rendered speechless. Deanna stock still on the back stoop and me standing there with a garbage bag reeking of excrement.

"I brought the certificates to a safety deposit box," I lied through my teeth. *I will take one stab at extricating myself from this,* I thought, *one outright denial.*

"Charles . . . ," she admonished me with my own name. As if that kind of blatant lying weren't worthy of me. And I wanted to say, *Yes, Deanna, it is. You don't know what I've been up to— it is.*

But I couldn't say much of anything—not yet, not when it concerned the truth. I was dead in the water, and I knew it.

"Charles, why are you lying to me? What's going on?"

I suppose I could've denied I was lying to her. I could've stuck to my ridiculous story about the safety deposit box— ridiculous not because it wasn't possible, but because even if she had believed me, I would have had to produce the stock certificates on Monday, and that *was* impossible. I could've said this is my story and I'm sticking to it, no matter what. But in the end, I had too much respect for her. In the end, I loved her too much.

So even though I knew what I was about to do, knew that now that I was about to take a stab at the truth I was going to be stabbing *her*—I went ahead anyway.

I started with the train. That hurried morning, the lack of cash, the woman who'd helped me out.

When I mentioned Lucinda, I could see Deanna's expression change—her features flattening, the way animals' faces do at the first sign of danger.

"Then I had a bad day at the office," I continued. "I was kicked off the credit card account."

Deanna was obviously wondering what getting kicked off an account had to do with $110,000 missing from Anna's Fund. And with the woman on the train.

I was wondering about that, too. I knew there was a connection, but I couldn't remember what it was. Something about needing to talk to someone, maybe—or had it simply been a precursor to what followed? One step taken off the ledge before the other foot followed?

"I ran into the woman again," I said. What I should've said was that I ran after, sought, meticulously looked for, this woman. But wasn't I allowed to soft-pedal just a little?

"What are you *talking* about, Charles?" She wanted the Monarch Notes version now—she wasn't interested in a prologue or an introduction, not when she could tell that her future with me was hanging in the balance.

"I'm talking about a mistake I made, Deanna. I'm so sorry." A *mistake*. Was that all it was? People made mistakes all the time, and then they learned from them. I was hoping she might look at it that way, even though common sense and everything I knew about Deanna after eighteen years of marriage told me there was no chance of that. Still.

Now Deanna sat on the stoop. She pushed her hair back from her face and straightened her back like someone about to be shot who still wants desperately to keep her dignity. And me? I raised the gun in my hand and pulled the trigger.

"I had an affair, Deanna."

P. Diddy was still seeping through the window. Curry was barking at a passing car. Still, the surrounding world was about as silent as I'd ever heard it. A silence even worse than the kind that had permeated the house ever since Anna got sick, silence so black and hopeless that I thought I might start crying.

But she did instead. Not loudly or hysterically, but the tears suddenly there, as if I'd slapped her hard in the face.

"Why?" she said.

I'd expected she would ask questions. I thought she might ask me if I loved her, this woman—or how long it had been going on, or how long it was over. But no—she'd asked me *why* instead. A question she was entitled to, absolutely, but a question I was unprepared to answer.

"I don't know, exactly. I don't know."

She nodded. She looked away, down at her bare feet, which seemed strangely vulnerable on the green step of our back stoop, like naked newborn mammals. Then she looked up again, squinting, as if looking directly at me were hurting her eyes.

"I was going to say, *How could you,* can you believe it? I was. But I know how you could, Charles. Maybe I even know *why* you could."

Why? I thought. *Tell me. . . .*

"Maybe I even understand it," she continued. "Because of what's happened with us lately. I think I can understand it, I do. I just don't think I can *forgive* it. I'm sorry about that. I can't."

"Deanna," I began, but she waved me off.

"It's over now? This affair?"

At last a question I could more or less handle.

"Yes. Absolutely. It was once, just one time, really. . . ."

She sighed, cracked her knuckle, wiped her eyes. "Why is *Anna's money* missing, Charles?"

Okay. I'd told half of it, but there was still a whole other half, wasn't there?

"You don't have to tell me anything else about the affair—I don't want to know anything else about it," Deanna said. "But I want to know that."

So I told her.

As sparingly as possible, as linearly as I could remember it— one thing leading to another leading to another—and I could tell that while it had all made sense to me, in a horrible, albeit panicked, way, it wasn't making any sense to her. Even when I reached the part where we'd been attacked and beaten and I could see actual sympathy in her eyes. Even when I reached the part where Vasquez entered our home and put his hand on Anna's head. Still it made no sense to her. Perhaps she could see what I hadn't been able to—could spot the moments in this tortured tale when I could've done something different, when this different course of action was *crying out* to be tried. Or maybe it was because I'd left something out, something significant and necessary to any true understanding of events.

"So I paid him the money," I finished. "To save her."

"You never thought about going to the police? About going to *me?*"

Yes, I wanted to say. I had thought about going to the police, or going to her, which was pretty much the same thing, really. But when I'd thought about it, I'd pictured the way she'd look—which was the way she looked *now.* So I hadn't. And now I *really* couldn't go to the police, even though it might not make much of a difference, since it was entirely probable the police were coming for me.

"That money," she whispered. "Anna's Fund . . ." saying it the way I'd heard investors mention one fund or another these past couple of years while perusing the stock pages on their way to work. *That Dreyfus Fund . . . Morgan Fund . . . Alliance Fund . . .* As if reciting the names of the dearly departed. Gone and never to return.

"You have to go to the police now, Charles. You have to tell them what happened and get our money back. It's *Anna's.*"

I'd told her a story with a hole in it, a hole I'd hoped would be big enough to sneak through. But no. She was making a perfectly reasonable request, only I didn't have a perfectly reasonable answer. Protecting Lucinda from her husband's anger wouldn't do now—not for Deanna, not when protecting her was costing our daughter over a hundred thousand dollars.

What she didn't know was that I was protecting *me.*

"There's more," I said, and I could see Deanna deflate. *Haven't you told me enough already?* her expression seemed to say. *What more can there possibly be?*

"I asked someone to help me," I said, thinking that I was still lying, since I hadn't asked Winston as much as *coerced* him. On the other hand, Winston hadn't actually helped me as much as set me up. "I asked someone to help me scare off Vasquez."

"*Scare off?*" Deanna might be in semishock, but she was still smart enough to see the inherent flaws in my plan, and she was calling me on it. That when you ask a man to scare off someone else, there was a volatility factor of plus ten. That what starts out as a fist in the face can end up as a knife in the heart. Or a bullet in the head.

"He was threatening this family, Deanna. He came to our house."

When something loves me I love it back, Deanna had said to me once. That was her rule to live by, her credo, her own *semper fidelis.* But she was in the battle of her life now, with bomb after bomb falling all around her, and it was anyone's guess if that love could actually survive. Judging by the expression on her face, I would've had to say no. She was having problems recognizing me, I imagined—recognizing this man as the generally loving and gentle husband she'd known for eighteen years. Not this guy, who'd had a seedy affair and paid blackmail money because of it and even enlisted someone to get rid of this blackmailer for him. Was it possible?

"I didn't know what else to do," I said lamely.

"What happened?"

"I think Vasquez killed him."

A sharp intake of breath. Even now, when I'd no doubt ripped apart every illusion she once cherished, I was still capable of surprising her. An affair—bad enough; but then *murder.*

"Oh, Charles . . ."

"I think . . . I believe, this man, the man who died, may have been taping me. Setting me up, sort of."

"What do you mean, *setting you up?*"

"He was an ex-con, Deanna. He was an ex-con and an informant, I think. He was obligated, maybe."

"You're telling me . . . ?"

"I don't know. I'm not sure. But I'm worried."

And so was she. But maybe the biggest thing she was worried about was where love goes when it *goes.* This steadfast devotion of hers, which had been pummeled and knocked around and stomped on. Where?

"I knew something was wrong, Charles. I thought some money was missing before—when you took the first ten thousand, I guess. Maybe it's my imagination, I thought. So I didn't say anything. Maybe I was imagining *everything*—the way you were acting. The hours you were keeping. Everything. I thought it might be a woman. But I didn't want to believe it. I was waiting for you to come tell me, Charles. . . ."

And now I had told her. But more than she could have actually imagined.

She asked me a few more questions—some of the ones I'd expected she would. *Who was this woman, exactly? Was she married, too? Was it really just that one time?* But I could tell her heart wasn't really in it. And then other questions that maybe her heart *was* in, or what was left of her heart—how much trouble was I really in with the police, for instance, things of that nature.

But in the end, she told me to leave the house. She didn't know for how long, but she wanted me out of there.

A few weeks later, weeks I spent avoiding Deanna and retiring to the guest bedroom after Anna went to bed, I found a furnished apartment in Forest Hills.

DERAILED THIRTY

Forest Hills seemed to be made up of Orthodox Jews and unorthodox sectarians. People who seemed alone, or who were without a visible means of support, or who didn't seem to really belong there. In that particular apartment or particular building or that actual neighborhood. I fit in perfectly.

For instance, I looked like a married man, but where was my wife? I was undoubtedly a father, but where exactly were my kids? And then I even became a little shaky on the means-of-support thing.

On the first Tuesday after I moved out, I took the train into work at Continental Boulevard.

I was called down to Barry Lenge's office. That itself was unusual, since office hierarchy dictated that bean counters—even the head bean counter—travel to *your* office when a face-to-face was needed.

I went anyway. After all, I think I was suffering from a kind of post-traumatic stress syndrome, and whatever self-confidence I had left was down to the approximate level of a whipped dog.

Barry Lenge looked even more uncomfortable than me. That should have been my first clue.

His triple chin made him appear physically agitated, in any case—as if his head couldn't find a position where it wasn't imposing on another part of his body. But today he looked worse.

"Ahem," Barry cleared his throat, which should have been my second clue; there was something in there he was going to have a little trouble getting out.

"I was just looking over the production bills," Barry said.

"Yes?"

"This Headquarters job. There's something I wanted to talk to you about."

Now it must have been me who looked truly uncomfortable, because Barry looked away—at his set of silver pencils—and I remembered how Eliot had doodled on his stationery the morning I was fired off my account by Ellen Weischler.

"The thing is . . . something's been brought to our attention."

"What?"

"You see, there's forty-five thousand here for music." He was pointing to a piece of paper sitting on the desk in front of him. The same bid form I'd looked at before.

"*See* that?" Barry asked him. "Right there."

I pretended to look, if only because that's what whipped dogs do when given a command—they obey. I could see a number there all right; it looked like forty-five thousand.

"Yes?"

"Well, Charles . . . there's a problem with that."

"Yes?" Was that all I was going to say—answer each of Barry's revelations with a yes?

"Mary Widger heard the same music on a different spot."

"What?"

"I'm *telling* you this same piece of music was on another spot."

"What do you mean?"

"Correct me if I'm wrong. Forty-five thousand dollars was for *original* music, right?"

"Right."

"So it's not original."

"I don't understand." But I did understand, of course. Tom and David Music had found a piece of music in a stock house, and they hadn't bothered to see if someone else had used it before. Someone had.

"Well, maybe it just sounds the same. It's just a bed, really."

"No. She brought it to the musicologist. It's the same piece. Note for note."

She brought it to the musicologist. Musicologists were generally consulted to make sure that any music we did wasn't too close to any other existing piece of music we might be trying to imitate. For instance, we might cut a commercial to Gershwin's "'S Wonderful," but if the Gershwin estate wanted an arm and a leg to let us use it, we might attempt to rip it off, but not too closely—because the musicologist would say no. Only in this case, of course, it wasn't Gerswhin who was being ripped off.

"I'll talk to the music house," I said, trying to sound as officially indignant as Barry did. Instead of scared.

"I talked to the music house," Barry said.

I didn't like the way Barry said that—*music house*—with a noticeable derision. A pointed sarcasm.

"Yes?"

"Yeah. I talked to the music house. So the question I have for you is *this*. How much?"

"How much *what*?"

"How much? If I was to give you a bill of what you owe this agency, how much should I make it out for?"

"I don't understand."

"You don't understand."

"Yes."

"I think you do. I think you understand perfectly. The music house is a paper company, Charles. It doesn't exist. It exists only to make illegal profits from this agency. So if I want those profits back—how much do I need to ask you for?"

"I don't know what you're talking about. If you've uncovered some kind of scam here . . ."

"Look, Charles . . ." And now Barry didn't seem the slightest bit uncomfortable anymore. He seemed right in his element. "Look—if you pay us back the money, there's a chance this won't end up in court. That *you* won't end up in court. Are you following me? Not that that would be my decision. If it was up to me, I'd throw you in jail. But since I'm the company comptroller, money's kind of close to my heart, right? Eliot feels differently. Fine."

Eliot feels differently. I'd been wondering if Eliot knew anything yet.

"Look, maybe I suspected something . . . I thought maybe something was . . . Shouldn't you be talking to Tom and David?"

"I *talked* to Tom and David. They both had plenty to say. So you want to keep fucking with me, fine, but you should know that if you keep this up, Eliot will reconsider his decision. Why? Because I'll *tell* him to. They don't want the bad publicity—I understand. But they want their money back. And you know something? When it comes to money versus a momentary smudge on their reputation, they'll take the money. Trust me on this."

It was clear I had a decision to make. I could admit taking the twenty thousand dollars. I could even pay the twenty thousand dollars back—if Deanna let me go near Anna's Fund again, which might not be so easy. On the other hand, I had the distinct feeling Tom and David had implicated me to a greater degree than the facts actually warranted—and that Barry wasn't going to believe twenty thousand dollars was the extent of my fraudulent activities. No, the bill was going to be higher. If I admitted anything, I decided, I was done.

"I didn't have anything to do with this," I said as forcefully as I could. "I don't know what Tom and David told you, but I wouldn't necessarily trust the word of two guys who've apparently been cheating you for years."

Barry sighed. He tried to loosen his collar, an impossible task since it was already two sizes too small.

"That's the way you want to play this," he finally said. "Fine. Your decision. You say you're innocent, we institute company procedures. Fine."

"Which are . . . ?"

"We suspend you. We hold an internal investigation. We get back to you. And if I have any influence on the powers-that-be at all—we fucking *arrest* you. Understand, pal?"

I got up and left the office.

DERAILED THIRTY-ONE

Time passed. One week, two weeks, a month.

Time I spent mostly wondering in lieu of working. I was wondering, for instance, if Deanna was ever going to forgive me and whether or not I was going to be arrested for murder or indicted for embezzlement. None of those things had happened yet. Still, there was always tomorrow.

I decided after my first day as a jobless person that I was a creature of habit and was habitually programmed to go to work in the morning. So I rode the train into Manhattan just like I always did and commuted back in the afternoons. My depressing environs had something to do with it; the furnished apartment was like a motel room without maid service. I felt a little like Goldilocks sleeping in someone else's bed. Someone who was about to show up at any minute and demand my immediate departure. There were clues who this someone was—little relics of actual habitation left behind in this now sterile desert.

A paperback, for example. A dog-eared copy of *Men Are from Mars, Women Are from Venus*. But was it a Martian or a Venutian who'd once owned it? It was hard to say.

A toothbrush discovered behind the stained toilet. One of those fancy ones with a curved brush for those hard-to-reach areas. Lavender. Was that considered a feminine color or a masculine color, or neither?

And in my one desk drawer: a sheet of lined paper filled with what appeared to be New Year's resolutions. "I will try harder to meet people," was the first one. "I will be less judgmental." And so on. I decided the writer of this list and the owner of the book were probably one and the same, since both pointed to a devotee of rigorous self-improvement. I wondered, if Deanna was from Venus, was I from Pluto?

I visited the 42nd Street Library. I strolled the Met. I spent an entire day half sleeping in the Hayden Planetarium, waking periodically to a canopy of stars—like an astronaut coming out of suspended animation, alone in the universe and so far from home.

I made sure to call Anna every afternoon—always from my cell phone, since the elaborate cover story we'd worked out to explain my absence was that I was shooting a new ad campaign in Los Angeles. Once, I'd spent two months out there doing just that; it seemed like an excuse that might actually work.

Where are you now? Anna would ask me.

The Four Seasons pool, I'd reply.

A studio in Burbank. A street in Venice. In a rented car at the intersection of Sunset and La Cienega.

Cool, Anna would say.

Deanna had told me she didn't wish to speak to me for a while. The torture involved how long a while that would actually turn out to be. Occasionally she would pick up when I called and I'd hope that a *while* had ended right then. But she'd call out for Anna and wait silently until our daughter picked up the phone. In a way, it wasn't that different from all our years A.D.—after diabetes—that stifling silence about things we couldn't mention. Only there was a terrible reproof in her silence now, as opposed to just plain grief. And where before silence had been filled with the inconsequential and bland, it was now filled with the kind of quiet western movie heroes were always running into just before an ambush. *It's quiet,* they'd say to their amigos, too *quiet.*

It was late February, the Monday of my third week of banishment and joblessness, when I saw Lucinda again.

My first instinct was to hide and duck back farther into the faceless crowd. My second instinct was to say hello. Possibly because it was good to see her up and about again; it alleviated my guilt a little. Up and about and even talking to someone.

I'd wondered about her, of course. If she could ever recover from what Vasquez had done to her. I hoped so.

And now I thought that maybe she could. The rings under her eyes had gone away. She looked beautiful again; she looked like Lucinda.

I was so entirely fixated on her, it was probably a minute or so before I even took notice of whom she was talking to. Was that her husband—glimpsed briefly that day in front of the fountain at the Time-Life Building?

No. It wasn't her husband she was talking to. This man was shorter, younger, frumpier. A fellow broker, perhaps—a friend from the neighborhood.

They seemed to be on good terms with each other, at least. They'd stopped in front of a newsstand and were engaged in a lively discussion.

I was in a kind of no-man's-land, I realized. Neither far enough away to be invisible, nor close enough to be conversational. One look to the left and Lucinda would see me for sure—stuck in limbo, the man who'd failed her, a reminder of all she'd been through.

I wanted to spare her that. Mostly, I wanted to spare *me* that. So I turned tail. I skirted the fringes of the slowly moving

crowd and tried to keep my face forward to avoid any acciden-
tal eye contact.

I made it through the crowd, a piece of flotsam moving with
the tide. All the way over to the stairway leading to Eighth Avenue. Home free.

Only, I'd peeked. I couldn't help it. I'd peeked over at Lucinda and her business associate to see if I'd remained unno-
ticed.

And noticed something.

I mulled it over on the cab ride to the National Museum of
the American Indian and decided I didn't know what. Whatever it was had been picked up in one quick, furtive glance.
And there'd been all these people between us, too. *Foreground
crosses*, we call it in shoot-speak. Where you walk the extra
back and forth between camera and actors to ensure it looks
real, that it doesn't look like some sound stage in Universal
Studios.

Only sometimes you put too many extras into the mix, and
they obliterate the actors entirely. It becomes impossible to see
them, and they themselves become extras in the shot. Then
you have to thin out the extras and rework the blocking so the
actors can be seen again.

That's sort of what I was doing in the cab.

I was trying to push the faceless crowd of commuters off to
the side so I could see Lucinda clearly. Lucinda and that business associate of hers, or neighborhood friend. Or . . .

Her brother. Yes, maybe it was her brother, only I couldn't remember if she had a brother or not. It seemed to me we'd spent
a lot more time talking about my family than hers. I'd poured
my heart out to her, hadn't I? About Anna and Deanna? I didn't
remember whether she had brothers or not.

But it seemed to me now that it must have been her brother.
Or perhaps her cousin. Yes, it could have been her cousin.

It had to do with what I'd noticed.

I was trying to push those other people out of the way to get a clear look, but they were getting annoyed and pushing back. They were telling me to get lost or busy looking for a cop.

Their hands.

I thought I saw their hands touching. Not interlocked, not intertwined, but touching.

Something you might do with a brother, wasn't it?

And even if it wasn't her brother, even if it was a friend of hers, a *new* friend of hers, could you blame her? I'd never asked her if I was the first. Why should I assume I'd be the last?

She was still stuck in the same awful marriage. She was desperately in need of someone to talk to. Now especially. Maybe she'd gone and found someone.

And for the briefest moment, I felt something suspiciously like jealousy. Just a quick pang, a phantom ache from a long healed wound.

Then I forgot about it.

DERAILED THIRTY-TWO

It was Anna's birthday.

I'd never missed one. I couldn't imagine missing one now. She might give a sullen shrug of her shoulders when I brought up things like birthdays—*Birthday, what's that?*—but I genuinely believed she'd never forgive me if I didn't actually show up for one. And then I'd have two Schines in a unforgiving mode, and I was having a hard enough time with one.

So when I phoned home and Deanna picked up, I said: "Please don't call Anna yet. I need to talk to you."

She sighed. "Yes, Charles?" she said.

Well, she'd used my name, at least.

"Anna's birthday is coming up," I said.

"I know when Anna's birthday is."

"Well. Don't you think I should be home for it? She'd hate me if she thought I'd stayed in California on her birthday."

"I'm not ready for you to come home, Charles."

Yes, that was a problem—Deanna not being ready. As for me, of course, I was more than ready.

"Well, couldn't we . . . what if I say I came back just for her birthday and then I have to leave again?"

"I don't know . . ."

"Deanna, it's Anna's *birthday* . . ."

"Look . . . you can stay the night, okay? But in the morning, Charles, I want you to leave."

"I understand. That's fine. Thank you."

It felt a little odd thanking my wife for letting me stay overnight in my own home. Not unjust, just odd. The important thing, though, was that she'd said yes.

When I arrived at the kitchen door, present in hand—I'd bought her three CDs based on the recommendations of a clerk at Virgin Records—Anna was sitting at the counter munching cereal and staring zombie-eyed at MTV.

"Daddy!" Anna, who normally liked to keep her childish enthusiasm under control, seemed unabashedly glad to see me. Only not as glad as I was to see her. She popped up off her stool in a flash and straight into my arms, where I clung to her as if my very life depended on it. And maybe it did.

I was about to ask her where her mother was, but just then she walked into the kitchen. I had no idea what to do—I felt as awkward as someone on a blind date. I wasn't sure how to greet her, what to say to her, and it occurred to me that she was probably a little confused on the issue as well. We both hesitated, then settled on a perfunctory embrace with all the warmth of a postgame hockey handshake.

"How was California?" she asked me, evidently determined to see the charade through.

"Fine. Not done yet, either. I have to go back in the morning."

This was evidently news to Anna. She immediately pouted and said: *"Daddy . . ."*

"Sorry, honey. There's nothing I can do about it." And here, at least, I was telling the truth.

"I wanted you to see me sing at the spring concert. I have a solo."

"Well, don't turn professional till after high school."

The attempt at levity failed; Anna turned back to MTV, looking hurt and upset with me.

"Can somebody get me some juice?" she said. Her hands were suddenly shaking; she was holding the TV remote, and it was jiggling up and down.

"Are you low, honey?" Deanna said, quickly opening the refrigerator.

"No. I'm shaking because I *like* to."

Deanna shot me a look: *See what I've been going through,* this look said. *She's getting worse.*

Deanna pulled out some orange juice and poured Anna half a glass. "There you go. . . ."

Anna took it and swallowed a little.

"I think you should drink a little more," Deanna said.

"Oh, is that what you think?" Anna, ever vigilant against any suggestions concerning what she should or shouldn't put into her own body. She was still shaking.

"Come on, sweetie," I said.

"I'm fine," Anna said.

"You're not—"

"*All right!*" Anna said, grabbing the glass and striding out of the room. "I wish both of you would get *off* of my back already."

After she left the room, Deanna said: "She's scared. She's been going up and down like a roller coaster. When she gets scared she gets angry."

"Yes," I said. "I know."

Why did you call me Anna? our daughter Anna used to ask when she was very small.

Because you're part of me, Deanna would answer. *De-Anna, see?*

"I have to get back to the bills," Deanna said. Which suddenly reminded me that we might soon be having a problem paying those bills. Deanna left the kitchen.

I still needed a birthday card. Since my daughter and wife were both mad at me, I decided it was a good time to go to the stationery store on Merrick Road and buy one.

When I walked into the store, an older woman was buying Lotto tickets at the counter.

"... eight ... seventeen ... thirty-three ... six ... ," listlessly spitting out a seemingly endless litany of digits. "... nine ... twenty-two ... eleven ..."

I walked to the back where the greeting cards were. Of course, there weren't just greeting cards; there were anniversary cards, get well cards, condolence cards, Valentine's Day cards, thank-you cards, graduation cards, and birthday cards. I planted myself in front of the birthday section, momentarily dazzled by all the subcategories: Happy Birthday, Mom, Son, Wife, Mom-in-law, Grandmother, Best Friend, Cousin. And Daughter—it was there somewhere. Of course, once I found the category, I had to decide on the tone. Funny? Respectful? Sentimental? I was inclined to go sentimental here, since that's how I felt these days. There were a lot of sentimental cards, too, most of them with flowers on the cover and little poems on the inside. Only the poems weren't sentimental as much as trite— the *roses are red, violets are blue* genre of poem writing.

For instance:

> To my daughter on her birthday
> I have this to say
> I love you very much
> Your smile, your spirit and such
> Even though we may be apart

You have your daddy's heart.

The end.

I was worried Anna might throw up if I brought that one home for her. On the other hand, if I wanted to be sentimental *and* halfway intelligent, the pickings were slim. There were cards with nothing on the inside, for instance, allowing you to be as intelligent or sentimental as you'd like. These cards tended to have moody black-and-white photographs on the cover—of a snowfield in Maine, say, or a lonely mountain stream. They basically said stupid poems are for the unenlightened masses—these are for the more soulful of you. I couldn't decide if I was up to soulfulness today, though. So what was it to be?

Just past the card racks there were more elaborate gifts. Ceramic hearts saying "World's Best Mom." A golf ball "Fore a Great Dad." Fake flowers. A bell that said "Ring A Ding Ding." And some picture frames.

I didn't notice it immediately.

I looked here and there, sifted through the ceramic and cheap plastic, picked up the golf ball, gently rang the bell. I even turned back to the card rack, intent on finally making a decision. Only I had what you might call an episode of peripheral vision—you *might*, except it wouldn't be strictly true. It wasn't that I saw anything out of the corner of my eye, just that I remembered seeing it.

The bell, yes. And the silly golf ball. And the ceramic hearts. Keep going. There.

It was in the second picture frame.

And the third one, too.

And three miniature ones set behind it. And the large frame decorated with a metal trellis of flowers.

"Can I help you with anything?" The voice seemed to be coming from far away.

The picture in the picture frames.

They put them there to show you how nice they'll look once you get them home and put *your* pictures inside them. You and your wife at that wedding in Nantucket. The twins as Hansel and Gretel from a long-ago Halloween. Curry, the sweet-faced pup. Because people lack the necessary imagination otherwise. They need surrogate faces in there so they'll know what to expect when it's sitting back home on the mantelplace.

"Can I help you with anything, sir?" The voice more insistent now—but it was as if it were speaking through glass.

Behind the glass of the picture frames was the picture of a little girl. She was on a swing somewhere in the country, with her tawny blond hair caught in midswirl. Freckle faced and knobby kneed and sweet smiled. The very model of carefree youth. Because she *was* a model. Behind the swing were makeup artists and hairstylists and wardrobe people—only you couldn't see them.

"Sir, are you all right?"

I'd seen this picture before.

I showed you mine, now you show me yours.

Remember?

She'd seen Anna peeking out from the inside of my wallet, so I'd asked to see hers.

I showed you mine, now you show me yours.

And she'd laughed. I'd made lovely Lucinda laugh out loud, and she'd reached into her leather bag and shown me.

The little girl on the swing. Out in the country somewhere.

She's adorable. That's what I'd said.

And she'd said thanks. *I forget sometimes.* Two parents complimenting each other on their respective progeny, commuter small talk, nothing to it.

Nothing at all.

I forget sometimes. Because maybe that was an easy thing to do, to forget something that you didn't actually have.

She'd shown me a picture of her child, only it wasn't *her* child. It was someone else's child.

"Sir? Is something wrong?" The clerk again, wondering just what had come over me.

Well, I would tell him. Amazing grace, that's what.

Was blind but now I see.

DERAILED THIRTY-THREE

I was helping Deanna clean up the plates smeared with half-eaten cake and dollops of melting ice cream.

I was asking myself how it was possible.

The birthday celebration had been strained and awkward. Anna had invited just one friend, possibly her only friend these days. It felt more like a wake than a birthday celebration, but then I was kind of preoccupied.

I was thinking about that resident in the ER who'd asked me about Anna's eyes. I was thinking he should've asked me about my own. *Are you having problems seeing?* And I would've said, *Yes, Doctor, I'm blind. I can't see.*

But not anymore.

My life had turned into a train wreck. I could hear the screams of the dead and dying. But all that time it had been Lucinda at the wheel. I knew that now. Lucinda. And him.

How was it possible?

A lie. A farce. A con—trying to stick a label on something that was clearly out of my experience. As Anna waited patiently for us to stop singing "Happy Birthday."

A setup. A hoax. As she opened her presents and read her cards. My card said: "Can't you stay thirteen forever?"

An out-and-out robbery. As Anna thanked each of us for her presents and even gave me a hug.

And this, too: *That man at Penn Station.*

He wasn't her brother, her neighbor, or her favorite uncle.

He was *next.*

Deanna and I had managed to put up a decent front. We'd smiled, we'd talked, we'd clapped our hands when Anna blew out her candles.

But now that Anna and her friend had been dropped at a movie and we were alone, it had grown deathly quiet again. Just the steady splash of the faucet and the sour clinks of plates and glasses being laid to rest in the dishwasher tub. And the awful shouting going on in my own head.

"Well," I said, trying desperately to tug my thoughts in another direction, *any* direction, and at the same time cleave the silence, "one year older."

"Yes," Deanna said without much enthusiasm. Then she placed the last plate into the dishwasher, walked to the kitchen table, and sat down. And, for the first time in God knows how long, *really* began talking to me.

"How have you been, Charles?"

"Okay. Fine." *Liar,* I thought.

"Really?"

"Yes. I'm okay, Deanna."

"I was thinking," she said.

"About?"

"I was thinking as we sang 'Happy Birthday' to her. To our Anna."

"Yes . . . ?"

"You said something once. About us, about being a parent. I wonder if you even remember it?"

"What did I say?"

"You said"—she closed her eyes now, trying to conjure up the exact words—"that it was like making *deposits.*"

"Deposits? I don't remember . . ."

"Anna was three or four, somewhere around there, and you'd taken her someplace she wanted to go—the zoo, I think. Just you and her, because I was sick. I don't think you were feeling so hot yourself—I think I'd caught your cold. And you just wanted to stay home and lie down on the couch and watch football all day, but Anna pestered you and you gave in and took her. You don't remember?"

I did remember now, vaguely, anyway. A Sunday long ago at the Bronx Zoo. Anna and I had fed the elephants.

"Yes, I remember the day."

"When you came back, I thanked you. I knew you were feeling shitty and you didn't really want to go. It wasn't a big thing, but I remember being really happy that you did it."

Deanna was looking right at me now—*directly* at me, as if she were searching for something missing. I wanted to say, *I'm here, Deanna. I never left.*

"You said something to me. You said that every day with Anna, every good moment you spent with her, was like a *deposit.* A deposit in a bank. If you made enough of them, if you diligently kept putting money away in that account, then when she was older and on her own, she'd be rich enough to get by. Rich with memories, I guess. I thought it was kind of sappy. I thought it was kind of brilliant. She's going to need dialysis soon," Deanna said.

"No, Deanna." All thought of zoos and elephants, of Lucinda and Vasquez, immediately disappeared.

"Dr. Baron did some tests. Her kidneys are failing—one of them is barely there at all. Very soon our daughter is going to have to be strapped up to a machine three times a week so she can stay alive. That's what he said."

"When?"

"What does it matter? It's going to happen, that's all."

Then Deanna was crying.

I remembered wondering not too far back if Deanna was all cried out. But then I'd learned differently—that day in the garden. And now.

"I think you were right, Charles."

"What . . . Deanna . . . how do you mean?"

"I think we did okay with her. I think we gave her a very nice bank account. I think we never forgot to put something in. Never. Not once."

I felt something itchy under my eyes, something hot and wet on both cheeks.

"I'm sorry, Charles," she said. "I never closed my eyes to what was going to happen. But I did in a way. Because I wouldn't let you talk about it. I didn't want to hear it said out loud. I'm so sorry. I think that was wrong now."

"Deanna . . . I . . ."

"I think we *should* talk about it. I think we should talk about what a remarkable daughter we have, for as long as we have her. I think that's very important."

And somehow, in some magical and unexplained way, we ended up in each other's arms.

When we stopped crying, when we finally disentangled and sat across from each other, holding hands and staring out the window into the black-as-ink night, I thought that Deanna was about to ask me to come home now. I could almost see her forming the words.

I deliberately broke the mood; I got up and said it was time to leave, to go back to Forest Hills.

I couldn't come home. Not now. Not yet.

Something had just been made clear to me. Crystal clear.

I had unfinished business to take care of.

I was out of one job, fine. Now I had another one. An even more important one.

I had to get Anna's other bank account back.

Somehow I had to find them.

Somehow I needed to get back my money.

DERAILED THIRTY-FOUR

It was impossible to miss Lucinda's legs.

I hadn't missed them that first morning on the train.

And I didn't miss them *now* when I saw them emerging out of the morning crowd at Penn Station. Striding forward from a sea of denim, serge, and English wool—sleek and sexy and belonging solely to her.

Her and that man.

I'd been waiting to see them for days. I'd taken the 5:30 into Penn each morning. I'd planted myself at approximately the same spot I'd seen them the last time. I'd diligently stood guard. When the morning crowd dissipated and they didn't show up, I'd walked from one end of the station to the other.

I'd done this day after day.

I'd told myself it was my only chance. I'd crossed my fingers and said my prayers.

But now that I'd spotted them, I had trouble looking at them.

I felt naked and vulnerable and scared.

I couldn't help looking at that man, for instance, and seeing myself. Once at an office friend's bachelor party, I'd turned away from the nubile young stripper in a gold lamé thong just long enough to see everyone *else* staring at her and thought with sudden dismay: *I look like them.*

This man was so evidently besotted with Lucinda—or whoever she was. He kept grabbing for her hand and gazing lovingly into her eyes.

I hadn't been wrong about who he was. She was playing him just as she'd once played me. He was *next.*

How pathetic, I thought. *How pitiable.*

How exactly like I'd been.

When I'd looked into the picture frame that day in the candy store, I'd asked myself what it was that had made me such a target. But only briefly. Because I knew the answer. In the cold light of day, it was so easy to see just how much I'd been asking for it. For something. Anything. Anything at all to come rescue me from me.

I'd spent a lot of time replaying all the moments I'd spent with her, too, my rescuer. Only now remembering them just a little differently from before. Running them back and forth and back in my head, the way, in the days before computer editing systems, I used to have to run strips of celluloid through Moviolas until they frayed and split. I had to patch them with tape again and again and again, until the images formed actual cracks and nearly disintegrated into dust. Take the first time I met Lucinda. *Here, I'll take care of it,* she'd said sweetly on the train that day, but when I looked closely now, I could already see ugly fissures crisscrossing her face as she offered a ten-dollar bill to the pissed-off conductor.

She'd picked me that day.

Lucinda and the man had worked their way over to the open coffee shop, where they sold fat-free peach muffins and doughy bagels. The man ordered coffees, and they stood elbow to elbow across a small table. Steam sometimes obscured their faces.

I kept my back to them. I flipped through newsstand magazines and peeked. I was worried about her seeing me, but less worried than I might have been.

My face had changed.

It had happened gradually, bit by bit. I'd lost weight. As my life seemed to implode, my appetite had lessened, waned, disappeared. My clothes began to hang on me. When Barry Lenge administered the coup de grâce and sent me into the ranks of the unemployed, I'd stopped shaving, too. My goatee had become a beard. A few days ago, I'd looked into the bathroom mirror and seen the kind of face you see in hostage dramas staring back. That haunted-looking overseas government official who's finally been released after months of dark captivity. I looked like that.

Only I was *still* a hostage.

I kept peeking now.

It became hard watching them without actually being able to go over and confront them. Because now, in addition to feeling scared and naked and vulnerable, I felt angry. It welled up in me like sudden nausea. The kind of anger I'd up to this point reserved solely for God—on those days I believed in God and on the days I didn't—for Anna's disease. The kind of anger that caused me to clench my hands into fists and imagine landing them in Vasquez's face. And hers.

But I resisted the urge to walk over and tell her that I was on to them. That I knew what she'd done to me. I needed to bide my time. To get Anna's money back, I needed to find Vasquez; and to find Vasquez, I needed Lucinda.

That was my mantra. This was my mission.

She would lead me to him.

I guessed that Lucinda wasn't a stockbroker anymore.

I overheard a conversation Lucinda had with the man at Penn Station on Wednesday morning the next week. The man mentioned *selling short* for a client, how this client was a veritable *meal ticket* for him, which meant that he was a stock-broker and Lucinda wasn't. Because another stockbroker might be inclined to know people in other brokerage houses and might be inclined to ask them about their co-worker Lucinda, who, it would turn out, didn't exist. No, Lucinda obviously had another occupation these days. A lawyer, an insurance agent, a circus clown. And Lucinda, no doubt, wasn't even her name.

I knew the name of the man she was about to con out of his money, though. I knew this because another man had come up to them while they were having coffee together that same morning and said: *Sam, Sam Griffen, how are you doing?*

Not too well, actually. Mr. Griffen blanched—his face turning the color of soap, as Lucinda turned away and stared at the price list on the wall.

When Mr. Griffin regained his voice, he said: *Fine.*

Then Lucinda got up and walked off with her coffee cup—just another commuter on her way to the subway. And Mr. Griffen sat and talked with this unwelcome intruder for five minutes. When he left, Mr. Griffen sighed and wiped his face with a stained napkin.

I thought it was unnerving being this close to a victim without being able to warn him. Like standing next to a child who can't see the speeding car bearing down on him but being forbidden to tell him to get out of the way. Watching this horrible accident unfold in close-up and super slow motion. The worst kind of voyeur.

I thought she saw me once.

I'd followed them to a coffee shop north of Chinatown one morning.

They'd taken a table by the window, and I saw Sam Griffin reach for her hand and Lucinda give it to him.

I couldn't help remembering the way that hand had felt in my own. Just briefly. Remembering the things the hand had done to me, the pleasure it had conjured up for me that day at the Fairfax Hotel. Like opening up one Chinese box and finding another inside, and opening that one up, too, and then the next box, each box smaller and tighter than the previous one, opening them faster and faster until there were no boxes left and I was trying to catch my breath.

I was still trying to catch my breath, still lost in memories of guilty pleasure, when they exited the coffee shop. I had to turn and dart across the street. I had to hold my breath, count to ten, then slowly turn back, fingers crossed, and see if I'd been spotted.

No. They'd gone off somewhere in a taxi.

Then I lost them.

One day.

Two days.

Three days.

A week. No Lucinda. No Mr. Griffen. Nowhere.

I scoured Penn Station from one end to the other, coming early, staying late.

But nothing.

I started to panic, to think maybe I'd missed the boat. That she'd already taken Mr. Griffen off someplace for an afternoon of sex and Vasquez had already caught them in the act. That he'd already taken their wallets and asked Mr. Griffen why he was fucking around on his wife. Maybe even called Mr. Griffen at home and stated his dire need for a loan. Just ten thousand dollars, that's all, and he'd be out of his hair.

When the next week came, and I still couldn't find them, I was ready to give up. I was ready to admit that a forty-five-year-old ex–advertising executive had no business thinking he could win here. That I was hopelessly out of my element.

I was ready to throw in the towel.

Then I remembered something.

DERAILED THIRTY-FIVE

Okay," the deskman said. "How long you want it for?"

This deskman was the very same one who'd given me the key to room 1207 back in November when I'd stood in front of him with Lucinda on my arm.

I was back at the Fairfax Hotel, and the deskman was asking me exactly how long I'd be needing room 1207 for.

Good question.

"How much is it for two weeks?"

"Five hundred and twenty-eight dollars," the man said.

"Fine," I said. So far, I was on paid suspension. And $528 was a bargain in New York City, even if the room had blood-stains on the carpeting and the stink of sex in the mattress sheets.

I paid in cash and received my room key. There was a pile of magazines sitting on top of a beat-up couch, the only true piece of furniture in the lobby. I stopped to peruse them: a *Sports Illustrated* from last year, a *Popular Mechanics*, two issues of *Ebony*, and an old *U.S. News & World Report:* SHOWDOWN IN PALM BEACH COUNTY. I took the *Sports Illustrated*.

I rode the elevator with a man wearing a University of Oklahoma jacket who actually looked as if he were from Oklahoma. He had the slightly bewildered look of a tourist who'd fallen for the picture on the cover of the brochure—the one taken in 1955, when the Fairfax wasn't being subsidized by federal welfare checks. He'd probably tried his hand at three-card monte and already purchased a genuine Rolex watch from the man on the corner. He looked like he was ready to go home.

So was I.

But I was on a mission now, so I couldn't.

For just a moment as I was opening the door, jiggling the key inside the somewhat resistant door lock, I couldn't help tensing up and waiting for someone to blindside me into the room. No one did, of course, but that didn't stop me from sighing in relief as soon as I made it inside and shut the door.

It looked a little smaller than before, as if my imagination had given it a size more commensurate with what had gone on there. But it was just a room in a cramped downtown hotel, big enough for two people who pretty much intended to stay glued to each other, conducive to sex if for no other reason than its restrictive dimensions. The kind of room where two is company but three's a disaster—remembering what it was like to be stuck in that bird's-eye seat on the floor.

I lay down on the bed without taking my shoes off and closed my eyes. Just for a few minutes.

When I woke, it was nearly dark.

For a few seconds, I had no idea where I was. Wasn't I home in bed? Wasn't Deanna next to me or downstairs whipping up something tasty for dinner? And Anna—chatting away on-line in the next room, homework spread out on her lap like a prop to throw me off the scent?

There was a musty odor in the room, mustier even than my furnished apartment; the mattress felt hard and lumpy at the same time; the ghost images of a chair and table I didn't recognize were hovering precipitously by the foot of the bed. And I finally woke to my current surroundings as to a radio alarm that's been set too loud—I groaned, winced, and looked furtively for a stop button that didn't exist.

I got up and made my way into the bathroom to splash some cold water onto my face. My body felt like pins and needles, my mouth dry and pasty. I looked down at my watch: seven twenty-five.

I'd slept the whole day away. When I walked back to the bed, I saw the *Sports Illustrated* I'd taken from downstairs lying on the floor.

I saw the date.

November 8.

One week before I'd walked onto the 9:05 to Penn Station and my world had come tumbling down.

DERAILED THIRTY-SIX

I was sitting on the beaten-up couch in the lobby.

I was wearing a baseball cap pulled down low over my eyes.

I was tracking human traffic like an eagle-eyed crossing guard.

How long do you want it for? the deskman had asked me when I checked in.

Why did I want it in the first place?

That day when we walked out of Penn Station and into a taxi, that day when she'd finally said yes. When she'd asked me, *Where?*

I'd gone and dutifully picked our hotel from a moving taxi.

But maybe not.

Now it seemed to me that I'd pointed one out to her, but she'd said, *Uh-uh,* then picked out another one she didn't like the look of; and then finally, when we'd made it nearly all the way downtown to the vicinity of her office, I'd pointed to the Fairfax and she'd said, *Okay.* So when you really thought about it, maybe I hadn't picked our hotel after all.

Maybe *she* had.

The hotel where I'd run into the wrong person at just the wrong time. Only I hadn't really run into anyone. They'd set a trap, and I'd walked into it.

Which brought me to my hunch. An idea that occurred to me when I was standing empty-handed and frantic in Penn Station.

There was no reason on earth for her to think I would ever find out about her and Vasquez. The last time she'd seen me, I'd been running for my life down that stairway in Spanish Harlem.

They didn't need to change addresses.

Just victims.

When she relieved Mr. Griffen of most of his cash and all of his dignity, odds were it was going to be in the very same place they'd done it to me.

So I sat on the couch in the lobby.

I waited.

I had a dream.

I was on the train again. The 9:05 to Penn Station.

I was looking through my pockets again because the conductor was standing over me, asking for money.

One hundred thousand dollars, he said.

Why so much? I asked him.

The fare's gone up, the conductor replied.

When Lucinda offered to pay for me, this time I said no.

I made it through both issues of *Ebony.*

Patience, I told myself as another morning went by without a sighting. Patience. After all, look how much patience Lucinda had exhibited with me. All those chummy lunches and romantic dinners she'd had to suffer through in order to get me to go upstairs to that room. If she could do it, so could I.

From *Popular Mechanics* I learned the basics of hot-water

piping. Which wrench was voted best overall value. How to tile a floor. Roofing made simple.

One afternoon, I called Barry Lenge from the room to see how the investigation was going. To touch base with the *real* world—isn't that what Vietnam grunts used to call the world back home, the one that existed far away from the front? Which is where I was now—on the front lines, pulling guard duty to prevent any enemy incursions.

And the military reference was entirely apt. Wasn't I exercising each morning now? Push-ups, sit-ups, jumping jacks, isometrics—the works. So the next time Vasquez said, *Good boy,* maybe I'd show him how good I really was.

And something else. I still had Winston's gun. I kept it up in room 1207 wrapped in a towel and hidden behind the bathroom radiator.

As far as the real world went:

Barry Lenge got on the phone and said there was no point in my calling him. They were still conducting their investigation. They were still crossing the *t*'s and dotting the *i*'s. It didn't look very good for me, though. I should've taken him up on his offer—that's for sure. He'd be calling me soon enough.

I thanked him for his time.

Then I checked my cellular for messages and found a voice mail from Deanna.

A Detective Palumbo called for you. He said it was important. I told him you were out of town.

Time was running out.

I knew that. Running out for me and Sam Griffen both. If it hadn't run out on Sam Griffen already.

It was Friday morning.

I was browsing through the out-of-date *U.S. News & World Report,* whose headline was SHOWDOWN IN PALM BEACH COUNTY.

Occasionally the deskman would glance over at me, the deskman and the bellman, too, look me over, up and down, all without saying a word.

It was that kind of hotel. People who came here had nowhere else to go, so no one expected you to go anywhere or do anything. You could loiter in peace here, sit on a couch all day and read out-of-date magazines to your heart's content.

"Gore is confident of ultimate victory," the magazine reported solemnly.

When I looked up again, the bellman had multiplied. He had some help for the afternoon rush; a black man dressed in a similar nondescript green uniform was leaning on the desk, talking to him.

I'd left my cell phone upstairs, and I wanted to call Anna. I got up and walked to the elevator. The bellman nodded at me, the black man who'd been talking to him momentarily stopped, turned around, then resumed his conversation.

I was thinking that I knew that bellman—the black one. That I must've seen him that day months ago when I'd entered the very same elevator with Lucinda. The elevator doors opened; I walked inside and pressed twelve. I got off on my floor, I hummed a song whose words I couldn't remember, I opened the door to my room and walked inside. Which is when I realized that I was wrong, that it wasn't that day I'd seen him after all.

I walked back into the elevator and pressed Lobby.

The black man was still yapping at the bell captain—his back directly toward me, so I couldn't actually tell if I was right.

They call you Chuck?

I took a loping circle over to the front desk, looking sideways the whole time, holding my breath as the man's face slowly came into view, a quarter moon into a full half, his features starting to fill in.

If you were my crimey, that's what we'd call you.

Remember? Biding my time that day on the corner of, what . . . 8th Street and Avenue C? Waiting for Vasquez in Alphabet City, but it wasn't Vasquez who'd walked up to me—or actually *into* me.

Why don't you look where you're going?

The face three-quarter now, and I was beginning to feel clammy and light-headed.

It was him.

Yes, it was.

The black man who'd frisked me up against the alley wall, who smelled of blood and pomade.

I quickly turned away—toward the deskman, who looked up as if waiting for a question. This question being, *How smart is Charles?* Very smart—or at least smarter than I was seven months ago.

Then again, even fools have their day.

After all, for once I knew something they didn't.

I knew how they did it.

I knew where they'd be doing it again.

DERAILED THIRTY-SEVEN

I bought a pair of sunglasses from the Vision Hut on 48th Street. I was pretty sure the black man hadn't recognized me the other day, that he hadn't matched the bearded and undernourished-looking man he'd seen sitting in the lobby to the man he'd led into that alleyway in Alphabet City.

Still, it wouldn't hurt to take precautions.

I completed fifty-two push-ups and seventy-five sit-ups before 7:00 A.M.

When I got downstairs, I walked over to the bellman's desk and said hello.

"Hi," the bell captain said.

"Not too busy today, huh?" I said.

"Nope."

Then I was pretty much out of things to say.

"How long have you worked here?" The good conversationalist will always ask the other person about himself.

The bellman looked kind of suspicious. He was about forty or forty-five, I guessed, greasy hair combed in a kind of pompadour, a style about forty years out-of-date.

"A while," he said.

"Get any days off?"

"*Why?*"

"Excuse me?"

"Why do you want to know if I get any days off?"

"I don't know. Just making conversation." That, at least, was what I was attempting to do.

"Oh, I get it," he said.

"Huh?"

"What kind you looking for? You want white, black, spic . . . *what?*"

"Excuse me?"

"You looking for a date or not?"

I blushed. "No. I was just . . . talking. . . ."

"Right," the bellman said. "Fine."

In this hotel, apparently the bell captain did a little more than carry your bags.

"Are you the only bellman?" I asked, trying to steer the conversation where I needed it to go.

"Why?"

"I was just wondering if you had any—"

"What *exactly* you looking for, mister?" He sounded irritated now. "You got something going with Dexter, ask him, okay?"

Dexter. That was his name. Dexter.

"When does . . . Dexter work?"

The bell captain shrugged. "Wednesdays and Fridays."

"Oh."

"You need your bags put somewhere?"

"Bags? No."

"Right. Well, I'm the bell captain. So if you don't need your bags put somewhere . . ."

He was asking me to shut up. I retreated back to the couch, where I sat for another half hour or so, or until lunchtime.

*   *   *

When I came back in from my 7:00 A.M. coffee run a few mornings later, Dexter was standing behind the desk.

I sat on the lobby couch and opened my coffee cup with trembling hands.

I was afraid Dexter would recognize me, and I was feeling kind of scared again; I might look like a dangerous man with my oversize shades, but looks can be deceiving. For instance, Dexter looked more or less harmless reading a magazine in that pale green uniform. He looked like a guy who might even help you with your bags if you asked him nicely. Not like a guy who'd slam you up against an alley wall and laugh when you were punched in the stomach.

I could feel a vague pain there, the vestige of that wallop to my solar plexus, which might have been the body's way of warning me. *What are you doing, Charles?* my body was saying. *Don't you remember how much it hurt? You were crying. You couldn't breathe, remember?*

I remembered just fine.

There was another reason my hands were trembling.

Wednesdays and Fridays, the bellman had answered me when I'd asked about Dexter's work schedule.

But today was Tuesday.

DERAILED THIRTY-EIGHT

I got the gun out from behind the radiator—it was hot to the touch. I just wanted to know it was still there, that it hadn't disappeared, hadn't fallen down the hole in the bathroom wall or been stolen by the maid.

I held it like a rosary—something that just might grant me my dearest wish.

I put it back into the hole.

When I exited the elevator into the lobby, I could see Dexter sitting behind the bell captain's desk with his head in his hands. He appeared to be reading a women's muscle magazine.

I walked slowly over to the front desk and perused an old stack of tourists brochures. "Ride the Circle Line," one said. "Broadway Tours." All the things New Yorkers themselves never get around to doing.

The lobby was fairly quiet this morning. There was a couple who seemed to be waiting for a cab; every minute or so, the man poked his head out the front doors and announced there were no taxis yet. His wife nodded and said they were going to be late. The man said you can say that again. When the man announced that there were *still* no taxis two minutes later, she did.

The man in the University of Oklahoma jacket I'd seen on the elevator was complaining to the deskman that there was no King James Bible in his room.

"Are you kidding?" the deskman said to him.

An old man stood hunched over his walker just to the left of the elevators. He might've actually been moving, but if he was, it was too slowly to register on the eye.

I was happy for the company. It was hard to imagine anything really bad was going to happen to you while an old man was shuffling along next to you in a walker and someone else was complaining about there being no Bibles in his room.

Dexter looked directly at me and asked if I had the time.

"Eight o'clock," I said.

And then I tensed up and waited for Dexter to recognize me. *Wait a minute, I know you—what the fuck are you doing here?* But Dexter went back into his magazine.

The old man seemed to be suffering from some kind of emphysema in addition to his leg problems; he wheezed, gurgled, and heaved with each tiny shuffle.

A woman with six-inch heels, who wasn't suffering from any walking problems, sashayed into the lobby with a fat little man in a bad suit. She detoured past the front desk without actually stopping and grabbed a room key the deskman had already laid down on the counter.

"Come on, sweetie," she said to the fat man. "Come on."

The fat man kept his face trained on the worn carpeting in the lobby. He remained that way until the elevator opened up to rescue him.

Two young couples walked in with luggage and asked how much a room was. But the two women—girls, really—spent the entire time peering around the lobby with obvious distaste. They looked at the old man as if he were walking around without any clothes on. They didn't seem to like the sight of me, either.

I heard them whispering to their boyfriends, who seemed interested in staying—the price was right, wasn't it? But the women won out—the guys shrugged and said no thanks, then all four of them left.

"Next month . . . is my . . . birthday," the old man in the walker said.

He'd maneuvered his way over to me. I remembered a game I used to play as a kid. It was called red light, green light, and the object of the game was for you to sneak up on someone without ever actually being seen to move. Whoever was "it" had to close his eyes and say, *Red light, green light, one, two, three,* then quickly turn around and attempt to catch the pursuers in the act of advancing. It wasn't fun being it. It was eerie—seeing someone twenty feet back, then turning and seeing them frozen not five feet from you. It was like that with the old man, who every time I'd looked had seemed stuck in place yet was suddenly there by my right shoulder.

"Eighty . . . three . . . ," he said again. He had to pause before every word or two in an effort to get enough air in his lungs. Vegas would've given you attractive odds on his making it to eighty-four.

"Happy birthday," I said.

"Lived here . . . twenty years," the old man said between gasps.

I imagined that was just about the time the hotel began its precipitous decline.

"Well, good luck," I said.

Ordinarily, I found it hard talking to old people. I resorted to hand motions and condescension, as if they were foreigners. But this morning, talking to anyone was better than not talking at all. Because I was harboring two terrible fears. One that Lucinda and Vasquez and Dexter had already robbed and beaten Mr. Griffen; the other that they hadn't.

The old man said: "Thanks."

I needed to go to the bathroom. Nerves. I'd needed to go for the last hour but kept telling myself I couldn't leave my post. Now I had to. I walked to the elevator and pressed the button.

The doors opened with a loud sigh; I entered and pressed twelve. I jiggled my legs, *Come on . . . come on . . .* trying to will the elevator doors to shut. Finally they began to close, the hotel lobby starting to narrow by inches, less and less of it until it was just about gone, a mere sliver of a view. I'd estimate ten inches—no more.

Just wide enough to see Lucinda and Sam Griffen enter the hotel.

DERAILED THIRTY-NINE

It's what I'd come for.

Even if I felt like shouting, *No, not today!*

Even if I wasn't ready.

Still, I made it up to the twelfth floor without passing out. So far, so good. I made it into my room without being assaulted. I was on a roll. I paced around the room, back and forth, like the big cats in the Bronx Zoo, only the truth was, I was more like that lion in *The Wizard of Oz,* the one searching for courage.

I *had* courage, though, didn't I—it was there somewhere, wasn't it? Yes, of course. Courage was hidden behind the bathroom radiator in a towel. I went in and got it, unfolded the towel and took courage out.

I glanced at the mirror and saw a blind man staring back at me. A blind man with a gun.

I walked out of the room again, but this time I took the fire exit down—the dark stairway, which would enable me to *peek* once I made it downstairs. I shoved the gun into my pocket.

The stairway had strips of what looked like asbestos hanging from the walls; rats were scurrying back and forth in the dark corners of the landings. When I reached the lobby floor, I slowly opened the door wide enough to put one eye there. Only there was nothing to see. Lucinda and Sam were gone.

I walked back out into the lobby. Dexter was still behind the desk, but he appeared to have just gotten there. Maybe because he looked jumpy. As if he were worrying about his tips.

I walked over to the front desk, although I couldn't actually feel the ground.

"Excuse me?" I said to the deskman. "Can I ask you something?"

"What?"

"That woman who walked in before?"

"Yes? Which woman?"

"The woman who walked in with the man. Just before. Dark hair. Very pretty. I think maybe I know her."

"So?"

"Well, I'm curious if that's her. What's her name?"

He looked as if I'd just asked him for his wife's phone number or the exact measurements of his prick. "I can't give out that information," he said dourly.

"Fine," I said, "just tell me what room she's in and I'll call her."

"You'll have to tell me her name first," he said.

"Lucinda?"

The deskman looked down at his register. "Nope."

"How about the man. Sam Griffen."

"Nope."

For a second, I was ready to tell the deskman to check again and, if he still said *nope,* to accuse him of lying. That it *was* Sam Griffen, no mistake about it. Then I realized it wasn't the deskman who was guilty of lying.

Sam Griffen wouldn't have registered under his own name.

"Never mind," I said. I walked over to the glass doors and stared out at the sunlit sidewalk.

This is how they do it, I thought. *Dexter knows the room number in advance.*

Lucinda picks the hotel. Then after Lucinda tells Vasquez when, Dexter tells Vasquez where. The exact room number. So Vasquez can be there waiting for them in the stairwell. Dexter is paid off, probably—each time he gets paid off. Dexter works Wednesdays and Fridays, but sometimes he works Tuesdays. If that's when Vasquez tells him to.

I went back to the front desk. Dexter was still reading his magazine over by the bell station.

I had to get that room number.

"Excuse me," I said.

"Yes?"

I leaned forward and whispered, "That woman I asked you about before. She's my *wife.*"

"What?"

"I've been waiting to see if she'd come here. You understand?"

Yes, he understood. He was a hotel deskman, so he understood perfectly. Only he still wasn't talking.

"I can't give out room numbers."

"Maybe for a hundred dollars you can."

But even though he hesitated, licked his bottom lip, and looked around the lobby as if for eavesdroppers, he still said no.

I had approximately $280 in my wallet.

"Two hundred and eighty dollars," I whispered, and then, after the deskman still didn't say anything: "And I won't tell anyone you run whores out of here."

The deskman of the Fairfax Hotel turned red. He stuttered. He sized me up. *How much trouble can this guy actually make?*

He whispered: "Okay."

"For two hundred and eighty dollars, I'd like the *key,* too,"
I said.

And the deskman said: "Room eight oh seven."

And when I slid the money across the counter, he slid the
room key back to me.

DERAILED FORTY

I went back up the stairs.

But this time I heard someone in there with me.

Not at first, though. I was concentrating too hard on simply walking up the stairs. Putting one foot in front of the other and eerily conscious of my own labored breathing. I thought I sounded like the old man in the lobby—like someone with one foot already in the grave.

Then I heard somebody else in there with me.

At least several floors above me and maybe drunk, because whoever it was was stumbling around up there and occasionally cursing at himself.

In Spanish.

Lucinda and Mr. Griffen would be in the room by now, I thought. Lucinda would be demurely removing her clothing. Turning her back to Mr. Griffen as she removed her dress and stockings. And Mr. Griffen would be thanking a benevolent God.

Vasquez? He would be positioning himself in the stairwell opposite their room.

I pulled the gun out of my pocket and took a few deep breaths and kept coming.

When I turned the corner between the seventh and eighth floors, I saw him wedged against the hall door, panting and sweating.

"Who are you?" Vasquez said when he turned around to see who'd come up the stairs. He looked stoned.

"Charles Schine," I said.

"Huh?"

"I need that loan back."

"This room's occupied."

The first words out of Sam Griffen's mouth.

I'd carefully opened the door to 807 with my room key, keeping my gun trained on Vasquez. I'd made sure he entered the room first.

Sam's statement had been directed at Vasquez. But when he saw me following him in with a gun, his expression turned from annoyed to panicked.

"What . . . who are you?" he said.

"Charles!" Lucinda answered for me. She was lying on the bed dressed in a lacy black thong, or *un*dressed in a lacy black thong. She'd evidently gotten the show on the road already.

Four of us—a horrified-looking Sam Griffen dressed in pale blue boxers, Lucinda in her black thong, Vasquez in a turquoise velour sweatsuit, and me in sunglasses, holding a gun.

"Hello, Lucinda," I said.

It felt strange holding a gun like that. Pointing it at the people who'd cheated me out of over one hundred thousand dollars—moving it back and forth between them. It felt powerful, like an extension of my hand, except my hand had mythological powers now—it could suddenly throw thunderbolts. They were all scared of the gun, even Mr. Griffen.

"Look," Mr. Griffen said in a very shaky voice, "you can have all my money." *You can have all my money*—isn't that what I'd said to Vasquez that day?

"I don't want your money," I said. "She does."

"What?"

"*She* wants your money."

Now, in addition to looking terrified, Mr. Griffen looked confused. My heart went out to him—sympathy for a kindred soul, for someone who was about to go through the same shock and disillusionment I had.

"I don't understand," Mr. Griffen said. "Who are you?"

"It doesn't matter," I said.

"Look, I don't want any trouble," Mr. Griffen said.

"They were going to take you for everything you have," I said. "You're already in trouble."

Lucinda said: "I don't know what you're talking about. Me and Sam fell in love . . . we—"

"You met on the train, didn't you, Sam?"

Sam nodded.

"By accident—it just happened. I understand. You talked and talked about everything. She was pretty and sweet and understanding, and you couldn't believe how attracted she was to you. She was too good to be true. Wasn't she, Sam?"

Sam still looked scared of me, but at least he was listening.

"Ask yourself that question. *Wasn't* she too good to be true? Ask yourself if she ever told you where she lived. Did she? The *address*, Sam. If she ever seemed to know anyone else on the train—her friends and neighbors. Most people know someone on the train, don't they. Even one person?"

"He's been stalking me, Sam," Lucinda said. "We had a thing once, before you. He's jealous. He's out of his mind."

You had to give her points for trying, I thought. She was good and she was desperate and she was trying.

Vasquez had moved a little. He seemed definitely closer to

me than he'd been before. He was playing red light, green light with me.

"Get back," I said to him. "One giant step back." I pointed the gun at him. Vasquez took a step back.

"I don't know who this crazy *fucker* is," Vasquez said to Mr. Griffen. He was playing along—he'd seen where Lucinda was going with this now, so he was playing along. "I was just walking in the hall, man, and this asshole pulls a gun on me."

Sam had a small potbelly and thin, blue-veined arms. He'd crossed them tightly over his pale, hairless chest, as if he were trying to keep himself from crying. He obviously didn't know whom to believe—maybe it didn't even matter now. He wanted to get out of there.

"Listen to me, Sam. What does she do for a living? Has she told you where she works?"

"She's an insurance agent," he said, but not too convincingly.

"What company, Sam?"

"Mutual of Omaha."

"Shall we call them, Sam? There's a phone right over there. Why don't you call Mutual of Omaha and ask for her. Go ahead."

Sam glanced at the phone sitting on the night table by the bed. Lucinda glanced at it, too.

"Did she show you the picture of her little girl, Sam? The cute little blond girl on the swing? The one you can get for yourself at any stationery store?"

"We got to take this crazy fucker down," Vasquez said. "He's out of his fucking mind—he's gonna *shoot* us. You with me, Sam?"

But Sam wasn't with him. Sam looked forlorn. He was still confused, but he was being worn down by logic. Maybe he *had* asked himself if Lucinda was too good to be true—maybe he'd always known she was too beautiful and too smart and too available.

"Whatever she's told you is a lie, Sam. All of it. You're being set up, understand what I'm saying to you? You were going to get a surprise. You were going to walk out of the room and Vasquez here was going to jump you in the hall. He was going to rob you. He was going to rape *her.* Only it *wouldn't* have been rape because she's already given her consent. They're in this together."

Vasquez was on the move again. He was edging forward.

"I don't understand why raping her . . . ," Mr. Griffen said.

"The rape is to make it look legitimate, Sam. And to make you feel guilty that you didn't stop it. That you didn't protect her. So when he starts blackmailing you—you and *Lucinda,* or whatever she calls herself—when he asks you for a little loan and then a not so little loan, you'll pay up. Even if you start having second thoughts about it, even if you start thinking about going to your wife and telling her everything. Because that would still leave her husband, wouldn't it? And she would've told you no, she would've *begged* you not to do it—that she couldn't have her husband know about it—about you and her and the *rape.* Even though she doesn't have a husband, Sam."

Mr. Griffen believed me now. Maybe not 100 percent, but enough.

"Can I . . . go?" Mr. Griffen said. "Can I just . . . get out of here?"

But Vasquez said: "Are you stupid? You gonna take off and leave us with this crazy motherfucker?"

"Look," Sam said, "I just want to go home. I don't know what's going on here, and I don't care. Really. I just . . . just let me go, okay?"

Vasquez reached back into his pocket and hit him across the mouth with something black, and Sam went down. That fast. His mouth began to leak blood.

Another gun.

I'd done just about everything right. I'd gotten the room key and surprised Vasquez on the staircase. I'd made it into the room. I was going to get my money back. Even if my plan was just a little bit murky on *how* I was going to get my money back. Maybe by keeping Lucinda at gunpoint until Vasquez came back with it—maybe by all going for the money together. But I'd made one mistake. I'd forgotten that Vasquezes carry guns. I hadn't searched him or patted him down or made him throw his gun away.

There were a few seconds when all wasn't lost. When I still had the advantage. Vasquez had a gun and Sam was down and bleeding, but I was still the only one in the room with his gun actually pointed at someone.

I could tell that Vasquez was thinking that it was one thing to hold a gun on somebody and an entirely different thing to pull the trigger. He didn't think I had it in me.

But he didn't know something. They say money is the great equalizer, but it's really, truly, desperation. It had leveled the playing field.

I pulled the trigger.

Nothing happened.

In the millisecond it took for Vasquez to realize his good fortune, to begin raising his gun hand, I understood *why* nothing had happened.

I'd forgotten to click off the safety.

I launched myself at Vasquez, using the only advantage I had going for me. Surprise.

My initial charge knocked the gun right out of Vasquez's hand, and it skittered somewhere under the bed. So now we were more or less even.

Maybe I even had the edge. Because there was a chance my desperation was even more terrible than Vasquez's. I had nothing much to lose. Detective Palumbo would be calling back any day now, and even if *he* didn't, Barry Lenge would. So I did have desperation on my side. And something was not quite right with Vasquez. He *was* drunk, or stoned, or something.

Vasquez had gasped from the initial shock of body contact, then immediately tried to separate himself from my grasp. But he seemed like a punched-out heavyweight in round twelve, sluggish and wobbly kneed. It gave me courage.

I could see Sam out of the corner of my eye—up on his knees and looking down at his hand, which was bright red because he'd just touched his mouth with it. He looked dazed and confused.

"Mother . . . *fucker* . . . ," Vasquez said, grunting now from the exertion of trying to get me off him but not having much success. I had my arms firmly around him, and I wasn't letting go.

Vasquez staggered into the wall. I had him in a bear hug, so he was doing what bears do when they want to get something off their backs. They rub themselves against the nearest tree trunk. Vasquez was using the nearest wall.

I held fast as I crashed into the plaster wall and dislodged a yellowed reproduction, my sunglasses spinning off onto the floor.

Then we fell to the floor with a loud crash; I could smell Vasquez now—the stink of garlic and cigarette smoke and fried eggs. The carpet was so thin that it was like rolling around on playground cement. And for the first time, I was absolutely convinced I was going to win. I'd moved my right arm around Vasquez's neck and was squeezing for all I was worth—and right at this minute I was worth a lot. One hundred and ten thousand dollars, at least.

Vasquez was sputtering, and I wondered if I was going to kill him. And I thought: *If I have to, I will.*

Vasquez gave one last effort at getting me off his back, but one of his arms was pinned between me and the floor, and I had the other one wrapped up tightly, so even though Vasquez gave an awkward lunge forward, he couldn't dislodge me.

He collapsed; I felt all the strength go out of him—whatever strength booze or drugs hadn't sapped from him already.

I hadn't killed him, but I'd won.

I'd won.

There were a pair of shoes standing just at eye level. At first I thought they belonged to Sam, but Sam was over there on the other side of the room, bleeding into his hands.

So I peered up.

"Lookit here," said Dexter, "it's Chuck."

DERAILED FORTY-ONE

Dexter had slipped in during the heat of the battle.

We'd been rolling around on the floor, and neither one of us had heard the door open. That allowed Dexter to enter the room, pick up my gun, click off the safety, and point the barrel at my head.

I was leashed and muzzled. My hands were tied behind my back with my own belt. They took off my shoes and socks and stuffed one clammy sock into my mouth.

They did the same thing to Sam. Sam resisted momentarily, and Vasquez kicked him in the head.

I could smell Sam's blood.

It smelled almost sweet, but since I knew where it was coming from, it was a nauseating sweetness. That was a problem. Because it made me want to throw up, and the thought of throwing up with a sock already stuffed into my mouth made me want to panic.

Not panicking was easier said than done. I was wondering, for instance, what they were planning to do with us, with Sam and me. I had the strong feeling *they* didn't know yet.

They seemed at loose ends. They kept muttering and whispering to each other—sometimes in Spanish, sometimes not.

"*Nosotros tenemos que hacer algo,*" Lucinda was saying now.

I'd taken just one year of high school Spanish, and the only word I actually remembered was *gracias*—but I could intuit their confusion anyway.

I overheard Vasquez whispering something in English to Lucinda.

"Afterwards . . . we can go . . . Miami and . . ." They were taking off.

It made sense. After all, Sam was useless to them now, a would-be cash cow that had been irrevocably damaged. All that time and effort put into leading him here and nothing to show for it.

They were legitimately upset. They were unhappy I'd shown up. I was the reason it hadn't worked out the way they'd planned. Me. I'd gummed up the works and left them with a problem they hadn't counted on. Their weapons, after all, were fear and deception, but now I'd made those weapons useless.

Which left what?

"You stupid *fuck* . . ." Vasquez was sitting on the bed with his hands on his knees. He was talking to me. "I told you not to pull this kind of shit again. I told you to go back to Long Island and stay there, right? You lost *money* before, motherfucker. *Money.* You should've thanked God. *Now* what you gonna do, huh?"

Perhaps pray.

It wasn't merely the words that were frightening, that made me think praying was in order—it was the fact that Vasquez himself seemed frightened saying them. *Now what you gonna do, huh?* As if it were a question they'd asked themselves, then come up with an answer they hadn't liked. When scary people start sounding scared, that's when it's okay to be scared yourself.

The three of them went into the bathroom together. Some-one—I thought it was Dexter—was arguing against doing something. I could hear his raised voice.

When they came out of the bathroom, Dexter didn't look very happy. It appeared he'd lost.

But Vasquez and Dexter were going somewhere now.

"Ten minutes," I heard Vasquez whisper to Lucinda, "and then we'll go down to . . . Little Havana . . . my cousin . . ."

Vasquez and Dexter left the room.

Which left the three of us. Sam, Lucinda, and me.

"What are you going to do with us?" Sam said through the sock in his mouth. The words muffled, but understandable.

But Lucinda didn't answer him.

"I won't tell," Sam said. "If you let me go, I won't say a thing, I promise. Please . . ."

Still no answer from Lucinda. Maybe she'd been told not to say anything—no fraternizing with the enemy. Maybe after having had to talk to Sam Griffen for months, it was nice not having to say anything to him now. Or maybe she knew exactly what they were going to do with us and thought it better not to tell.

"The sock . . . it's choking me," Sam said. *"Please . . ."*

Lucinda finally responded, but not with words. She got up and walked over to Sam—a short walk of five feet, maybe.

"Please," Sam said, "take it out of my mouth . . . *please . . . I'm choking . . .*"

So Lucinda reached down to pull out the sock.

As soon as her hand reached into his mouth, he bit down on it, and Lucinda screamed.

Maybe he'd been asking himself the same questions I had and come up with the same answers. So maybe he'd decided he had nothing to lose.

She kicked out at him—*"Motherfucker!"*—trying to get her hand out of his mouth, but Sam was holding on like an attack dog, the kind trained to take down robbers and not let go, even if you shoot them dead. Lucinda, screaming and punching at Sam's head with her free hand, but Sam *still* not letting go, holding on for dear life.

I tried to get over there, but I had to worm my way to them, because my hands were tied behind my back. I had to move in sections. I was trying to help Sam. Because something bad was going to happen now. I could see that.

For one thing, Lucinda had managed to get her hand out of his mouth. Finally. For another, she was raising the gun in her left hand and beginning to bring it down on Sam's head. Sam's mouth was bloody, her blood and his seemingly mixed together, as Lucinda brought the gun down on his face again. Then again and again.

"Please," Sam said, "please, I'm a *father.* . . . I have *three children,*" as the gun smashed into his cheekbone. As it smashed into his nose. Hoping, I guess, that this might give her pause, might make her stop hitting him. But it only seemed to make her madder. Sam kept pleading, "Three children . . . please . . . a *father,*" but Lucinda kept hitting him. Harder and harder—I could hear the sound of metal hitting bone. As if he were saying, *Hit me,* and she was just going ahead and obliging him.

I'd managed to get eight inches, ten inches, a foot closer to them, when I finally realized it didn't matter.

Not now.

Sam was dead.

Vasquez and Dexter walked back into the room.

Dexter was carrying two garbage bags—the large, industrial-strength kind, big enough for an entire lawn of leaves. Or a couple of bodies.

Maybe that's why when they saw Sam was dead, when Vasquez kicked him softly with his shoe and actually confirmed this, no one seemed particularly upset about it.

"He bit me," was all Lucinda said, and Vasquez nodded.

Then Vasquez picked up a pillow and said to me: "Time to go to sleep."

Vasquez has a gun, but he can't take the chance of someone hearing it.

They were going to suffocate me.

I'd been doing something while Lucinda killed Sam. While she'd gotten up and gone into the bathroom to wash the blood off her hands. While Sam lay there without breathing. I'd remembered something. Dexter had come in and picked up my gun, and then he'd given the gun to Lucinda when they went out.

Which still left one other gun.

Vasquez's gun. Where was it?

Under the bed. Where it had come to rest when I'd knocked it out of Vasquez's hand.

Maybe five feet away from me. That's all.

They were going to suffocate me.

I'd begun to inch my way over to it.

Something else. I'd begun to test the quality of the knot that Dexter had tied with my belt. It wasn't meant to be used as a rope; it wasn't supple enough to make a good knot. There was some give there.

They were going to suffocate me.

By the time Vasquez and Dexter reentered the room, I'd opened a tiny hole in the knot. I'd moved myself to within two feet of Vasquez's gun.

Close enough to reach it. If I could get my hands out in time.

"Bedtime," Vasquez said.

Your life does not flash in front of your eyes.

I would like to tell you that now.

That's what they say happens to you when you face your own death, but it's not true. Not for me—my entire life did not play itself out before my eyes. Just one small part of it.

When I was seven years old and at the beach.

I'd been playing in the surf and not paying attention, and a rogue wave had come along and knocked me under. By the time they pulled me from the water, I was purple, cyanotic, and—if not for the ministrations of a first-year lifeguard—*dead*. From that day on, I was forever scared of drowning. From that day on, when I had dreams about dying, it was always that way. With no air in my lungs.

That's the part of my life I saw now.

Before Vasquez placed the white pillow down over my mouth, I managed to gulp in one deep breath.

There was a game we used to play as a kid. It was called No Breathing. A game I played with nearly maniacal devotion after that incident at the beach—as if I knew it just might save me one day.

I used to be able to do three minutes. Maybe even four.

Go.

The pillow smelled of sweat and dust. I began to work my hands back and forth against the knot in the belt.

I pushed outward with both wrists. Then relaxed. Then pushed. Then relaxed.

It was like a painful isometric. Vasquez had all his weight pressing down on me. It was hard to move my hands.

I kept my wrists pushing, though. Even though the belt was cutting into my skin like a dull blade.

It was slow going. I heard someone pacing a few feet from me. The bed squeaked. Lucinda cleared her throat. Someone turned on the radio.

My hands were going nowhere. I kept pushing and pushing, but it was like pushing against a locked door. Like running in quicksand. I was pushing, but nothing was giving. My chest was starting to ache. My arm sockets felt as if they were being pulled apart. They were screaming at me.

No, they screeched. *Not on your life. Not possible. Forget it.*

Stop!

My lungs were on fire now. I couldn't feel my hands.

Then the belt began to give.

Just a little.

Just loose enough to get a little piece of my hand through.

I pushed with all my strength. Then again and again.

My wrists were bleeding. I kept pushing.

I got my hands halfway through. Both hands were sweating. The sweat and blood was helping them slide through the belt. That was good, that was *wonderful.* I kept pushing.

My hands were three-quarters out. I needed to push just a little bit more, just a little bit. It was my knuckles, though.

They were a problem. *Please.*

I gave one last push—one last push for everything. For everything I needed to make it back to. For Anna. For Deanna. Now.

I pushed and pushed and pushed . . .

One hand came free.

I'm dying.

My left hand, the arm closest to the bed.

It's black. I can't see. I'm dying.

I heard Vasquez say, "Huh."

I heard Dexter say, "Watch out."

I frantically felt for the gun under the box spring. My lungs were bursting. I slid my hands this way and that way under the bed. Where was it?

I felt the gun. I got my fingers around it.

What's this? What's happening?

I brought it out from under the bed.

And at that very moment, at that very instant in time when I might've turned the tide, I died.

ATTICA

Fat Tommy was right.

They'd sent me notification in the mail.

"Dear Mr. Widdoes: This is to inform you that State budget constraints will no longer allow for an adult education program in State prisons. Classes will end on the first of next month. A formal notice of termination will follow."

This meant I had two classes left.

Just two.

The COs kept their distance from me now, as if I had a communicable disease. Was it possible state layoffs were contagious? When I slipped into the COs lounge for coffee, they gave me a wide berth—wider even than before, when it was simply my job that had rubbed them the wrong way. Now it was my lack of one.

I sipped my coffee alone, over in the corner of the room known as the museum.

The *museum* had been so dubbed by a long-ago correction officer whose name no one remembered. It was a loosely arranged collection of prison-confiscated weapons. *Bangers, shanks, gats,* and *burners*—what the cons call knives. Forged from bedsprings, hollowed-out pens, smuggled-in screw-drivers—whatever the prisoners can get their hands on. But there were also crude guns—ingenious things put together with odds and ends from the machine shop, capable of putting a reasonable facsimile of a bullet into a man at close range.

It was constantly being added to. After each clear-out there'd be one or two more donations.

I stared at these crude instruments of death until the silence at my presence there grew intolerable, or until it was time for class.

Whichever came first.

The writer had kept it up with monotonous and painful reg-ularity.

Every class I found another installment sitting there on my desk.

My own story slowly being fed back to me, chapter by painful chapter. It was a torturously slow indictment of Charles Schine. I was convinced that torture was *exactly* what the writer had in mind.

There were other things, too. Another note appeared at the end of chapter 20.

"Time we got together, don't you think?"

Written in brown ink, except it wasn't brown ink. It was written in blood. It was meant to scare me.

And I thought, *Yes, it is time we got together.* Even if I felt my palms grow sweaty and my collar tighten like a noose.

The writer wasn't in my classroom. I knew that.

The delivery boy was.

A few classes after I received the last note, I dismissed the class and someone stayed behind.

When I looked up, he was sitting there and smiling at me.

Malik El Mahid. His Muslim name.

Twenty-five or so. Black, squat, and tattooed.

"Yes?" I said, even though I knew what was coming now.

"Like the story so far?" he said, still smiling. Repeating the first words the writer had scrawled to me.

"You," I said. "You've been leaving it for me."

"Thas right, dawg."

"Who?"

"Who *what?*"

"Who's giving the chapters to you?"

"You sayin' I ain't the writer?"

"Yes. I'm saying you didn't write it."

"Fuckin' right. I didn't read none of it either."

"Who?"

"You know who, dawg."

Yes.

"He wants to see you now, 'kay?"

He wants to see you now.

"All right," I said as calmly as I could.

But as I gathered the papers on my desk, I noticed my hand was trembling. The papers were clearly fluttering right there in full view of Malik, and even though I willed my hand to stop shaking, I couldn't get it to listen.

"Next week," Malik said. "All right?"

I said yes. Next week was fine.

But I have to get back to the story now.

I have to explain what happened.

DERAILED FORTY-TWO

When I brought the gun out from under the bed, the world collapsed. It ended.

There was a flash of light, a blast of heat, and then the earth imploded and went black.

Then I woke up.

I opened my eyes and thought: *I'm dead.*

Vasquez has killed me. I am dead. I am in heaven.

Only I couldn't have been in heaven.

Because I was in hell.

Pick up Dante's *Inferno* and go right to the sixth circle. The black sulfurous fumes. The inferno of boiling oil. The screams of agony. I opened my eyes and couldn't see. It was still morning, but it was night.

This much was clear. The eighth floor of the Fairfax Hotel had somehow become the basement. The seventh floor down had become a grave.

The room itself was half standing. It was spring, but it was snowing (plaster powder, I discovered when I tasted it on my tongue). An entire air-conditioning unit was lying on top of my left leg.

This is what I know now, but not then. What I pieced together from newspapers and TV and my own limited observations.

That women's health center next door to the Fairfax Hotel provided federally subsidized abortions, which meant that to certain people out there it wasn't a women's health center as much as an *abortion* center.

That man in the University of Oklahoma jacket whom I met in the elevator the day I checked in and then later saw in the lobby, complaining about having no Bibles in his room? He was one of those people out there. A muscular Christian, a devout right-to-lifer, but one with an aggrieved sense of injustice and a fascination with explosives.

It turned out he wasn't spending his time playing three-card monte and buying fake Rolexes on the street. He was spending his time up in his room, painstakingly putting together a bomb made out of fertilizer and acetates. When it was done, he strapped it carefully to his body.

He took the elevator down to the lobby of the Fairfax Hotel with the intention of walking into the women's health center next door and blowing it and himself up.

Let me explain the volatility of this kind of bomb. According to later reports in the papers, it is not your most stable kind of explosive. Not like dynamite, for instance, or plastic explosives. It's extremely volatile, very transmutable.

He never made it out of the elevator. Something happened. The elevator stopped short. Or he was jostled. Or he pressed the detonator by mistake. Something.

The bomb exploded at the very epicenter of the building. If you were trying to take down the Fairfax Hotel and not the abortion center next door, and you were smart about blast ratios and shock indexes and structural weaknesses, this is where you would do it.

In the elevator directly between floors five and six.

And the Fairfax Hotel was a structural weakness waiting to be put out of its misery.

Its bones were cracked and creaky and brittle. Peeling asbestos made it a model firetrap. It had several leaks in its gas heating system, or so it was later determined. In short, it was a disaster waiting to happen.

Steel beams. Sections of roof. Plaster wall. Plate glass. People. All hurtling up in the air and then, true to Newtonian physics, *down*. On top of what was left of the Fairfax Hotel. Flattening it like a crushed wedding cake.

One hundred and forty-three people died that morning in the Fairfax Hotel and four surrounding buildings.

One hundred and forty-three and, eventually, one more.

I heard a voice.

"Anyone alive down there? Anyone?"

"Yes," I said. *If I hear myself,* I thought, *then maybe I'm alive.*

"Yes," I said, and heard it.

Arms grasped my arms. Lifted me out of the rubble and carnage and blackness, and I was suddenly alive and breathing.

This is what I know now, but not then.

Two rooms had remained intact—or mostly intact. Who knows why? When someone decides to strap a bomb to his body and obliterate himself, rhyme and reason take a holiday. Some people that morning went to the left and survived. Some people went right and didn't. One person lay this close to death on a hotel floor and made it out alive.

And pretty much unscathed.

They brought me out of the rubble and laid me down on a stretcher at the side of the street, and they went in and brought out anyone else they could find. Including Vasquez and Lucinda and Dexter and Sam. Of the four, three of them were dead and the other one almost. Dexter and Sam and Lucinda had blankets pulled up over their faces. Vasquez was unconscious and bloody and barely breathing.

They laid him next to me on the sidewalk, and a fireman took his pulse and shook his head. When someone with a red cross on his arm came running over, the fireman said, "Take care of the old woman over there," and pointed at a woman whose clothes were smoldering.

"He's not going to make it."

Eventually I decided to get up and leave. To just walk away.

Even though I must have been suffering from some sort of shock, I felt terrifyingly lucid.

Visibility was almost zero. But I could see Lucinda's body not five feet from me. I could touch Vasquez. Firemen and policemen were running back and forth in a choking maelstrom of black smoke.

I got up. I began walking. I vanished in that maelstrom.

I walked quite a while. I was wondering if Deanna had been right all along, that things happened for a reason. I wasn't sure now. People stared at me as if I'd just landed from another planet. But no one stopped me—no one asked me if I was hurt or needed a doctor or an ambulance. Maybe they were immune to this kind of thing now. I walked straight down Broadway. I thought my hair was singed—when I ran my hands through it, it crackled like static. I ended up hailing a taxicab somewhere near Central Park.

I went back to my apartment in Forest Hills. The taxi driver had the radio on. Someone was talking about the explosion. Possibly a gas leak, a woman was saying—she was interviewing a fire captain. It would be a while before they'd find evidence to the contrary. The taxi driver asked me if I was all right.

"Yes," I said. "Couldn't be better."

When we got to Forest Hills, the street I lived on was deserted. Maybe everyone was glued to the news. No one saw me enter the building, go into my apartment, fall into a stupor.

I slept an entire day.

When I woke the next morning, I went into the bathroom and didn't recognize myself. I was in blackface—I belonged in a minstrel show.

I turned on the news. Three talking heads were debating figures. What figures, exactly? It took me a while to figure it out. The number of dead—that's what they were talking about. Somewhere around 100 was the consensus. On another channel they claimed it was 96, 150 on another. The hotel dead and the peripheral casualties in the four surrounding buildings. But who knew how many died, really? That's what the talking heads said. The bodies were burned up, crushed, incinerated. It was impossible to tell, one man said, they might never know. If someone who was in the hotel showed up, they were alive—he said. If they didn't they were dead. People had already begun scouring hospitals and Red Cross shelters, putting up pictures on walls and fences and street lamps—a hollow-eyed and desperate army of bereaved.

I watched for an entire day without moving.

I didn't call anyone—I didn't speak to anyone. I was more or less paralyzed. All that horror. I couldn't move—I couldn't eat. I couldn't speak.

The illusion of invulnerability I used to carry around like a birthright—the one Vasquez and Lucinda had stripped me of—had now been taken from 143 others. No one was safe anymore. No one.

The rubble from the explosion was taken by truck to the city dump. To the dump in Staten Island. To the place you can get to by following the stench straight down Western Avenue.

To make room for the tons of debris, they first had to move

other tons of debris. Move those piles of debris from one place to another. And amid the pile of twisted steel, crushed cardboard, tin cans, broken bones, rotten food, cracked brick, and human waste—they found a wasted human.

They finally found Winston.

This was all the police had been waiting for. A body. They had me on tape telling Winston what I wanted him to do, but they didn't have *Winston*.

Now they did.

I discovered this when I finally called Deanna three days after I stumbled away from the blown-up buildings. From what looked like downtown Beirut. She was happy to hear from me.

"Thank God, Charles," she said. "I thought you were *dead.*"

DERAILED FORTY-THREE

That's when it first occurred to me.

When Deanna got on the phone and said, *I thought you were dead.*

Or maybe it wasn't exactly then. Maybe it was later, after I'd told Deanna what I'd been up to—what had happened to me in the Fairfax Hotel—and she gasped and went silent and then told me the police had come to the house with a warrant for my arrest. Because they'd found Winston's body in the Staten Island dump.

Or it might've been later that day, when a somber and pale-looking city spokeswoman read a list of the dead on a news program. The confirmed dead and the *presumed* dead—otherwise known as the still missing.

My name was on it.

It was kind of surreal, listening to myself be declared officially missing. It was like attending my own funeral—my very own memorial service. The city spokeswoman said this list was carefully compiled from the hotel's computer hard drive, recovered in the rubble—people who were known to have been

registered guests at the time of the explosion. And from be-
longings found here and there, scattered around the blast site
and stored in the hotel safe. Briefcases, PalmPilots, engraved
watches, and jewelry. My watch, for example, was missing. "To
Charles Schine with all my love," it said on the back. The
spokeswoman explained they'd matched this list to the people
who'd made it to emergency rooms and hospital beds.

I was picking up the phone to call someone—anyone—and
explain that I wasn't dead after all, that I was still here. I was
getting dressed at the same time, because maybe a phone call
wouldn't be enough, it was possible I would have to show up
and produce myself in the flesh. I was rummaging through my
sock drawer, and I came across Winston's wallet.

Which is when the idea *really* occurred to me.

When it changed from the ridiculous to the possible. From a
wishful notion to an actual plan. I'd buried Winston's wallet in
my sock drawer and forgotten about it. But I remembered
something Winston told me now.

The easiest thing to get—new identities, he'd said.

His wallet, for instance, had four of them. Driver's licenses.

A Jonathan Thomas. A Brian McDermott. A Steven Aimett.

And a Lawrence Widdoes. The only one of the four who
looked even remotely like me—younger, of course, but the
same basic coloring.

I thought you were dead, Deanna said.

So did a few other people.

I'd checked into the Fairfax Hotel, but I'd never checked out.
Or maybe I had, but only in the vernacular sense of the term.
As in, *Did you hear what happened to Charley? He, well, checked
out. He* died.

Which reminded me of one other popular saying.

I'd be better off dead. Yes, we've all heard that one, too. An expression we use in times of crisis, when things are absolutely
hopeless and there seems to be no way out.

Unless there is. Unless you think that you're good and trapped, but there is a way out after all.

Being dead.

Maybe that was the way out.

If I showed up, I'd be alive.

But what if I *didn't?*

DERAILED FORTY-FOUR

I was standing on the corner of Crescent and Thirtieth Avenue.

In front of a place called the Crystal Night Club. It didn't look like a nightclub. It was just an ex-VFW lodge—the pale imprint of "VFW Lodge 54" still lingered on the brick facing. But it was past midnight, and I could hear music inside. A Latin-looking man was throwing up on the sidewalk.

When I walked in, I was immediately aware that I wasn't exactly in my element.

Remember that scene from *Star Wars* where the hero strolls into that alien bar? I felt like that. Only these aliens were of the terrestrial variety—the kind you see on the evening news when the INS conducts its periodic roundups on the border. The kind you see on any lawn crew on Long Island. If I hopped a plane to Santo Domingo and stepped off onto the runway and into the nearest bar, it might look like this.

I was pretty sure I was the only white American in the place. Possibly the only legal American, too.

Salsa music was blaring from two enormous speakers. Spanish was flowing freely around the room.

Everyone seemed coupled up, but they were oddly paired. The women were dressed up—short flashy skirts and high heels. The men wore dirty jeans and T-shirts. It took me a while to understand what was going on.

The women were hostesses. That's the way one of them introduced herself—first in Spanish, *huéspeda*. Then in English, when I looked perplexed and she got a good look at me and realized I wasn't her usual clientele.

For a moment she hesitated, as if she expected me to realize my mistake and leave. But when I stood there and waited politely for her to continue, she did.

"I'm Rosa," she said. "Want a hostess?"

"Yes," I said. "Fine."

Return for a minute to that moment I was taken out of the hole in the ground that had once been the Fairfax Hotel.

I was laid on the sidewalk as they waited for the ambulances and doctors to arrive. They came out with other bodies; they placed a dying Vasquez next to me on the ground.

The fireman who laid him there was covered in soot. His eyes were like white ash on burning charcoal. He asked me if I was okay.

I said yes. I could hear the faint wail of a rushing ambulance. I knew I had just a few minutes.

When the fireman went back in for more bodies, I leaned over Vasquez as if I were comforting him. Seeing if he was all right. I put my hands into his pockets. First the front pockets, then the back.

In his front pockets was some change. A vial with white powder in it. Some matches.

His back pocket was bulging with his wallet. I quickly removed it and put it in my pocket.

I got up and left.

In the taxi to Forest Hills I rifled through it, returning the favor Vasquez has done for me in the Fairfax Hotel.

In this wallet: a phony police badge; a suspicious-looking driver's license; more white powder wrapped in aluminum foil; two hundred dollars; a business card for something called the Crystal Night Club. Proprietor listed as Raul Vasquez.

On the back was some Spanish writing. *Veinte-y-dos . . . derecho, treinta-y-siete izquierdo, doce . . . derecho.*

The next morning, the morning I woke in blackface, I looked it up on-line. Google.com—Spanish Dictionary.

Once I translated the first word, I knew they were numbers.

Twenty-two right.

Thirty-seven left.

Twelve right.

I was pretty sure it wasn't a football play.

This is the way it worked in the Crystal Night Club.

You ordered overpriced drinks, and Rosa talked to you.

That's what the other men were doing.

Rosa explained it to me, as something to talk about.

"You ain't no wetback," she said. "That's what we get in here. Usually," she added, not wanting to offend me.

"Where do you come from?" I asked her.

"America," she said, *"where do you think?"*

"No. I meant where do you live?"

"The Bronx," she said. "All of us do. We get bused in."

"Oh."

"These guys"—she pointed around the room with evident disdain—"they live on crews. You know . . . like six to a room."

"And they come here to drink."

"Right," she said with a little smile, as if I'd said something funny, "to drink. Want another?" she asked me, reminding me that that's exactly what I was doing. Drinking.

I'd barely touched my ten-dollar tequila sunrise, but I said sure.

"They're lonely," she added after making a hand signal to the man behind the bar. He had a thick neck festooned with tattooed crosses. "They come here to like . . . you know, bullshit. They got no one to talk to. No one *female*," she said. "They like, fall in love with us, you know. They blow all their *dinero*." And she laughed and rubbed her fingers together.

"Yeah," I said. "I understand."

"Oh yeah . . . you understand. So what's your story?"

"Nothing," I said. "I don't have one. I just wandered in."

"Yeah, well, that's cool."

Rosa was thick hipped and fleshy—most of the hostesses were. I was picturing Lucinda. I was wondering if she'd worked here, too; I took a gamble.

"Actually," I said, and Rosa leaned closer, "I came in once before. I think."

"You *think?*"

"I was drunk," I said. "I think it was the same place. Not sure."

"Okay," she said.

"There was this girl here." I described Lucinda in detail, all the detail someone who'd spent countless hours staring at a woman would know. I left out things like her sexy pout and liquid eyes.

"Oh," Rosa said. "You're talking about *Didi*." But she said it in a way that made me think she hadn't exactly liked Didi.

"Didi? Yeah . . . I think that was her name. Sure."

"She was a fucking *puta* . . . a player, you know. . . ."

"No."

"Oh yeah. She comes in and sees what's what in like two minutes, right? Sticking her tits out . . . her skinny little ass . . . parading it for the boss. I could see what she was doing. I'm

down like James Brown on this bitch, right? She's here like two
days, two fucking days, and she's doing him."

The boss. Raul Vasquez.

"Where is the boss?" I said.

Rosa shrugged. "Don't know. He hasn't been around. Why?"

"No reason." And I thought: *They don't know.* I had his wallet, and he wasn't registered at the hotel. They had no name
and no one to notify. No next of kin to break the news to.

"So, you married?" she asked me.

"No."

I was trying to put it all together. I was trying to picture how
it started. These poor wetbacks came into the Crystal Night
Club to blow all their cash on hostesses who basically looked
down on them. Lucinda was one of those hostesses. That faint
accent I'd asked her about on the train—Spanish? But Lucinda
hadn't remained a hostess for long. She'd flashed her *skinny ass*
instead and hooked up with Vasquez. You could see why he'd
want to. She didn't look like the rest of them here. She looked
like someone who spent her day buying low and selling high in
some office tower downtown. The kind of woman other white-
collar commuters would drool over behind their morning
papers.

Was it his idea, I wondered, or hers? Who got the idea—who
looked around the depressing environs of the Crystal Night
Club and saw the possibilities?

"You ain't drinking," Rosa said. "The rule is, if you don't
drink, I gotta talk to somebody else, okay?"

"I'll order another," I said, and Rosa smiled.

Maybe it was her. Didi. Maybe she saw how ridiculously easy
it was to make these day laborers far from home fall in love
with her and knew it would be even easier with guys like me.
Married guys who weren't far from home, but maybe were
wishing they were. Guys who wanted someone to talk to just
as much as these guys. Guys with *real* cash.

When the bartender brought over another tequila sunrise, I opened my wallet to pay.

Rosa said: "Widdoes? What kind of name is that?" She was looking at a piece of my new driver's license. Yes, my first night as a new man. Charles Schine was dead.

"Just a name," I said.

"It's depressing," she said. "Like *widows,* you know. . . ."

"Yes, well, it's spelled differently."

"That's true," she said seriously.

"Where's the bathroom?" I asked her.

"Over there—" She pointed to a back hall. "Most of them use the sidewalk," she said, and snorted. "You should smell it at four in the morning. They don't know no better."

"Well, I'll use the bathroom," I said.

"Sure. Go ahead."

When I got up from the table, I saw the thick-necked man behind the bar staring at me. I walked to the back of the room, passing Colombian, Mexican, Dominican, and Peruvian men engrossed in conversation with their respective hostesses. The conversations were kind of one-sided, though, the men leaning over the tables and talking in slurred Spanish. I thought that my conversations with Didi had been pretty much like that, too.

One of the bathrooms said "hombres" on the door.

I walked in that one. There was a man kneeling over the toilet. I could smell his vomit.

I walked into a stall that had graffiti over every inch of it. Mostly in Spanish, but some English, too.

"I have an ten-inch dick," someone had written.

I sat on the toilet and took a deep breath. I'd seen a third door here in the back hallway. His office?

I waited till the other man left, then I got up and walked back into the hallway.

There was no one there. I walked to the third door.

It wasn't locked. When I opened it, its rusty hinges shrieked at me and I stopped and waited, my heart somewhere in my throat.

Nothing. The salsa music was pounding away out there.

I slipped inside and closed the door.

The room was dark. I felt for the light switch and found it just behind the door.

Yes, it was his office. Had to be. It wasn't *much* of an office, but there was a desk, a swivel chair, a beat-up couch, a file cabinet.

I was thinking about the man behind the bar. How he'd stared at me when I walked to the back hallway. The tendons on his neck had looked like thick strands of rope.

I scanned the walls—they were made of fake wood. Nothing there. No wall safe, for instance. No picture that could be hiding a wall safe. Those numbers on the back of his card—they had to be the combination to a safe. If not here, somewhere. He was dead, and I needed that money back. I had to chance it.

There was a ripped calendar hanging on the wall, but when I pushed it to one side there was nothing behind it.

I heard footsteps outside the door. I held my breath.

They kept going; I heard the bathroom door open and shut.

I tried the file cabinet—it was locked. The desk drawer was open. In the back of the drawer was a sheaf of yellowed newspaper. It was a bunch of clippings. The first was an old cover of *Newsday*. COMMUTER JUMPS OFF LIRR was the headline. There was a picture of a body wrapped in a white sheet, lying at the side of the railroad tracks in Lynbrook, Long Island. A somber-looking policeman was standing guard over it.

The actual article was there, too.

"A Rockville Center man apparently committed suicide last night by jumping off a Long Island Rail Road train," the article began. It went on to say that he was married with three children, that he was a corporate lawyer, that he'd left no suicide note. He'd been experiencing some unnamed personal problems, a family spokesperson said. Other than that, there was no explanation. Witnesses on the train said the man—his name was John Pierson—was walking to the back of the train with other commuters in order to find a seat when he simply, and without warning, jumped.

I might've stopped reading right there, except one of the witnesses' names caught my eye. The last person to see him alive—the one who actually saw him jump.

Raul. No last name given. It listed his occupation as bar owner.

The door opened.

The thick-necked man was standing there staring at me.

I was standing behind the desk with the newspaper clippings in my hand. The desk drawer was open.

"Astoria General," he said softly.

"What?"

"The nearest hospital. So you know what to tell the ambulance driver."

"I'm sorry . . . I was looking for the bathroom . . ."

"I'm going to have to fuck you up bad," he said, still in that soft voice. "Two, three weeks in the hospital before you get out, okay?"

"Look, really, I was just . . ."

He closed the door behind him. He locked it.

He began to walk toward me.

I stepped back, but there was only wall behind me.

He stopped and took something out of his pocket. A roll of coins that he wrapped his right fist around.

He walked around the desk; he was close enough to smell.

Then I remembered what I had in my pocket. I pulled it out and flipped it open.

He stopped.

"Detective, NYPD," I said. Vasquez's phony police badge. I'd stuffed it into my pocket and almost, but not quite, forgotten about it.

"We have reports of illicit drug activity," I said, wondering if that was how policemen actually spoke. I tried to remember the way Detective Palumbo had spoken to me that day in the office.

"There's no drugs here," the man said. "You got a warrant?"

I didn't, of course, have a warrant.

"You just *threatened* me. Do I need a warrant to *arrest* you?"

"There's no drugs here," the man said. "I'm going to call our lawyer, okay?"

"Go ahead," I said. "I'm done."

And I walked out right past him.

I counted in my head. *One, two, three, four* . . . wondering how many seconds it would take me to get out of the bar and onto the street. And how many seconds it might take him to reconsider letting me walk out without checking my badge again or asking me to wait for his lawyer to arrive. I was up to ten when I passed Rosa, who said, "Hey, where you goin'?" . . . fifteen when I walked through the door without answering her.

DERAILED FORTY-FIVE

I came back to Merrick later that same night.

When no one could see me. When I could scurry up the driveway and sneak in the back door. Curry whimpered and mewled and licked my hand.

Deanna rushed into my arms and we held each other until my arms went numb.

"Do you know you've been listed as missing?" Deanna said.

"Yes, I know. You didn't . . . ?"

"No. I told the detective who came here that we were separated, that I hadn't heard from you, that I didn't know where you were. I thought I should probably keep to that story until you told me differently."

"Good." I sighed. "Look, I need to talk to you about something."

"Wait a minute," she said. "They found something of yours, Charles."

"My watch?" I said.

"No." She went into the den and came back with it in her arms.

"They told me to come down and pick it up today. It was in the hotel safe."

It was big, black, and bulging.

My briefcase.

The one I'd handed to Vasquez in Spanish Harlem with one hundred thousand dollars of Anna's money in it.

What was it doing here?

"They found it in the safe. It had your name on it."

My name, in embossed gold, as plain as day, even though the briefcase was covered in fine white powder. *Charles Barnett Schine.*

"It's really heavy," Deanna said. "What do you have in there?"

I went to open it, to show her what I had in there, but it was locked. It *was* heavy—heavier than I remembered.

And I thought: *Yes, of course. If you had a lot of money and you wanted to put it somewhere other than a bank, because you weren't exactly bank material and you maybe didn't trust banks anyway, maybe you would pick a hotel safe in the care of your friend and partner, Dexter.*

"They didn't want to break into it," Deanna said. "Not unless it went unclaimed."

I'd never used the lock before, of course. I seemed to remember that you had to program it yourself, put your own three-digit code into it. I'd never bothered to.

I started to walk to the kitchen drawer where we kept the knives I would use to force it open, when I remembered something.

I reached into my pocket and pulled out Vasquez's business card. I turned it over.

Twenty-two right.

Thirty-seven left.

Twelve right.

I moved the tiny cylinders. It clicked open.

In the briefcase was the $110,000 of Anna's money. And hundreds of thousands more.

Things happened for a reason, Deanna always believed. And now, finally, I agreed with her.

We talked.

And talked.

Straight through the night.

I told Deanna what was on my mind.

At first she was incredulous; she made me repeat it because she didn't think she'd heard it right.

"You're not serious, Charles?"

"As far as anyone knows, Deanna, I'm dead, understand? I think I should stay that way."

I told her everything I hadn't before. The T&D Music House. The investigation they were conducting at my company. The charges that would no doubt soon be filed.

Deanna still resisted. She put up coffee; we huddled in the basement so we wouldn't wake Anna.

We imagined the future. But we imagined it two ways.

We imagined me walking down to the police station in the morning and giving myself up. We imagined it first that way. Giving myself up to the police and getting a lawyer and going to trial. And possibly losing. Conspiracy to commit murder, with exhibit A being an audiotape where a jury of my peers would hear me asking Winston to more or less go kill someone for me. A tough thing to explain your way out of. So I might end up looking at fifteen years, possibly ten with time off for good behavior, even with that *separate* indictment hanging over my head for embezzlement.

Ten or fifteen years. Not the longest time in the world. Maybe even doable time. Maybe. Only there was another sentence to consider here.

Anna had been handed a sentence, too. An uncertain sentence, true, a reprieve from the governor always a possibility. But not likely. Probably, more than possibly, a death sentence. Which meant that when I'd finished serving my ten or fifteen years, when I came out to find my family waiting for me outside the walls of Attica—it would be diminished by one. It would be just the two of us. And maybe sooner rather than later. Because there would be other nights where Anna would be found unconscious and shaking; other injections given with a trembling hand to my comatose daughter. Keeping Anna alive was a two-person job—it had always been a two-person job.

And since we were both sitting there and imagining this kind of future, I imagined all of it. Getting the news in prison, by letter, maybe: "We regret to inform you that your daughter, Anna, passed away yesterday." Begging for permission to attend her funeral. Being turned down. Having to see Deanna's ravaged face through the plastic partition the next time she came to visit me.

We imagined that future first.

Then we imagined another. A different kind of future.

A future someplace else. With other names. A future that would include both of us there to share in it.

With $450,000 to support it. To support Anna.

That's how much was in the briefcase. One hundred and ten thousand dollars of Anna's Fund and $340,000 from the other men they'd taken to the cleaners.

Which was another reason to consider this second future. That briefcase. Someone might come looking for it.

There were times that night it seemed like we were talking about someone else. That it couldn't be *our* family we were discussing, that it had to be someone else's. A more or less ordinary middle-class family suddenly becoming a *different* ordinary middle-class family. Was that possible? Sometimes things like that happened, didn't they? Entire families whisked off into witness protection programs, new identities, new lives. This was different, of course.

We weren't going to be hidden by the government. We were going to be *hiding* from the government. From the New York City Police Department.

Hiding from everyone from now on.

In the end, it came down to a simple question. It came down to Anna. What was her best chance? What promised a longer future for her? With me or without me? It was possible I could beat the charges. After all, even with adultery thrown into the mix, I might have sympathy on my side—and a clever lawyer, too. I *might* beat the charges, but it was only fifty-fifty at best.

Could we take the chance? Could we roll the dice?

The reason to do it was Anna.

The reason not to do it was Anna.

I would have to disappear first—tonight. And Deanna? She might have to wait a long time to join me. Six months, maybe even a year. And all during that time, Anna couldn't know—we both realized that. She might say something, give me away. For an entire year or so, Anna would have to believe that her father was dead.

We went round and round, back and forth.

Maybe it was simple fatigue that finally beat us down. We kept hammering away at the rational and logical until they both finally switched sides.

By five in the morning, the most logical, the most reasonable thing in the world seemed to be to disappear off the face of the earth.

I never turned myself in.

I died.

DERAILED FORTY-SIX

I left that night.

But before I walked out, before I held Deanna for what seemed like twenty minutes with neither of us saying a word, I tiptoed upstairs and looked in on my daughter.

She was fast asleep, with one arm thrown over her face as if she didn't wish to see something. Bad dream, maybe. I whispered good-bye to her.

I didn't have a destination.

My destination was anywhere far from there.

I took a Greyhound bus at 6:00 in the morning that was headed to Chicago. It seemed as good a place as any.

I sat next to a thin and restless prelaw student who was on his way back to Northwestern.

"Mike," he said to me, and put his hand out.

"Lawrence," I said. "You can call me Larry." It was the first time I'd really used my new name—that I'd said it out loud. It felt odd, like seeing myself with a beard. I would have to get used to it.

Mike was a sports junkie; he wanted to be a players agent when he graduated, he told me. I was going to tell him that maybe I could help him, that I *knew* one or two agents, having used athletes in commercials for years, but I stopped myself. From now on, I wasn't in advertising. From now on, I'd *never* been in advertising. Which got me thinking about what I did do if someone asked. And what I would do whenever I got to where I was going.

Except for a teaching degree I'd gotten from Queens College—not because I particularly wanted to be a teacher, but because I didn't know what else I was going to do back then—advertising had been it. How was I going to make a living now?

I fell asleep a few times on the way to Chicago. And dreamed. About Winston. He was sitting with me in my old office, and we were talking about the Yankees' chances in the coming season. Then Winston heard a dog barking—he got up and left. When I woke, Mike was looking at me oddly, and I wondered if I'd talked in my sleep. But Mike just smiled and offered me half of his tunafish sandwich.

When we got to Chicago, I shook hands with him and wished him luck.

"You too," he said, and I thought that I would probably need it.

I found an apartment over by the lake.

I'd brought enough money to tide me over for as long as it might take. More than enough, anyway, for one month's security and one month's rent.

The neighborhood was largely Ukrainian.

Neighbors sat on brown stoops when the weather was nice. Kids rode bicycles in the street and played stickball. One month after I moved in, they held a block party. A bald, sturdy-looking Ukrainian man knocked on my door and asked me if I wanted to chip in.

I gave him twenty dollars, and he seemed very happy. He made me promise to come down and join them later.

I wasn't intending to; I was going to stay put up in my apartment and read the *Chicago Sun-Times*. The torrent of articles about the Fairfax bombing had slowly lessened to one or two a week. But there was an updated death list in today's issue. Even though I was expecting to see it there, even though I was *looking* for it, the sight of my own name in stark black and white caused me to turn pale and nearly drop my coffee. My name had migrated from the missing to the dead. It was official now.

And someone else's name had finally shown up on the list of victims as well. *Raul Vasquez*—they'd finally ID'ed him.

I got up and walked to the window. I could hear music and laughter drifting in from the street below. I suddenly realized how lonely I was.

I went downstairs.

A local band was playing Ukrainian folk songs—at least I assumed they were, since everyone seemed to know the words and at least twenty people were in the middle of the street dancing to them. Portable grills were set up on the sidewalk. A young woman offered me a kind of sausage wrapped in sourdough, and I thanked her and dug in.

Then a policeman came walking toward me.

"Hey you," he said.

I froze. Every fiber in my body told me to run, to throw down the sandwich and take off.

"Hey." The policeman held something out to me.

A beer.

He was off duty and lived in the neighborhood. He was just being friendly.

I let the air go out of my body; for the first time since I'd

come to Chicago, I relaxed. I stayed down there till midnight.
I drank beer and ate sausages and clapped to the music.

The second hardest part of all this was not seeing them.
Deanna and Anna.

The *hardest* part was knowing what Anna was going
through.

Once a week, I called Deanna's cell. From a public pay
phone, just to be on the safe side.

Once a week, I asked Deanna how Anna was dealing with it,
and Deanna would sigh and tell me.

"It's so *hard* not telling her, Charles. The other day . . ." But
she didn't finish.

She didn't have to.

I could picture Anna clearly. I spent hours and hours up in
that apartment doing nothing else. I tried not to, but it was like
trying to keep those pictures of Winston out of my head.

"Maybe we can—" I started to say, but Deanna interrupted
me.

"No, Charles, not yet."

"They want me to hold a memorial service for you," she told
me a few weeks later.

"Aunt Rose and Joe and Linda. . . . I told them you were
missing. That until they officially declared you dead, I was
going to hold on to the hope that you were still alive. Joe thinks
I'm delusional, of course. He thinks it's been long enough and
I have to face reality. I told him to mind his own business. He
didn't take it very well. I think the family's starting to choose
sides, Charles. All of them against the lunatic."

"Good," I said.

That, more or less, was our plan.

In five months, six months, seven months, Deanna and Anna
would be coming to join me. And leaving all family behind.

They belonged to our other life. They couldn't be part of this one. It would help, we thought, if they were all estranged from each other. Deanna's refusal to face facts and her family's insistence she do just that gave us an unexpected way to accomplish that. The flood of sympathetic phone calls from close and distant relations had already thinned to a trickle. Walls were being erected, barriers put in place. The one exception was Deanna's mom. We'd agreed that at some point we'd have to cross our fingers and tell her.

It was becoming more and more apparent that disappearing off the face of the earth wasn't easy—ties had to be cut, loose ends knotted up. It was like planning a long and complex vacation, only a vacation you weren't intending to come back from.

"Oh, your company called about your insurance, Charles," Deanna said. "I was all ready to tell them that I wasn't ready to admit you were dead yet. That they could keep their insurance, but she said she was calling to say they were *fighting* it. Because of your suspension—they'd stopped payments. She wanted me to know."

Life was nothing if not ironic, I thought.

There were other ways I passed the time up in my apartment.

I set about creating more ID.

I had a driver's license. I wanted more.

Winston had said getting a false ID was the easiest thing in the world, and he wasn't far wrong. These days you just needed the Internet.

When I logged on at an Internet café and typed in "False ID," I found at least four sites all too willing to help.

The secret was simply getting that first piece of ID. That one enabled you to get more. And thanks to Winston, I already had the first piece. A driver's license, which, according to a Web site called Who Are You, is considered primary ID. That is, it enables you to get everything else. A Social Security card, for example, obtained through a simple application in the mail.

Slowly, I built up an identity.

A credit card. A voter's registration card. A bank card. Discount cards for Barnes & Noble and Costco. A library card. All the things you would be expected to carry in your wallet.

But now that I had an identity, I needed a job.

One day the *Chicago Tribune* ran an article about the education crisis in the state. Apparently there was a dearth of teachers in Illinois. Qualified people were going into other, more lucrative fields and leaving schools terribly short-handed. Classes were being piggybacked with other classes. Programs were being cut. The state was considering running a TV recruitment campaign. And something else. They were down to letting even unlicensed people teach—anyone who'd taken some teaching courses in college and promised to complete the necessary credits concurrent with their teaching job.

It seemed like an opportunity for me.

The hardest-hit area, according to the article, was called Oakdale—about forty miles outside of Chicago. Once a mill town, it was now largely destitute. Mostly blue-collar and minority, and struggling along with sometimes seventy kids to a class. They were virtually begging for teachers.

I went there one day to look around.

I got off the bus and wandered down its main street. There were a lot of shuttered stores and broken windows. Parking meters had no heads on them. Only the bars seemed to be doing a decent business. It was just early afternoon, but they seemed filled with out-of-work men. I heard someone shouting from inside a bar called Banyon's.

"*Motherfucker!*" Then the sound of breaking glass.

I hurriedly walked on.

I went into a luncheonette and sat at the counter.

"Yeah?" the luncheonette owner asked me. He was fat and

tired looking; his apron looked as if it hadn't been washed in years.

"A hamburger," I ordered.

"How you want it?"

"Medium."

"Okay." But he didn't get up from his seat.

After a few minutes, I said: "Are you going to make the hamburger?"

"Waiting for the cook," he said.

"Where is he?"

But just then a woman came out through the doorway behind the counter. His wife, I guessed. She was smoking a cigarette.

"Burger," the luncheonette owner said to her. "Medium."

She took a frozen pattie from under the counter and placed it on the grill.

"Want fries with that?" she asked me.

"Sure."

"Just move in?" the owner asked me.

"No. Maybe. Thinking about it."

"Uh-huh. Why?"

"Excuse me?"

"Why are you thinking about it?"

"There might be a teaching job for me here."

"Teaching, huh? You're a teacher?"

"Yes."

"I was never good at school," he said. "Didn't have the head."

"Well, it looks like you're doing all right."

"Oh sure. It's okay."

His wife placed the burger in front of me. It looked pink and greasy.

"What happened to the parking meters?" I asked them.

"Oh those," the man said. "Someone stole them."

"They never replaced them?"

The man shrugged. "Nope. Wouldn't matter. We don't have any meter maids or anything, so no one was using them anyway."

"No meter maids. Why not?"

"Because we don't have anything. The city's broke. We share a police force with Cicero."

"Oh," I said. Most citizens would be alarmed at having no police force to themselves, I thought, but not me. I found that piece of information comforting.

Oakdale, Illinois. It was seeming more and more like a place I might like to hang my hat.

I sent out a résumé and letter to the Oakdale School District.

I wrote that I'd taken teaching courses back in college but had gone in a more entrepreneurial direction after graduation. I'd run several successful businesses out of my home. Now I'd gotten the urge to give something back. To mold and shape young minds. Oddly enough, I wasn't being untruthful here. I'd spent most of my life attempting to sell another credit card or slice of pizza; the thought of doing something that would actually benefit someone other than me was genuinely appealing.

I kept the résumé purposely vague. I wrote down "City University," not specifying what *college* in the city university system I'd actually attended. I was banking on the fact that beggars can't be choosers. That an underfunded and overworked school system in desperate need of teachers is not going to have the time or inclination to check facts.

I sent out the letter and résumé in July.

By August 10 I had my answer.

They requested I come in for an interview.

DERAILED FORTY-SEVEN

I started teaching the day after Labor Day.

Seventh-grade English. They gave me a choice of grades, and I picked the one closest to Anna's age. If I couldn't help her at the moment, I thought, I could help kids like her.

It was balmy, but I could already feel hints of fall in the intermittent breeze, like icy currents in an August ocean. I stood outside in shirtsleeves on the steps of George Washington Carver Middle School and shivered.

My first day was the worst.

The bell stopped ringing, and I found fifty-one skeptical students staring up at me.

The class was two-thirds black and one-third black wannabe. Even the white kids wore those low-slung dungarees with the elastic bands of their underwear showing. They practiced the strut that seemed to come naturally to their black peers; they'd stand in the schoolyard before first bell, making up raps.

When I wrote my name across the blackboard, the nub of chalk broke and the entire class laughed. I opened my desk to find another piece of chalk, but there wasn't any—something I would discover with all my school supplies that first year.

"Mr. Wid" remained on the blackboard.

So that's what they began to call me. Mr. Wid.

Hey, Mr. Wid, what's shakin'? Yoh, Wid . . .

I didn't correct them. It broke the ice that first day, and as time went on I grew almost fond of it, with the exception of a certain piece of graffiti I read on the wall of the boys' urinal one day.

I'm holding Wid's head in my hand!

I became fond of them, too—even the graffiti writer, who sheepishly admitted it when he was caught adding to his collection and spent two afternoons in detention for it. His detention supervisor, as it happened, was me. I volunteered for it; I had nowhere to go and no one to go home to. So I supervised detention, I taught an after-school study hall, I helped out the school basketball team.

The graffiti artist was named James. But he liked being called J-Cool, he told me. He came from a one-parent household— just *his mama,* he said, and I instantly thought about Anna.

I told him if he stopped writing that he was holding Wid's head in his hand on the bathroom wall, I would start calling him J-Cool.

Deal, he said.

We became friends.

I became kind of popular with everyone. Not just with the kids, but with the faculty, since I was always volunteering for things they themselves would otherwise have had to do.

Being liked, however, had its drawbacks.

When people like you, they invariably ask you questions about yourself. They're curious about where you came from, what you did before, if you're married or not, if you have any kids.

Lunch hours became awkward for me. An obstacle course I

had to negotiate for forty-five minutes every afternoon, maintaining just enough concentration to avoid tripping up. At first, I'd be talking to someone and would forget what I'd told someone else—Ted Roeger, eighth-grade math teacher, for instance, who'd invited me to play weekend softball with him in his over-forty league. I politely declined. Then there was Susan Fowler, a thirtyish fine arts teacher who seemed unattached and desperate, who always seemed to find an empty chair at my lunch table and turn the conversation to relationships and the difficulties thereof.

Eventually I went home and wrote out my life as Lawrence Widdoes. From childhood to now. Then I practiced it, asking myself questions about myself and answering them.

Where did you grow up?

Staten Island. (Close to home, yes, but I needed to pick a place I would at least know something about. And since I'd passed through there a million times on the way to Aunt Kate's, I knew enough about Staten Island to avoid looking stupid if a Staten Islander decided to ask me questions about it.)

What did your parents do?

Ralph, my father, was an auto mechanic. Anne, my mother, was a housewife. (Why not? Auto mechanic was as good an occupation as any, and housewife was what most women did back then.)

Did you have brothers or sisters?

No. (Absolutely true.)

What college did you go to?

City University. (That's, after all, what I'd put on my résumé.)

What did you do before this?

I ran a beauty care products business out of my house. Hairsprays. Facial creams. Body lotions. (A friend of mine had done that back in Merrick, so I knew something about it—enough, anyway, to get by.)

Are you married?

Yes. And no. (This was the tough one. There were no wife and children with me in Chicago now, but if things went according to plan, soon there would be. Suddenly they would just appear. Why? Because we'd suffered the great malaise of the twentieth century—marital difficulties—and we'd separated for a time. But just for a time. We were working at a reconciliation—we were hopeful it would happen and that they would join me.)

Do you have any children?

Yes. One. A daughter.

I stayed close to the truth in almost everything. It made it easier when my mind went blank, when someone cornered me with a question I wasn't prepared for. The life of Lawrence Widdoes was different from the life of Charles Schine, yes, but not *that* different, and those differences slowly and haltingly became second nature to me. I became familiar with them, nurtured them, trotted them out and took them for strolls around the park, and finally adopted them as my own.

"She's begun dialysis," Deanna said.

I was standing at the public pay phone two blocks from my Chicago apartment. It was October now. Wind was knifing in off the lake and rattling the phone booth. My eyes teared up.

"When?" I asked.

"Over a month. I didn't want to tell you."

"How . . . how is she taking it?"

"Like she's taking everything else these days. With this horrible silence. I beg her to talk to me, yell at me, scream at me, *anything*. She just looks at me. After you left, she just closed up, Charles. She's holding it in so tightly I think she's going to explode. I took her to therapy, but the therapist said she didn't say a word. Usually you can wait them out—the silence becomes so uncomfortable they become desperate to fill it. But not our Anna. She looked out the window for fifty minutes, then got up and left. Now this."

"Jesus, Deanna . . . does the dialysis *hurt* her?"

"I don't think so. Dr. Baron says it doesn't."

"How long does she have to sit there?"

"Six hours. More or less."

"And it doesn't hurt her? You're sure?"

"Your being gone is what's hurting her. It's killing her. It's killing me not being able to tell her. I don't think I can *not* tell her anymore. Charles . . ." Deanna started crying.

I suddenly felt as if every useful part of my body had stopped working. Someone had just plucked out my heart and left a hole there. It was waiting for Anna to come and fill it. Anna and Deanna both. I began to calculate. It had been, what . . . four months?

"Have you put the house up for sale yet?" I asked her.

"Yes. I told anyone I'm still *talking* to that I have to get away. There are too many memories. I have to start fresh."

"Who are you talking to?"

"Hardly anyone. Now. My aunts and uncles have given up on me—I had another fight with Joe. Our friends? It's funny . . . at first they give you the song and dance how nothing's going to change—you'll still get together for Saturday night dinners and Sunday barbecues. But it does change. They're all coupled up and you're alone and they feel awkward. It becomes easier to just not invite you. We were worried how we'd manage to cut ties with them, and it's happening on its own. Who do I talk to? My mother, mostly. That's it."

"The first decent offer you get on the house—sell it," I said. "It's time."

DERAILED FORTY-EIGHT

I found a house outside Oakdale.

It wasn't much of a house, a modest ranch built sometime in the fifties, but it had three bedrooms and a small garden and lots of privacy.

I rented it.

And waited for them to come join me.

Deanna sold the house.

It wasn't the best price we could have gotten, but it wasn't the worst, either. It was expedient.

When Deanna told Anna they were going to be moving, she had to weather a storm of protest, however. Deanna was ostensibly moving to be rid of the memories—Anna wanted to hold on to them. Deanna said it was done; there was no going back. Anna retreated into stony silence.

She left most of the furniture. We didn't want a moving company having an address of delivery.

They packed up the car and left.

*   *   *

Somewhere between Pennsylvania and Ohio, Deanna pulled the car over and told Anna I was alive.

We'd agonized over this.

How exactly do you go about telling your daughter that her father isn't dead? That he didn't die in that hotel explosion after all? I couldn't just pop out of the woodwork when she got there. She had to be prepared for something like that.

We'd also wondered *what* should be told to her. *Why* was I alive? Or, more to the point, why had she been allowed to think I was dead all these months?

She was fourteen—half kid and half not.

So we decided on a story that was half true and half not.

Deanna pulled the car into the parking lot of a Roy Rogers along Route 96. Later, she told me how it went.

"I have something to tell you," she said to Anna, and Anna barely looked at her. She was still on a kind of speaking strike, using silence as a weapon, the only one she had.

"It's something you're going to have a hard time believing, and you're going to be very, very angry at me, but I'm going to try to make you understand. Okay?"

And now Anna did look at her, because this sounded serious.

"Your father is alive, Anna."

At first, Deanna said, Anna looked at her as though she'd lost her mind. And when she repeated it, as if Deanna were maybe playing some kind of sick joke on her. A look of near disgust passed over Anna's face and she asked her mother why she was doing this to her.

"It's the truth, darling. He's *alive*. We're going to meet him now. He's waiting for us in Illinois."

And it was at that point that Anna finally believed her, because she knew her mother *hadn't* lost her mind and wouldn't have been cruel enough to joke about it. She broke down, finally and completely and spectacularly broke down. She cried rivers of tears, Deanna said, cried so hard and so much that Deanna didn't think the body could contain that much water. She cried out of happiness, out of sheer relief.

Then, with Deanna stroking her hair, came the questions.

"Why did you tell me he was dead?" Anna said.

"Because we couldn't take the chance you would tell somebody. Maybe that was wrong—I'm so sorry you had to go through that. We thought it was the only way. Please believe me."

"Why is he pretending to be dead? I don't understand. . . ."

"Daddy got into some trouble. It wasn't his fault. But they might not believe him."

"They *who?*"

"The police."

"The police? *Daddy?*"

"You know your father, Anna, and you know he's a good man. But it might not have looked that way. It's hard for me to explain. But he got into trouble and he couldn't get out."

Deanna told her the rest. Their names would be different. Their lives. Everything.

"I have to change my *name?*" Anna asked.

"You always said you hated it, remember?"

"Yeah. But . . . can't I just change my last name?"

"Maybe. We'll see."

All in all, Deanna said, she thought the overwhelmingly good news that I was alive canceled out the overwhelmingly bad news that her life was being turned upside down. And that we'd lied to her all these months.

Anna said, "Jamie."

"What?"

"My name. I like Jamie."

*   *   *

I was waiting for them in Chicago.

The car rolled up to the curb and Anna jumped out before the car actually stopped and flung herself into my arms.

"Daddy," she said. "Daddy . . . Daddy . . . Daddy . . ."

"I love you," I said. "I'm so sorry, honey . . . I'm so—"

"Shh," she said. "You're alive."

DERAILED FORTY-NINE

Our new life.

I got up at six-thirty and made breakfast for Deanna and Anna. For Jamie. She went off to school to me. I was able to enroll her at George Washington Carver. When the principal asked if they could have her previous academic records forwarded to them, their favorite new teacher said sure—he'd notify her last school and they'd be there in a few months or so. The principal said fine and never asked me again.

I'd scouted out a local endocrinologist named Dr. Milbourne, so Anna could continue her dialysis without interruption. He asked for her records. I gave him the same answer I gave the school. He didn't seem overly concerned because Deanna had Anna's blood journals for the last five years. That and her current blood sugar reading and medical work-up seemed to tell him all he needed to know. He put her on dialysis in the office, and wrote her a prescription for a portable machine we could use in the house. My new medical insurance, courtesy of the Illinois Board of Ed, took care of everything.

I managed to find a drugstore in Chicago that carried the

special insulin Anna needed, the one made from pig cells that was slowly being phased out in favor of the synthetic insulins that Anna didn't respond to as well.

Deanna, who used her previous middle name of Kim, took a part-time job as a receptionist to help out with the family finances.

And an odd and wondrous thing happened.

We became happy again.

It dawned on us gradually, in small increments here and there, until we could finally and fearlessly say it out loud.

We'd been given another chance at this thing called *family*. We grabbed it with both hands and held on for dear life. It felt a little like when we'd first started out, newly married and imbued with passion and hope. We didn't know how long we'd have Anna for, that's true, but we were determined to appreciate every single minute we did. We talked about it now, comforted each other, found strength in each other. Silence was forever banned from our doorstep. We became a kind of poster family for communication.

And slowly, intimacy came back as well. The first night we were together again, with Anna safely asleep in bed, we tore into each other with a kind of desperate abandon. Sex had taken on a new edge and, with it, a new excitement. We mauled each other, we banged bodies, we screwed ourselves sweaty, and in the end we looked at each other with a kind of amazement. Was that really us?

Two months later, Deanna announced she was pregnant.

"You're what?" I said.

"With child. Knocked up. Preggers. So," she said, "what do you think? Should I have an abortion?"

"No," I said.

We'd wanted another child once. Anna's getting sick had changed our minds. But now, I believe I wanted it as much as I've ever wanted anything.

"Yeah," Deanna said. "I kinda feel that way, too."

Seven months later, Jamie had a brother. We called him Alex. Call it a homage to Jamie's previous incarnation—and to my grandfather Alexander.

I had one close call.

I was coming out of Roxman's Drugs with Anna's prescription. I was marveling at the actual severity of a Chicago winter; Windy City didn't quite do it justice.

Frigid City. Subzero City. Frozen Stiff City. Yes.

I was wearing a parka, knit cap, earmuffs, fur-lined gloves. I was still quivering. Strands of frozen moisture sat on my upper lip. I was looking for my car in an outdoor parking lot and hoping it would start.

I walked past an office building and bumped into someone with blond hair.

"Excuse me," I said, turning around to face her.

It was Mary Widger.

"That's okay," she said.

I whipped back around and kept walking. I remembered—one of our packaged goods clients had its headquarters here. She must've been coming from a meeting. When I turned the corner and peeked, she was still standing there.

Did she recognize me?

I don't think so. I still had my beard. I was bundled in leather and fur. Still, it felt like my heart went on hiatus for a while. I found it hard to breathe.

I waited a few minutes, enveloped in my own clouds of hot vapor, then walked back to the corner and peeked again.

She was gone.

DERAILED FIFTY

Alex was two.

He was talking up a storm, doing calisthenics on the living room furniture, and generally delighting, amusing, and captivating us on a daily basis.

Kim was back to working as a receptionist.

Jamie was holding her own. Medically, scholastically, even socially. She'd made friends with two girls who lived down the road. They had sleep-overs and pizza parties and went to the movies together.

Mr. Wid? He was teaching *A Separate Peace* and several works of Mark Twain in seventh-grade English.

One of Twain's classic lines seemed remarkably apt these days.

The reports of my demise are greatly exaggerated.

Jamie wasn't the only one who'd built up a social circle. After keeping a low profile for a good part of a year, I'd finally taken some of my colleagues up on their invitations. Slowly, we began to see people. A dinner. A movie. A Sunday get-together.

My previous life began to fade. Not just because time had

passed, but because this life was better in so many ways—all the ways that really counted, I now knew. I'd made more money before, that's true. By all the usual standards of American success—a prestigious job, a nice salary, a large house— this life was a come-down. But in *this* life I could measure job success in something other than dollar signs. My annual bonus was seeing children who came into my class struggling and un-motivated leave it on track and engaged. It was good for the soul. And I didn't have disgruntled and demanding clients looking for my head every day, either.

And married life? It continued to surprise in ways big and small.

Lawrence Widdoes was a happy man.

One Saturday in the summer, I took Alex with me into Chicago.

I had to pick up another prescription for Kim, and I thought I'd take Alex to the Children's Museum.

First, we went to Roxman's Drugs.

The druggist greeted me by name. We were old pals now. He asked me how I was doing.

Fine, I said.

He said the weather was too hot.

I agreed with him—we were stuck in the middle of an un-relenting heat wave. Something I was only too aware of, since I was teaching summer school in a building with no air-conditioning. At the end of each day, I came home drenched.

The druggist slipped a lollipop to Alex, whose eyes went wide, the way kids' eyes do when you present them with their version of money. He made me unwrap it for him, then popped it into his mouth and smiled.

Then the druggist's assistant walked over and said: "Mr. Widdoes? I'm sorry, I thought you understood. I said the in-sulin won't be in till Monday."

"What?"

"Remember, I said Monday."

"You said Monday when?"

"When you called. I told you that."

"When I called?"

"You asked me if the insulin was in. I said Monday."

"You mean my wife. She must've called you."

He looked puzzled, shook his head, shrugged. "Okay. Well, it's not in till Monday."

"Fine. I'll come back."

We went to the Children's Museum.

There were several hands-on exhibits. Alex climbed through a giant left ventricle and into a model of a heart itself, where he sat down and refused to budge. He knew I couldn't climb in there with him, and he relished this momentary independence. I had to wait him out.

Eventually he appeared from the right ventricle.

He saw what his weight was on Mars.

He tapped in Morse code.

He finger-painted on a computer.

He put on bird's wings.

I took him to the museum café, where I bought him a hot dog and fries—but only if he promised not to tell Mommy, who was waging a personal crusade against junk food these days.

Sitting there eating, I had what you might call a flashback.

Something was bothering me. It was sitting on my shoulder and buzzing in my ear. I tried swatting it away, but it wouldn't leave. I couldn't kill it. It was maddening.

I remembered sitting and eating with Lucinda, Didi, whatever her name was. I remembered pouring my heart out to her the day she'd asked about my daughter. About Anna. I remembered telling her something.

I suddenly felt cold.

I took my cell out and called Kim.

"Honey?" I said when she picked up.

"Yes, hi. How's it going?"

"Fine. After this we're going to the museum of dead parents. I feel like I've run a marathon."

"Then he must be having a good time."

"You could say that. Look, I wanted to ask you something."

"Yes?"

"Did you call Roxman's this week? About Anna's insulin?"

"Roxman's? No. Why?"

"You didn't call? You're sure?"

"Yes, Charles . . . woops . . . yes, *Larry,* I'm sure."

"It isn't possible you did and forgot? Isn't that possible?"

"No. I didn't call Roxman's. I would remember. You want me to sign an affidavit? Why?"

"Nothing. Just something they said to me. . . ."

I said good-bye. I hung up.

I stared at my son. He was munching on his last piece of frankfurter. Voices were echoing off the museum walls, a child was screaming bloody murder at another table. He looked up at me.

"Daddy . . . okay?" he said.

DERAILED FIFTY-ONE

I went on-line.

I went back three years. I went back to the day of the explosion.

There were 173 entries for "Fairfax Hotel."

Everything from newspaper articles to magazines articles to mentions in TV shows and even Internet jokes.

Did you hear about the new rate policy at the Fairfax? It bombed.

Most of the articles were what you might expect.

Stories of heroic firemen and innocent victims. And among the stories of innocent victims, I saw my name there again—among the missing at first, then onto the list of the dead.

Charles Schine, 45, advertising executive.

And Dexter's and Sam's and Didi's names, too.

And his—placed alphabetically right at the end of the roll call.

I kept reading. There were other stories there, stories about the bomber.

RIGHT-TO-LIFER BOMBER'S HOMETOWN REMEMBERS, one of them was titled. Jack Christmas was born in Enid, Oklahoma. He was a friendly boy who washed blackboards, his third-grade teacher said. Though one school friend remembered him as *kind of spooky.*

There was an article about the hotel itself.

HOTEL'S UN-FABLED PAST GAVE NO CLUE. It was built in 1949. It originally catered to a mostly business clientele. It fell into disrepair and became a haven for short-rate prostitutes and low-income residents.

There were several entries about domestic terrorism.

An article about an organization called the Children of God. A manifesto from an army of antiabortionists. Several items about survivalists. A recounting of the Oklahoma City bombing and its similarities to the one at the Fairfax Hotel.

And later on, another list of the dead—with brief obituaries this time.

Charles Schine was employed as a creative director at Schuman Advertising. He worked on several major accounts. "Charley was an asset to this company, both as a writer and a human being. He will be greatly missed," Eliot Firth, president of Schuman Advertising, said. Charles Schine leaves behind a wife and daughter.

Samuel M. Griffen was touted as "a shining star in the world of financial planning." His brother said, "He was a generous and loving father."

There was something about Dexter. "He was one of our own," the holding company for the Fairfax Hotel said. "A dedicated employee."

Even Didi received an obituary—at least I assumed it was her.

Desdemona Gonzalez, 30. A loving sister to Maria. Daughter to Major Frank Gonzalez of East Texas.

I took a detour. I looked up East Texas newspapers. I knew

the hometown papers would have been falling all over themselves to write up the stories of their local victims.

I found her. An article from a *Roxham Texas Weekly*.

Retired Major Frank Gonzalez sits on his front porch
nursing a very private pain for his youngest daughter,
killed in the Fairfax Hotel bombing. Desdemona Gonzalez, 30, had lived in New York City for the last ten years,
her father said. "She didn't keep in touch much," he said,
but she'd "call on holidays and things like that." . . . Family friends admitted that the elder Mr. Gonzalez and his
daughter had been estranged for a number of years. . . .
There had been a drug arrest when Desdemona was a
teenager and allegations of child abuse against her father.
A family friend who wishes to remain anonymous added
that these charges were all "unsubstantiated."

I clicked back to the general obituaries.

There was one missing.

I felt something in the small of my back. A trickle of ice
water in reverse—it began crawling up my spine.

I went back and clicked each entry again. I reread everything. Nothing. Not one mention.

I logged on to the *Daily News* Web page. I typed in "Fairfax
Hotel."

Thirty-two articles.

I started with the one written on the day of the explosion.
There was a picture of the bomb site. An old woman crying on
a corner curb, firemen standing in the middle of the street with
their heads down. I scanned the entire article. I went on to the
next one.

Pretty much the same stuff I'd read elsewhere, except in
chronological order. The bombing, the dead, the heroes, the
villain, the investigation, the funerals.

It took me two hours. Still nothing.

I was beginning to think I was wrong. I'd misinterpreted an offhand comment, that's all. The kind of thing that happened all the time.

I would look at one more week—the week of the last article, four weeks after the actual bombing. That's it.

Then I would log off and go and kiss my sleeping children good night. I would crawl into bed with Kim and mold myself against her warm body. I would fall asleep and know that everything was okay.

I started with Monday. I went on to Tuesday.

I almost missed it.

It was a small item—buried in an avalanche of the Middle East war, a triple murder committed in Detroit, a marital scandal involving the New York City mayor.

HEROIC SURVIVOR NOT SO HEROIC, it said.

I clicked on it, held my breath, and read.

It was kind of a human-interest story, the kind they start running when they run out of stories about heroes and victims, a story meant to make you shake your head at the sad ironies of life.

Body pulled from wreckage . . . no identification . . . in a coma for several weeks . . . brain surgery . . . fingerprints revealed him to be . . . previously identified as dead . . . his car in hotel parking garage . . . hadn't shown for sentencing . . . police spokesperson . . . prison infirmary . . .

I read it slowly, from beginning to the end. Then once more, making sure.

Anna's insulin.

It was made from a pig's pancreatic cells, which is the way all insulin used to be made. Until they figured out a way to make it synthetically in the laboratory. This was a fairly recent development; Anna had been using pig insulin since she'd gotten diabetes. When she'd tried the synthetic stuff, her numbers had strayed high and stayed there.

That happened sometimes, Dr. Baron had said. Some people responded better to the real stuff. So he'd kept her on it.

Even though they'd begun phasing it out—even though it was becoming very hard to get hold of. But there was no need to worry. There would always be some drugstores that carried it, he said.

I was talking to Jameel Farraday, a guidance counselor, in the school lunchroom.

Once a year, Jameel brought convicts from state prison into the school auditorium in an effort to scare George Washington Carver's students straight. The convicts, some of whom had even grown up in the neighborhood, would talk about drugs, about the wrong choices they'd made, about life behind bars.

Then they'd take questions from the audience.

Ever kill anyone? one student asked an ex-junkie who had a scar running the entire length of his jawbone.

He said no, and the student body groaned.

"I'm thinking about having my class write letters to men in prison," I said to Farraday. He was eating milky mashed potatoes and greasy chicken fingers.

"For what purpose?" he asked me.

"Well, kind of like the thing you do—but in writing. My kids can practice their penmanship, and these men can provide some life lessons, maybe."

"Okay," he said.

"I was wondering . . ."

"Yes?"

"I *knew* someone who ended up going to prison—from my old neighborhood. I thought I might start with him."

"What did he do?"

"I don't know, exactly. Drugs, I heard."

"Uh-huh."

"You have any idea how I could find out where he is?"

"You mean which prison?"

"Yes."

Farraday shrugged. "I don't know. I can ask my contact in Chicago Corrections, I guess."

"Would you?"

"Sure. If I remember. Where's he from?"

"New York."

"Uh-huh. What's his name?"

"Vasquez."

"*Vasquez?*"

"Yes. Raul. Raul Vasquez."

DERAILED FIFTY-TWO

He knew where I was.

They'd pulled him half-dead from the rubble, but only half.
He was in a coma for weeks. They didn't know who he was.
His car had been parked in the hotel lot. He hadn't shown up
at work. He was listed as dead.

They ran his fingerprints in a last-ditch effort to find out his
name. Raul Vasquez. He had a "did not show" for sentencing
for two counts of assault and battery and one for pandering.

He was transferred to a prison infirmary until he recovered
sufficiently enough to be brought into Bronx Superior Court
for sentencing.

This I knew from the article. The rest of it I imagined.

He'd sat there in prison. He'd thought and he'd remembered.

What Didi had told him. About my daughter. About the special pig insulin she needed to survive. *Why pig insulin?* She had
asked me, remember? Like a concerned lover, instead of an ex-
tortionist wheedling the details out of me.

Vasquez sat there in prison and fumed. I was hiding from

him. I was gone. But then he understood there was something I would have to do. No matter how carefully I was hiding, I would have to do this thing.

This is Mr. Widdoes. Is my insulin in?

How many drugstores must have said no. Must've said, *Widdoes who?*

But he kept going. He kept calling. He had all the time in the world. He had all the motivation necessary.

Maybe he started in New York. Then on to Pennsylvania. And so on.

One day, he'd reached Illinois.

Roxman's Drugs.

And this time when he asked if his insulin was in, the druggist's assistant didn't say no.

He said not yet.

But it'll be in Monday.

Two weeks after I'd talked to Jameel, he found me after class and handed me a sheet of paper.

"What's this?" I said.

"Your guy," he said. "But there's three of them."

"Three?"

"Yeah—three Raul Vasquezes. But if he's from New York, I'd imagine he's this one." He pointed to the first name on the sheet. "I'd imagine he's here."

I lay upstairs in bed. I couldn't sleep.

Kim was attuned to my nightly rhythms and knew without even looking that I was lying there wide awake and staring at the ceiling.

"What's the matter, honey?" she said. "What's wrong?"

I couldn't tell her yet. I didn't have the heart. We'd escaped from catastrophe once; we'd made a new life. We were happy. I couldn't tell her that we hadn't escaped after all. That the past was reaching out for us with icy fingers.

"Nothing," I said.

I was thinking.

What was parole for a twelve-year sentence?

When would he be getting out?

He would come for me then—I knew that. For my family. And then he would do what he'd done to Winston and Sam Griffen and the man he'd pushed off the train in Lynbrook, Long Island, and God knows how many others.

That day he came to our home as a chimney cleaner.

I heard about a family that went to sleep and never woke up.

Yes, he would be coming for me.

Unless—I whispered it like a fervent prayer.

Unless I get to him first.

He didn't know that I knew he was alive. He didn't know that I knew he'd found me.

But what did that matter?

He was in prison. He was locked up.

To get to him, I would have to get inside Attica.

Now—how could I do that?

ATTICA

It was my last class.

I'd circled it in my calendar. I'd rehearsed it in dreams.

When I walked through the metal detector, a CO named Stewey said, "Last day, huh," and I thought he looked almost despondent. Maybe people get used to the people they belittle, and who knows if they'll ever find anyone as good again?

Before I went to my classroom, I stopped off in the COs lounge.

It was just a room with folding chairs and tables and a thirteen-inch TV usually tuned to *Dukes of Hazzard* reruns. The COs evidently had a thing for Daisy Duke—those high-cut shorts of hers, probably—because an old poster of her still hung on the wall. Someone had penciled in nipples on her white blouse.

I poured myself some coffee. I put powdered milk into my cup and stirred it with a plastic swizzle stick.

I casually walked over to the COs museum situated in the left corner of the room.

"You got your twelve oh-one, brother," Fat Tommy said. He

was spread across two metal chairs with a Jenny Craig TV dinner on the table in front of him.

It's only natural that employees pick up the lingo of the workplace; Attica guards often talked like Attica prisoners. And 12:01 meant gaining your freedom—getting your walking papers.

Maybe, I thought. *We'll see.*

I sipped my coffee, I perused the collection of gats and burners, as Fat Tommy chomped away on a meal he could only find ultimately dissatisfying. He was the only other person in the lounge.

When I finally turned and left, Fat Tommy looked up but didn't say good-bye.

From the lounge to the classroom, I first had to go through a black locked door—knocking twice and waiting for another CO to clear me. Then I walked down the "bowling alley," what they call the prison's main walkway. It's dissected down the middle by a broken yellow line, like a state highway. One side is for prisoners. The other side is for COs. Or for people who fall somewhere in between.

I passed a CO called Hank.

"Hey, Yobwoc," he said. "I'm gonna miss you. You were my best boon coon."

Translation: best friend.

"Thank you," I said, but I knew he hadn't meant it.

When the class settled in, I told them it was the last time I'd be seeing them. That it had been fun teaching them. That I hoped they'd keep reading and writing on their own. I told them that in the best classes, the teacher becomes the student and the students the teachers, and that that's what had happened here—I'd learned from them. No one looked particularly moved; but when I finished, one or two of them nodded at me as if they might even miss me.

Malik wasn't one of them. He'd passed me a note last time. Where the writer would be waiting for me.

I told the class we might as well use this last class for creative reflection. I wanted each of them to write an essay on what the class had meant to them. This time, I told them, they could even put their names to them.

Then I excused myself to go to the bathroom.

I passed the black CO who was supposed to be stationed outside the door and who, this time, actually was. I said I'd be back in ten minutes, and he said, "I'll alert the media."

He'd be waiting for me near the prison pharmacy, the note said.

He worked there.

A pharmacy job gave you *shine,* a student had explained to me, since it gave you access to drugs.

It also gave you access to something else, I knew. Drug manufacturers. You could call them up to find out things if you wanted to. Like maybe where a certain rare insulin was being distributed.

It probably hadn't taken him years to track me down after all.

I walked back down the bowling alley. I followed the signs.

The pharmacy consisted of one long counter protected by steel mesh. There are prisons within prisons, I noted, an axiom also true of life. The kind of insight I might've pointed out in my class, if I still had one.

I continued past the pharmacy, striding down an empty hallway that veered sharply left and seemed to lead to no place in particular. But it did.

Malik had told me where he'd be waiting for me, and I'd gone and scouted it.

An alcove in the middle of the hall.

A kind of blind. In an older institution like Attica, there were lots of them, hidden little corners where the prisoners conducted business, where they sold drugs and got down on their knees. Where they evened scores. A blind. An appropriate description, except I was walking in with my eyes wide open.

I walked into the alcove where it was quiet and still and stopped.

"Hello?"

I could hear him breathing in there.

"Hello," I whispered again.

He stepped out of the shadows.

He looked different—that's the first thing I thought. That he looked different from the way I remembered him.

His head. It seemed smaller, reshapen, as if it had been squeezed in a vise. He had a scar running down from his forehead. That was one thing. And he had a *tat* on his right shoulder. A prison blue clock face without hands—doing time. And farther down on his arm a tombstone with numbers—*twelve*—his prison sentence.

"Surprise," he said.

No. But that's what I wanted him to think.

"How you doin', Chuck?" he said. He smiled, the way he'd smiled at my front door the day he'd come to my house and put his hands on my daughter.

"Larry," I said.

"Larry. Yeah, I'm down. That was some cool shit you pulled off—playing dead like that. Had everyone fooled, huh, *Larry?*"

"Not everyone. No."

"No, not everyone. You're right. You shouldn't have let my girl see your wallet, Larry. Bad move. Stupid."

The hostess in the Crystal Night Club. Widdoes . . . *what kind of name is that?* she'd said.

"I thought you were dead."

"You wish."

Yes, I thought. *I wish.* But there comes a time when you have to stop wishing.

"I've been looking for you, *Larry.* Like all over. You took something of mine, you know. I want it back. So I've been looking for you. And I *found* you, too. I found you twice."

"Twice?"

"Once in *Chicago.* Oh yeah . . . that's right. Surprised by that, huh? Yeah, I knew *exactly* where you were. Oakdale, Illinois. Then you moved on me."

"Yes."

"Bennington. Right down the fucking road. How's that for lucky?"

"That's lucky."

"Uh-huh. You know how I found you?"

"No."

"Your kid. Through the drugstores. First Chicago. Then *Bennington.* And then the next thing I know, the very next thing I know, you're waltzing in through the fucking front door."

"Yes."

"I said to myself, Here's your twelve oh-one, nigger. Here it is on a platter."

"Why didn't you say hello?"

"I did. I did say hello. I got my boy to write up my hello *for* me."

"Your *boy?* He can't even read."

"Not Malik. My boon. A Jew literary professor who eighty-sixed his wife. Writes all the pleas for parole here. And very cool jerk-off stuff. 'Charley Schine Gets Fucked'—his latest. He thinks I made it up in my head. He thinks I'm creative."

"Yes—it was very effective."

"I thought you might run. Seeing your life story and all."

No, I thought. If I was going to run, I would have done it back in Oakdale. It's what Deanna said to do—*Let's run,* and I said, *Okay, but if we run, we will have to keep running. For all time. So maybe we shouldn't.* So I'd taken a leave of absence and we'd come here.

"You have something of mine, *Larry*," he said.

"Some of it was mine first."

Vasquez smiled. "You think this is a fucking *negotiation?* You think I'm bargaining with you? You're fucked. It's your role in life. Accept it. Get down on your knees and open your mouth and say please, Daddy. I want my *money.*"

Someone was shouting in the pharmacy: "The doc says I need this shit, understand?"

"You're in prison," I said.

"So are you. You're locked up. You're doing time. You think you're safe out *there?* Think again, motherfucker. I can turn you in—I can tell them, *Here's Charley*. If you're lucky I could. 'Cause I might send someone to your house to fuck your wife instead. I might. How old's your daughter now—ready to get stuck with something else now, huh?"

I went for him.

Reflex simply took over my body and said: *Listen up—we're going to stop this man, we're going to shut this man up forever. We are.* But when I lunged at him, when I went for his throat, his knee came up and caught me in the stomach. I went down to my knees. He stepped behind me and slipped his arm around my neck and squeezed. He whispered in my ear.

"That's it, Charley. That's right. Got you mad, huh? Here's the thing. How lucky was it that you showed up in Bennington? Forty miles from here. In my own fucking *backyard?* And then, if that isn't lucky enough, you walk in the goddamn door and start teaching here. How lucky is *that?* Is that lucky or *what?* Or is that like, *too* lucky? What do *you* think, Charley? You think that's too lucky? I don't know. You got something for me, Charley, do you?" He reached his hand down and patted my right pocket. He felt it there—the gat, the one I'd taken from the COs museum. "You got something you want to stick me with? Huh, Charley?" He took it out of my pocket—he showed it to me.

"You ought to know me better by now, Chuck. *Sure I'll meet you by the river. Sure I'll come alone.* Sure. But I met your mail boy at the river first, huh? Took his head off, huh, Charley? Who the fuck you think you're dealing with here? You think this is punk central?" He put the knife against my throat. He pressed it against my jugular. Then he smiled and pushed me to the floor. I could smell something acrid—urine and ammonia.

I wanted to answer him now.

To tell him yes, I did know who I was dealing with. To tell him that that was why I'd waited six months in Bennington before applying for the teaching job here. Why I'd made sure he'd found me there first, living in Bennington and teaching in high school, so that it would just seem like some kind of fortunate coincidence that I'd later taken a teaching job here. In the very prison he was incarcerated in. And I wanted to tell him that's why I'd purposely left my keys in my pocket that day I walked through the metal detector—to see if it would be possible to smuggle in a weapon. A gun. And that when I learned it *wasn't* possible to smuggle in a gun, how I'd started making visits to the COs lounge because I'd heard they had a kind of museum there.

I wanted to tell him that it was true—I hadn't known who I was dealing with when I sat with Winston by the river, and later back in the Fairfax Hotel—even then I hadn't. But that I did now. That I'd learned.

And one last thing. One very last thing. How when I stood there in the COs museum with my back to Fat Tommy, I'd *whispered* this thing I'd learned to myself. Like a prayer to the God of screwed plans. Because I'd learned if you want to make God laugh, that's what you do—you make a plan; but if you want to make him smile, you make two.

Two.

I reached into my *left* pocket. I took out the spring-loaded gun made of soapwood and tin that I'd carefully loaded in the COs lounge.

I shot Vasquez directly between both surprised eyes.

Times Union

Prisoner killed on Attica attack.

by Brent Harding

Raul Vasquez, 34, an Attica prisoner, was killed yesterday when his intended victim managed to wrest a prison-made gun away from him and fatally wound him. Lawrence Widdoes, 47, who teaches English to Attica prisoners two nights a week, was assaulted by Mr. Vasquez near the prison pharmacy. A witness who works in the pharmacy saw Mr. Vasquez physically attack Mr. Widdoes. "He was choking him good . . ." Claude Weathers, an Attica prisoner, stated. "Then pop—Vasquez goes down." Mr. Widdoes, who suffered a bruised neck, is unsure what provoked the attack, but believes it might be related to some negative criticism he leveled at a student who is the cellmate of Mr. Vasquez. Mr. Widdoes, whose teaching duties are ending due to state budget cuts, is simply glad to be alive. "I feel like I've been given a second chance," Mr. Widdoes said.

DERAILED—END

I came home.

Kim came rushing out of the kitchen and stopped and stared. As if I were an apparition.

I nodded at her, I whispered, "Yes."

She slowly walked toward me and curled herself around my body like a blanket.

It's okay, she was saying, *you can rest now.*

Alex came running down the stairs, crying, "Daddy's home." He tugged at my shirt until I picked him up and held him. His cheek was sticky with chocolate.

"Where's Jamie?" I asked Kim.

"Doing her dialysis," she said.

I kissed her on the top of her head. I put Alex down. I went upstairs to Jamie's bedroom.

She was hooked up to the portable dialysis machine. I sat on the bed next to her.

"We'll be going back to Oakdale soon," I said. "Back to your friends, okay?"

She nodded.

She did this three days a week now.

There was some talk of getting her on a list for a kidney-pancreas transplant—the newest hope for diabetics like her. But then there would be antirejection drugs to worry about the rest of her life, so it was hard to know if it would really be better for her. As for now, we hooked her veins up to this terrible machine three days a week, and I sat there by her bed and listened to its whir and hum as it pumped blood through her failing body.

Sometimes I drift off to this sound, and Anna is suddenly four years old again and I'm back at the zoo with her on that long-ago Sunday morning. Feeding the elephants. I lift her up into my arms, and I can feel her tiny heart running to greet me. There's a soft chill in the air, and the leaves are drifting down from a swaying canopy of dark russet. Just Anna and her dad, walking hand in hand together in search of memories.

And I know I will sit here forever.

I will sit here as long as it takes.

More
James Siegel!

Please turn the page for
a preview of

DETOUR

now available
from Warner Books.

They were back in the hotel room.

Galina had left for the day. Joelle was asleep in her crib. Slats of amber light were slanting in through the window.

He'd remember this exact moment for a long time. Just about forever. He'd remember the way it looked—how the rays of light crisscrossed the bedspread and seemed to cleave Joanna's naked leg in two. He'd take a photo of this moment and paste it into the album of very bad things.

Joanna was lying half in and half out of the bedsheets, staring straight up at the ceiling. She looked kind of morose.

Once upon a time Paul had resisted asking Joanna why she looked unhappy, because he always knew what the answer would be, and it always involved him. He was hoping things were different now—that the two of them were positively *suffused* with happiness—so he went ahead and asked.

"What's wrong?"

"You're going to think I'm crazy," she said.

"No, I'm not."

"Yes, you are. You don't know what I'm thinking. It's ridiculous."

"Yes, I do. You're thinking I'm going to think you're crazy."

"Besides that."

"What, Joanna?"

"It's nuts."

"Okay, it's nuts. Tell me."

"She smells different."

"What? *Who?*"

"Joelle. She smells different."

"Different than what?"

"Different than . . . before."

Paul didn't know quite how to answer that.

"So?"

"So?"

"So she smells different. I'm not—"

"Don't you understand what I'm saying?"

"No."

Joanna rolled onto her side and faced him. "I don't think it's *her.*"

"What?"

"I don't think it's her," clearly enunciating each word this time so he'd know exactly what it was she was saying. Which was clearly and patently, well . . . nuts.

"Joanna—of course it's her. We took her to the doctor today. You were with her the whole day. Are you . . . ?"

"Crazy?"

"I wasn't going to say that," Paul said. Of course, that's exactly what he was going to say. "I just . . . I mean, it's just so . . . She's Joelle."

"How do you know?"

"What do you mean how do I know?"

"It's a simple question. How do you *know* it's Joelle?"

"Because I've been with her two days. Because . . . it *looks* like her."

"She's one month old. How many other babies have you seen here that look exactly like her?"

"None."

"Fine. Well, I have."

"Joanna, because she *smells* different? Don't you think it's kind of . . . paranoid?"

"You mean like when we thought Galina kidnapped her?"

"Yes."

"Maybe we weren't being paranoid. Maybe Galina *did* kidnap her."

"Do you hear what you're saying? Do you? It's ridiculous."

"You didn't think it was ridiculous yesterday."

"Yes, I didn't think it was ridiculous yesterday. That was before Galina came *back* with her. She had a fever, so Galina went to get her a thermometer. Remember?"

"Joelle didn't have a fever when we went for a walk, did she?"

"How do we know that?"

"Because I'm her mother. I held her before we left. She was fine."

"Babies get fevers, honey."

Joanna sat up. She took Paul's hands in hers—her palms felt cold and clammy.

"Look. Joelle had a beauty mark on her left leg. Right here." She reached over and touched his leg, just below the knee. It nearly made him jump. "I saw it. I felt it. When you fell asleep the first night, I went to her crib and just . . . well, looked at her. I couldn't believe we *had* her. I woke up and thought I was dreaming maybe. I had to see her again. To know she was real. You understand?"

Paul nodded.

"Okay. When the doctor examined her today, I didn't *see* it. I told myself *maybe you're wrong, maybe you didn't really see a beauty mark before*. It was dark in the room. Maybe it was a speck of dirt, a smudge. Only . . . all day today I was thinking that she smelled different than she did before."

"Honey . . ."

"Listen to me. Please." She squeezed his hands, as if she were trying to physically press her belief into him, as if it were something that could be caught, like a disease. Only he didn't want her disease.

He wanted her to stop this, to go back to being the ecstatic new mother who woke up in the middle of the night just so she could gaze at her daughter. "Joelle had this . . . I don't know, musky smell. She had it when we picked her up at the orphanage, and she had it here. She stopped having it when Galina brought her back."

"Okay. Why didn't you say anything then?"

"Because I knew you'd think I was crazy. Just like you're thinking now. I told *myself* I was crazy. But I didn't see the beauty mark today. So maybe I'm not."

"Why would she switch babies, Joanna? Why? For what earthly reason?" Paul was trying to make her see how silly this all was. Belief was immune to logic; it operated by its own laws. And this scared him, if only because there was a tiny part of him that was, well . . . starting to listen to her. The fact was, Joelle *had* smelled a little musky. Now that Joanna had mentioned it, okay, yes, she had.

"I don't know why she'd switch babies, Paul. Maybe because of our fight."

"What fight? You mean about putting her to sleep?"

Joanna nodded.

"That's ridiculous."

"Okay, it's ridiculous. I'm ridiculous. I just think that two days from now we're going to be leaving this country with the wrong baby. Then it'll be too late."

"What do you want me to do, Joanna? Even if I believed you. What would I tell the police? *What?* That I know we apologized to them for insisting our daughter had been kidnapped, but guess what, now we think she was *switched*?"

"We can go back to Santa Regina," Joanna said. "We can have them check her out for us."

"And what do you think María would say about that? How stable would she think we are? How much would she want us to have one of her babies? Nothing's final yet, Joanna. They can still take Joelle back."

"This baby's not Joelle."

"I happen to disagree with you. Okay? I happen to think she is. Because the alternative makes no sense. None. Listen to yourself. You're basing this on a *smell,* for chrissakes. On something you *think* you saw in the middle of the night."

"Let me ask you something, okay?" Joanna said.

No, he wanted to say—it's not okay.

"Let's say there's a one percent chance I'm right."

"What?"

"That's fair, isn't it? One percent?"

"Look, I—"

"I'm asking you a simple question. You want to attack me with logic, fine, I understand. So I'm asking you a logical question. You love percentages, don't you? You're an actuary—pretend it's one of your insurance charts. Is there a one percent chance I'm right?"

"You want me to put a percentage on something I think is totally ridiculous?"

"Yes, I want you to put a percentage on something you think is totally ridiculous."

"Okay, fine—there's a one percent chance she's not Joelle. And a ninety-nine percent chance she is."

"Okay. Are you willing to leave the country with even the *chance* she's not ours?"

For a moment he was going to say Joelle wasn't theirs anyway—because in the usual God-given sense, she wasn't. But he couldn't say it. It wasn't true anymore. From the second he'd clasped her to his chest, she'd become theirs.

She was their daughter.

So now what?

It seemed an eternity before Galina opened her door.

Maybe because Paul was no clearer about what he was going to say to her than he was before, and so was standing there frantically trying to come up with something. In addition to hoping she wouldn't be home, that no one would actually answer Pablo's knock.

Pablo had driven the three of them to Galina's house in the Chapinero district, a working-class area of dun-colored apartment buildings and modest homes. When they'd slid into the backseat, Joanna hadn't taken their daughter from Paul's arms as she normally had in the two days they'd been with her.

She was making a statement.

This isn't my daughter. You hold her.

Well, Paul thought, they'd see.

"Hello, Galina," Paul said when the door finally opened.

She seemed surprised to see them, but not in a way Paul construed as alarmed. In fact, she smiled, then leaned over and whispered a sweet hello to her very favorite baby. Paul felt like turning to Joanna and saying *see, satisfied now?* Joanna didn't look any different than she had during the ride over, which was nervous and unhappy.

Galina invited them in.

The door opened onto a small living room. It had a brown leather couch and two worn but comfortable-looking chairs facing a television. A lumbering yellow dog barely shifted from its sprawled position on the floor. Galina had been watching a soap opera; at least Paul assumed that's what it was. A perfect-looking young woman was kissing a perfect-looking young man.

"Please sit," Galina said, gesturing to the couch. *Do you see this,* Paul kept up his running, albeit silent commentary to Joanna, *she's inviting us in. She's asking us to sit on her couch.*

Galina brought out cookies and four cups of industrial-strength Colombian coffee in what must have been her fine china. She turned down the TV.

They made small talk.

"How did the baby sleep last night?" Galina asked.

"Fine," Paul answered. "She woke up once around two, I think, and then went right back."

"You're lucky. She's a good sleeper."

"Yes," Paul said. Joanna remained conspicuously silent.

"You have a lovely house, Galina," Paul said, continuing to search for anything to talk about except the actual reason for their visit.

"Thank you."

"What's your dog's name?" he asked.

"Oca," Galina said. At the sound of his name the dog lifted his head and sniffed the air.

"Did Pablo take you to the doctor yesterday?" Galina asked.

"Yes."

"And what did he say?"

"Everything's fine."

"Wonderful," Galina said. She smiled; her laugh lines fairly cackled.

Then Joanna spoke.

"Her fever was gone."

"That's good," Galina said.

"I wonder what it *was*?" Joanna added.

"Who knows?" Galina lifted her hands up in the universal gesture of the human limitation to understanding the mysteries of the universe.

Which is what Joanna was trying to do, of course. Understand, at least, one mystery.

Paul knew that he was expected to take over.

If he sat back and said nothing, Joanna would accuse him of non-support, of aiding and abetting the enemy. Except the enemy was treating them to coffee and cookies and the general hospitality of her home. The enemy had run to a *farmacia* to buy Joelle a thermometer when she was sick. Still, he was counted on to do certain things. Support her, for example. Something he hadn't done when she'd insisted Joelle, the *real* Joelle in her mind, had been put to sleep the wrong way. Something he was firmly and unquestioningly expected to do now.

"Uh, Galina . . . we were wondering about something," he started.

"Yes?"

"This is going to sound a little silly, okay?"

"Okay." Galina repeated his American slang with evident amusement.

"My wife . . . both of us, really, have noticed this difference. About Joelle."

"Difference. What do you mean difference?"

"Well, I said this is going to sound silly, but the fact is, she kind of smells different. Than she did before."

"Smells?" She looked over at Pablo, as if for confirmation she'd heard him correctly. Apparently, she had. Pablo looked as confused as she did.

"She had this kind of musky smell," Paul blundered on, "and now she doesn't. It seemed to change after, uh . . . when we thought she was . . . when you went to get her the thermometer."

"Yes?"

"We were just wondering about it," Paul said. "That's all."

"All right."

Evidently, Galina still had no idea what he was talking about.

"We were hoping maybe you can account for it?"

"Account for what?"

"Why she seems to be . . . different."

Galina put her cup of coffee back down on its china saucer. The sound seemed to echo unnaturally. Maybe because the room had suddenly turned uncomfortably quiet, the only sound a vague murmur emanating from the lowered TV. If the five of them were on that soap opera, Paul thought, there'd be a dissonant organ chord now to signify the portent of something dramatic. In this case, Galina's growing realization that she was being accused, albeit clumsily, of something she still didn't understand.

"What are you saying?" she asked now. "Are you suggesting . . . *what?*"

"Nothing, Galina," Paul said, a little too quickly. "We were just curious, that's all."

"About *what?*"

"About why she smells different."

"I don't understand. What are you asking me?"

We're asking you if you stole our baby, Galina. If you switched her.

"Nothing."

"Then why are you here?"

Paul felt like asking Joanna that himself.

"We wanted to know . . . ," and here Paul suddenly went blank.

"She had a beauty mark," Joanna said.

"What?" Galina turned to look at Joanna.

"She had a beauty mark when we got her. It's not there now."

"Beauty mark?"

"My daughter had a beauty mark on her left leg. And she used to smell like . . . well, like her. The beauty mark's gone. She smells different. *I want to know if it's the same baby.*"

Okay, Paul thought, Xena, warrior princess, was in full battle mode. The cat had been let out of the bag. Only it wasn't a cat as much as a Tasmanian devil, something large, carnivorous, and repulsive-looking. Probably the way the two of them looked to Galina right at this moment. After all, her back had physically stiffened—one of those clichés that evidently rang true. Her gentle gray eyes had turned hard as glass.

Paul found himself trying to look anywhere but at her, searching for a hole he might be able to hide in.

There was a box of cigars sitting on her mantel.

It had a photograph of a man in a white panama hat.

Paul wondered if Galina smoked cigars. A pair of brown slippers nestled like cats on her front welcome mat. The dog, who'd roused itself from its semicomatose state, had picked up one in his mouth, then dropped it by Pablo's feet, where it landed with an uncomfortable thud.

He forced himself to turn back to Galina. She still hadn't said anything—Joanna's accusation had turned her mute. She looked more or less horrified.

Later, much later, Paul would wonder if there's such a thing as peripheral hearing. Something that impinges on the ear but only announces itself later on.

He was trying not to stare at Galina's pained expression. He was wondering whether he should apologize to her. He didn't notice the muffled sound emanating from the inner recesses of the house.

Galina did. Which accounted for her expression.

Joanna had noticed it too.

Because she reached out and dug her fingernails into his arm. He almost cried out. Which would've made it two people crying in the house instead of just one.

Him and the baby.

There was a baby crying in the house.

He'd finally heard it.

He'd finally processed it. Because when he looked down at Joelle, she was sleeping. Which meant that there was a baby crying in the house, yes, only it wasn't this baby.

"Who's that?" That's the first thing he said. Stupid, okay, but then, he was obviously a little slow on the uptake today.

Galina didn't answer him.

"Whose baby is that?" he said, even though he was starting to have a good idea whose baby it might be.

"Pablo. Can you go see who it is?"

Pablo didn't move.

"Galina?"

She hadn't changed expression. Or maybe she had. The hardness in her eyes was still there, and there was something else now, a scary sense of focus and fortitude.

"Galina, is that our daughter? Is that *Joelle*?"

It took Paul a while to realize that Pablo *still* hadn't moved. That Galina still wasn't answering him.

Paul stood up with the baby in his arms—the question was, *whose* baby? He felt faint. "Okay, I'm going to see who it is." Announcing his plan out loud as if seeking approval.

He reached out to give Joelle to Galina and then, of course, stopped himself. Galina wasn't exactly his nurse anymore; it was possible this baby wasn't Joelle. He felt as if he were teetering on the edge of a deep and dangerous abyss—physically and emotionally hovering right over the edge. The room itself seemed to be swaying.

Then things flew into motion.

Joanna stood up and said *I'll go look,* and immediately began walking toward the sound of the crying baby. Pablo roused himself from his chair.

Paul offered up the baby in his arms so he could go join his wife, but it seemed to take an enormous effort to lift her.

"Sit down, Paul," Pablo said gently.

He was offering to look himself. He was telling Paul to sit down and take care of the baby. Pablo was being Pablo.

Paul gratefully reclaimed his seat as Pablo followed Joanna into the hall. The baby was crying louder, screeching even. And Paul finally and completely acknowledged what Joanna had feared was true.

He *recognized* that crying.

He remembered it from the first day in the hotel room when their daughter had wailed endlessly for food. Until Galina had shown up and made everything all right again.

Galina was still stiffly seated in her chair—only she appeared to be physically closer to him than she'd been before. How was that possible?

For a minute or so nothing happened.

The baby continued to cry from somewhere in the house; Galina continued to stare at him with an odd and unsettling calm.

Then Pablo reappeared, walking back into the living room while supporting Joanna with one strong arm. She was leaning against him, her head laid back on his shoulder as if she were very close to fainting. Where was the baby?

Joanna clearly looked distraught, while Pablo appeared helpful. There was undoubtedly a causal connection between those two things, but Paul wasn't sure what it was.

Something was wrong.

Look closer.

Her head on his shoulder. It took Paul a few seconds—seconds in which the world changed from A to Z—to understand that the reason it was lying back on Pablo's shoulder like that was that Pablo had his wife's dark luxuriant hair wrapped tightly in his fist.

Pablo was pulling Joanna into the room by her hair.

Her mouth was open in a half-muted scream.

He threw Joanna down onto the couch, flung her backward as if she were a piece of luggage he'd thrown into the car at El Dorado Airport.

"*Sit,*" he said. The way one barks commands at a dog. A stupid, stubborn dog, a dog who should know better.

Paul felt rooted to the couch, a spectator to a horrifying drama that had suddenly and inexplicably become real. He was waiting for the intermission, when he could stretch his legs, shake the cobwebs out of his brain, and thank the cast for their stunningly convincing performance. The play continued.

Galina stood up.

She methodically began closing the wooden shutters on each side of the room as she talked to Pablo in a steady stream of Spanish. As if he and Joanna weren't even in the room. She seemed to be chastising him—Paul's Spanish was beginning to come back like a long-repressed memory, and it seemed like he could understand every fifth word or so. *You. Called. Not here.* For one regrettably stupid moment Paul wondered if she was yelling at Pablo for throwing Joanna down on the couch like that.

For not getting their baby.

For *turning* on them.

But that was like hoping you're asleep and dreaming when you're completely and terrifyingly awake.

Paul handed the baby to Joanna—the baby he'd thought was his daughter and that he now knew wasn't—and stood up to protest Pablo's treatment of his wife, to reason this out, to get Joelle and have Pablo take them back to the hotel this instant.

"I told you to sit down, Paul," Pablo said.

Somehow he delivered this statement over Paul's prone body. This was an enormous surprise to Paul. That he wasn't standing. He was lying down on a wooden floor smelling of wet fur and shoe polish. *How had that happened?* He heard Joanna's sharp intake of breath.

"I'm okay, honey," he said. Oddly enough, he didn't hear the words. His tongue was strangely obstinate; it had decided to lie down on the job. Just like the rest of his body, which felt absurdly heavy. There was a strange metallic taste in his mouth.

He tried to lift himself up from the floor. No go. He felt vibrations traveling through the floorboards, some kind of rebalancing of weight from one place to another. He heard heavy shuffling and sensed a quickening in the air itself.

They looked like marines.

Five men in mottled green uniforms who'd suddenly flowed into the room like a brackish river breaching its banks. Young faces with stolid expressions of dumb determination. Each of them carried a rifle.

"Please," Paul said.

The room was eerily dark; Galina had closed all the shutters but one. It felt like the moment before everyone yells *surprise.*

The surprise is for us, Paul thought.

Then he passed out.